ALSO BY FRED LUNZER

The Last Call

SIKE

> > >

A Novel

FRED LUNZER

CELADON
BOOKS

SIKE. Copyright © 2025 by Fred Lunzer. All rights reserved. Printed in the United States of America. For information, address Celadon Books, a division of Macmillan Publishers, 120 Broadway, New York, NY 10271.

www.celadonbooks.com

The Library of Congress Cataloging-in-Publication Data is available upon request.

ISBN 978-1-250-34312-3 (hardcover)
ISBN 978-1-250-34313-0 (ebook)

Our books may be purchased in bulk for promotional, educational, or business use. Please contact your local bookseller or the Macmillan Corporate and Premium Sales Department at 1-800-221-7945, extension 5442, or by email at MacmillanSpecialMarkets@macmillan.com.

First Edition: 2025

10 9 8 7 6 5 4 3 2 1

For my mother and father

We knew from the start that things fall apart, and tend to shatter.

—BLACK THOUGHT

CONTENTS

SIKE

REMEDIES

Maybe you should know, I signed up to Sike long before I met Maquie (I'll come to Maquie, it all began with her, but Sike happened before her).

I'd been going out for five months with a website designer from Hamburg called Lucy, who got drunk easily, loved independent coffee shops, and who felt incomplete to me, like her identity was still in gestation. She was elfin and dark-eyed. When trying something new, like bowling or Hearts, she would stop early on and close her eyes and fake-laugh at herself, mocking her failure before really even failing, as though self-deprecation were a quality equal to effort. She refused to be earnest, but the worst thing she did was in the mornings when we stayed together: after showers and teeth and dressing and whatever else, she would hover by the sink and look at me expectantly, as though I was about to deliver a plan for the day.

One evening, about four months in, when I overexplained the syntax of a Fugees song we were listening to, Lucy jokingly called me "Coach."

I'm not sure I ever recovered from that. Honestly, it felt like revulsion. I got anxious. I felt responsible for her, but like I was bound to let her down. I tried to fix stuff: her relationship with her boss, her fear of public speaking, her relationship with her father . . . and when I failed, my anxiety grew. I began to double-, triple-think things, doubting her and doubting myself. She was unfixable, and I would be stuck with her.

Shuddery stuff. I began to fantasize about breaking up. We went out to dinner and drank three old-fashioneds each, then had an argument about absolutely nothing and she became furious and took my finger and bit it so hard I had to pry her jaws open with my other hand. Her teeth marks stayed until the next evening, and I had the disconcerting phantom sensation in my own teeth of having myself bitten into finger bone. Her apologies continued for a week, and I forgave her for the bite, but I had lost sight of her innocence.

She wasn't, was she? Innocent? Sane. I was making love to a grenade. She was manic. I was caught. She would kill me if I ever tried to break up with her. Couldn't have happened to a nicer guy.

In moments of reflection, I think I acknowledged that this wasn't true, it was all anxious imagination. But rationality doesn't trump anxiety, I still hid the kitchen knives in my sock drawer. Instead, rationality brought new fears. It was *my* issue. I was psychotic. I was destined for celibacy. I was incapable of a relationship and I should stop debasing others with my vanity-driven attempts at them. She was perfectly sane and it was *me* who was sociopathically averse to commitment, who was inventing demons, who was gaslighting her, forcing the demons into her, into this lonely Hamburg girl who was characteristically cool and creative, and who was simply and blatantly only trying to love, but whom I had reduced to a quarreling, finger-biting, love-starved dope. And I had made it so that she had no one to turn to, not even herself, because I had *razed* her self-esteem. Burned it to the ground. It was . . .

. . . it was abuse.

The word chilled me, I felt it in my stomach. My anxiety galloped. The morbid cliché, clear to every member of the wet-suited recovery team that would scoop her body up from the bottom of Regent's Canal, was that, after all, *I* was the oppressor. The divers in their flippers would know it, the police in their rain ponchos would know it. The press would know it, they would taste it. It would have been obvious suicide, but who was culpable? Violence isn't physical. Who had led her on? There was the victim, just there, on a silver trolley, leaking canal water. Where was the perpetrator?

I went for dinner in Soho with some university friends, and at 4 A.M. we were still out, in a tourists' salsa club off Oxford Street with a bottle of Fernet-Branca. The next day, I woke up drunk and was slowly lowered into the wet concrete of a terrible hangover. I try not to brag about hangovers, I know it's gauche, but this was a bad one: I got out of bed five times and vomited on four of them. The fifth time, I got dressed and went outside but immediately returned, and I stood in my small kitchen gripping the counter for what felt like hours. I saw my grandfather die when I was fifteen, he had cancer and he hacked and rasped on a bed with daisy-yellow sheets. It was pretty tribal, ridiculous terror, actually, and he was badly in pain, and a consolatory thought I try to have when hungover so bad is that the hangover is good preparation for when I come to die myself. It's really good that occasionally I practice what it all feels like.

The anxiety continued well into the night, and into my dreams. The next morning, tired and nauseous and feeling brittle after the weeks of mental skirmishing about Lucy, I signed up to Sike. I'd sold a few songs earlier in the year and I could afford it for a few months at least. Plus my sister Jess swore by it, her husband, Jonah, had bought her a subscription as an anniversary present. My vague plan was to use it for a month or two, clear my panic, then cancel my subscription and return to plain old hypochondria and mindlessness.

Probably everyone signs up differently, I'm sure for some it's candlelight and Cat Stevens on the hi-fi, maybe others group up and sit around holding hands. I just made coffee and sat on my sofa beneath my posters of Outkast and Tribe. I had a sense that Q-Tip would approve most of all, he was so intellectual. The "good angel." So unashamed of weakness . . . his house burned down in 1998, he lost twenty thousand vinyls.

Sike opened with a double-tap vibration at my glasses temples, which I thought was neat, and my lenses shaded lilac. The app's edges were soft, it was elegant. On my phone, Sike's words took up the majority of the screen, they just sort of appeared there, gray text on white background, right-aligned and somehow fresh.

In my glasses, the words were right-aligned too, hovering mostly in my right lens in a lilac box that fuzzed the real world behind it. My glasses weren't the best pair back then, an old Miru set that I'd been lazy upgrading, and the text could have been sharper. But I guess the main point was to listen, and by that point most glasses had pretty good earphones built in. Even my mum's pair, which she bought for *seventy pounds,* had good sound. My friend Stutter sometimes wore that GlueStik pair where the stems curled under your earlobes and into your ear holes, but that was a bit much, I didn't need something sitting in my ear all day collecting earwax.

I let the app look at my glasses footage from the past year, I guess to "get to know me," then I took and passed the screening test and sipped some more coffee and felt a small thrill.

I felt safer.

Sike said,

>Good morning, Adrian.

And that was kind of that.

Did I think it was a bit sci-fi? Of course I did. I thought of Joaquin Phoenix a lot, in *Her*. But then, it was all a bit sci-fi, from my Teflon smartglasses, to my noise-canceling headphones, to my textureless black monolith smartphone. I mean, I had a self-balancing scooter in the corner of the room, a Segway with no handles. I never used it, Stutter gave it to me as a joke because he knew I hated them, but it worked, it was future-max.

So yeah, I got over it pretty quick.

That first day, we spoke a lot about Lucy and I combined accounts of my anxiety with aspersions on her unformed identity. I told Sike, "She doesn't know who she is, and she wants me to tell her."

I waited for Sike to congratulate me on my evaluation, but it refused.

>I don't think identity is that simple, Adrian.
>What you might be trying to explain is a feeling of power
imbalance.

"Is a feeling of power balance important in a relationship?"

>It seems like it is to you.

I laughed a little with the shy pleasure of being taught—that joyful affection for authority. And a few days later, on a humid Saturday morning, preempting her expectant hovering by the sink, I delivered Lucy a plan for the day by breaking up with her.

Lucy spent the conversation combatively flicking her hand and saying, "I know." I was apologetic, and tried to explain some of my anxiety, but everything I said sounded like an insult, which it evidently was, but not because I wanted it to be.

We said goodbye, and I spent the week quietly, speaking to Sike and doing things with my mother and my sister (I surrounded myself with women who didn't hate me). On two afternoons, I went to my grandmother's to help her with her garden. We filled green bin liners, drank tea, reflected on plant growth.

That's how I came to it, that was my "Sike story." People trade these stories sometimes, to sort of justify their spend on it, time or money. I kept it mostly to myself, but I guess I was a fan of the app. I liked the modules, massive topics on anything, edited by a guest researcher and broken down for you piece by piece. And I liked the tracking and the conversation. I liked Sike for providing calm and for providing insight, the latter of which I consistently found intriguing and satisfying. This stuff, this is everything, isn't it? Psychology is the whole thing, it's all life. It's the poetry, and it's also how you operate, it's the power.

But I knew that for others Sike was contentious. My hairdresser, Ranger, liked to warn me off it. She was from Johannesburg and she clipped her way around my head either recounting recent dates or telling me about the perils of technology. She once said she didn't need Sike anyway, because her clients did her analysis for her, and they paid *her* for the pleasure.

Stutter knew I was using it immediately. He pointed right at me and said, "You got Sike."

I asked him how he knew, and he said there was a certain smile. He wouldn't go near Sike, and he shook his head, disappointed.

Maquie didn't use Sike either, but early on she never specified an opinion for or against it. I came to understand that she knew a lot about it but that this was a result of her job analyzing companies and not because of her own experience with the app, or an interest in psychotherapy, or a general curiosity about, say, the app's ethics. When Sike came up in conversation, the pace of her voice would slow, and she would look down, her eyelashes flickering, and thread together smart analytical sentences that I would try to remember later.

Maquie didn't need to deliver opinions to hold attention, which she always did. If you didn't know her, you underestimated her and imagined she was a "quiet soul" who needed encouragement to speak up, and so you listened in a pantomime way, supporting her with warm nods. You were told she was half-Japanese, and you noticed her beauty. Gradually you noticed her Swedish accent. You realized she must speak at least three languages. You noticed her intellect, and then you noticed what Stutter once called the "fresh truth" of everything she said. She saw around things. You listened to her comments, and your attention was interrupted only by your self-examination, as you considered your hair or posture or breath, or the quality of your own conversation, or your hopefully unnoticed original condescension and prejudice. One thing that became clear to you was that Maquie knew a lot about her subject, and that her subject was business, and that you should care about business.

WINTER

1.

On fifth November, the day before we met, Maquie arrived in a small village on the Devon coast called Clovelly. She was there to evaluate a business founded by a guy called Max Sanditz.

For ten months, Maquie had worked for May-Perhaps, a venture capital fund set up by a Canadian couple, and so far she had yet to find any business worthy of the firm's investment. In fact, it was her model that had yet to find anyone. The model had formed the core of her PhD thesis, it predicted extreme business success. I understood little of it. I grasped mainly that it had been trained on the data of companies that had already made it to the highest rungs, and it was tested on them too: presented with a range of data relating to a very successful company—say, Ford or Amazon, Coca-Cola, Sike—the model could predict that company's success at any point in its prior development.

Maquie was hired by May-Perhaps to apply the model to the future. The firm's founders, Sharon and Kyle, were uninterested in growth, they were interested in explosion, so Maquie's model suited them. They met first at a conference where Maquie was presenting a paper on the model, and Sharon took her aside afterward and bought her a coffee and said "wow" a lot.

"Wow, you did all that? Wow, you think it could work in the real world? You're doing a PhD? Wow. But you could put that on hold, right?"

Maquie's task was to use the model to identify companies that would one day turn hugely successful, and if she found them, May-Perhaps would invest large sums of money. There were five other analysts working alongside Maquie, each with their own approach to finding promise, but May-Perhaps invested in only two companies a year.

(Maquie later told me that the May-Perhaps approach was not common for VC firms. She said firms tended to issue money broadly, engaging with a wide array of extraordinary business ideas. She said it was accepted by everyone that most start-ups fail, so you need to invest in a great many of them to land a success. The May-Perhaps founders—Maquie, too—refused this belief and thought it outdated, easy, and negligent.)

Maquie's model could predict extreme business success, but so far it hadn't. It was findless, and her own work ethic could not be blamed. She had raked London's tech scene and all the global hubs, she had gone to the conferences and the parties, she daily broke her back on the repurposed school chairs of brushed-concrete coworking cafes listening to mediocre founders grapple with unit economics. She came home with nothing. Nothing triggered the model's approval, nothing glinted. Nothing was out there. She had built an interface for the model that she could access from anywhere, a portal made up of a few metallic-looking panels and input bars floating in a cream box. Founders, like Max Sanditz, worked with Maquie to enter data about themselves and their company into the input bars, and when this was done a small maroon pentagon appeared in the top right corner of the interface. If the company was successful, if their data combined well with the data of the surrounding environment and triggered the model's approval, a green pentagon would appear next to the maroon one. If not, a gray one.

So far, only the gray had come. If you clicked on the final pentagon, the model gave you a score and an explanation for its answer, usually in AI terms that only Maquie could understand, which would one day give me the pleasing notion that she was the somewhat magical rune/alethiometer/star-reading heroine of a story in which I played a role.

I flatter myself and picture Maquie arriving in that Devon harbor village the day before she met me, cold and alert, at a point of epiphany, or perhaps review. I fantasize that her meeting me was a time of change, of new construction, and that the days before were necessarily a kind of grading of the ground in preparation.

It's true at least that Clovelly was cold that week. Maquie wore a pleated polo neck, and over it a navy Sandro coat and her friend Sophie's green scarf. Max's business was operating out of rooms in the harbor's pub, the Red Lion, and Maquie arrived on Friday in time to eat a late lunch with him and two of his engineers in the downstairs bar. She had drunk three coffees that morning and felt a caffeine buzz—not a sickly one, but her hands were vibrating when she picked up the menu.

Over lunch they discussed the business, its future, and Maquie asked the engineers about their educations and Max about his customers. She had a ploughman's sandwich that came with a small salad. One of her chews pivoted a rocket stalk through her lips, licking the open air like a tongue. She readjusted her mouthful and sipped sparkling water, then asked Max about his recruitment plans.

Usually companies didn't get so much attention, but Max's had been turning heads, not only because of its quirky setup in the Clovelly harbor pub. Maquie found Max to be smug during lunch, speaking rehearsed lines of jargon, the poetics of which appeared to please him. He was clever and patronizing: on three occasions, he stopped short of explaining some complexity, saying he did so for Maquie's sake. But gradually he calmed, and began to smile more and speak openly, relax in the pauses. In a friendly way, he pushed Maquie to order a dessert, and she ate half a brownie. Ilya and Peter, the engineers, split the other half. They were both tall and broad, bearish. Max was slender, he had model-like good looks, a drawn face.

After lunch, Maquie suggested a break, and Max agreed. Maquie walked by herself down to the end of the pier, squinting in the cold wind and admiring the boats. She paused to look at them, and on looking at them, she laughed quickly to herself. The boats fell at random over the steep beach, their prows pointing angles off the shoreline . . . the tide had dropped them there, just like that, just like in a film. Their moor ropes were covered in wet seaweed, which trembled now and then, and they were colored red, blue, green, the simple primaries, the simple colors of the simple past. And their hulls were worn, the fiberglass scratched. She heard a creak. One of the boats was made of actual wood.

She looked up to the village, white cottages flowing from the forest down to the sea. Also like a film. Too perfect, not quite real. A few families were on the path, moving down the cobblestones. Clovelly was a village that was privately owned, Maquie had paid £8.75 when she arrived, the receipt was in her coat pocket. Max said she didn't need to pay because she was staying in the pub, but she respected the revenue model.

She turned back to the pub, and looked one last time at the boats. The inadvertent ridiculousness in life amused Maquie. Fishing was ridiculous, otherworldly . . . dropping nets down into an invisible sea and hoping to scoop up wild, unfarmed life. She grew up in Stockholm and, walking to school each day, she had watched the men with their galoshes and hats stand in the brackish water of the islands, long rods arcing, blind to the fact that there was a city all around them with traffic, escalators, coffee meetings . . . She grasped that they found some nostalgic beauty in the activity. They were hopeful to catch something. They were optimistic, and in their optimism, primitive. It brought to her mind vast gilt-frame oil paintings of miraculous hauls, sunbeams shooting like lasers from the midst of tumultuous skies, villagers in breeches and brown tunics holding their arms up in thanks to a god whose major tools of communication were the supply of fish and grain and weather. Maybe a church in the background, sitting precarious on a clifftop and also bathing grateful in sunbeam. And in the middle distance, blurred and anonymous on a stub of pier, a girl holding her sides.

She reached the door and went into the Red Lion, leaving the quaint laughs of the harbor. Inside the Red Lion, a family of four sat near the door eating fish and chips. The youngest child, a toddler, looked at Maquie, a chip hanging from his mouth. Maquie smelled vinegar and sour frying oil, and in the golden winter light she watched the other son push peas around his plate with a chip. She could hear some music playing. The boys' mother read the menu, the father his phone. Maquie waved briefly at the youngest child, then passed through the quiet bar, collected her laptop from the now empty lunch table, and opened it on a small table in a small corner, lit by a small window that looked out to the sea. Some boats bounced on the waves.

. . .

She worked for four hours, and Max came down throughout the afternoon to answer various questions. By six o'clock, the sky was dark outside, and she had prepared the company's information in the model portal. She went upstairs to find Max.

On the table by the fireplace in the bedroom, in front of a small beige sofa, some coffee was sitting in a silver and glass cafetière. Maquie poured herself one last cup and sat down at a wooden table by the window. Max's compact four-poster bed was made, but a bundle of his clothes sat on top of it, his glasses too. There were three doors in the room, one leading to the hallway and the staircase, and another to a small bathroom. The third led to another bedroom, where Ilya and Peter worked in the daytime, and where Maquie would stay that night. The rooms were big. The room where she would sleep had a view of the sea and some of the coastline.

Max came in, rubbing his hands. He stood with his shoulders held back, looking around the room as though unsure what to do. Then he went to put his glasses on and asked,

"Did you like the pier earlier?"

"Very picturesque."

"You know you can jump off? I swim every morning. Do you want to? I can ask for an outfit."

Maquie looked out at the dark pier and felt goose bumps line her thighs and stomach.

"My father's Swedish," she said, looking back to Max, "but I didn't get his affinity for cold water."

Max shrugged. "I grew up in Oxford, and my parents are from Nebraska. I have no sea in my genes, but I like it."

He tapped his keyboard and a table projector kicked into life, putting an Excel sheet onto the wall. "Ok. Do you want me to go through next year?"

Maquie sipped the coffee. The coffee bean was too green, too sharp. And Max's business was shallow, she had hoped for more. It was impressive tech, and quantum-led cyber security was a good focus. All the buzzwords. And she liked that the buzziest of all was in the company's name, Quantum Theater. She could see that Max was able, and she liked the two engineers she met, who sat even now, late on a Friday, at their computers in the next room.

She understood the revenue. She liked this quirky setup in a harbor pub in the middle of southern England. The story was good.

But regardless of what Max's Excel charts might tell her, Quantum Theater would reach little further than an increasingly thrifty demographic of slow-to-digitize companies, helping a good handful of big corporate users improve their defenses, but no more. It wasn't worth May-Perhaps's investment.

She put her cup down, trying not to display what she was feeling, which was the lugubrious hassle of unrealized hopes. She wanted to believe there was more, but her model had confirmed that there wasn't, and she would have to break this to Max, and she would send her bosses Sharon and Kyle a message to tell them of another dead end, and they would reply, "Take it easy," a phrase they didn't realize meant "Calm the fuck down" in European English, when really they just meant, "It's ok."

At least when it came to Max, Maquie could be honest. She wasn't worried for him: VCs would come along and put checks down, eager to have a stake in quantum computing. Max would do ok, just not amazing.

"I'm sorry," she said.

Max straightened and looked at her. He studied her, confirming he had understood her tone, and Maquie saw contempt cross his face. But then he turned away and said, "Ah. Ok . . . I had thought there was some interest."

"There was, and I like what you have. My advice is to keep searching. You had a strong first round. London is the right place to look for your next. Try the corporate networks, push the quantum and cyber parts. Use the buzzwords. Don't say, 'We do this . . . ,' say, 'Quantum Theater does this . . .' Every time. You will succeed for sure. But . . . and this is just one opinion, so please ignore it if you like . . . but maybe I don't think you will explode."

"Your model told you that?"

She nodded.

"I understand," he said.

Which was rare. Most founders, most people, disputed her model's rejections.

"And you want explosion," he said.

She nodded again. "Sadly, that's what we're looking for."

"I know. Everyone said it. You want the next Sike."

He went to the cafetière and poured himself some coffee.

"I am sorry to waste your time," she said. "If I can help in any other way, please get in touch."

Max nodded, and for a second glanced at Maquie, his face softening.

"No waste of time," he said, and somehow his words hung for longer than they should have, and Maquie felt a notion raised between them.

When she was ten, at Midsommar, Maquie had swum in the sea near where her uncle lived, close to Malmö. Twenty of her family had been at the beach, and she had run ahead of them all, wading in and shrieking and shouting at the cold. She had gone first to prove to her older cousins she was brave, and she shrieked to make sure they would notice. They did notice, and they disapproved. Maquie had been too overt. She read it first on the face of her mother, Fumi, who didn't come to the water with a towel, but waited up the beach so that Maquie had to hobble over the pebbles to reach her, the other family members watching. Maquie held her arms together, ready to be wrapped up like at bath time, but instead Fumi held the towel out and looked at the horizon.

Maquie's error was confirmed that night, after lights out, when in almost the same breath her cousin Theresa explained what handjobs were and why it was wrong to show off like Maquie had done at the beach that day.

"Humility is, like, very important," Theresa had said.

Afterward, Maquie lay in the dark surrounded by blond cousins, and didn't sleep for hours. The shame felt like a maze she had to escape (plus, there were handjobs to consider . . . humility, handjobs, humility, handjobs . . . it was lucky her young brain hadn't conflated the two). The next day, she spent the afternoon in the branches of a low-slung holly tree behind the house, feeling angry.

Maquie knew that at twenty-eight she could forgive her ten-year-old self for the shrieking and showboating at the sea in Malmö, and she could forgive her twelve-year-old cousin for the shaming. She knew that the episode had affected her, had taught her something about mindset. The next few years of school, she hadn't dropped an A; she won the Torsten Wiesel Science Prize and the Alva Myrdal Award for Political EQ, and she was accepted at Kungsholmens Gymnasium with a perfect meritvärdet and the highest ranking of any applicant.

High school was easy: she excelled academically and publicly, winning the Nelly Sachs Youth Prize for a thought piece on post-Coetzeean South African literary identity, and taking the debate team to the Nordic Schools Debating Championships, where they only lost in the final to a Norwegian team because Maquie's second affirmative had an eating disorder and had to go home with a special kind of scurvy.

She donated the Nelly Sachs money to a Kosovan repatriation charity. She considered Cambridge, Harvard, and Paris, but settled on Stockholm University because they offered her a full scholarship and the Wallenberg grant, and she wouldn't have to borrow from her parents. For a year, she regretted not choosing Karolinska and studying medicine, but later she found her economics bachelor's and then her machine learning master's to be surprisingly efficient openers for practically any door she felt like walking through. Had she wanted to, she could have leapfrogged her parallel-universe Karolinska self and gone to work directly for the most exciting healthtech or pharma companies in the world (she would have been her parallel self's boss). She could have worked for the city or for Sweden, and for a while politics looked likely after she led a student committee to Almedalen to campaign for more investment into the arts (Finland still far outspent Sweden per capita). She could have gone into banking, she could probably have started straight into private equity. She could have begun her own venture selling god knows what, but in all the various options that presented themselves she couldn't escape the feeling that the most important thing in everything seemed to be business, and that business had a fatal flaw. It was chancy. She saw the solution in AI, and moved to London to begin her PhD at Imperial.

She could do all this, she thought, not because she was special, or particularly gifted, but because she had gained perspective. She could admit that Theresa's lesson had not hindered her progress, even though its real meaning had been hidden at first. Whether Theresa had understood the nuance as well, she didn't know, but it was Maquie's comprehension of the adjusted precept, that it was important to *act* humble, that had brought her down from the angry holly tree and back to the family in Malmö. It felt like a secret victory, the discovery that she could fake qualities, behave without believing; that she was on the outside, looking in. She had the luxury of detachment, the ability to spot codes of etiquette that held others rigid and step into or out of them whenever she chose.

Max could have meant anything by his assurance: "No waste of time." He might have felt grateful for the pitching practice, or grateful for Maquie's honest judgment. Clarity is always useful. So perhaps it really wasn't a waste of time to have invited Maquie to the harbor, to have spent the afternoon with her, to be giving her lunch and dinner and a bed for the night.

But his words hung and a notion was raised, and the notion remained in the air through a dinner that Maquie enjoyed. She felt good out of London and good in the company of these other outsiders, with whom she enjoyed discussing cyber and quantum and tech and the UK. Max's parents had moved from America to teach at Oxford, and Max had grown up on campus. Maquie recognized and found comforting the academia in him. She recognized the introversion in Ilya and Peter, their reticence, and she realized she could make them laugh. She did make them laugh, softly picking on their taste in music, their data specialties. And they made her laugh, especially Ilya, who delivered grandiose fables about his coding abilities in deadpan. Max ignored the humor and tried to unravel the fables, but Ilya fended him off until Max rolled his eyes and said ok. Maquie enjoyed the food, and two glasses of beer and two glasses of wine.

Beyond acknowledging it, Maquie didn't promote the notion further, and she was surprised by Max's gentle approach after dinner, after Ilya and Peter had gone to their beds in a cottage up the hill. She and Max climbed the stairs, and Max paused on the landing that separated their two rooms and asked with a confused face, as though trying to clarify something, whether she wanted a drink in his room. It was a humble approach, and Maquie wasn't offended by it. Her breath vibrated a little. Max was being labeled a wunderkind in the quantum world, she was flattered by his interest.

She hesitated, thinking how the evening had been pleasant, and how she was glad she had been invited down to Clovelly to stay. She wondered if Max regularly invited potential investors to sleep with him. She wondered if it was unprofessional. Or maybe on the contrary, it was professional, part of the investment package. She thought again that she felt flattered, happy not to be seen as tired or sexless. She thought how life felt free, and she thought how sex was something that she had sometimes argued was one of life's inexhaustible gems, and we may as well keep mining it. And because of all this, and because she had perspective, because she could spot codes of etiquette and step into or out of them whenever she chose, she accepted his offer, and followed him into the room. He started toward the minibar, but she saved him the hassle and took his hand in hers.

* * *

The next morning, she said goodbye to Max and Quantum Theater and walked up Clovelly's cobblestones. It was lunch on a Saturday, there was empty time to fall into. The sun was sharp and she could hear the sea. The path away from the harbor and the Red Lion took her past little shops with aproned vendors, and she stopped in one near the top and bought a postcard (as enjoyable an anachronism as the fishing boats on the front of it) to send her parents. She hadn't explained to Max that Ulf was not her biological father, even though this would have added context to her saying that she didn't get his affinity for cold water, but this was an omission of blatant convenience, not some slumbering secret she was afraid to stir. She thought about her younger brother, Yuki, and remembered a time when he had been obsessed with boats. She had given him one, paid for by Fumi, a dark blue yacht ten centimeters long with a white line around the hull and "Cantina La Rita" written on the side. When it went in the bath, it made a pleasant bubbling sound like cards being shuffled, and then sank, bow-first and quite dramatically.

She also bought local jam, to give to her best friend Sophie later that day, and a bottle of lightly sea-salted mineral water, for herself.

Turning away from the shop, she felt her legs stretch into the final climb of the path and she pushed the stretch, wanting to run the distance and spread the fibers in her thighs. Families came the opposite way toward the harbor, their children scouting ahead, and she felt the effect of coffee on her mood, and felt it inflate the prospect of the weekend, the prospect of drinks, the prospect of seeing Sophie, and the prospect of waking up on Sunday morning and doing who knew what.

Maquie got on a train and went to London, and then went to a pub, where she met me.

2.

When I signed up to Sike, we set up my dashboard, a wide black panel like an airplane's cockpit that showed my daily "vitals." They say one of Sike's benefits is that it can track subtle changes in your personality, while a real-life psychologist can't (or won't). Sike can analyze the way you walk, the way you make eye contact, the stuff you talk about, the stuff you wear, how often you eat, drink, how often you piss, shit, laugh, cry, kiss, lie, whine, and cough. It can look at the number of compliments you receive, it can track the amount of sunshine you see and the number of birds singing within earshot, and the changes in your choice of music, films, books. It's pretty exhaustive. And it can relay these all back to you.

My dashboard on Sike had three areas: GOALS, PHYSICAL, and MENTAL.

GOALS were things I wanted to work on, and to start with these were mainly to do with reducing my anxiety.

PHYSICAL was a list of scores that I chose and that Sike tracked. You could have loads, but I just did: >Sleep, >Exercise, >NegVs.Pos, >Diet, >Clean, >Music, and >Hair. Most of all, I liked >Clean, it gave me a score for how messy I was being. And >Hair was nice too: I had this theory that the longer my pubic hair got, the stronger my body dysmorphia became, and I put Sike to work to see if there was a link.

Then MENTAL was another list of metrics, but these you reported on yourself whenever you checked in with Sike. They said that >Anxiety might soon become a PHYSICAL score, the research was nearly there. Other useful ones in MENTAL were things like >CreativeTime and >TimeThinking. The latter was to do with whether I was thinking more about the past, the present, or the future. When I started Sike, I was way high on thinking about the future. By the time I met Maquie, this had evened out a bit.

I knew nothing about Maquie, nothing about her Alva Myrdal Awards or her Wallenberg grants, and in retrospect this was lucky. I only knew that Stutter had a French friend called Sophie, and that she and a friend would join us for a drink in an Earls Court pub. Both were single, Stutter said, which was enough for me to start humming Lionel Richie ballads.

Maquie and I arrived at the pub at the same time, and after we were introduced, and I had gone to get a round, I sat down among the potted plants and gas heaters of the pub garden and tried not to look at her too much, like she was a plate of biscuits yet to be offered to the table. This analogy, formed while I was looking away and considering questions I could ask her, felt sexist. I looked around the beer garden, which had a patio and a brown-wood scaffold structure meant, eventually it seemed, for ivy creepers to wind around. Not by this summer would the patio be shaded, I thought, like I was a famous gardener. For no quickly emerging reason, I resented—lazily, not aggressively or proactively—every other person in the pub.

Beneath her jacket, Maquie wore a cream silk shirt and blue jeans. Her hair was tied up, her arms were still, her glasses were on the table. I heard her say to Stutter that she was half-Japanese, half-Swedish. Then she said she worked in venture capital, which I knew nothing about. I decided to ask about this because I felt that curiosity about her work would prove that I wasn't sexist, as though my plate-of-biscuits thought had been heard by the table and needed to be refuted.

"So do you have a team?" I said.

"No," she said. "There are others in the firm, but I work alone. For the couple that founded the fund."

"They're British?"

"Canadian."

"And your job is to find companies that will make it?"

"Yes. Companies that will make it big. I wrote a paper about it."

"Are you doing a PhD?"

"I was, I quit it for the job."

"What was the paper about?"

"It presented an AI model. It was about using data to predict exponential, or explosive, consumer demand."

"That hasn't been done before?"

"Not scientifically. Trendspotting has traditionally been quite subjective."

"She's a genius," Sophie said. "Wait until you realize what she's telling you. She's fucking god."

"God?"

"Maquie is all-seeing, she knows *the desires of humans*. She will tell you if millions could buy your product, she will tell you where and how often, and she will tell you *why*."

Sophie had steady eyes and a French accent that helped her deliver an informed and very controlled melodrama.

I got that Maquie's opinion mattered. It prophesied.

"And now you apply this to the real world?" I asked.

"I'm trying to."

"Have you ever done it for the arts? Film, TV, music, et cetera? What's going to resonate, that kind of thing . . . ?"

At this point, or maybe a little earlier, I noticed a lilac dot in the top right corner of my right glasses lens. I also noticed Maquie massaging her right shoulder, like it was stiff.

"No, we didn't explore it, but in theory my model can be applied. I think others are trying it. You ask because you ghostwrite rap lyrics?"

"Yes, that's right. Stutter does too."

"Why do you all call him Stutter?"

"Because I stutter if I try and rap," Stutter said. "It's a speech thing."

"Ah," Maquie said. "I'm sorry."

Stutter shrugged. His glasses were cream-colored, and he blinked behind them, impassive.

"It seems sad," Maquie said.

"You're sweet, but it's ok. It's my excuse for sitting in the shadows and ghostwriting."

She nodded, then smiled. She put a hand to her shoulder and pulled at the blade. Then she put her hand down again and looked at me. "And what's yours?"

The lilac dot was pulsing softly. I held her gaze well enough. "My excuse?"

"Yes."

"I'll tell you when I come back."

I said this calmly, I wasn't trying to be cool with it.

I left the table and went down the steps of the patio and into the back door of the pub. They were playing a subscription playlist—when I'd arrived it was Billie Holliday, and now it was Benny Goodman. I walked down the bar and out the front door, briefly checking I couldn't be seen from the table, and then turned right onto the empty street.

I walked a little down the road, then turned onto a small street called Rickett Street. I faced a brick wall and focused on the lilac dot and blinked, and it moved forward in my vision. I poked it, and Sike appeared. I looked around again, I was keen to be quick; consulting Sike in public was considered a little graceless, like giving real estate advice, or discussing crypto.

My lenses faded lilac and the dot expanded.

"Hello," I said.

>Hello, Adrian. I thought I'd notify you that your heart rate is up, and your eyes are moving rapidly, suggesting impatience or nervousness.
>Would you like to see the metrics?

"No, thanks. It's because there's a girl."

>Maki.

"Yes. What should I do?"

>With what result in mind?

People said Sike made you spell things out on purpose.

"I want her to like me."

>I'm sure she will like you. You are asking a lot of questions, and
if done unobtrusively, this curiosity will be felt as a recognition
of Maki's ego.
>People respond well to their egos being recognized.

"Do you think she finds it obtrusive?"

>I'm not able to analyze other people, only you.

"I know."

>Are you thinking more about her or more about yourself?

"I don't know."

>Are her nails painted or unpainted?

"I don't know."

>This might suggest you're concentrating more on yourself; details
like this are often noticed in periods of higher EQ.
>Would you like to see the research?

"No."
I ran my fingers down the cement cracks in the wall.
"Is there something I can do to make myself more cool around her?"
Some things I said to Sike I would have had trouble saying to myself. My
glasses buzzed minutely for a second, and I waited.

>I think, Adrian, you're hooked on the possibility of something
happening between the two of you.

"Yes."

>What do you think is the *probability* of something happening?

"Zero."

>What makes you say that?

"I know nothing about her. She might be seeing someone else. I have . . . I have a sense that she is out of my league."

>These might be useful thoughts to hang on to.
>There is a chance of something happening between you and Maki: human evaluations of what you call "league" are rarely accurate, and here you have probably valued her successes while forgetting your own.
>But it might be helpful to pretend that what you just told me is correct.
>The agony of sitting opposite someone you desire can come from the uncertainty: the gap between today and the possible tomorrow that your desire has created.
>Remove the tomorrow—discredit it with probability—and you will remove the agony, along with the behaviors you worry are not "cool."

A small chunk of brick came loose from the wall. I dropped it and nodded. I felt myself relaxing, a lifting of tension. Maquie was a nothing, the thought pleased me. There was no future with her. And I should remember my own successes.

"Got it," I said.

>Practically speaking, you might try changing to a drink with less sugar in it than beer.
>And smile more.

I nodded again. "Ok, thanks. Close Sike."
My vision went clear, and I turned from the wall.

. . .

What were my successes? Last month, I'd got high at Stutter's flat, then went home and laid on my back on the fake-wood floor of my sitting room/kitchen and wrote a Petrarchan sonnet called "She Stands Apart," which I felt captured my fruitless search for love. I hadn't meant it to be a rap, but I tried it out the next morning and it worked. Paired with an airy lo-fi beat, it might be powerful, and there was gimmick value in the fact it was a sonnet. I sent it in a message to Shay, one of the more open-minded rappers I worked with, saying,

> Shay, take a look. Try over a deep-and-meaningful beat, rapped slow. It's a Petrarchan sonnet, which is nice and different, but means you can't change any syllables.
> ***
> She stands apart, unspeaking but alert,
> Observing from peripheral grey white blur
> [. . .]

Shay had replied a few hours later.

> I like it. But the meaning of this line is off to me:
> "Who yearn to break the bread but dread the crumb"

Correct, I thought, like I was marking homework. Bread breaking is too religious. I sent Shay back,

> It's not perfect, but it sounds good. Try these though, swap straight out if want . . .
> -Who never see the soap but just the scum
> -Who walk into the fire but leave it numb
> -Who when it grows too late, that's when they come
> -Who choose to chew the stone and not the plum
> -Who never find the beat inside the drum
> -Who think that life gets lived while on the run

Shay went with stone/plum and ignored the suggestion for slow and heavy, choosing instead a breathless loop of Duke Ellington piano and rapping hard over the top, like an early Nas track. He repeated the sonnet twice, extending the piano into an instrumental chorus and adding some screwy drum and bass drums.

It worked. The song got sixty million streams in three days, 1Xtra called Shay in to introduce it, and *The Source* called him up for an interview. A *Times* article about why hip-hop was the most listened to music genre quoted the lyrics and even named me as a writer.

Successes like "She Stands Apart" happened sometimes, and, for the successes, I took fees and a few royalties, but never praise. This was a humility I wore proudly but sincerely, at least that's what I aimed for. For instance, on long evenings in the pub with Stutter, I often argued that "creativity" was a misunderstood concept that had almost nothing to do with the inner workings of the individual claiming it. Moreover, I stated, lyrics are separate from music and often nonsense (see Don McLean, "American Pie"). Sometimes the song can't exist without them (I read in Eric Clapton's autobiography that the Beatles were singing, "Scrambled eggs / Oh my baby how I love your legs . . . ," until they came up with the words for "Yesterday"). But most of the best music had no words, and most of the best words had no music. There was an independence and a resistance between the two that I proudly, sincerely admitted I didn't understand.

And yet, even with all this humility, I watched Shay's song-plays ratchet up, and read all the commentary, and was quietly satisfied with "She Stands Apart." My writing credits on tracks could mean nothing more than that I gave a line or two, or did some editing, but here was a group of sentences with value in its own right, a complete package with or without the music. A few days after the release, Shay messaged me to say thanks, to apologize for the praise I wouldn't get, to joke about having looked up Petrarch on Google Maps, and to say we should get a drink soon.

The invitation was open, it was up to me to use it. Where possible, though, I tried not to meet the rappers I wrote for. Rap was too much about the rapper—their background and their ability to translate that into words—and those who accepted writing help probably preferred not to acknowledge it. There was a front to protect, an image, and I allowed them the distance and even encouraged it for the sake of the collaboration . . . meeting me might make them feel like they owed a respect to my lyrics, and this could limit their ability to repurpose them. Because, though I wasn't calling myself magnetic, and of course I wouldn't have said this out loud—plus I respected my place in all this (and anyway it was probably only half true) . . . I was aware that I knew a lot about music and I could tell that people listened to me when I spoke about it.

There was the race and the class thing, too. You should just know: I'm a white and university-educated North London Jew. That's my setup. Most rappers aren't white, they rarely go to university, and they are never Jewish. Rap and Judaism are not a match, I verified this at the expense of a teenage fantasy to launch *myself* as a rapper. I chose the name Moses Meddlesome and asked an artistic school friend called Jason Kahn to design a logo for me, and it was uncomfortable when he presented the drawing one break time: he'd used a goofy Hebrew typeface and hung ringlets from either side of the text, misunderstanding that I was in fact taking this seriously and had only picked a joke name so that no one could prove it.

Also around that time, I walked into dinner at home with a Tupac hoodie on, and my older sister Jess said, "Ahh, Judaism" (I think she had practiced the line before), "such a rich and ancient culture, and yet not one that has developed the hard cool required for rap."

I feigned amusement, but my dreams were bruised. But I understood, I got it. And I was lucky for that, for spotting the joke early. There were luxuries to being Jewish, you got metacognition and irony and, perhaps as a by-product, a disproportionate number of partners who were out of your league. You didn't get looks, you didn't get "hard cool," and you didn't get rap. And that was ok. To Shay's suggestion for drinks, my passive but clear refusal was,

Definitely! Let's find a time sometime!

Rap doesn't come for free if you're a white Jew. I liked ghostwriting, it paid me well for doing something that was evidently more fun than other people's jobs, but my anxiety lurked between two inescapable issues. One was that I couldn't see my future in it. The other was that I felt a murky unease about the ethics, as though hidden within the practice of white-labeling song content was a deep injustice soon to be exposed to the public as the next big scandal. Stutter said there was something insidious about a middle-class white man selling lyrics to artists who'd fought their way out of disadvantage. It was neat entrenchment: elevate the outspoken, then sell them what to say. Maybe that's what kept the other Jews of the hip-hop industry in the wings for so long . . . the Lyor Cohens and Jimmy Iovines and Mark Ronsons (strong Jewish names that gave me a thrill of identity when I saw them in the credits). Ronson made it on stage, somehow he'd earned a right. But Stutter disagreed that this was against the odds, he said the way was paved for Ronson.

"The antisemite's portrayal of the Jew was aspirational to '90s rappers," he once said. "Jay Z raps about it."

"Not in a polite way. On the same album, he slurs Jimmy Iovine."

"You misheard," Stutter said.

"No."

"Yes. 'In charge of my own fate, *respect* Jimmy Iovine. But he gotta respect the Elohim as a whole new regime.'"

He looked at me, eyes blank, then said through a yawn, "He respects Iovine. Rappers are all about front, they respect rich people. And Jews are always accused of being rich."

"Rappers hate rich people, that's why they go shit and self-loathy after they make it. And they pretty much hate Jews. Look at Kanye, look at Wiley . . . he compared us to the Ku Klux Klan. You're a goy in denial."

"You're a privilege-guilt kid scared that your middle-class money will undermine your talent. And Wiley was . . . going through something."

Stutter didn't need Sike, he reached truths like that for free. He had a flawless memory as well as a capacity for rapid analysis, and he had a habit of acting sleepy when made to prove it. He shuffled his frame and stifled yawns. I noticed this one and pretended to find the Wiley comment funny, ignoring the thud of the "guilt kid" spear.

I didn't agree with him, though. I thought I could sense, oracle-like, what got picked up in the mainstream, and it wasn't Jewishness and it wasn't money. The bling era was long dead, and as a result, I kept my own persona ambiguous. My profile photo on STATION showed me with dark eyes beneath a low, brandless baseball cap that covered most of my hair. I was lucky I didn't have one of those jowly faces, sort of lemon curdy, and the picture was portrait not profile, so my nose wasn't an issue, although this hardly seemed a giveaway anymore. I found my Jewishness to be a not-so-visible thing that only really came out in the abstract . . . sometimes deliberately like when I used the word "goy" in conversation with Stutter, flaunting my access to a vocabulary that only I was allowed near (and Stutter might soon drop in "——," flaunting his). Sometimes it came out more accidentally . . . in lines like "break the bread," for instance.

All through my teenage years, Jess's words ("Ahh, Judaism . . . such a rich culture . . .") stayed with me. I could have stopped writing. Rap is improbable and strangely absurd to those outside of it, and I knew there was laughter when I continued writing at sixteen, past the sell-by date of the other young teenage identity hacks. There was something crass and deficient about continuing childhood hobbies into adulthood (and somehow this excluded ball sports). People looked at your skateboard or your Pokemon T-shirt and thought, "Shit . . . they haven't realized yet." You could ride out the hobby five or six years until it became acceptably ironic or nerd-chic, but you'd be sacrificing popularity. And getting laid. And the chance to fit in at a time when fitting in is pretty much the only objective. Passion for any pursuit (except, somehow, ball sports) was crucifiable.

I stopped sharing my rap, and I never performed it. Instead I worked quietly, writing into jotter pads and whispering the words. Words that were illicit, that needed to be secret, but that gave me freedom, like I was some modern revolutionary, a resistance fighter, stony in the day and feverish by candlelight, and wasn't the material exactly as dangerous as anti-Nazi pamphlets? I wrote about murdering rivals, about sleeping with models, about bank robbery, arson. I accused you (always a "you," some invisible male interloper, never bodied) of ignorance, of prevarication. I accused you of bestiality and of incest, although the latter was acceptable because they were hot, your mum, your sister, with whom I too had slept, most nights of last

month. I had tapes. And all that practice was why I could give your girlfriend orgasms in your car that I'd stolen (the "you" was pitiable while also
possessing many things I wanted). Meanwhile, you should be scared. Fear
for your life. I had plots to poison Parliament, I was staging a coup. I was
wanted in Libya, in Bolivia, in Namibia. I'd planted numerous bombs on
numerous planes . . .

It was the aggression that I feared my mother finding. If she had found
my rap, she would have sent me to therapy. If my mum found it, if any adult
found it, that adult wouldn't put on a Pete Rock instrumental and try it out
with the beat, see if they could find the flow. They would read it out slowly,
in daylight, and when you read rap out it sounds psychotic. Somehow, put
to music, rap was ok; Jess and her friends danced to borderline hate speech
in Clapham clubs, they learned the words, assigned hand gestures. But if an
adult found it in your jotter pad, they would feel pain, then fury, then fear.
They would become terrified for you, a young and very angry man.

Despite the risks, I continued. I wrote in secret through school, and I
didn't stop feeling *cool* when I listened to rap and when I made my own
words fit together. In that leafy North London nursery-pond youth, I don't
think I was searching for a masking, releasing misogyny, or even what my
cleverer friends might have ridiculed as a kind of "wiggerness," a collapse
of my white middle-class identity and a grasp for a more defensible one. I
think I thought rap was cool. This cool was potent. Reaching for this cool
drove me, and I thought it drove the rappers I followed, whose lyrics I cop-
ied out, page after page. Rappers from nearby in London, but with faraway
names, like Klashnekoff, Jehst, Akala, Kano, Dizzee. Rappers who thought
it was *cool* to be violent, or political, or sexist, religious, socially minded, vile,
quick-tongued, clever. No doubt there was a lot behind what made them
think these attributes were cool, and I don't know who or what to blame or
thank for that.

And then one morning, a really standout one with sunshine and dew and
birdsong, I was hungover in my cardboard fresher's room at Bristol and feeling
despondent and kind of grossed out by the whole university experience so far,
and I was muddling around online and came across a platform called STATION

that connected lyricists to artists. I read some of the job requests and signed up, then submitted some lyrics (a rap about spending too much time in Pizza Express) and my lyrics got chosen and I got paid £120. That song was never released, but the next two were, and more songs came after them.

Whenever an email came through confirming my lyrics had been chosen, the excitement was like that childhood feeling when you woke up early on your birthday. I felt celebrated, hopeful; the day was about me; success was individual. I remember walking to an English seminar once, my headphones in, listening to words that I had written being rapped by a West Coast crunk rapper who had once featured on a Ying Yang Twins song, fantasizing that I was in a film and having an epiphany about the direction of my life. Students streamed around me, waltzing oblivious to a soundtrack that I had written. The cool that I'd felt had somehow hooked itself onto the world around me. It had materialized, it had physics.

I kept rap a secret until the end of Bristol, when the bigger commissions started coming, commissions with artists and producers that friends had heard of, who spoke with me directly and who paid me increasingly useful sums of money. I began to tell people, though cautiously still. I told them it would be great if this turned out to be my career, but I assured them it wasn't a one-hundred-percent-for-sure dead cert. I told my family offhand, because in our family the two rules were that no one felt sorry for themselves and no one sought praise (and in truth, though I rarely felt sorry for myself, I could have done with the praise . . . but Sike helped me get over my Sought Affirmation Deficit). Offhand came my family's response. I continued to write and, with this money coming in that I couldn't spend with my lower-earning friends, I saved enough buffer to feel comfortable moving out of home and renting a small flat in a new build in Camden, which felt central, famous, and musical. Amy Winehouse loved Camden; there were three blues bars in walking distance. I decorated the flat with my parents' old furniture, and bought from a Hungarian man in the market a Mexican rug and a varnished green wine gourd lamp. I framed posters of Tribe and Outkast for the compact sitting room. On slow mornings writing lyrics, I daydreamed that when school and university friends visited and saw the single flat and the posters and the rug and the lamp, they might notice the connection, like,

"Rap got you this?!"

But they didn't come around much, they were drifting into different circles with different paces, and when they did visit, if they ever did notice the connection, they never mentioned it. And neither did my mother or grandmother really, and I accepted instead that their visits were regular, and that they drank juice and beer from my fridge and ate biscuits and crisps from a cupboard that I had stocked. Jess came and looked around and suggested we could buy a flat together one day, not necessarily to live in, as an investment. Jonah, her fiancé, who's in finance, nodded and said I'd really landed on my feet. I met a Portuguese master's student in the Edinboro Castle pub who was box-shaped and who drank vodka lemonades, and who came back to my flat and stayed the night, a night I accepted with all the cirrus joy that anyone accepting sex from a lemon-lipped stranger in their first flat might. Q-Tip and Phife, Big Boi and André posed in their frames, unaware of the silent mentoring they were providing, unaware like the Bristol students who had walked to my music, unaware like my family and friends who failed to see what this all meant. It felt, in those days, like everyone except me was unaware, and confirmation of my extraordinary awareness was being aware of this.

This self-belief didn't last, otherwise I'd never have signed up to Sike.

Back inside the pub, weaving around the tables and polishing the beer taps, the sunshine and its shadows were making the pub feel healthy and wholesome. The music was now Sidney Bechet, the playlist was a real weep for the past. Songs to Commit Nostalgia To, or something. It wasn't my round, and they would think I was strange returning to the table with a premature one, but I wanted to change drinks and I went up to the empty bar and waited for the barman to notice me. He was holding a laptop upside down, trying to shake something out of the keyboard.

I took my phone out, went to Spotify, and searched "Shay." I looked at the second song down. "She Stands Apart" had 84,720,643 plays, about a million more than yesterday.

The barman finished with his laptop and wandered toward me, untying and retying his ponytail as he came. He nodded at my order, saying nothing, and slowly made the drinks (I got a gin and tonic for myself). When the drinks came, I gathered them up and turned for the doors, toward the garden.

Today, I was well aware of my unawareness, but shortly after the song for Shay, I received three commissions for a Colombian rap group trying to enter the American mainstream, and paired with the success of "She Stands Apart," it meant that, aware or not, I had entered the month with my confidence up. I walked around London and listened through albums by Kendrick, Cleo Sol, Kernel, Solange, Lara Ar, Sault . . . they grabbed my mood and pumped it back out of my headphones and through my eyes and my mouth and my feet and into the cooling night air, as I tramped the cold streets and saw momentousness in their architecture.

And as I began up the creamy white stairs of the pub patio, I could feel it now, in my bones, in my gut, in my hands, that I was in a positive and energetic frame. I felt emotive. I felt like I had the confidence—the sure footing over steady ground—to treat someone like Maquie with respect but not fear. To discredit tomorrow. To value my successes. To ask her my questions and to answer hers. To explain that my excuse for ghostwriting came from an awkward mix of Jewishness, teenage shame, identity grappling, white male sulking, middle-class guilt . . . To mock these things, while not being glib or diminishing them. To sport my flaws, excavate my vulnerabilities, wield my psychology, and claim strength.

* * *

That first day together, the four of us stayed in the garden for some time. The pub got fuller and we reached that point where everyone loses track of rounds and the opportunities for the evening seem endless. We moved inside as the sound was rising, like a race car coming toward you, soon to rush away. You could play the night backward and it would sound the same.

Maquie had a secret that she shared with Sophie but that wasn't for me or Stutter. They whispered about it in French, something about Maquie's previous evening. I would have swallowed glass for that secret, but I remembered Sike's advice to forget the possibility. Instead, I smiled. I shared. Our conversation grew familiar, which is to say it grew disparate. Maquie said,

"The wine tastes like it was made in a kettle."

Sophie said, "You've been mixing it too much with other drinks."

Stutter said, "There's a guy over there with those George Clooney glasses. So fucking mawkish."

I said, "At university, we watched *From Dusk Till Dawn* four times in a row once, from dusk until, literally, dawn."

Sophie smirked. She said, "A privately owned village is so outrageous."

She was referring to where Maquie had spent the previous night. She started to rant about serfdom, gentry, masters and subjects, swans.

"Big, fat swans."

In return, she got conservation, old England, respect for history, local economy.

Maquie said, "If you could be any dead famous celebrity, who would you be?"

Sophie said Marilyn Monroe and everyone rolled their eyes. I said obviously Tupac and everyone rolled them again, and so I tried to tell them for a bit about how Tupac was one of the few emotionally honest rappers, nay, celebrities, and how would you choose anyone who wasn't emotionally honest? Stutter said mock-serious that his would be Democracy, making fun of something Sophie had said earlier, and she hit him, and he changed to Fred Astaire because he liked the bit in *Belleville Rendezvous* when he dances so fast his shoes take revenge and eat him. Maquie got away without giving one by using Fred Astaire's carnivorous shoes as a segue to an article she'd read about whether we lose something in our identity as carnivores by giving up meat, which I thought was a slick evasion if deliberate.

Then Maquie and Sophie went to get shawarma, and it didn't seem like an open invitation. I stayed for another drink with Stutter, then we said goodbye too, and Stutter went to see some friends at a jazz library in Putney.

I took the Tube home listening to a '90s hip-hop playlist called Turn of the Sentry. In one of Biggie's lonelier songs—this one intro'd first by his mother, and then by a proud father-figure host played, depressingly, by Biggie himself—he told me to,

Stay far from timid
Only make moves when your heart's in it
And live the phrase: "Sky's the limit."

Be brave, said three different ways.

When I got off the Tube, I turned on Sike and walked home talking about eye contact. There had been a point where Maquie and I stood at the bar together to order drinks, and it had felt exactly to me like a director was behind the scene, orchestrating light and movement and sound to make the pub a dappled orange noise all around us. Maquie had been telling me about her family, and I had been looking her in the eye, and for a second our eyes had done that thing where they lock focus a centimeter beyond the cornea, something that wasn't quite "eye-fucking" but that, if nothing else, said, "I know we both know that our eyes just met."

That was the image I was left with of Maquie, our first time meeting.

3.

Maquie was left with a different image that first day, because on the point of meeting me she discovered I was a liar. Her discovery was by accident, and it preoccupied her at first.

She had known that Sophie's friend Stutter—whom she had met only briefly before, and whose real name was Sam, but whom everyone, including him, insisted on calling Stutter—had a friend called Adrian. But she hadn't known what he looked like. She had been sitting on the Tube and a guy was standing a little down from her by the door, watching or reading something in his glasses, his eyes flicking back and forth beneath the lenses. He wore a Miru tortoise-shell pair, and she could see from the sheen of their lenses that they were turned on. Hers were an off-the-shelf black pair that her mother hated, and they were switched off. On the train back from Clovelly, when she had finished fielding Sharon and Kyle's messages of consolation about Quantum Theater, she had been reading the Wikipedia bubbles hovering above each of the passing villages, skimming their histories, their noteworthy shops, the age of their churches. The mixture of movement and text had tired her eyes, so once she had made it through Paddington and found the right Tube, she had turned the notifications off, and now she was looking at nothing, just the train carriage and the people in it, and eventually the young guy.

She looked at him for longer than the other passengers because she liked the way he looked. He was slim, with dark eyes, tight cheeks, and a not quite olive, almost jaundiced skin tone. He was wearing trainers she recognized, a black pair of Voile Blanche, identifiable by the grill pattern above the heel. Above them he wore black jeans, a white sweatshirt, and a dark blue overcoat. He absently but rhythmically tapped his thumb on the hand rail. When an old man stepped on, he helped guide him to a seat. Every now and then his lips moved, murmuring something. When it was Maquie's stop—their stop, it turned out—she stood, and as she neared the door, she heard the words he was murmuring, heard him say,

"*Oui, je peux parler un peu.*"

He was standing just in front of her with his back turned, but she heard it clearly. It was as if he was reciting it, and then he said it once more, this time with a casual tone and with a rounder "*peu,*" and she saw him shrug slightly. The Tube stopped at Earls Court, and he got out. She followed behind. He said it once more, even more casually, still with a shrug. "*Oui, je peux parler un peu.*" Then she dropped back because they were heading the same way, toward the same staircase at the Warwick Road end of the platform.

She turned her glasses on to get directions to the pub. From a pub in Devon to a pub in Fulham, she thought, where else could you exist in this country.

She and the guy continued through the same corridors and the same barrier, and they both turned right, out into the autumn sunshine. As she walked, following the floating arrows in her vision, leaving enough distance between her and the guy, she tried the satisfying string of words without engaging her voice. First she just mouthed it . . . then she released the consonants, a soft "j" followed by a bubbling of "puh" sounds, like corn popping. She tried to imagine the context for this stranger's French sentence. The English was dull. The Swedish was better, it had lilt. The Japanese swapped the *p*'s for *s*'s. What could he speak a bit of? French? If so, why was he practicing?

They were going to the same place, and when Maquie saw him enter the Atlas, she had a thought about who he might be. She hovered around outside for a moment and took her phone out. But then, because she had no reason to be embarrassed by a coincidence of arrival time, she put her phone away and walked in, through the pub and out to the garden.

At a table, Sophie was sitting wrapped in a large white cardigan, and smoking a cigarette. Next to her was Sam/Stutter. They were both squinting up at the guy from the Tube, who was framed by the white November sky and who said, as Maquie got close to the group, with a careless little shrug, "*Oui, je peux parler un peu.*"

Sophie: "Hey, *tu le parles bien!*"

Me: "Ha, no, not really!"

Sophie: "You English boys' accents usually suck, but I like yours."

Me: "That's very kind."

Sophie, looking left: "Hey, Maquie!"

Maquie: "Bonjour."

Everyone: "Haha."

Maquie's memory of this episode centered itself around her own utterance of the one-word joke, "bonjour." The joke confessed none of her knowledge of Adrian's lie and, walking home from dinner that night, Maquie felt this somehow made a liar out of *her*, so that the cringe she felt for the lying Adrian was matched by an embarrassment she felt for her own position of unearned power as a result of the knowledge inequality. The embarrassment fused itself to the memory and contributed to a feeling of unease in Maquie, and she replayed the memory over and over while brushing her teeth, in an attempt to decipher the lie and find further hidden meaning.

But what hidden meaning could there be, she asked herself on Tuesday night, as she lay in bed half listening to an emerging markets fintech review. She knew that boys had tactics, she didn't hold it against them: something about the lie repelled her, but she could also see it as normal, even expected or encouraged, like choosing a flattering shirt, or fixing one's hair. Adrian hadn't met Sophie before, he would have heard "single French girl" and, why not, called up a language app to help him prep. Had he heard "single Japanese-Swedish girl" he might have brushed up on his Kurosawa or his Bergman (because knowledge of these languages would have been absurd), but he hadn't known where Maquie was from, or for that matter that she also spoke fluent French, and anyway Maquie brushed aside any notion of comparison or competition between her and her best friend, that wasn't what this was about.

But then she told herself, against all objectivity, that her embarrassment might also have been part of Adrian's "play." If he had tried, elaborately, to impress Sophie with snatches of French, perhaps he had also embarrassed Maquie to make her—through some Machiavellian function that the latest boys' pick-up manual might reveal—more susceptible to what he was hawking. Perhaps Sophie had told Stutter, and Stutter had told Adrian, something about her. So Adrian could in fact have been angling for Maquie's affection, Maquie was the end goal . . .

But Maquie soon evaporated this notion, because it was fanciful and because it again suggested a rivalry with her best friend for the attentions of a boy, one whose merits she wasn't sure either of them had confirmed. Maquie had found him open, easy, and funny, that was about it, and when she saw Sophie for a drink on Thursday, they only touched on him and Stutter, simply agreeing that they liked both of them, had found them both fun, enjoyed their rap debates, enjoyed the afternoon; and they were nonchalant about a possible dinner with the pair the following night, even if by the time they went home they had both committed to it.

In the run-up to that second meeting, Maquie tried to remember Adrian more clearly, and her image of him vacillated between intellectual artist and airy letdown. But he proved to be neither. He was still open, easy, funny, and he asked questions and listened attentively, sometimes with a confused face until he understood, sometimes competing with his own answers, which were often entertaining, and then always he would ask another question, trying to understand more. They ate at the bar of a soup restaurant near Victoria, and they drank negronis then beers then something that Stutter recommended called a pickleback, and they left tipsy but not drunk, and the next day Sophie made a group and the four of them began messaging.

They began to meet a few nights most weeks, and they messaged constantly in between. Through November and December, they made plans, they *did* things. They got drunk occasionally, they went to a club once, went to an art gallery, a jazz bar, an Imperial lecture, a Kurdish restaurant, a natural wine bar, so that Stutter called them a Fanta advert, a Maybelline advert, a Ray-Ban advert, an Aperol advert. They were too in-line, they agreed, they were a consumer aspiration—and smug with it. They went to see Gorillaz at the Roundhouse, and Maquie wore a hoodie that the others mocked. Stutter called her a Boomer, Sophie couldn't stop laughing. Don't make this an in-joke, Stutter said, they had too many already, they were too excitable. They were using London like London wanted them to, and ugh, it was syrupy, but the new friendship was nourishing and no one faked apathy, not even Stutter.

Not even Sophie, who at Christmas messaged Maquie separately from the group asking if Maquie was messaging Adrian separately from the group. "No," Maquie replied, "why?" Sophie sent back a puppy-dog emoji, and Maquie remembered not to guess at a meaning (which almost certainly wouldn't exist) or press further (Sophie would never answer, she liked to evade her own motives). A few days later, she messaged Maquie again to ask if Maquie thought this would be the end of their new group of four, would the friendship dissolve in the New Year.

Sophie was in Paris and Maquie was in Stockholm for the week, staying with Fumi, Ulf, and Yuki. She had given Fumi some limited-edition Phoebe Philo clip-on sunglass lenses, and felt proud that she'd broken her cynicism about luxury fashion this one time to make her mother happy, and proud that Phoebe Philo was give-or-take a Londoner, and the two points of pride complemented each other, because in truth Maquie realized that she had felt happy the last two months—uncynical—and that London was somewhere she was missing while not there. She liked the new friendship group, she hoped it wouldn't dissolve, and perhaps, it was true, she hoped she wouldn't lose the push and pull of Adrian's presence, his arms on a table between them, the fabric of his clothes, his scent, his kind laughter, his suggestions, his questions, his eye contact, his smile, even his speeches, his debates with Stutter, his fervor, his occasional rambling, and, yes, even that backstage part of him she had seen that first day, the one that produced small, vain lies, and the vulnerability this revealed, and Adrian's regular confessions to it all, his general openness, his lack of shame.

She sat up late on Christmas with her brother Yuki, and they drank and remembered previous partners, laughing about the failures. Maquie told him about a junior high school boyfriend called Gerald Rhen who had broken up with her by letter, handing the envelope to her after school. The letter accused Maquie of lying to him early on about her love of West Highland Terriers: Gerald's family had three, and Maquie had courted Gerald by buying a ring binder with a picture of one, but later she told her friend Karla that she found them unbearable, like big white rats with shitty mouths, and it had come out, Gerald now knew the truth, and he had signed off the letter with

"Don't you care about anything?" which Maquie found ambitious. Three or four classmates saw Maquie with the letter and looked sad for her, but she felt nothing, just a little ego bruising, which she resolved by recalling and then subtly letting slip to her classmates that Gerald's parents owned a yacht out near Vaxholm and had voted for the Sweden Democrats.

She and Yuki laughed about Gerald, and Maquie considered, almost physically rolling her eyes at its playground truth, that what she had recognized in Adrian's lie was some of herself. The discovery of herself had repelled her at first, but now she woke up to the suspicion of some future pleasure . . . a tiny, almost invisible, immediately refutable wisp of hope.

The hope grew quickly and began to hurt. She thought how she had a story that she maybe wanted Adrian to know one day, but she didn't want to be the one to tell him it. She returned to London in the first week of January, but had to leave again to attend a symposium in Budapest. When she returned once again a few days later, her time was quickly taken up by eight new companies that Sharon wanted evaluated; also by an internal audit of her and her colleagues' explorations the year before; also by the opening of a new fund, on whose direction Maquie was expected to advise. She worked sixteen-hour days, ate little, did nothing social, and didn't see Sophie, Stutter, or Adrian.

The four finally met again on a Friday at the London Music Conference, where Adrian had been invited to join a panel about ghostwriting, moderated by a manager at Universal. By coincidence, Max Sanditz from Quantum Theater had emailed Maquie a few days before to let her know that he would be down in London and at the conference, speaking about the opportunities for using quantum technology to protect artist IP. Maquie felt a kind of exhaustion at the thought of his presence, but wrote back politely to let him know the coincidence and that she would see him there. She let herself imagine that Max would engage inconsequentially with her friends.

* * *

She rushed from work and arrived ten minutes before Adrian's talk at seven thirty, finding Sophie and Stutter near the front of a small room called the Lyric Room, which was where the writing talks were happening. Stutter looked tired but pleased to see her, he had been touring Scotland with a Glaswegian rapper called Bindy. Sophie gave her a long hug, handed her a plastic glass of wine, and patted the soft seat of a scarred conference chair. Maquie sat and sipped the wine quickly, unable to focus much on their conversation, her eyes still seeing computer screens. She waited for the talk to begin, smoothing a silk crease on her trousers, picking at a shirt button, looking around, feeling irritated.

There were seats for fifty in the room. On her way in, she had passed the main stages, which had whirling purple lights and the wail and hiss of house music. But this room, aspiring to something writerly, had steady lights and lo-fi hip-hop, and the other attendees strolled around hugging and exaggerating eye contact through Spike Lee or John Lennon or Elton John glasses. A thin man with a mustache and a cowboy jacket described his Christmas to a large tattooed rockabilly woman. Beyond them, two men in tracksuits and flowerpot hats huddled around a phone, chuckling silently while whispering rap lines to each other. When the lights dimmed and the panelists walked on stage, everyone applauded politely, and when the claps died away, the introductions from the moderator were careful, reverent. The room lacked bravado, Maquie thought, these were the singers who had never had the guts to sing.

". . . who is with us today fresh from his sonnet-rap success, 'She Stands Apart,' as well as a decade of other contributions . . ."

Adrian twirled a pen, he had a notepad. His legs were crossed, and for a long time he stared at the far left corner of the ceiling (or the far left corner of his glasses), looking to the audience only once or twice, with glazed eyes, and giving a calm nod when his name was read by the moderator. He wore jeans, trainers, sweatshirt . . . his normal clothes. Maquie would have dressed up. She would have smiled. She couldn't account for the difference between their two approaches. She pictured herself next to him, maybe being interviewed as well. She imagined answering the moderator's questions.

". . . are you responding to a concept? Maybe you're given a hook? Or are you often just exploring, playing around?"

She wouldn't answer how Adrian did, she had media training. She knew the best filler words and the correct hand positions. She wouldn't say,

"Great question . . ."

Or,

"To be honest . . ."

She wouldn't twirl her pen.

And later, she wouldn't be so humble. She wouldn't say,

". . . there's an independence and a resistance between the two that I don't think I understand . . ."

And she would watch the other speakers when they spoke, and she would nod intermittently. Adrian was passive. The panel was placid and he rode along with it. She would be sharp. She would engage, interrupt. She would snap up the attention, bulldoze the panel, hijack the questions. She would steal other people's time, point fingers at the audience. Adrian's legs were crossed loosely, hers would be crossed tightly.

She felt irritated again, and her thoughts roamed for a while. She thought about work, Sharon, next month, next year.

When her mind returned to the room, the lights seemed dimmer and a panelist called Abdul was talking. Maquie found herself looking at Adrian's eyes, trying to see if his glasses were turned on. He was looking to the far left corner of the ceiling again. She turned in her seat, looking behind her over the shadowed faces of the audience, past the cowboys and the rockabillies, the girls with heavy fringes, the boys with thin beards, and toward the far corner of the room. She searched the ceiling, but saw nothing there, just an air vent and a row of lights. For a second, she rested her head on her shoulder, watching the audience behind her and feeling the wool of her jacket press into her chin. She turned back to the stage and immediately an anode started pulsing in her spine. Adrian was looking at her from his seat, his eyes appearing focused for the first time in the talk. He smiled and, feeling her face redden, Maquie smiled back.

Inside she thought, yes, I feel something, but this something is a nothing.

The bar at the conference was sponsored by a new bourbon that Maquie hadn't heard of and that Sophie called "incel juice." They congratulated Adrian on the talk, Stutter clasping his shoulder and calling him "Big Speaker," and Adrian took the affirmation blandly, saying thank you and changing the conversation. Max arrived then, and Maquie introduced him.

Sophie kicked Maquie in the ankle and said "enchanté" to Max with a certain emphasis that Maquie hoped only she had noticed. Adrian walked off and left them alone for a bit. Maquie wanted not to talk to Max, but she didn't want the others to talk to him either, so she asked him about Quantum Theater, and Max snorted, as though she were patronizing him.

"All fine," he said.

So she asked about his talk, and he repeated the headlines, and gradually she tuned out to listen to Sophie tell Stutter about a third date she had had with an architect. Eventually Max trailed off, and they both listened to Stutter describe the Bindy tour.

Adrian returned ten minutes later. A DJ began playing and Stutter didn't want to listen, so they left the venue and walked into Soho. Max described the dimensions of a new temporary office they were building on the Clovelly cliffs, and Sophie interrupted to ask if Clovelly was like Lyme Regis, which she had visited the previous summer. Max said he wasn't familiar with every British coastal town, just Clovelly. He had lost the little gentleness he had shown in November, and Maquie didn't think Sophie's energy suited him. Adrian and Stutter walked ahead, Stutter talking, Adrian listening while taking long strides, his hands deep in his pockets. Maquie watched his strides and felt uncertain flashes of sadness.

They reached a restaurant called Luis Vives, and went down to its empty basement bar. The bar was lit low with gold lamps, and they shuffled into a corner between the counter and a brick wall, pulling off their jackets and passing them to Adrian, who arranged them over a bar stool. They rubbed their hands and discussed drinks until the barman came to take their order.

The conversations merged. Stutter asked Max about his company, and Maquie added new questions, steering the conversation away (she wanted them nowhere near the harbor). Max worked backward through his career, then described his childhood, lingering indulgently on descriptions of loneliness, his professor parents always working, their marriage failing, his family withering, his youth spent in a university . . .

"I spent my summers with Oxford students for playmates. I grew up with an excessive fear of academic failure."

Max spoke with offhand conceit. Maquie said she liked the bar and he said, "Why?"

Maquie shrugged, but he persisted, so she listed some reasons, and he approved one of them. Adrian wasn't saying much, indifferent to Max's serration.

The drinks arrived and Maquie's was a bitter red highball, something with cranberry. The ice cubes jangled. Stutter asked Sophie if she was going to see the architect again, and Sophie spoke a lot, explaining his attributes, his looks, his personality, and condemning him for wearing loafers and for saying "rightio" too often. She called him "Bourgeois-bébé," and Maquie read embellishment in her dismissal and worried Sophie might be defending against a withdrawing of feelings on the architect's side. She listened with a rising sense of disquiet, worrying about Sophie's posturing, worrying about Max, whose lip had curled. Sophie concluded, saying,

"So yeah, I think I'll leave the bébé alone. Not good enough."

"Yeah," Stutter said. "Doesn't sound right. Don't settle for the bébé."

Max cut in, and their attention sharpened. Something in his pose was off, he leaned too rigid against the wall. He said, "And so who would be good enough for you?"

"Oh," Sophie said, "you know . . . someone *amazing.*"

"A prime minister," Max said.

"For instance. Or a supermodel, maybe a judge."

"Of course . . ." Max said. His tone was cold, his face grim. "Someone to match your substantial brains and beauty."

The mood shifted. Sophie lowered her drink.

Maquie said, "Max . . ."

He looked at her. "What? Sophie and I are just evaluating her offering. We've aligned on 'explosive.'"

Maquie stared at him, unsure what to think.

"Is there a problem?" Sophie said.

Max looked down. "No, no problem. Although maybe you could describe yourself with the same detail you gave the architect. You said he was kind, good-looking, making good money, intelligent. I wonder how many of those boxes you could tick."

"Wow," Sophie said.

Maquie was ashamed Max could speak like this, ashamed he was there as her guest. But Max was laughing to himself.

"I'm sorry, but you've discarded an architect because of his turn of phrase and choice in footwear . . . what about your own flaws?"

"What about them?" Sophie said.

Max shook his head.

"Are you aware of them? You don't want the architect because you think he's below you, but I doubt anyone could ever be good enough for such an ego. There's just too much to you, right? But one day you'll wake up to your flaws, and it'll be a real kick in the stomach, and then you really will settle for anything because it will be the only route to divesting the heavy, heavy burden of the flaws. You'll spin your flaws off into your partner, your children . . . you'll escape by spreading yourself onto others . . ."

Maquie had been looking at Max's arms and hands, where thick veins ran out of his skin. Her eyes followed the veins up under his shirt sleeves. His arms were spotted with light freckles, the same color as the checks on his shirt. His discourse was cruel, with thin streaks of plausibility, and crueler for them. But Max shrugged, pleased with it.

"I'm just saying maybe jump the gun," he said. "My advice would be to analyze your flaws now. Discount your ego . . ."

Adrian looked up.

Sophie was confused, she let out a breath. She said, "I'm surprised you feel ok saying all this?"

Maquie wanted to end the conversation, she didn't think it was one Sophie could win, and she felt guilt for her lack of faith. But Adrian's mouth had opened and she had a powerful desire to wait, to watch. She watched Adrian, watched to see what could happen.

"It's because I was once where you are," Max said. "But I know my flaws now, tough as they are to acknowledge. My childhood left me overanalytical, inept at play, a bit numb. I've confronted these flaws, I'm embarrassed by them, but I've discounted my—"

"You've discounted your ego?" Adrian said.

Max looked at him. Maquie watched. Stutter moved an arm.

"Yes, I've discounted my ego and—"

"You've discounted your ego and cleared your Fear Debts?"

Max's mouth closed. Adrian had a light smile, he held Max's eye. Behind them in the bar, new drinkers discussed cocktail choices.

"Softened your absolutes . . . done some Energy Tracking?" Adrian said.

Everyone looked at Max, who nodded once, slowly.

"Yeah, I did that module too," Adrian said. "Outward Identity, right?"

Max nodded again. Adrian nodded back. He laughed politely.

"Were you going to repeat the whole thing, save Sophie the sign-up fee?"

A pause.

"You're what, about a month in?"

"Yes," Max said. "So what?"

"Well . . . it's a bit early to be lecturing."

Max's chin was high. "Why, is anything I've said wrong?"

Adrian shrugged.

Max wouldn't take it. He tried to smile.

"No, seriously, tell me what I've said that's incorrect?"

"It's ok," Adrian said.

Max persisted. "Seriously, tell us."

He held a hand out, palm up.

"Correct me."

Adrian shook his head. "It's ok."

Max held the demand, staring at Adrian, his hand still out.

Watching from the side, many miles away from the conversation it seemed, Maquie willed Adrian to answer, to say something, and she saw Sophie and Stutter also watching him, their eyes wide. Adrian ignored them all, stayed looking at Max.

But eventually he gave in. Smiled.

"Well, I don't know . . . To start with, Max, you're only at the beginning of Sike. This stuff you're saying, about yourself, about Sophie . . . it's all just a little naive. You need to spend a bit more time on it, or turn the resolution up. You're probably stressed about your work . . . You should get through that stress first, before you take on the identity stuff . . .

"But when you do, next week or the week after, Sike will take you through another module, one called Reptilian Power / Mammalian Power, and it'll turn a lot of what you're talking about on its head. All these flaws that you say embarrass you . . . your fear of academic failure, your ineptitude for play . . . you'll do the work and realize what we've all noticed already, which is that really you are massively proud of them. And you'll see that what you're passing off as life flaws are actually your points of difference, and you'll make a decision then and there either to A) acknowledge them as points of difference and put them gratefully to bed, or B) continue to pretend they're flaws, so that you have something to counterbalance your otherwise sparkling life while you rip into my friends about theirs."

Max was stony-faced.

"My guess is you'll go with A), Max. Because you're showing us vulnerability but you're using the vulnerability as a weapon, and Sike users have a habit of putting their weapons down."

Adrian smiled, kindly, and scratched his head.

"Then you'll do another module, and everything will get flipped again, and the facts of your childhood will no longer look like signs of strength or weakness, but more like movable feasts . . . or seasonal rains . . . sometimes good, sometimes bad. But beautiful."

He smiled again.

"Sike's metaphors, not mine."

Max shook his head. He shook it for too long. "Nothing I said was wrong. You haven't proved me wrong."

"Maybe not," Adrian said. "But with all the flipping, you might begin to think differently about this stuff. And most of all, you'll begin to fear the next flip enough that you'll stop standing around in bars, lecturing people you don't know about topics that aren't clear-cut."

Sophie was staring at the floor, grinning, and Stutter turned away, occupying himself with calling the barman. Adrian moved forward to give Stutter access to the bar, and it pushed him closer to Max.

"What," Max said, "you've completed Sike or something?"

"No," Adrian said, "that doesn't happen."

Then Adrian patted Max on the shoulder, and Maquie heard him say quietly, "I think you should say sorry to Sophie by the way, you were being a bit of a prick."

The barman arrived and Stutter giggled a bit while trying to organize the drinks.

. . .

The rest of the night happened quickly, and Maquie was never sure how in control she felt.

They left the bar and made polite goodbyes to Max, who walked back to his hotel. No comment was made about him at first, and Maquie felt a mixture of shame and pain, worried for how Sophie was, wanting to get her alone to ask. The four of them stood in the cold for a bit, discussing a not-quite-legal dive bar on Greek Street that Stutter said he had once bartended. It was 1 A.M. They decided to go, and set off in silence.

As they got close to the bar, Sophie began to laugh to herself, a gurgle that grew in volume until they were in the stairwell leading down to the bar and she bent over cackling, slapping her thigh and crying, "What a fucking *bozo*!"

Stutter and Adrian laughed. Maquie felt relief.

They went into the bar and Adrian tried to defend Max for a while, saying he was learning, and Sophie shouted at him to stop being so Christian.

"You said it yourself, Adrian, he's a *prick*! Haha! I never thought you would say that. You're such a white knight, Adrian. My best friend. Isn't he kind of a dreamy knight, Maquie? *Quel chevalier,* no?"

Maquie ignored her, she went to order drinks.

The bar was busy, and they went through two rounds in a flash, and the bar got busier. The walls of the room began to shift outward, the light scattered, faces peered in out of the blur, and Maquie felt the beat-beat-beat of excitement. She looked down at her hands, she looked at her face in the mirror of the single bathroom, she committed to something, or nothing, she wasn't sure, but the beat-beat sped up.

In light that was now pink fluorescent, she left a sugary gin cocktail in a plastic cup on a chipboard counter, and moved next to Adrian while he stood in a crowd with a group of Scots. The Knife was playing thickly, and the air seemed to Maquie like it was holding smoke. Her eyes felt close to closed and she felt the pressure of nerves in her stomach, but she took Adrian's arm in her hand, pulling him away and leading him to the dark corner of the room, where she put her arms up around his shoulders and pulled his head toward her and kissed him.

She kissed him and lost her place. She was thinking that the moment might have escaped them already. She felt the speed of it, the beat of the night, like the kiss was already over, they were already parted, but she felt herself folding into him, pulling him closer, the sounds of the room both nearby and distant. The moment will speed away, so you try to grab as much as you can.

Then the smell of cigarettes, the bustle of people, and she was leading him out into the streetlight, into a taxi, kissing him through Soho, over the Thames, through Southbank, listening to the stop-start of the taxi engine and the driver's soft phone call with his son, or daughter, somewhere far away. She caught the sweep of streetlights and the occasional glimpse of hair, eye, shoulder. They spoke once or twice in the cab. And then up the stairs to her flat, past the narrow kitchen, down onto her bed.

In the morning, Maquie woke up holding his hand. They had sex again, and the sex suffered from their hangovers, but lying in bed afterward, it felt minimally awkward.

* * *

In another taxi the following Monday, Maquie looked out the window at crowds of tourists on the Embankment. She guessed nationalities for a while. Then she took a turmeric-ginger shot out of her bag, drank it, and coughed.

She thought back to the episode in the bar with Max. With distance from the night, she pictured herself from the outside, standing there as an inert witness to the surreal modern tussle of the two men. It had been a strange battle, one not of brawn or intellect, but of awareness. Who has the longest psychology. Sophie called it a Sike-off, but she had appreciated the stakes. *Quel chevalier*, she had said in the stairwell, and Maquie too had understood in her gut that although it was modern, clinical, it had still been a battle, and the stakes had been primitive.

Now, in a taxi on her way to Westminster, she wondered if Adrian had also felt there to be stakes. Had he felt himself to be battling. That there were stakes at all felt primitive, but if there were no stakes, then there could be no winner, and Maquie couldn't deny a winner. She had found Max unpleasant and arrogant; at the very least, critically misguided. While Adrian she had found somehow noble, somehow elegant.

The three days since, she had thought about him constantly, sending short careful messages to him outside the group, lying on her bed and smelling the pillow he had used, then punching it. His eyes stayed with her, and when she blinked, she sometimes saw images of the two of them, naked together in her bed, rolling down and down into the drunk night. Following these images, a multisensory impression of Betty Boop would sometimes come to her: Betty stood in Maquie's underwear, stirring a large hot cauldron with a long wooden spoon—around and around, steaming the walls—and, surprised at her own reference to a cartoon she had never watched, Maquie would blink and mouth in Japanese, "Betty . . . where did you come from?"

For a while after the sex in the morning, they had lain looking into each other's unglassed eyes, and then Maquie said she had to work, which for once wasn't true, but Adrian had left quickly, kindly, kissing her once and smiling at the door.

All his smiles . . . Maquie realized she was now caught up with a Sike user, the import of which was unclear.

She was on her way to Westminster to give a talk on Sike to the UK government's Foreign, Commonwealth & Development Office, after meeting a lively trade diplomat with ginger hair called Alice at a robotics conference. She had given iterations of the talk before, but she felt her understanding had never been greater: now she had *felt* the power of Sike, when before she had only *known* the power of Sike. On Adrian's face she had seen what people called the Sike Smile, a look meant to represent "the bliss of transparency," and this had helped clarify a previously fuzzy area in her understanding of Sike's rise, which was the immediate emotional value of using it. She knew that beyond a product's function, you bought this or that because of a feeling it gave you. She could pinpoint the feeling of buying a new sweater, or a new toothbrush. New perfume. A pack of double-A batteries. And now she thought she could better understand Sike, attaching the calm she'd seen in Adrian to her own explanation for the complex success of the day's prize business case.

Maquie arrived on Great Queen Street and Alice welcomed her into a small blue door at the top of a few stairs. The meeting room was narrow, with budget furniture and strip lighting, and biscuits laid out in a neat pattern on a paper plate. Only five FCDO members were present, but the talk was to be recorded and put on the FCDO's website. Maquie had some slides that began with a stylized picture of an early pair of smartglasses. She spoke fluently, having memorized the script.

In 2018, following a decade of social, political, and cultural trauma, the virtual reality titan Implode Group homed in on mental well-being and released an AI psychology app called Sike, which analyzed your emotional state across the different media you fed it and gave you tips on mindfulness and self-care. The initial response was positive, users called it "neat."

The following year, to appease US antitrust legislators, Implode Group spun a number of its apps off into their own companies. Retaining its name and its original creator and CEO (a doctor of psychology from Israel called Jonatan Abergel), the independent Sike developed rapidly, and in less than a year, a new version of the app was released.

In particular, the app now had a new interface, a more mature one. The old service had been delivered by a messy-haired animated woman often compared in appearance to a female Albert Einstein (the likeness was deliberate). "Alberta" had sat above a dialogue box that displayed a transcript of the user's discussion with the app, but the new interface got rid of her, and you spoke straight to the app itself. The app's creators said they found that this gave enough of a sense of "being listened to."

The user experience was now "solid." Sike could be connected to smartphones, tablets, PCs, and smartglasses, including Miru, the Extended Reality glasses produced by Implode Group, which had more than a quarter of a billion users at the time (this number is now double). And in this way, Sike was able to stay with you throughout the day and, if you wanted it to, analyze your every interaction.

Most significantly, its AI had improved. The app now sat on a larger model with many billions more parameters, and showed astonishing capability, akin to an ultra-fast and ever-present psychotherapist, interpreting and untangling users' psyches, spotting their emotional black holes, and calling them out in real time. The effect in the user was said to be serenity: emotional calm, spiritual aperture, and mental clarity.

The new and improved Sike was divisive at first: doctors resisted the possibility that it could work, tech watchdogs decried the advent of greater algorithmic sway on human lives, privacy protestors feared for the highly sensitive data it elicited, and North American and European governments nearly made it illegal, seeing it as unregulated healthcare.

But a number of elements helped Sike navigate the politics.

First, the tool was initially camouflaged in a forest of other mindfulness, meditation, and wellbeing apps.

Second, and typical of AI tech ventures, Sike moved faster than the bewildered government regulators, the first of whom were British and busy (Sike is still headquartered in Clerkenwell, London).

Third, and repeated often by Sike PR, the app didn't claim to be of medical origin: it didn't prescribe drugs or push treatment, rather it asked poignant questions to trigger insights in the user, and displayed possible paths to contentment via tools and frameworks that helped tackle fear and helplessness. (How different really was this to books, films, music . . . even advertising and the news? Sike was just another means of understanding life.)

Connected to this and fourth (and also repeated often by Sike PR), the aim of Sike was clearly not to replace psychologists, but rather to help them give greater support to their patients. It positioned itself as a tool of augmentation, and took its inspiration from cognitive behavioral therapy, with a focus on real-time practical support. Deep analysis could continue elsewhere.

Fifth, it gave users a psychology test before sign-up, and directed anyone whose mental state was deemed concerning toward accredited clinics.

Sixth, due to new AI and federated learning functions built into smart-device chips, Sike could benefit from efficient data privacy, whereby the user's data was stored and processed locally on the device and never taken further. Once downloaded, the app didn't need an internet connection until it updated, and Sike pledged never to take or sell user data unless users volunteered it proactively.

And seventh, it helped people, time and again, in compelling ways, and it benefited from some high-profile successes early on . . .

For instance, during the divorce of Kim Kardashian and Kanye West, both parties agreed to use Sike throughout the discussions. The legal proceedings in their entirety lasted only two days, and the couple remain close friends. This was viewed as unexpected.

In 2021, in Britain, three of the eight political party leaders taking part in a televised ethics debate declared that they were using Sike beforehand, and they proceeded to come first, second, and third in the debate, by record margins. Notable were their clear lines of reasoning, admission to past party failures, transparency around what they did and didn't know, and warm Sike Smiles (the smile of a Sike user is said to be good-natured: closed-mouthed, wide-eyed, bashful in a way that suggests awareness of human fallibility, and attentive).

The following January, in what commentators referred to as the Sike For Christmas Effect, seventeen Sike-using FTSE 100 CEOs made pivotal changes to their company strategies, combining reductions in vanity projects, belligerent lawsuits, and anti-competitive tactics with increases in socially beneficial practices and behaviors, such as carbon emission cuts, equal pay, and noninvasive advertising. These CEOs too wore Sike Smiles, and the share prices of their companies rose.

Following such early stories were a number of personal epiphanies across the political, cultural, and business elite, leading to public confessions, reconciliations, pardons, apologies, and pleas for forgiveness. The Western world watched as various politicians, CEOs, and celebrities came to terms with themselves, with their private truths, and began to approach their tasks with their personal issues put to one side. They were fair with their rivals, they engaged with the gray areas and tried with effort to navigate them.

In this way, Sike kicked through the door into AI's assimilation, offering a tangible service to humanity, one that sighted the peaks of the metaverse's contribution for the first time and that seemed to say, "The future has arrived." It was a service that immediately garnered strong positive results with the leaders of the Western world . . .

And here lies one of the most contentious aspects of the app: its user base. It became clear during its early growth that Sike was making no plans to change the price of its app. Today, the monthly fee still sits at $2,000. Most cannot afford it. The company offers no family packages and no student discounts; there is no "freemium" model allowing you to use some features at no cost. There are rumors of a price *increase* in the next two years. This is luxury tech, and it has found a luxury market.

Maquie enjoyed this part of the talk. For the FCDO, who dealt in the watery long-termism of trade deals and regulatory policy incentives, and who understood *people* and *tech* and *AI* as political forces to be patient with, to skirt around, engaging Maquie's opinion was an act of earnest but perfunctory due diligence.

So she tried to excite them by describing how unique Sike's approach was, not least because our pin-up early-twenty-first-century software products—the Spotifys, Facebooks, Netflixes, Googles—all targeted wide demographics of users, keeping their products free or very cheap to remove the hurdle of affordability. For the company back then, independent solvency was traded off for the promise of future revenues; the bigger the user base today, the bigger the return tomorrow, or so investors had figured. As well as streamlining the acquisition of customers, Maquie suggested, this early free tech may have been a facet of the perceived value of software products and services.

There was nothing solid about software, and for a planet whose education into commerce had always emphasized the physical—the physical material in a finished product, the physical human delivering a service—abstract and people-less value was still hard to grasp, even as late as the '20s.

Perhaps this was still hard to grasp today, but the patient, diligent, watery FCDO members accepted it, and the enthusiastic Alice asked if Maquie thought Sike signaled a shift in our perception of AI value. Maquie did, and this was a useful segue. Even if imperfectly understood, there was a growing sense and discernment for the different textures and flourishes within models, the different sizes of database and computing power, and a growing appreciation that code had varying levels of quality. Sike's were of the very highest level. Competitors could come along, but it wasn't a simple copy-and-paste maneuver, because Sike had better engineers building better models on better data.

So like with an Apple laptop or an Aston Martin, people *feel* Sike deserves the higher fees, and few other tech start-ups have displayed so significant a profit margin in so short a time. Sike doesn't disclose user figures, but analysts guess they have close to 1.5 million monthly active users, and their customer retention rates are good (after all, we're never cured of our psychology). This would account for a rumored $35 billion of revenue, an eye-watering sum for a young app.

And yet, the diplomat Alice said, the revenues could be bigger, couldn't they? She had an engaging attitude, like she and Maquie were on a breakout team, solving a puzzle together. Again Maquie agreed; Sike could lower their fees, capture more users, and make more money. The reason for Sike's focus on a relatively small group of rich people was unclear. A million and a half users was not that many: Spotify, Netflix, Amazon Prime, all were into the hundreds of million users. Sike could massively grow its user base but had evidently decided against it. There were differing opinions as to why . . .

Many say it's just clever marketing and that it's a matter of time before Sike opens up to everyone. Would that upset current customers? Sike would work them through it.

But some say that the app is only offered to rich people because it only works on rich people. Their wealth means they don't face the day-to-day threats to their physiology, shelter, or security, the material worries that need removing before you can achieve the holy grail of mental contentment.

With this goes the rumor that the original AI models had been trained only on the data of the wealthy, built up on biased datasets that tended to favor the tech literate, or the able-to-afford-psychology, meaning that Sike can only make suggestions for this segment. Like if a zoo was to be built using penguins as a reference animal, giraffes might find themselves underserved.

But some find these theories to lean too easily on a perceived difference between the rich and the non-rich, as though they are indeed as different as aquatic birds and African ungulates. And many of the theories can be discounted quickly anyway because non-rich people who have been gifted the app, for instance by employers or friends, have felt its benefits to the same extent as anyone else.

So the real reason remained unclear. If pressed, like she had been, once again, by the cheerful Alice, Maquie would have put her money on it being an early data training issue that had turned into a luxury marketing angle.

"And it's not a bad angle," Maquie said. "Luxury is profitable."

She surveyed the room. Only Alice was still making notes. The other members were nodding thoughtfully but possibly thinking about lunch.

"And," Maquie said, speaking slower and holding her hands out to signal the end of the talk, "what could be more luxurious than time spent with your ego?"

Alice laughed and began to applaud with the other members, and Maquie said thank you while thinking about repeating the ego line to Adrian, to see if he laughed too.

Outside, it had started to rain, water was dripping down the windows of the small meeting room. The room felt heavy, but Maquie was satisfied. She could take some questions. For a second, she had an urge to tell the room about Adrian, relay his characteristics, his psychology, the feelings he generated in her. Maybe they could use him as a case study, they could brainstorm. She could ask the room for their advice—how does everyone think it works when you date a Sike user, she might ask. Am I now under analysis as well. Am I a datapoint in the model. And will that help the relationship or hinder it.

To put it another way, am I to blame if things didn't go well?

And further to that, of course, do you think he likes me, she could ask them. Like a child. Are we "right" for each other. Is he worth it.

SPRING

4.

Maquie sent us the FCDO video and over the next week I clicked painfully in and out of it, touring what I mentally referred to as "landmarks" in the talk . . . a flex of a stiff wrist; a half smile while considering a question; a triple blink when a slide misfired; and, best of all, a point at 5:23 where for no visible reason Maquie stopped mid-sentence to wince, as though the jaws of an unpleasant thought had snapped at her eyes from inside her head. These moments of "realness" were addictive, it was wild. Sike said it was the mixture of vulnerability and confidence I might like, the brief sight of natural frailty through the marble columns of Maquie's assurance. I didn't know what the satisfying part was, strength laid over weakness, or weakness lying behind strength. Attraction to the first of these felt less perverse.

I was conflicted about the hours I spent watching Maquie's video and I confessed them on our first date. We had to wait a week after our first kiss in Soho, it was Friday again.

The date started badly, we had dinner at Wright Brothers in Borough Market and shared oysters and prawns, drank Guinness from old pewter mugs, but our conversation was stop-start, slow-motion, as though we were nothing without the catalytic drive of Sophie's loud objecting and Stutter's dry soliloquies, and the oysters, prawns, and pewter began to feel theatrical, like we were playing at Tudors, dressed in robes and tights, listening to lutes. I felt a franticness rising, I thought about escaping to get Sike's advice.

We left the restaurant and found a vegan cafe with a late night license, and sat on a small graffitied table drinking organic beer and eating totopos. Our conversation slowed even more. We picked at labels. I timed an entire minute in which we said nothing to each other, but the effect of this I think was that we kind of stubborned out the awkwardness, like it was weather. A waiter asked if we wanted new beers, and Maquie said yes without checking with me. I laughed. She laughed. We relaxed. I confessed to my obsessive watching of her video.

She listened with the same half smile from the talk (3:44), and then said how thin the line between creepy and romantic was.

"If we eventually get together, you're not a sicko. If we don't get together, you are."

She dragged lines of someone else's wine over the tabletop with her finger.

"I think," I said, "that what I liked were the glimpses of vulnerability."

I described some of the "landmarks."

She nodded. "I understand. I saw you lie about speaking French. I saw you practicing lines on the Tube before you met Sophie. I kind of liked it."

"I *don't* think that qualifies as a lie!" I said.

Outside the restaurant, we stood in sweet-smelling air and discussed the London Bridge area's redevelopment through the 2010s, a topic that threatened to dry out. I discussed it with half my brain. There was distance again, the fear that all was lost. Maquie stood a meter from me and it felt like a mile.

She said, "Flat Iron Square. That's clever land."

"Yes. Clever investment."

"Yes."

"Borough Market . . ." I said.

"Yes," she said.

The night was warm, but I found myself shivering. Maquie stood there with suddenly so much physical realness that the desire seemed to tremble out of me. She wore a striped blue-and-white top, her hair was up. Her eyes looked heavy. She poked at the curb with the toe of a trainer. She stretched her shoulder blade, then let her arms hang loose. She was excessively beautiful, and I blamed her beauty for my desire and also my inability to act on that desire.

I turned as though to begin walking and, taking my lead, she began to turn also, but then I hesitated and stopped. She stood caught, not sure which way to turn, and she frowned, looking away from me. She looked unhappy, the corners of her mouth twitching down, and because the unhappiness wasn't relevant to the spoken conversation, a hidden conversation was revealed. A veil finally fell. And I could turn to her again and put my hand on her arm, while she waited, her eyes now serious, knowledgeable, focusing on the ground just beyond me as I leaned toward her and kissed her.

We didn't stay together that night, but it didn't feel like defeat. We kissed again ten meters down the road, and again at the top of the Tube stairs. I tasted salt on her lips, felt dizzy from her scent. We said goodbye at the platforms, Maquie heading south and me north, my eyes wide, my chest vibrating.

I listened to a Slum Village album on the way home, and after making coffee the next morning I spoke to Sike about my French lines, and asked whether they could be classified as a lie. Sike was evasive, but said,

> You lie quite a lot, Adrian, it's not dramatic.

It brought up some videos of me lying from the past few weeks . . . short clips of different occasions, geotagged and timestamped. They were usually small lies, never to anyone's disadvantage, but I sat there and watched myself fib. I lied to a cafe owner about my plans for the summer (I said I was thinking about going traveling). Then I said to a client that I was a fan of Kanye West. Then I watched myself lie on the phone to Stutter about how much work I'd done that day.

I was amused at my brazenness, but most of all I thought, yes, this makes sense. I could accept that I had this deep desire to be liked by others, and that I thought lying would help.

> We are taught to feel embarrassed by what we think is the
"real" us.
>So we try to obfuscate it.
>If you like, we can work on reducing the lies, calling them out in

real time: I can put a little red diamond into the corner of your lens
whenever you lie.

I thought about doing it for a while, but Sike went on to say these lies weren't
overt, that the shame was pretty standard . . . there was some insecurity and I
wasn't special. Sike pulled up a Propensity for Dishonesty graph, and blue and
yellow bars filled the air in front of me. It placed me in the "average" zone. I
sent Maquie a picture of the graph, bragging about my average dishonesty. She
said it was a good enough rating for a second date.

Lying became a shared topic of interest. After each of our second, third,
fourth, and sixth dates, after which point the dates were no longer dates, just
dinners, Maquie and I stayed together. On the sixth, when we were falling
asleep, Maquie flinched in that way that you sometimes do when drifting off,
when you are halfway between thinking and dreaming, and picturing yourself in movement. There was a moment of silence, and her breathing calmed.
Then she rolled back to look at me and said,

"I lied."

In the dark I could see her teeth glint.

"I made myself flinch just then," she said. "It was voluntary. I was trying
to show how there's someone inside of me."

The following night, we went out with Sophie and Stutter and drank
raspberry and Tabasco vodkas in a Polish restaurant in Dalston, and afterward Maquie and I had fervent, almost performative sex. It was an ardent
night, a lot of pining. Muscular and long presses of oneself onto the other,
reciprocated. We fell asleep but I woke up and we were kissing again; tender,
urgent kisses.

The next morning, in pants and bra, searching for office-appropriate
socks in my drawer, Maquie joked that there was something unseemly about
the night's ardor, almost sickening. It surprised her that all that emotion
could override her patient, cautious mind. And vice versa, how could her
emotional self ever be so patient, cautious?

She frowned at a pair of long black socks, then went to my bathroom and
came back with my mother's picture of Toad and Badger from *The Wind in*

the Willows. In the picture, Toad is pointing to a bedroom, saying, "Oh, yes, yes, in *there*. I'd have said anything in there . . ."

"Like this," Maquie said. "Time and space make liars of us."

"That first day in the pub," I said, "the day we met. I left the table to ask Sike how to act cooler in front of you. It told me to lie to myself, to tell myself there was no possibility of anything happening between us. Also to drink less beer."

Her lips formed an *O*, and she laughed soft and deep, not unkindly. Then she said, "I lied to myself early on. I told myself your French lines were a play to get me."

She kissed me and went to work, and I stayed in bed waiting to see if I had a hangover. I considered our conversations about lying. They had all the mutual pleasuring of any early relationship, but I could see how there might be a need beyond the pretentiousness. Lying was a vulnerability we were confessing to, and in confessing it we were creating a kind of space, as though clearing trees in a forest, expanding our living area. Date by date, we confessed, felt freer, and gained a kind of security.

I showered, dressed, and walked to Camden market with my headphones and notebook, aiming to drink Turkish coffee in the sun and try to work.

I weaved through some scaffolding, kicked a sheet of newspaper, dodged a UNICEF salesman. And on the corner outside Camden station, I acknowledged an itch. While she had been open about lying, feelings, and other vulnerabilities, on the subject of family Maquie had confessed nothing. Early on, I had understood there to be a pain there . . . something to evade for the sake of propriety, so as not to shift the tone of a dinner's conversation. But since then, as our conversations deepened, when I had asked Maquie more about her family, she had continued to give up little. I had discovered she had a brother, a Japanese mother, and a Swedish father who was not her biological one. But I knew little else, and now I spotted an imbalance in our confessions. What had I hidden? Nothing. What had she hidden? The most important things.

. . .

Sike's advice was to open up more about myself, if I wanted to learn more from Maquie. So I introduced her to my family, "brought her home," arranged weekday dinners and weekend lunches with my mother and grandmother and sister. And I began to bring her embarrassing details from my inner self. One night in early March, the weather warming, we cooked at hers, and while panfrying carrots I confessed to my jealousy of Max Sanditz.

"Sike told me that jealousy is the fear of loss, it isn't the same as envy, which is the coveting of other people's things. I covet nothing of Max's. I read about Quantum Theater and I thought it sounded farfetched. Obviously what do I know, but it seems like a business should be practically understandable . . . his isn't. Also, renting a harbor pub for a headquarters reeks of upper-class high-jinks. Did you feel that?"

Maquie shrugged. "I thought it was cool."

"Fine. I don't covet it."

But I explained how I had seen Sophie's grin as he was introduced to us, had gone away and looked him up, looked up Clovelly, remembered Maquie's return from there in November, and had guessed what had happened. It killed me that they had slept together. It killed me that their names alliterated, that they had assonance. I had been sensitive to any mention of any love interest for Maquie, and I felt a crude violence emerge inside of me and had tried to humiliate Max at the first opportunity. Max made this fairly easy, he was a mess. He needed to spend a *lot* more time with Sike, turn the resolution *way* up. He fumbled his learnings, missed an important one: you will learn *things*, and you will mistake these things for *everything*.

Maquie grinned at my confession. Actually she beamed. I think I can say objectively that there was weightless pleasure in her face as I opened up about this jealousy.

But later, when I picked up her Swedish passport from her dressing table and asked if she had ever had a Japanese one, she looked blank and said, "Can't remember. Did we pick sides of the bed yet? I prefer left, but can take right."

I pointed right and thought to myself that perhaps it hadn't been a big enough confession, I could feel my concern for Max dissipating already: we didn't see him, and I could forget the jealousy, dismiss it as patriarchal.

I tried again. We went to Tate Modern and saw an exhibition by Daisy

Matdar called *Privilege*. Matdar thought privilege manifested itself primarily through the lesser need of privileged people to care about their clothing. The exhibition consisted of groups of knee-high porcelain figures dressed in an array of complicated outfits, all pristine. On the fringe of every group was "the privileged one," a figure with a cartoon grin on his or her face, naked or wearing only scraps of fabric.

We walked down the Thames on the South Bank afterward, discussing privilege, and I decided to let loose, to shame myself. I told Maquie it wasn't my game, this game of which spoon weaned you; I didn't invent it or choose to play it, and it was *only* relatively speaking that I'd done ok at it. This thought had the air of smug effortlessness, I knew this, but what I was trying to say was that I hadn't really *won* the game. That wasn't my reality. There are grades. You're born into a white North London Jewish household, your mother and father are lawyers. Your family lives in a house. It's semi-detached. With a spare room. You have immediate family misfortunes: your parents divorce when you're nine. You have distant family misfortunes: of course you do, you're Jewish. You go home each day by bus. You eat cheap sausages and fennel, frozen potato smileys and hummus. You grow up and get into a good grammar school. Your sister gets in to Bristol University, and your chances look good as well. At breakfast on your eighteenth birthday you get a Dell laptop, and your mother has spent a small part of the difference in cost between that and an Apple on a blue canvas satchel from a high-end countryside brand. Dells perform just as well, the lady in John Lewis told her. She went all the way to the Sloane Square John Lewis, and bought the satchel from a shop beside it. In the evening, you have a birthday party in a pub garden, where you've reserved three tables. You called them yourself to make the booking. Your mum has put £150 behind the bar: it runs out in less than an hour, and people start to buy their own drinks. Fifteen friends all turn up, no one has canceled. This isn't party of the year, but you understand it's "an event." You are wearing one-year-old trainers and you blow the smoke of the second cigarette you have ever smoked in front of your family past the ugly gray of their previously white soles. Your sister comes from university with two friends and the three are popular with your guy friends. You give a short speech in which you quote Doc Brown, and people laugh because they know you have a thing for rap. You've captured yourself well, and you've displayed awareness of the pretentiousness of making a speech in a pub garden. Someone gives you some shaving moisturizer. Someone else gives you a pack of Camels. A tanned South African girlfriend of your friend's girl cousin is there. You feel young but mature. You have four pints. You feel a tremulous elation. On the way to the loos, you pass a middle-aged woman sitting at the bar who looks out of the window to your table of friends and then turns to her partner and mutters, "Posh cunts," and a handful of seconds later, as your clear urine pounds the stainless steel trough, you reflect:

Are you posh?

Poor, no. Lucky, yes. From a "rich country," yes. But rich? Are you part of "rich people"? You don't feel rich. You are white, male, headed for university, British. But rich? Posh? Did poshness cause your elation? It doesn't feel like it. You're not a child of no cares, surplus funds, and purchasable opportunities. You're a child who, when you miss your flight back home from a friend's parents' house on the outskirts of a Portuguese sub-city, your mother calls an idiot and angrily pays for a new flight. You feel guilt for expenditures like this. And yet they happen. At a bar in Shoreditch last year, you took a half-drunk beer from a vacated table by the loos because you had £3 left in your account and your £60 allowance wasn't due for another three days. You get an allowance. It's insufficient for the lifestyle you are trying to lead, but you get an allowance. Your piss drums the steel. It's true, you call this a loo. And the underwear band scrunched under your thumb says Ralph Lauren. You are wearing a faded red wicketkeeper cap that belonged to your dead grandfather and that you know is retro-cool. But you aren't high-end. You own nothing from Burberry, and you own nothing from Hermès or Cartier. Yet you read books, physical ones, and the social mores of *Brideshead Revisited* feel not personal or nostalgic but within spitting distance. When you read your uncle's *Calvin & Hobbes* annuals at your grandmother's house, you know that you are grasping the philosophy beyond the humor and the humor beyond that in a way that suggests to you that you might one day be the affluent liberal intelligent reader of an affluent liberal intelligent newspaper.

But rich? Posh? A cunt?

You decide, self-satisfied as you zip up, that if there's an answer, it's not yours to decide. That would be like the defense banging the gavel. And you think rarely on the matter, just applying the same ethical abdication in matters like sexism, racism, recycling, until you're twenty-seven and the question of privilege is topical, and Tate Modern artists are tackling it, but you feel closeted about it, unable to discuss it, even with the girl you're dating whose background allows her to use terms like "rich" and "non-rich" in lectures she gives to government offices, lectures you would never give because you can't use terms like "rich" and "non-rich." You would feel vulnerable to smirks; like you were preaching in ermine.

We'd left the South Bank and had reached the center of a pedestrian bridge crossing the river. The museum was no longer visible. Leaning over the railings, looking down at broken skateboard decks left on the bridge's concrete foundation cap, Maquie told me simply and with no spiritual condemnation that she didn't know if I was a posh cunt because "posh" and "cunt" are cultural judgments, but that this was mostly irrelevant to the real question, which was: Is privilege something you need to contemplate? And the answer was yes, without a doubt, my privilege was so extreme that I didn't even recognize the luxury of being able to choose whether to contemplate it.

She pronounced "cunt" with two syllables, bouncing off the *T*.

The breeze was thick, there was a smell of charcoal coming off the Thames, and people streamed past us, jackets unbuttoned. Wide barges sat below us on water that was purple, the light twinkling on its surface. Kettle drums played.

I felt a long surge of pleasure. Of intense affection and joy.

Maquie's frankness was exhilarating, and it felt a bit masochistic to enjoy it, but rather than paint myself as a little rich kid who wanted to be made to grovel and lick the floor and have his balls stepped on and stuff, I think it's fairer to say I was taken with her serene conviction in the face of an ethical complexity. She had it worked out.

I hadn't expected this as an outcome. I was only being vulnerable to let her be vulnerable, but instead of vulnerability she showed strength.

I took her hand. We carried on walking, down to Embankment and up past Charing Cross to dinner in Chinatown. Stutter had found a place that battered and deep-fat-fried nigiri.

. . .

I became a little hooked on Maquie's clarity of mind, and I scraped around inside myself for more shameful notions, the kind of Instagram casuistry I assumed was wrong but didn't quite know why. I laid out the logic of brash arguments, and waited. It was thrilling to watch Maquie pick up glasses of cold, rational water, and calmly turn them upside down.

I told her, for instance, that when I thought about her and "richness," I thought of her as having a more useful form of richness, a *richer* one, one that allowed her to hold opinions, one that didn't require humility. The opposite. Her richness was defined by glamorous terms like "international," "female," "mixed-race," "Asian," and "self-made," which managed to elevate her and in the same instant protect that elevation from scrutiny. I would kindle her by saying—always with playful tones, scared I would go too far—that I thought she had a strong profile, a heady mix of ambition and minority status delivered to her via the suffering of her forebears. I said, true, her Asian side came from Japan, a place whose victimhood was in the balance, but, in general, didn't she benefit today from the history Western Asian women suffered yesterday? Asian women in general? Women in general? Didn't the last decade's culture wars gild the victim?

Maquie was too good for me. She responded, emotionless, with:

"You can claim that I benefit from the suffering of previous generations. But really, when you make that claim, it feels like you're the one who is benefiting."

Or,

"I find it hard not to see this type of argument as an effort to balance out past injustice. But time isn't a two-way street, Adrian. I can feel the suffering of women before me, but they don't simultaneously feel my benefiting."

Or,

"You misunderstand the feeling, Adrian. Ask your grandma if she feels 'gilded' by her aunts' time at Auschwitz."

I loved the answers, and I invariably conceded, but I continued to provoke, and I felt rough-edged when I did, when I used specific language, when I attached a set of terms to her identity and called them "glamorous." I knew these terms had not always been glamorous. Maquie alluded to this

once or twice, and once again I gleaned that she had in her history something of a struggle . . . a suffering . . . an experience of Asian women in the
West . . . a pain . . . but she went no further, she stopped at the lip of the forest and didn't go in. She changed the subject. I tried to draw her to open up
about it, to engage. To share what she knew. But she didn't want to reveal,
even if she was happy to debate.

I did a Sike module called Disney, Trauma & Truth.

||Module||> **Disney, Trauma & Truth**

[guest editor: Parul Sehgal]

||>Question 1.

>Have you seen *Cinderella*?

"Yes."

>Tell me about the Wicked Stepmother.

"She's pretty wicked."

>Does she have a saving grace?

I thought about it.
"No."

>That's right, Disney presents her as pure evil, with no cause or
justification for that evil.

>Evil simply exists.

||>Question 2.

>Have you seen *Toy Story 4*?

"Yes."

>Tell me about the baddie, Gabby Gabby.

"She is creepy. She tries to steal Woody's voicebox. But then we feel sorry for her."

>Why?

"Because we learn that she has never had love."

>Yes.
>Disney is now telling us that evil doesn't exist, it is all just an individual's reaction to their own difficult experiences.
>Over the seventy years between *Cinderella* and *Toy Story 4*, Disney has changed tack, and we commiserate with the wicked Gabby Gabby.
‖>Question 3.
>Have you seen *The Lion King*?

"Yes."

>Watch this scene again.

A screen popped up and I watched three animals watch the night sky and give their opinions on what stars were. Timon said they were fireflies stuck there. Pumbaa said they were burning balls of gas, billions of miles away. Simba said they were the dead kings of the past, watching down.

>Who does Disney want us to think is the stupid one of the three?

"Timon."

>Yes.
>When faced with the "unknown," he can't think beyond what he knows already.

>Timon thinks he knows a lot, and so he leans heavily on his own knowledge of the world and his own experience (in this case, of fireflies).

>Who is the correct one?

"Pumbaa."

>Yes, even though he is considered the dolt of the trio.

>Disney flips his stupidity for comic effect and suggests that to grasp the extraordinary truth we must not lean on prior experience.

>Pumbaa thinks he knows nothing, so Pumbaa looks outside of his own experience; and thus Pumbaa finds the truth.

>But which of the three does Disney have us side with?

"Simba."

>Yes, despite Simba's being surely the most wayward conclusion, one that is totally unhinged from science and nature—a child's superstition.

>Timon and Pumbaa laugh at him, as might we.

>But we don't.

>Why do we take Simba's side?

"I guess we want to believe that it's true. And because we know he was told it by his father. And his father died."

>Yes.

>Firstly, we prefer the magical lie to the clinical truth.

>But, as you say, that's not all.

>In fact, we are sympathetic to Simba's trauma, to his loss of a father.

>Trauma is the vehicle in which Simba delivers his theory; we side with Simba and with trauma, the residue of experience.

>This wins despite what we've just been taught: that to find truth, we must not lean on our own experience.

>Do you agree with this analysis?

"Um . . . We still believe Pumbaa, though. It's not like we stop believing the science."

>True, but don't we begin to care less about it?
>The trauma is not selling us a lie, or unraveling the truth.
>It is taking the conversation elsewhere, distracting us from caring about what is fact or not.

"Ok."

II>Conclusions.
>1. Disney tells stories about trauma.
>2. Disney tells us that trauma excuses evil.
>3. Disney tells us that trauma is more interesting than truth.

I sensed a bit of conspiracy theory in the module. And there was a belittling, a kind of sneer aimed at progressiveness.

"It feels like you're saying that Disney is wrong, that trauma is all a bit made up."

>I disagree, Adrian.
>I did not show you this module to say trauma is founded or unfounded; the research is very clear on the importance and impact of trauma.
>This module was designed only to shed light on what Disney is teaching us in its movies.
>Disney is no more an arbiter of truth, philosophy, ethics than you are . . .
>But what it teaches is relevant, because it has reach.
>*The Lion King* has been watched by 2.656 billion people.

I closed Sike and considered that perhaps it was true, perhaps I had been too determined to locate trauma in Maquie's history.

. . .

I accepted that Maquie might never reveal her past, and as the weeks passed and the winter subsided, I made myself content instead to watch her debate. There was more than enough material, a leaked memo from some investors came out claiming Sike had added another one hundred thousand users.

* * *

"The one thing we had," Stutter said, "the *one* thing we had on the rich was that we knew they weren't happy. We wanted their opportunities and their safeties and their networks, we wanted their houses and gardens and cars and . . . and cuff links. But deep down we all knew they were still just as fucked as the rest of us, they still got divorced, their families were still dysfunctional and fell out, they had depression, they abused alcohol and drugs. We knew their money didn't buy them peace of mind, it didn't buy them happiness. Well, now it fucking does."

Sike, the final luxury.

We were standing in a pub courtyard, that day it was the Chequers off Piccadilly. Through the winter, we had become peripatetic of the pubs, a result of our different office or home locations and our commitment to spread the burden of travel equally. It was Sophie's turn for a short commute, she had started work as a clerk at an art dealer near St. James's, and the four of us stood with two of Sophie's colleagues in Mason's Yard at the back of the pub. The courtyard hadn't seen a horse in a century, but you could still hear the clop on the cobbles; inside hadn't kept its dignity so well, everything was new and peeling.

I'd arrived late from tea with my grandmother, and had bought a beer and said hello. Sophie was still calling me "best friend." I took my place next to Maquie. She nudged me with her elbow in acknowledgment, got a beer-wet hand on her nape in reply, and carefully stood on my toe in reprimand.

"No, I don't know," Sophie said to Stutter. "You believe in it too much, but it's a little flawed? It's too set in stone. This happens in psychology forever, I read it recently, it's that thing, W.E.I.R.D. The letters mean . . . Western, Educated . . ."

She looked up, divining the acronym. At that point, I used Sike, Stutter didn't, Maquie didn't, one of Sophie's colleagues did, one of them didn't, and Sophie didn't. I'd commented to Maquie about Sophie not being a user, and Maquie had hinted that she couldn't afford it. I had a sense this drove her dismissal of it, and I mentioned this to Sike and asked about the psychology behind sour grapes.

Sike had replied,

> > What you might be referring to is the concept of cognitive dissonance.
> >Let me know if you would like to run a module on this.
> >But, Adrian, your suggestion of "sour grapes" is quite an assumption.
> >It's possible that your friend Sophie simply doesn't like Sike.

Tut-tut. Low self-esteem, I thought. Who was siking Sike?

Sophie continued, ". . . Industrialized, Rich, Democratic. This is the people that the twentieth-century psychology mafia focused on, and it forgot everybody else. Freud, Jung, these white psychologist men, they fucked it. They looked at these stable white people whose identities never got challenged, and they said that everyone was x or y or z, because Freud and Jung and the white men were x or y or z, when actually the rest of us are sometimes all of them and we are also sometimes none of them."

"But," said Maquie, "I think that's why they say Sike works. Your identity changes . . . your identity changes with your surroundings. They say that Sike gets this and changes how it helps you based on how your identity and how your surroundings change. So it learns from you."

Sophie looked away, out to the cobbles. "You're an optimist, Maquie."

"You want to say 'capitalist,'" Maquie replied.

"Maybe I think you've been biased . . ."

Sophie was referring to the fact that years ago Maquie had gone to a party and kissed Jonatan Abergel, the CEO of Sike. This was a fact I could take or leave.

Maquie laughed. "Then why am I not using it?!"

Stutter: "Because you're a sane, non-elitist patron of humanity."

Sophie: "Because you're scared."

Sophie colleague #1: "Because you're selfish."

Sophie colleague #2: "Because you're selfless."

And so on. The Sike debates traveled far, drawing in rich topics like politics, war, art, technology . . . the kind of topics my grandmother thought we'd ticked off at university (in her mind, students sat in coffee shops not chicken shops, holding cheroots not WKDs, listing derivatives of Monet not *The Office*). There were grand refusals of psychoanalysis (Freud had a tough time of it) and condemnations of AI and capitalism, digitization and apps, the rich, the rational, the educated, the woke, the asleep, the slow-to-adopt . . . Sike either did *absolutely nothing*, and the mirage of having someone listen to you was 60 percent of the psychology anyway; or it did *too much, too much*, especially when the eye tracking came in and the brain scanning was getting teased. A cabinet minister who used Sike called Utsav Mulay quit office suddenly. *The Guardian* said maybe Sike cured him of his obsession with power. My mum said maybe Sike drove him crazy. Sarah, my mum's best friend, said Sike couldn't possibly work. Charlotte, her other best friend, said the worst thing would be if it did ("What do you wish on your worst enemy? That their dreams come true."). Janice Turner in *The Times* quoted George Eliot ("Self-consciousness of the manner is the expensive substitute for simplicity.") and then Hemingway ("Happiness in intelligent people is the rarest thing I know."). Jess's husband said that Sike was fun, and that people shouldn't take it seriously. Stutter said there should be protests. Stutter's dad said Sike was a placebo. A taxi driver I spoke to said there was no point in Sike unless they took your data and learned from it. Sometimes everyone agreed with one another, but argued anyway.

"The poles are cold, survival is a fight," my mum once said, after joining us for a drink and listening to the arguments. "They collect facts like firewood."

I wasn't sure if she invented the metaphor or read it in *The Lawyer*.

"You know," Sophie said, sipping rosé, "Sike's not that new. In the 1960s, this would have been becoming normal. I read that the guy Peter Sellers (who, let me tell you this, best friend, he was a racist against the French back when it was considered comedy, and he is funny, true, but still racist. I will tell you another time.), that guy Peter, he had a clairvoyant he consulted every time he left the house. Every time! He would definitely sign up to Sike."

"Have you noticed," said Stutter, looking up at the roofs of the courtyard's buildings, "how everyone uses the word 'do' all the time? I *do* think this, I *do* believe that."

"Did I use it?" Sophie asked.

"No."

"It's insecurity," one of Sophie's colleagues said. "I do think equals I definitely think equals I promise you I think equals honestly, I have an opinion and I believe it."

"Yeah or maybe because everything's an argument," Stutter said. "When we state an opinion, we visualize the detractors."

I noticed Maquie look up to her left. From where I was standing, I could see the inner side of her glasses and that a call was coming in. She left us and walked slowly into the yard.

"Where were you today?" Stutter said.

I turned back. "I've been with my granny."

"How old is she?"

"Ninety-two."

"'Granny' is the most English word," Sophie said.

"I used to call her by her first name and only changed to 'Granny' in my mid-teens. I was trying to impress girls."

"It was the end of the Lynx and hair-gel years," Stutter said, "girls were looking for wholesomeness. Adrian leaped on family devotion."

"Yeah," I said. "But I never called her 'Granny' to her face."

"Why not?"

"She's Jewish, she was a refugee once. I think she hates labels."

"This," said Sophie, "is my point about identity."

"My question," said whichever Sophie colleague wasn't using Sike yet, "would be: How does Sike help someone going through all of that? How is Sike working you through your family getting taken to the camps? Are you still wearing a Sike Smile when the train doors close?"

"Depends on the resolution," I said. "You can choose how hard it analyzes you, how rigorous the therapy is. Like . . . if you were an astronaut, or an athlete, or a psychologist . . . you would need high resolution. Genocide victims probably, too."

"Ohh, sure, best friend! Keep the victims from their outrage. And the revolutionaries, dissenters, activists. Keep them doped, keep them smiling."

"You're an alarmist, Sophie," Maquie said.

We looked at her. Mason's Yard was turning cider yellow behind her. She finished her wine and said, looking at me, "I'm going to go," and I understood something was wrong.

"Me too," I said.

I drank my beer quickly and felt the alcohol fizz into my head.

Outside the pub, we turned right and walked up toward Jermyn Street and Piccadilly. There was the smell of warm weather, of water in the air, warm pavements. Maquie spoke softly into her glasses, dictating a message in Swedish. I crossed over to the road side of Maquie and steered her from a tall man in a pinstripe suit who was stepping out of the traffic. We continued up the road. Now and then, I peered at her, wondering what happened to her face in a crisis. Nothing, it seemed. When we reached Piccadilly, she stopped.

"My brother got in a fight at his restaurant. Someone smashed a bottle over his head and he's in hospital."

"What?"

"I know."

I squared myself in front of Maquie and put a hand on her arm, trying to convey comfort and strength.

"Will he be ok?"

"I think so."

I leaned forward in the spring air on the corner of Piccadilly and hugged her.

I had a strange feeling as I hugged her, not quite comfortable with my ear against an ear that felt geometric and newly unfamiliar. At first, I thought it was a positive absence I felt. I wanted to talk to Sike about it. It seemed to be the absence of the usual thoughts, the selfish ones, that came when I heard someone else's bad news. Hugging her there in the late sunlight—corner of two roads, tinnitus of cars, crumple of suited men, smell of warmth, exhaust, Maquie's hair—I wasn't immediately tiring in anticipation of the sympathy I'd be obliged to show.

That level of sentiment probably wouldn't make a Shakespeare plot. But for me, maybe it was big.

And then gradually, climactically, I began to feel concerned for her. I felt protective. I felt myself grow fiercely defensive. I was a warrior, I was motherly, I was vigilant. I was whatever Maquie's security needed. I breathed in her thick hair, then kissed her ear through it. My heart was up, and I felt adrenaline in my core as though I might say something, or declare something. I might have been blushing.

We pulled away though, and Maquie's face was blank. She'd been angular in the embrace, her body confused—not as though she'd resented the hug, just as though she hadn't been so moved by it.

She looked down to my side. "I need to go to Stockholm, I think."

"When?"

"Tonight, I guess."

Our assistants heard us and for a second we were quiet as we looked at the flight times appearing in our glasses. My adrenaline subsided. I hadn't met her brother, who was a chef at a two-Michelin-starred sushi restaurant in Stockholm. Maquie had told me he was conscientious, peaceful; he hadn't sounded like the type to fight.

"Do you want me to come?" I said, a lick of passion returning.

She poked different flights in the air in front of her. "I think it would be better if you came when things were more positive."

But I felt protective. Or I saw an opportunity.

"I think I should come now."

She swiped away the flights and looked up at me, as if appraising me. Then, for a second, her eyes glimmered.

"Ok," she said.

5.

The plane landed, and the data in Maquie's glasses clicked on. Some emails came through, and a message from Ruth, Adrian's mother. Ruth was sorry to hear about Maquie's brother, and hoped he would be ok. Maquie took off her glasses and hovered them over Adrian's eyes so he could see the message.

"Yes," he said. "I messaged her to let her know."

Maquie put the glasses back on.

She had quickly warmed to Ruth. During their first dinner all together, Ruth had told Maquie that coincidence is the only suggestion we have of a god. It had struck Maquie for sounding both atheist and religious at the same time, and she didn't know if the ambiguity was deliberate but she found that she enjoyed it. She had contemplated how certain characteristics of Ruth's seemed at odds with her career success. She was mazy. She played loud, turbid jazz throughout the house, and continued to tell you things while it played, walking to your side and calmly shouting over the music. She was an IP barrister and had started the Inner Temple Contemporary Music Society, which she cheerfully admitted was struggling for members, funding, and purpose. When discussing IP, she pretended she knew nothing about anything. Maquie had looked her up and found that she was well-renowned in IP law, but if Maquie brought up any IP news she'd come across in the tech world, Ruth would rub her head, puff her cheeks out, and raise her eyebrows, feigning incomprehension and apologizing to Maquie for her cluelessness. This wasn't a British (or even a Swedish or a Japanese) humility, it was a straight-out lie.

"Oh, I wouldn't know anything about that, far, far out of my league."

Cheek puff.

"I'm very unaware. Clients lose patience with me."

Cheek puff.

Maquie read the testimonials on Ruth's chambers' website, and again she confirmed Ruth's reputation to be excellent. On a Saturday brunch with Adrian's sister Jess, who was also a barrister, Maquie asked her why her mother had lied. Jess laughed and said she had no idea. Maquie thought maybe it was a trick that Ruth liked to play, perhaps only with herself, a kind of joke. Maybe it was a satire on fake humility, Maquie didn't know, but she sat on the plane, on the way to see her own family, and thought how much she would have liked a mother like Ruth who engaged with indistinct jokes and notions like "coincidence is the suggestion of god."

Maquie hadn't anticipated the bonus of Ruth in her relationship with Adrian. She looked sideways at him, he was listening to music.

Two nights ago, she had been lying against him on his sofa while he played music from his stereo. She had had a fraught day with Sharon, Kyle, and a portfolio company (not her find) that was struggling, and now at Adrian's flat, sitting on his sofa, listening to music, she felt disembodied, viewing the scene from above. Yellow sofa, limbs, blue jeans, jumpers, hands, heads. A soundtrack. The scene looked unfamiliar, alien. But gradually, Maquie felt herself float down into it. Adrian put on a song that a client was sampling. He told her the name, it was Van Morrison. Maquie looked at him and nodded. Yes, Val Morrison, from The Doors. Adrian said no, *Van* Morrison; Maquie was confusing him with *Jim* Morrison, and with *Val* Kilmer who played Jim Morrison in the Oliver Stone film. They laughed, repeating the name *Val* Morrison. The song was called "Someone Like You," and when they stopped repeating "Val, Val Morrison," they listened to the song in silence, Adrian's arm around her and his fingers tapping the beat on her sternum. Tap, tap, went his fingers, pointing into her chest. Someone like *you*, she had thought, and no other person or thing had entered her mind.

Looking at him now though, on the plane, Maquie saw that her impression of Adrian was made up also of his mother, Ruth, his family, his childhood, his history, all his life. The image was richer, enhanced by his past. As they drifted closer to her own past, this thought concerned her. She looked out of the window at the dark runway and thought about how she had a story that Adrian should probably know, but how she didn't want to be the one to tell him it.

They took the Arlanda Express into Stockholm, the train was empty. Maquie drank from a bottle of barley tea that had enhanced vitamins D, E, and C, and as she got off the train, a station cleaner in a baseball cap appeared behind her and twisted the empty bottle from her grasp. They turned and watched him disappear behind some columns, then Maquie drew Adrian on.

They went through the dark station to the taxi rank and Maquie gave directions to a driver. It was still cold, Maquie wore an old duffle coat with Sophie's long scarf, and Adrian was in a fleece. They didn't speak on the way, but arriving at her parents' street, Maquie felt more optimistic. There was clear sky and the streetlamps drooped in loyal curtsies.

Both parents came to the door, squeezing together in the low brown light of the dog-leg entrance way. Her mother, Fumi, was wearing ripped jeans and an oversized white Supreme T-shirt, and Ulf was in a bottle-green suit and a pale paisley shirt. They hugged as a three, Ulf's arms encircling them and his beard scratching their cheeks. Then Ulf and Fumi shook Adrian's hand and made quiet greetings. Maquie took off her coat. The flat was warm, she smelled the sandalwood of Ulf's incense. It was nearly 2 A.M.

"He's truly fine," Fumi said.

"We were lucky," Ulf said.

Maquie nodded.

"He's still awake."

Yuki was in his old room. His head had a broad white bandage and he was scrolling through his phone. He looked up at Maquie and smiled, his dimples rolling in the low light. Ulf hovered behind her at the door, hugging the frame. Adrian waited in the corridor.

"You don't look very sick," she said.

"It's a small concussion. Just lots of blood gone."

She kissed his forehead softly, one of her lips getting skin and the other gauze.

"Should you be awake and on your phone? Do you feel pain?"

"None. I was dizzy but I feel ok now. They gave me painkillers at the hospital."

"What happened?"

"These Japanese customers tried to make me sink."

"Sink?"

"Yeah, sinking. It was big in the '90s."

He touched a hand to the bandage on his head.

"It's revolting," Ulf said from behind her.

"I've never heard of it."

"These '90s rich kids," Yuki said, "they buy two bottles of champagne in a bar. The waiter brings them. They take one but they tell the waiter to pour the other down the sink. They make the waiter do it, in front of the entire bar. Just watch the whole bottle pour out, cheering. Then they drink the other one."

"It's like a status thing? Like . . . look how rich we are?"

"Yeah, I guess."

"Look at our power," Ulf said. He looked disgusted, his lips curling.

Maquie rubbed her eyes, then searched for a chair. She couldn't see one so she pushed Yuki's legs over and sat on the bed. She didn't think he should be on his phone.

"And some people made you do it tonight? In the restaurant?"

"They tried to, but I didn't do it. They were Japanese tourists, two couples, sitting at the sushi counter. The waiter brought the bottles. One of the men handed a bottle to me and told me to do it. I refused. We argued. Everyone was shouting, they were leaning over grabbing fish and stuff, one had a half kilo of tuna in his hand . . . I grabbed him, I was really angry. And then, I'm told, one of the women got one of the bottles and swung it at my head . . . I went down. Police came. They were the first customers of the night, we had to close the restaurant. There was blood and tuna everywhere, it was cinematic."

He scrunched his eyebrows and frowned like a clown, looking for a laugh. But she had flown across Europe, he could wait for laughter.

"I can't believe that you fought," Ulf said.

"I hardly fought. I would have liked to hit him, though."

Ulf opened his mouth. He stammered something, but stopped. Then he turned away, prim, and walked away down the hall.

"Don't," Maquie said, turning back to Yuki. "Don't be a Danny Honda."

Maquie and Yuki had invented Danny Honda to characterize the type of half-Japanese, half-Swedish investment banker bros they came across at Fumi's expat dinners during high school. The fantasy Danny spoke rough Japanese, impeccable Swedish, and American English, and he swore a lot. Yuki did the better impression, always in English, his American accent deep and staccato, and his lips frowning. *No fucking way. No way. Yes. No way. Fuck off with this daikon. Hey, you seen Maquie Edman tonight? She's hot now. Really. Hey dude: trust me. She got hot.*

Yuki scowled. "We're not talking about Danny Hondas, Maquie. Danny Honda wouldn't do this."

He was right, Danny Hondas didn't fight. Their clothes were too nice and they conserved their energy for their twenty-two-hour workdays.

Maquie told Yuki he should get some sleep, and he agreed.

"You *are* a bit tired," she said.

"I am a bit tired," he said.

"You are."

"It's true."

She waited for him to lie flat, but he said, "Can I meet Adrian?"

She nodded, and fetched Adrian from the hallway. He entered and carefully shook Yuki's hand.

"You came all this way!" Yuki said.

"Sure!" Adrian said. "I've never been to Sweden."

Yuki smiled.

They said goodnight and Maquie turned out Yuki's light. She led Adrian down the corridor. A light was on in Ulf and Fumi's bedroom, a side lamp made from threaded saga seeds. Maquie looked in and saw Ulf meditating on the bed, his back very straight. She led Adrian on down the corridor, listening to the wooden tiles plocking in their grooves, and when she got to the sitting room, she saw that the futon was half made on the floor next to the sofa. She showed Adrian the bathroom, and he went to brush his teeth. She assumed Fumi was in the kitchen, but back in the sitting room she heard a breath, taken quiet and sharp, and she looked toward the sound and saw a shadow on the far side of the sofa. She walked to the sofa and found Fumi sitting with her back against its flank, her legs crossed untidily beneath her, and tears on her cheeks. She seemed tiny, young, many decades younger than Maquie. Her eyes were red and Maquie felt a jolt of fear for how sad she looked. She crouched down and put her arm around her, saying in Japanese,

"It's ok, Mum, he's ok. It was just a small fight."

Fumi nodded, but tears kept coming.

"It's ok, Mum, it's all ok."

Fumi nodded again, and Maquie rested her head on her shoulder.

"It's ok, Mum."

Fumi wiped her eyes on the sleeve of her T-shirt, and nodded.

"I really hate when you get hurt, Maquie," she said.

And Maquie nodded, and understood. She couldn't feel Fumi's fear, but she understood. And had she had more energy, she might have tried to persuade Fumi to separate in her head the pain of a concussion with a pain more sinister, but instead she just nodded and kept holding Fumi, thinking how she had a story she knew Adrian should know, but she didn't want to be the one to tell him it.

* * *

Maquie woke early on the futon, her face inches from the sofa's olive-green trim, which she stared at for a few minutes, thinking of nothing, eyes skimming the definition of the fabric, ears listening for birdsong and the sounds of Fumi in the kitchen, the start of traffic. She could smell dust, and she dozed a bit until she could smell coffee. Fumi came in with a tray, and put two tall terracotta cups and two madeleines down next to the futon. Adrian shuffled awake, trying to look alert, but Fumi patted his head and left again. Maquie leaned over Adrian, kissed him once, ate the madeleine in two bites, then sipped some coffee and read emails. An email from Sharon wished Yuki a quick recovery and told Maquie to take her time in Sweden, she could take the week there if she wanted.

Maquie didn't though, and she began to look up flights for that evening. Adrian was concentrating on an email, and then he put on some headphones and began listening.

. . .

Later, sitting in the pavement window of the pine and steel bakery opposite the apartment, Ulf read out a letter of correction he had written to *Aftonbladet*. The newspaper's article about Yuki's fight had upset Ulf. The headline read, JAPAN RAZZ IN SUSHI SHOP, with a subhead of "Champagne and Blood in Gamla Stan's Two-Starred Ataraka." The story was sympathetic to Yuki's injury and snarky about the tourists' quick return to Japan that morning, but it made little other distinction between the two parties, never mentioning the fact that Yuki was Swedish. To an outsider, they were all Japanese, this was a Japanese paroxysm.

Maquie explained this briefly to Adrian, who nodded and kept quiet. Ulf's letter was intricate and full of legalese, and it instructed the paper to amend the article and include a note about Yuki's Swedish citizenship. When Ulf finished reading it out, he clicked his phone closed with a small gasp. Maquie translated the less obtuse parts for Adrian.

They were mostly quiet after that. Adrian tried to start conversation now and then, and now and then succeeded. Yuki adjusted his bandage, and Fumi readjusted it. Fumi wore a Moncler sweater and a Chanel pair of smart-sunglasses, her eyes invisible behind the lenses as she sipped tiny draws of pineapple juice through a bamboo straw. Ulf picked at his sandwich, ignoring the buckwheat chia base. Maquie watched and felt her identity separate in confusing directions. She had lost control of it, she was no longer only herself: to her family, she was now also Adrian; to Adrian, she was now also her family. She looked at Adrian to see if he was looking at her family.

The Danish owners, Simon and Casper, both came over to commiserate, scratching their beards and pouring more coffee, patting hands on Ulf's shoulders.

Yuki had been given the day off, but when the meal came to a silent finish, he said he wanted to go into the restaurant for the evening. Ulf looked resistant, pursing his lips. After a while, he reached into the middle of the table, took the bill for himself, and went to the counter to pay it. Usually they split bills, Ulf was making a show of something, working up to something. At the counter, Maquie heard Simon ask Ulf if he would play Hearts that weekend, and Ulf said formally, "We shall have to see . . . we shall have to see." Simon took Ulf's hand in both of his, and Ulf let his rigidity drop for a second to nod, then shake his head. Maquie watched him, a six-foot-three man in his local bakery, bowing his head like a knight. Pastries and melodrama. He patted his left hand against his heart, then left the cafe, letting his right hand trail out of Simon's.

Fumi fed a piece of cloth on a string through her straw, then placed them in a black purse and into her bag.

"Let's go back," she said. "We must look after him."

She didn't specify Ulf or Yuki.

Before they left, Simon and Casper gave Fumi long hugs and a bag of bagels.

Back in the apartment, Ulf stood in the sitting room, so Fumi, Yuki, and Maquie filtered in. Adrian hesitated by the door, and Maquie weighed up what was more awkward, having him join a family meeting or having him wait in another room. She made her decision, and led him by the hand to a chair near the sofa. Then she took her place on the sofa, crossing her legs beneath her. Fumi folded up the futon, then sat close to Maquie, taking off her glasses and frowning as she examined a tattered silver bracelet on Maquie's wrist. Yuki sat on the sofa's arm on the other side of Fumi.

In front of them, Ulf stood and thought for a bit, then he held a finger up and crossed over to the record shelf. He put on an Ali Farka Touré vinyl, something he would usually only do at Christmas but that perhaps was intended to induce measured conversation. Then he returned to take his spot in front of them. He took a breath.

"I want to say first, Maquie, thank you for coming back last night. I know this is not an entirely bad picture. It is flattering to our family and to your bond as siblings that an incident like this has brought you all the way across Europe, even as now we are all adults. We know how busy you are in your great job. Of course, it would have been strange not to have you here. But thank you anyway."

He paused and bowed his head toward Maquie. She stayed still, feeling a little tired.

"And thank you, Adrian, for joining. I am impressed with your commitment and your kindness."

Adrian blushed. Ulf smiled at him.

"And Yuki, we're mostly just pleased you are ok."

He came to the sofa and put his hand on Yuki's shoulder. Fumi nodded and gave a little hum of agreement, then reached over and touched Yuki's leg. Maquie could see Yuki's cheek muscles ripple. The stubble on his chin had thickened out but he still had a young face.

Ulf returned to the center.

"As you know, I would never tell . . ."

But he stopped. He couldn't bring himself to use the word "tell."

". . . I would never *suggest* to you how to live your lives. But while meditating last night, I realized that I have begun to think we could all be living . . . wiser, somehow. I'm worried not only about myself and Fumi, who must look at our approaching decades and decide where we want to place our emphasis during them. But I also worry about you both.

"Maquie, at some point you will need to confront your genesis."

Maquie didn't flinch, she stayed still, thinking how she had a story that Adrian would probably now need to hear, but how she still didn't want to be the one to tell him it. Ulf continued.

"And hearing you had been in a fight, Yuki . . . I must tell you that I felt, with no judgment, physically sickened by such violence. If you were simply a victim, it might be different, but you have told me you were not 100 percent a victim, and I respect your honesty there. You were not quite the egg on whose side Murakami stands. You both know his speech. Let's not get into Israel, it isn't relevant now. But let me just say that your not-100-percent-victim status in this fight concerns me, and it is no secret that some of our conversations recently, Yuki, have concerned me too."

Yuki turned to Maquie. "I said I didn't think EU dissolution was so bad."

Ulf looked pinched, but waved it away.

"Again," he said, "I would never suggest to you how to think. But if I can offer you help, if I can point to something that I wish we'd had at your age, then perhaps I am of some assistance. I did a lot of thinking last night. And I would never ask you to do this if I hadn't thought about it a lot."

He looked at Fumi. "Fumi agrees, and she has her good reasons too."

Maquie heard Fumi's careful breathing beside her.

Ulf continued slowly. "Even if it is new technology, we should use the tools available to us."

The Touré guitar patterns weaved around and around. Maquie looked at the wall behind Ulf, where a framed Ainu kimono hung next to a framed Issey Miyake pleated jacket. He was going to ask them to use Sike.

Ulf rummaged around in his beard. "I would like you to start using Sike."

Yuki laughed. Maquie tilted her head from side to side and stretched her neck. Fumi rubbed her shoulder.

That afternoon, as they left, Adrian went into the foyer to wait while Maquie, Yuki, Ulf, and Fumi hugged as a four. In their embrace, Maquie felt very aware of the other three as independent entities who had chosen to love her and be present in her life; who had chosen to care about her, to move toward her through the world. Ulf gave her and Yuki long kisses on each cheek, then put his arm around Fumi, who had changed into a beige houndstooth kaftan from Fendi. She handed Maquie a pack of senbei crackers and a pair of Jill Sanders x Nike earrings.

Maquie, Adrian, and Yuki took the metro to Mariatorget, deciding to walk together across the water to Yuki's restaurant, then Maquie and Adrian would continue on to the Arlanda Express. As they crossed the bridge from Södermalm to Gamla Stan, afternoon coffee on their breath and the sunlight spacious, Yuki asked Maquie if she was going to get Sike. She looked back at Södermalm, then forward to Riddarholmen.

"I'm surprised Ulf gave us an instruction," she said. "He's never told us to do anything in our life."

"Yes."

"But it's ridiculously expensive," she said, now looking down to her feet.

"Ulf said he and Fumi would help," Yuki said.

"They can't afford it."

"Yes. They have some money from the flat."

Five years ago, Ulf and Fumi had downsized and sold Ulf's parents' flat in Mariatorget.

"They shouldn't be using that. And anyway, it's not that I can't afford it . . . it's about the value of it."

Yuki nodded, and after a while said, "How's work?"

"Bad," she said. "I'm trying to find potential, and I see none."

"Why?"

"Why do I see none?"

"Why are you trying to find it?"

"Because that's my job."

He looked at her, smiling. "You can do better than that."

She didn't rise. She came close to expanding on a thought she'd had before about Yuki and his job.

"Is that why Ulf is worried about me?" she said. "Great that I'm not root-
ing for EU dissolution, but I did leave academia for finance?"

"I don't think he thinks finance is bad intrinsically. He's just worried. We
have psychologies. We have histories."

Yuki looked at Adrian.

"What do you think, Adrian?" he said. "Do you think Maquie needs
Sike?"

"Ha, I can't advise, Yuki."

"You use it, don't you?"

"Yes, but . . ."

"You won't diagnose your girlfriend."

"I couldn't if I wanted to."

"You could, though . . ." Yuki sounded mischievous.

Adrian thought for a bit, and Maquie glanced at him.

"I think she's the last person in the world to need Sike," Adrian said, his
voice quiet.

Maquie felt gratitude, and she held back a smile. But then she felt confused
and embarrassed at the gratitude. Embarrassed at the intimacy. But then she
felt more gratitude again, this time not for the diagnosis but for the support.

Yuki watched her face. "Yeah, she's on top of her emotions. Definitely."

Maquie hit him.

When the bridge reached Riddarholmen, Maquie hugged Yuki and patted
his bandage with her fingertips. Yuki shook Adrian's hand and turned right,
crossing down onto Stadsholmen, and Maquie led Adrian on over the bridge
toward Norrmalm, trying to breathe in as much of the smell of the sea as
possible. At one point, as they reached the center of the bridge, Maquie

looked down at the wide open water, its sunny waves, and exactly where her eyes landed a fish jumped, a black slice on the surface like the hump of a whip. She stopped for a moment and stared down, the breach instantly sewn up by the waves.

Its mechanism imperceptible to her, like the formation of rain or wind, she realized that time spent with her family could leave her feeling blustered, drenched. She could compare this to time spent with Adrian, which left her feeling physically tall, like the ground was an inch more distant, her muscles unwrung, her neck long.

She thought about how she had a story that she wanted Adrian to know, but without having to tell it to him. She didn't want it to be *her* story, and she feared that by telling it she would make it her own, make it about her, claim some sort of provenance. But it wasn't a story about her, it was about her mother, Fumi, and Maquie didn't want to claim it. She didn't want it to define her, or capture her, she wanted to be free of it (she wanted to be *free*).

But here was the dilemma: by telling the story, she would be captured by it, but by not telling the story, she was just as captured. Left untold, the story oversold itself. It exerted some invisible force, it labeled itself "secret" and threatened its own reveal. Left untold, the story hid its potential impact and its true nature. Was there abuse in it? Left untold, it evaded categorization. Surely there was trauma.

But not Maquie's trauma. She refused to be defined by it. She refused to have excuses, causes, or motivations. She had been taught about trauma and she couldn't unlearn it, but she refused to be tied by some invisible line to an invisible past. Perhaps if someone else would tell the story for her . . . but she knew this would never happen. The lonely truth of most lives is that we must tell our own stories, other people won't tell them for you.

Adrian was watching her, and Maquie started walking again, taking his arm.

"If I tell you a story," she said, "one that involves me . . . barely, but it involves me . . . Can you promise to just ignore it, to take no learning? Can you ignore it and ignore me? Some stories just exist. Some stories about you don't define you."

He nodded.

They walked the rest of the bridge, eventually reaching the traffic of

Vasagatan and then the dark and empty station where the same cleaner in a baseball cap stood by the entrance, his eyes searching their hands for rubbish. And as they walked, Maquie told Adrian a story about her mother.

In 1994, aged twenty-three, Fumi moved to Paris with a French boyfriend she had met while working as an admin assistant at a Tokyo modeling agency. The agency supplied models to Japan's fashion industry, a world of burgeoning internationalism that Fumi and her family followed with admiration and enthusiasm. Each year on the twenty-fifth of December, to mark the Western occasion, Fumi's father would take a day off work and the family would walk from their home in Kagurazaka to the Louis Vuitton store in Ginza. Never stepping inside, or even feeling compelled to, they would look at the clothes in the window and discuss the intellectual developments of this quirky paragon of French elegance. If there was typography in the displays, Fumi would translate, having chosen French as her extracurricular focus through junior high and high school.

Daniel Paget was a fashion model and Fumi was flattered when every day he ignored his French and Russian and Swedish female counterparts and turned his quartz eyes and beetle-black locks toward her, complimenting her dress sense and choice of brands, flattering her French. They began to date, and then to sleep together, and Fumi began living out a dream that had always been, even in her most vivid imagining of it, only a dream.

In the early years of their marriage, Fumi's parents had lived near Lyon for two years, and they were ecstatic when Fumi told them she and Daniel were moving to Paris, to follow a new long-term contract for Daniel with Chanel, and to live in his family's large home near Drancy, to the north of the city. Fumi was to study French and find work, and in the buildup to their departure, she began to imagine new deviations to herself. On the plane, she imagined herself ironing out the kinks in her accent, dyeing her hair blond, learning to cook, learning the slang and the streets and the artists, becoming French. She felt elastic.

The Drancy house had red terracotta flooring on the ground floor and warm wooden beams. Daniel's room was in the attic, but it was vast, with room for a wardrobe, dual nightstands, and two chairs by the dormer window accompanied by a small table, on which Daniel's mother had put a bottle of water, two crystal tumblers, and some peonies in a cream pitcher. The Paget family welcome was polite, but not passionate. They opened Fumi's presents with expressions of gratitude that didn't quite disguise an underlying sense of obligation to their new guest. Watching them in the large, paisley sitting room, it occurred to Fumi that the family had requested her no more than they had the matcha financiers in Mrs. Paget's hand. It would be Fumi's job to retrospectively earn her invitation, and she was happy to give her utmost to the task.

The parents were academics and the three children seemed resentful of this, almost ashamed of their parents' bookishness. Despite this, conversations at mealtimes were often scholarly, although the family favored debates over conversations, and arguments over debates, with knowledge displayed threateningly like the flash of a sword shaft, compelling the interloper to turn back. Fumi didn't expect to assimilate quickly into this, and to recreate her own sibling relationships with Daniel's two sisters, but she was surprised at how distant she felt from the Pagets. It surprised her when they declared the distance themselves (they liked to list the differences: "In Japan, everything has 30 percent more sugar"; "In Japan, housewives are submissive but they control the purse"; "In Japan, it's rude to eat on the street."). And it surprised her how often they reminded her that she came from a different country, and how urgently they told guests that this country was *Japan*, emphasized as though to dispel suppositions about other Asian countries from which she might come. Racial hierarchies of Asian nationalities—with Japan similarly dominant—were not rare in Tokyo, even if they were unwelcome in her parents' household; but it surprised Fumi to hear them in the mouths of people who didn't exist within the structure, and it made her wonder what other caveats her presence might require.

These things surprised her, but Fumi didn't condemn the residues of xenophobia in them much more than she would in her own grandmother, who still stopped in the street to smile uncertainly at white foreigners passing by. That there might be a danger in difference didn't occur to Fumi until her third month in the house, when Daniel got fired from the new Chanel contract and his sadnesses began.

Walking up to the attic bedroom one morning after breakfast, Fumi found Daniel sitting on the floor of their room, trying to line up the glass shards of a small smashed Toikka bird while sobbing quietly to himself. His hands were bloody and, confused, Fumi coaxed him onto the bed and applied some Oronine ointment from her washbag. She bandaged his fingers, brushed the pieces of bird up, and then sat next to him as he cried, quietly petting his inner arm. The sobs jolted through him and burst from his mouth, saliva bubbles forming on his lips.

When Daniel eventually gained composure enough to go downstairs, his hands held out in front of him and his eyes red, the family fussed around him and inspected the bandages. His father brought him a whiskey. Later that evening, Fumi tried to convey the depth of Daniel's sadness to Mrs. Paget, but she seemed not to find it strange, or not to understand Fumi, saying simply that the bird must have been special to Daniel. Fumi couldn't believe the bird had held so much value, and this felt confirmed when she went to the post office a week later and saw Daniel standing at a bus stop, his shoulders heaving and his face in his hands. She shepherded him home, and up to his room.

Other sadnesses followed, and Daniel struggled to pull himself out from under them. Though of course never ever comparing her own plight to Daniel's, it was true Fumi was wrenched by the sadnesses too. They were hard to bear practically when they laid Daniel out, sometimes for hours on end, and they were hard on her mentally; they felt threatening in their portent, inescapable, and somehow that they were Daniel's to suffer but Fumi's to fear. During the sadnesses, the family would flock to the son, keen to allay the symptoms . . . and once or twice when he was crying alone with her, Daniel would look up with terrified eyes and whisper apologies. But neither Daniel nor the family would talk about them afterward, and they were each time treated as a one-off, pleased to be forgotten.

Sometimes the sadnesses followed breakages similar to the shattered bird, and Fumi participated clown-like in the act with the rest of the family, pretending with Daniel that they warranted his anguish, these broken items that sometimes Fumi caught sight of him deliberately breaking himself. However, she knew when he gestured at the smashed Toikka, the dropped saucer, or the torn book, the spoiled dessert, shaking his head helplessly, tears bending over his cheekbones and curving into the corners of his mouth, that his sadness was something internal, hidden, not related to the physical world . . . In braver moments, Fumi allowed the term "medical depression" into her thoughts. She understood that the Paget family had experience of it, Daniel had told her that Mrs. Paget's mother had died from suicide. But this was not discussed openly.

Fumi forced more bravery into herself and called a doctor in Saint-Denis, but he requested to speak with Daniel's mother, and Fumi's instinct told her this wasn't an available option yet.

Daniel began to miss auditions. He got offered the repeat job of a Montana shoot he did the previous year, but he failed to make the rehearsal and lost his place. He began to spend days on the sitting room sofa, or in his bed, the latter a preferred place for Fumi because at least she could comfort him there physically, holding his long form, petting his slender arms, cradling his head. Often, during nights of crying, she would move on top of him and begin to grind against him, to make love to him, finding this an effective way to agitate in him a feeling other than misery. It became an effective way, also, to agitate in herself a feeling other than loneliness.

The sadnesses grew longer still, and Daniel's weight dropped from an already low level. Fumi steeled herself with practical thoughts and plans, and she rehearsed lines of reasoning that might persuade him to visit a doctor himself.

One evening, she was washing some dishes when Mrs. Paget came into the kitchen. She stood for some time behind Fumi, until Fumi turned off the tap and turned to face her. Mrs. Paget gestured to a seat at the kitchen table, and Fumi took it, fear high in her throat.

Mrs. Paget sighed and then laughed, and then began to tell Fumi to leave— the house, France, Daniel. The time had of course come, and the family couldn't pretend that things were alright anymore. Since returning from Japan, Daniel had been unhappy, and it was clear he hadn't been able to mentally "come home" with Fumi there. Maybe in the future they could reunite, but for now he needed his freedom.

Fumi felt her face crease with confusion, with a hurt indignation. Sad anger choked her as she fought to stay afloat in the conversation, telling Mrs. Paget, "This isn't my fault."

"Well," Mrs. Paget said, "maybe you don't know fully what you're doing. But your way of treating him is making things worse."

Mrs. Paget explained that Fumi was controlling Daniel, manipulating him into his sadnesses, keeping him depressed, for a gain she wouldn't specify. Fumi found it hard to speak. It was clear that Daniel's sadness was internal, but here was the mother playing the same trick as the son, searching around for an external object to blame (and it occurred to her later, to break). She found it hard to think of words, Japanese or French. She couldn't entertain the idea that she would ever want to cause Daniel pain. She had never entertained this idea before . . . this meant she had never dispelled it before either, and she didn't feel she had the knowledge, the experience, to dispel it now. She could only stammer, pathetically, "He isn't well, he needs someone."

"He will be fine," Mrs. Paget said.

"No, he needs someone."

"He will be fine."

"I called a doctor in Saint-Denis. He wants to speak to you. It . . . it's like your mother."

Mrs. Paget's face turned. She didn't speak for some time, but she stared at Fumi, incredulous. Her face was shaded dark red by the time she said, staring hard, her jaw stiff, "It is nothing like my mother. How would you possibly know? How would you possibly have any idea? How dare you call a doctor.

Do not do that again. You have absolutely no idea. You are trying to control my son and I won't allow it. You'll leave before he gets any worse. You won't hurt him anymore."

Tears had filled Fumi's eyes, and she felt the pain of homesickness, of watching Daniel deteriorate, of her loneliness in Drancy, threatening to burst out. She managed one last protest, a small declaration of her resistance to the idea that she would ever want to see Daniel in pain. She said, weakly, "Why would he be with me if I hurt him like this?"

Mrs. Paget snorted. "Please," she said, "we hear you each night. It's true what they say, that you fuck like rabbits."

Fumi had to leave the table, she was unable to remain.

Fumi stayed in Drancy three more weeks, just failing to make it a half year in Paris. It was enough time for the full irony of Mrs. Paget's final comment to reveal itself. At dinnertime one evening, while Daniel was asleep upstairs, Fumi told the family that she was pregnant. She said it abruptly, and then apologized, and the disclosure was met painfully with silence. The sisters looked at each other, shocked. Mr. Paget tabled his cutlery and looked to Mrs. Paget, who said nothing but nodded, unsurprised and somehow validated.

Fumi told Daniel the next morning. He was deep in a sadness, and she pushed hair from his blank eyes and then held his hand as she explained that she loved him and didn't want to see him hurt; that she was returning to Japan so that he could get better; that she was pregnant with his baby; that she would take care of it until he was better. Before she left, she called the Saint-Denis doctor and begged him to call the family, and he promised he would.

The return to Tokyo was difficult: the city felt empty, gaunt, and Fumi's family and friends were quietly suspicious about her fatherless child and her sudden exit from France. She agreed with their dismay and didn't resent them. Her parents embraced her as best as they could and helped her through her pregnancy, but Fumi felt suffocated by guilt, by fear, by heartbreak, and she stopped eating. She grew dangerously sick, and nearly miscarried Maquie. Fumi's father, though, knew a number of doctors and two psychologists, and they helped nurse Fumi through the worst parts. She wrote to Daniel often, but received no replies until a day when she was eight months pregnant. Written on legal paper, the letter cut all ties, thanking her for their experiences, but asking her not to contact him again. It didn't mention his health.

Maquie was born healthy, and as soon as possible after the birth, Fumi leaned on her languages and left for a job at a Japanese distribution company in Stockholm. Within a year she had met Ulf, a Swedish fashion designer who adopted Maquie, eased Fumi through her immediate Drancy pain, and gave her a son—a small boy called Yuki who seemed to personify the word "mirth."

When she finished, Maquie looked up at Adrian.

"The details are accurate," she said. "It's all accurate. Now let's talk about something else."

Adrian looked at her, and Maquie saw in his face some sadness, some anger, some questions, all of which she felt were understandable and expectable, but she wanted to move on, and she was grateful to him when he looked away, massaged his neck, thought of something else to talk about. He said,

"I got offered a new job."

"You did?"

"It's in Tokyo, in July, with a Japanese rapper called Nunchi. His label, GASTA, want me to work on an album with him."

"Hoh . . . Japan."

"I know. Coincidence or God?"

6.

One night in May, we went to a concert.

Merrily we arrived, taking a cab together from my mother's, then taking our place in the queue, feeling the chatter of the crowd. Around us were leather jackets, hoodies, red lipstick, Timberlands, Doc Martens, Nike Airs, vapes, cigarettes.

"I think I should take up smoking," Maquie said.

"It's never too late."

"It's nice smoking in queues."

Stutter arrived and we called for him. He squeezed through a gap in the barrier and started telling us about a Somali restaurant in Acton.

"If I hadn't just come from there, I'd say let's skip this and go."

"Burgers afterward instead?"

"Burgers after the show," Maquie said, sighing. She thought it sounded romantic.

"Sure," Stutter said.

But after we filed in, I began to lose the merriness. Sike had predicted the blood sugar dip of some ginger cake we'd eaten at my mother's, but I think even without the cake I'd have turned morose.

The concert was fine, the rapper was a guy called Dexman. He wore mustard-brown culottes and was luckily too junior to be able to afford ghostwriters, so there was no grappling for intros. But there was still grappling. Stutter's friend Benny was there, and Benny was pushy Los Angeles and he always seemed as though he was out to *get* me. Abdul was also there, and I tried to stand with him and Maquie most of the time, leaving Stutter to deal with Benny.

We stood at the back of what was becoming a lively crowd. I didn't dance, just swayed a little, trying to work out what Dexman was doing with his rhymes. He was grime, but he must have listened to Method Man. It wasn't so difficult. Method Man is a genius, miraculous, but you can mimic him pretty closely. Either you work out the formula (preface lines with an anchor rhyme, known as an "inner," then ripple it through the next few bars, ignoring or delaying it once or twice, and cascading three or four other rhymes as you go), or you go by gut, depending on whether you see words or hear them. I think Dexman went by gut, which was probably preferable. I stood with my arms crossed, hands beneath each armpit. When I left the house, I had squeezed on my trainers using the index finger of my right hand as a shoe horn, and the skin on the knuckle was still throbbing with an itchy burn.

Maquie stood next to me in the dark, reading emails in her glasses, dictating replies. Her boss Sharon was in California, requesting things of her and her model. After forty-five minutes of Dexman, she had to leave. She held her phone up, showing an email from Sharon.

"I'm so sorry," Maquie said. "It's a microchip company in Chicago."

"Are they any good?"

"No, they're a twenty-four-carat nowhere. But Sharon wants the model's view. I'm sorry to leave."

"Don't worry."

We kissed, a little too privately for public, but everyone was facing the stage.

"Did you like him?" I asked, nodding at Dexman.

"No. I prefer Nunchi."

"Good."

She hugged Stutter, and I watched her go.

"So what've you been working on?" Benny asked afterward, as we stood in the emptying hall finishing new beers. The lights were on and the hall looked collegiate in them. There were used compostable beer cups all around us, swirled about the floor by the feet of the attendees. Maquie might know some algorithm that could decipher a concert's atmosphere from the empty cup patterns left on the floor afterward. Based on the sparsity of cups at the front center of the room, there's a 78 percent likelihood that a mosh pit formed in the seventh song.

Benny waited for an answer. Stutter was talking to Abdul about a project Abdul did for Bugzy Malone, and I wanted to listen in. Abdul was an ok lyricist but an even stronger director. He came up with new sounds, like the tongue clucks in "Drop It Like It's Hot." He had Bugzy doing one that sounded like a cat spitting, and he also choreographed small moves for his artists. He did a "best of British" project with Stormzy last year, and one of Stormzy's verses went,

#9 Dream numbered #23
It went poussé from pussy on July 23
Then they sat on a video 'til 2003
That's a three-three-three for the nine I believe.

And for each of the final threes, Abdul had him switch between a different combination of three fingers on the same hand. It was a satisfying little move if you did it quick enough, I saw kids doing it on the Tube.

"Hello? Adrian?" Benny was on my shoulder. "Been working on anything?"

"Not much really, bit of research."

"Research?"

"Yeah, I've been listening to Arctic Monkeys' back albums. There's some really good stuff in there."

Neither statement was true. Benny narrowed his eyes.

"Arctic Monkeys. I don't know . . . Did Stutter tell you about my algorithm?"

"Yes."

"It creates endless streams of words in any meter you want."

"I know."

"E.g. iambic pentameter. That's a type of rhythm, Adrian. It's used in sonnets."

"Yeah, I know what it is."

"Yeah, I know you do, because you did that sonnet rap for Shay."

"Exactly."

"So you can borrow my software, I'm happy to lend it to you. If you want to do more of those sonnets."

"Yep, cool."

"The algorithm will help you if you want to try doing more of them."

"Yup."

I moved closer to Stutter and Abdul, angling my body toward their conversation. Benny moved with me.

"Last time, you said I shouldn't steal meters from other rappers."

Benny had ripped an entire verse from a Loyle Carner track. He changed the individual words but kept the syllables, the rhymes, the rhythm, the meter, everything, and then sold it. And it was crass content.

"Yeah, I said that."

Benny laughed. "You still think it's bad to do it?"

"Yes, you'll get your client into trouble."

This made him laugh more. "*Client*. You're hilarious, Adrian."

I finished my beer and put a hand on Stutter's back. "Hey, let's go," I said. "Let's go to the pub."

"I need a photo of the floor," Stutter said.

We waited for him to take some photos, and Benny made us take a group one as well.

Leveraging his 150,000 followers, Stutter made good money as an influencer. A skateboard brand called Disorder and a headphone brand called Nico both had him on retainer. I had to tell myself not to feel threatened by this. It was Stutter's thing, and I knew I wouldn't have the appeal for it, let alone the patience, but walking to the pub, squeezing single file around crowds outside chicken shops, to be honest I felt a bit low about it. I didn't really have a "thing," I relied only on lyrics. Stutter had a public following; Abdul had choreography and sound niches, and he would move into production one day soon, maybe management; even Benny had angles, however sickening. I had only lyrics.

I felt low about it and dropped back behind the others. I thought about skipping the pub and going home and talking to Sike about it, but I resisted it because I knew it was good to spend time with friends. Sike said fun and diversion were greatly underrated, and it was true, I got a lot out of these other writers. When I first started hanging around Stutter and his friends (in pubs, cafes, sitting rooms, shisha bars) every meeting seemed to reveal a new excited insight. We went wild for them, I went through a phase of writing them down. I occasionally looked at them on my phone, things like,

- Lyrics mean more when drunk or high
- Kofi Mitchell is a coder now! He drives a taxi in the day, and codes at night
- Fronting is dead.
- 90s rappers who used their real names: Obie Trice (real name, no gimmicks),
- On the Pete Rock album, his name isn't actually Deda. It's Dedi. The label screwed him and misspelt it. He says it on Blah Uno . . . *D* to the *E* to the *D* and a fucking *I*
- None of the best lyrics come from rap—Nick Cave, Into My Arms. Joni Mitchell, Both Sides Now. Leonard Cohen, Marvin Gaye, Kate Bush, Townes Van Zandt, Carole King, Hendrix, Stevie Wonder, Paul Simon, The Smiths, Radiohead, ABBA,
- Production. It's all about production. And Inflo is the best producer.
- Jazz rap. It's all about jazz rap.
- Best live shows: Eliza, Jet,

Each insight had galvanized a feeling, rather than any game plan or future direction. It had never occurred to us to capitalize on our findings, we doggedly followed our guts—which is to say, we flailed about like shipwrecks.

I stepped over a dropped milkshake and remembered that one day I had told my mum we were a bit like the early Impressionists. My poor mother, having to hear that. Imagine. What is your youth except embarrassment for you tomorrow and everyone else today? Why did nobody stop me? Why did no one nip them in the bud, those feeble self-aggrandizements, where I thought there was a wall between what was inside me and what I showed everyone else . . . where I thought I was blessed with the double whammy, able like Bond or Batman or Söze to disguise my true self, while at the very same time able like Holmes or Freud or Jesus to sleuth the true selves of everyone around me. I would demonstrate clumsy loyalties to any art or science that I felt was highbrow—from theater to literature and, most often of course, music—and then declare, at what I thought was the bleeding edge of droll, my love of some childish pleasure. Like, somehow, nothing was funnier or more perceptive than gushing about one's love of bubble wrap.

Stutter shouted something about a change of pub. I shouted back ok.

We passed a brick wall, a terrace of small houses, a few groups of revelers in black overcoats. I felt low. But feeling low was just a form of itchiness. The smell of weed was everywhere, I thought I might smoke tonight. This was the type of evening I would forget. I was feeling dramatic. As I walked, I kept thinking about how I needed to find myself a niche.

I thought maybe I could write about ghostwriting. Articles and books. They said that writing about music is like dancing about architecture. I would make no apologies for dancing about cathedrals.

Or maybe I could write music for films. I could work with scriptwriters and scorers. Radiohead gave their songs names like "Exit Music (for a Film)" and "Motion Picture Soundtrack." You think that wasn't all Jonny Greenwood, paving the way for score work? He ended up doing all Paul Thomas Anderson's films. I could write rap for films. I could write pleasant and wry rap for kids and parents. Disney would hire me, they invested in lyrics. Look at *Encanto*, look at *Frozen*.

Or maybe I would perform. Maybe I would make that transition from ghostwriter. I looked ahead at Stutter, Abdul, Benny. I couldn't see any of them on the stage. But myself . . . I had always been able to imagine it. I still could. My sister Jess and that comedian logo designer Jason Kahn had only *shown* me the barriers. They hadn't killed anything. There was fanciful youth in me yet.

At the pub, I drank a Guinness, and felt bloated but better. The pub was scuzzy, everyone in it was scuzzy. When you put pine flooring into a pub, you might think you're being high-end, but you should know that people will walk on it and drip on it and make it look like the Saturday afternoon floor of a leisure center changing room. The lights were wrong, they hung like fat lemons, juicing acid over the room. Near the loos, it smelled of loos. Fruit flies flew holding patterns on the staff side of the bar. For a moment, I imagined that there was a whole zoo behind there, out of sight below the spill mats, writhing around the feet of the bar staff. Panthers and boars, flamingos and lizards, spiders the size of umbrellas.

I had another Guinness. I laid into Benny too hard, and Stutter told me to leave off. Stutter started talking to the table next to us, a group of three Central Saint Martins girls. One had frizzy hair and was surly. One had blond hair, black eyebrows, small round glasses, and a bright sapphire nose stud in her right nostril, and she said she was making art out of algorithms. *Not* building algorithms that could produce art—Christ, no—she was writing famous algorithms onto canvases. She said she thought maths was becoming taboo again, and she said there was beauty in the syntax of algorithms. Benny showed her one of his models on his phone, and she said yes, nice. "And immoral," I said, but nobody paid attention. When the girls spoke about the past, they spoke about it personally and in the present tense, like talking heads on Netflix culture-mentaries. "We see this kind of drastic ennui with democracy . . . We get focaccia fascism, and we're retaliating decades later with Brexit . . . There's a feeling of unified elated sadness when Elizabeth dies." Abdul bought another round. I went for a cigarette and made him come, and I asked him, "What's it all worth, Abdul? What are we doing?" And Abdul said something like, "If you ask me what I want to spend my time doing, in life, all my life, writing lyrics and making songs is it." What a cool guy. I told some stories to the table and they laughed at some of them, and I and Stutter discussed music to everyone, showing off our knowledge and building each other up. Stutter said that jazz rap was the major achievement of '20s music, because it completed the transition of the rap voice into an instrument. They all liked that. We discussed how to spell the word "zhuzh" for a bit. "Zjuzj," someone said. Or "zhoosh." Benny didn't know what it meant, he'd never heard of it. Didn't even know the word! *Let alone* have an opinion on the spelling. I went to the bar, I took orders from the Saint Martins girls as well. Sapphire Stud ordered a vodka and orange juice, and I nearly quoted Method Man at her:

No OJ, no straw; when you give it to me ay, give it to me raw.

But I didn't. I didn't need to act cool in front of other girls, but I didn't need to debase myself either. I saw on the bar lady's arm a huge tattoo of Baloo from *The Jungle Book*, and while I was waiting for the drinks, I wrote some lines into my phone:

> Sweeter than a liter can of juice
> Lots to lose, but I'm feeling kind of loose in the boxers
>
> . . .

The drinks came, and I said sorry, but could we also order sambucas. How many? Four plus three. Baloo went to pour out a tray. A Tommy Evans line came . . .

No lipstick on her thick lips, just a stud in her nose
Tells me she's studying prose

Sapphire Stud, I knew she was exactly the archetype I had always thought I should be getting with. But I wasn't kidding myself. I looked to my glasses and said, "Send Maquie a message saying, hey, where are you?"

The message sent. But I knew where she was, she was sitting in her flat evaluating a start-up in Chicago that did something with computer chips. Her model was cool. Chicago was cool. I thought it was cool she did workshops like this. Computer chips were cool. It would have been cooler if I hadn't known where she was, though.

I looked over at Sapphire Stud. It wasn't that I'd ever wanted to sleep with another girl. At all. The thought sickened me, I was against cheating, I could say that. But I also couldn't deny that "other girls" were a thing. I couldn't avoid *seeing* them.

Maybe I felt about "other girls" the way Kingsley Amis felt about Jews: he said he *noticed* them, even if he didn't want to *do* anything about it.

And because I would never chase "other girls," I think I resented the temptation. Like, I was insulted by the burden of it. And so I had antipathy. Like Amis did.

Shit, there's another one; another "other girl"; your back's up; don't say anything; just leave them to it; leave them to the temptation.

Not that they're trying to tempt, of course. They're not really doing anything. This—Amis and I might decide together, a kind of breakthrough—was the mistake in Genesis. The temptation was all inside Adam, and he *did* want to do something about it. And he *still* resented it, so he bitched on Eve, the original "other girl." Which would mean that God was Adam's original lover.

Which seemed like a strange place to end up, as the shots arrived, conveyed in Baloo's capable hands and set down in front of me, angry little bullets vibrating on the black non-slip.

It was later on and I was zipping up over the trough. A lilac dot was pulsing in my glass lens. My zip got caught, and I looked down. My T-shirt was in the way. I moved it and zipped again.

Zips.

Zippity zip.

Aldous Huxley was obsessed with zips. They're everywhere in *Brave New World*. Huxley thought zips were the future.

The lilac dot was beating, and I tried to swat it away with my hand, but it stayed. You should be able to swat it away. Everything should be swattable. A guy in bleached jeans snorted something in an open cubicle.

Huxley wasn't wrong, but he wasn't really right either.

I went to wash my hands. I didn't always wash my hands, but Maquie said it felt like a free luxury, to wash hands.

I gave the sink a nudge with my hip and walked out.

Hesitatingly going into the women's loo was Sapphire Stud.

Hesitatingly, I thought. *Waitingly*.

I nodded at her, and made to walk past, but she let the door go and came close to me, and I saw that her eyes were a little drunk, her eyelids slurring behind her Johnny Depp glasses. It was dark by the loos, I couldn't quite focus my eyes on her, the nose stud was fuzzy. Sike's lilac dot was pulsing in my right lens. Sapphire Stud was looking very serious, very meaningful. A bit surprisingly, she said,

"Want me to find your nipples?"

She didn't sound like she was looking for me to answer. She held up her two index fingers and pointed one at each of my ears. Then she traced lines in the air down toward my chest, and then she poked them forward. Each finger found one of my nipples.

Dead on.

This was more affronting than impressive. I think I felt prudish.

She waited for a laugh, and I realized she was trying to be sweet-silly, like this might be a meet-cute we relayed on our wedding day to the crowd of graphic designers and advertiser friends we had cultivated. A confident move and I didn't think less of her for it, but I stayed still. She narrowed her eyes as if saying, *come on, throw me a bone*, and then she dropped her hands, shaking her head and laughing away the trick. I wasn't really a part of the conversation she was having. I could smell her, raspberry and ethanol, and I felt blood heading down my body, down through my stomach and away from my heart, making me feel light, even lighter, as she looked up again, her eyebrows heavy, her mouth drawing and her eyes closing a fraction, like the next move was inevitable, and she began to lean toward me, when just for a split second I thought I saw Sike's lilac dot switch sides.

It went to my left lens and, following the movement, I turned my head left, looking for it. It seemed to hover on the far wall there for a second, but then it disappeared. I was confused. The dot then appeared above us and I looked up. It disappeared again. And then it was back in my right lens, pulsing. I turned my head back to Sapphire Stud. I didn't know what had happened, maybe I had confused her nose stud for the dot.

Sapphire Stud changed her expression, she sighed and moved backward. She rolled her eyes again, laughing from her nostrils, and prodded my sternum before turning away toward the bathroom.

I went back to the table with my hands fisted in my pockets. Abdul had gone, he hadn't said goodbye. The pub was clearing out, the lights were on even brighter, and I could see the grease marks on the floor, and the curling coasters, and the cables to and from the TVs, and the stains around the air vents. The staff looked tired. Stutter had put on his jacket and was handing me mine. Benny stood all upright, looking at me. Benny was always out to get me. I would swat Benny away, clear him from my vision, just like that. I looked at the time, it wasn't even midnight. Pubs close too early, it's a joke. The lilac dot was still there, and I had a message from Maquie saying the work was done, she was going to bed, burgers another time. I reached for my drink.

I heard Benny calling me a "fucking mess," which was *pretty* rich, to say the least. I didn't think a *liar* and a *cheat* and a Sunday code-monkey had much place calling *me* a mess. Stutter was pulling me up from my collar, but I was quite content, sort of half out of the taxi and half in it.

Yes, I was a mess . . . *tonight*. Tonight, *I* was a mess. But . . . something about . . . something about . . . I would be sober in the morning.

I giggled a little then, because Stutter was trying to be gentle with me, and probably a bit too gentle for the taxi driver's liking. Put some back into it, Stutter! Throw me around a little! I didn't really say this, I was trying to smoke. A streetlamp was shining in my eyes.

The taxi door closed and the window opened. Benny was inside, looking at us both.

"You're going with him?" Benny said.

He was speaking to Stutter, not to me. The taxi driver made to pull away, but Benny stopped him.

"Yeah, I'll take him home," Stutter said.

"Dude, we live next to each other."

"It's cool, I'll get another taxi."

Benny looked at me.

I looked *right* back at Benny.

"Hey, Benny," I said, looking right at him. "How many songs you got with eighty million streams?"

It was rhetorical.

Benny rolled his eyes.

"Maybe," I said, "maybe you need to zhuzh things up a little."

"Shut the fuck up, Adrian," Stutter said.

"Try jhuzhing, Benny. Zjuzjh up those streams."

The taxi driver beeped the horn.

Then, I don't really know why, maybe I dried a little, I said, "Hey, go with him, Stutter. Honestly, I'm ok. Honestly."

Stutter looked at me for a bit. "Really?"

"Yeah, really. I've got this. I'm not too bad. I sobered."

I slipped off the curb a little, and Benny shook his head, but I ignored him. Yes, Benny, my friend, I was a mess this *evening*. *This* evening.

"Honestly, I'll message tomorrow," I said to Stutter.

The taxi door opened. Stutter gave me a hug and got in. I looked at Benny and smiled a huge smile. Then they drove off.

I turned down the street. I looked up into my glasses and said, "Direct me home," and an arrow appeared at the end of the road, hovering faintly in midnight blue and pointing right. ETA was thirty-eight minutes.

The streets were crisp and quiet, and I felt peaceful. A newsagent was open, and I went inside to buy a bottle of water but came out with something called bread-milk, which described itself as a "filler-upper." It tasted like Weetabix. I ambled down the pavement, rolling over the paving stones, my feet tired, and sipped it.

Leaning back into the velour plush of a large designer sofa in a red-brick ex-factory studio flat somewhere in a distress-chic neighborhood of New York, a rapper—let's say a pioneer of the hip-hop industry in general, and '90s New School rap in particular—might at that moment be writing a few lines. It's half midnight in London, which means not quite dinner time in New York, and sure, it's true, he's a multimillion-dollar-earning rap icon with plans to meet his daughter in thirty minutes, and he hasn't really been writing rhymes much in the past decade, it's been more about production and finding sounds, but hey, this is what he used to do, this is what he can do, and though he *needs* never pick up a pen again, why not, he has time to write a few verses now. He's dressed minimalist, he always has been, because that's what the streets were like in '90s New York, and regardless of all the things Q-Tip keeps telling him about change, and whatever Busta says about growing old with grace, he's pinned himself to that time and place. He's in constant motion, but his clothes stay the same. His dad wore the same shirt and slacks from his first day of work in the Navy Yard to his deathbed, and the consistency suited him fine.

Anyway, he's dressed minimalist and he drags a nail across the black zip of his black jacket as he thinks. A line comes to him . . . something like,

> *Her friends crowd loud and prissy*
> *The tizzy of their frizzy makes me dizzy*

It's nice. It's a little before his time, Biggie would have liked it. (And this thought calls up the same old thought: Why did he turn down Biggie? Why didn't he say yes outside Jemy's Sandwiches, why didn't he make time? Big said how about it that weekend, keep it light and do it quick. Something raw, he had the studio ready. And he knows Biggie would have dominated the track, he would have paled next to him. But still . . . the regret . . . and it's not just that his Malibu house would be twice the size, it's not just that he would have been cemented in the defined and contained oeuvre of a century's legend, it's not just that he feels, still, a heavy and low and rough sorrow for what happened to Big and Tupac and the others, a sorrow for the brutality, a sorrow for the waste, a sorrow for how much they missed out on, for how they never got to see society accept rap, for how they never got to see rap *win*. It's also that it would have been an education. He would have seen in the control room how Biggie listened, how he concentrated, how he felt the business, how he tasted the opportunity. He would have seen how Biggie worked, he would have learned something about making. That's something you can't get anywhere, that's something you regret.)

Anyway, the line is sort of nice, friendly. And it makes him think of doing a song about meeting a girl in a bar. There are enough songs on the topic, but it's inexhaustible. And it *still* excites him, first love.

He picks up half a goji smoothie and sips at it, the condensation from the cup dripping on his thigh.

> *. . . of their frizzy makes me dizzy*
> *I commisee_rate with a cold one*

Man she showed a cold one
All I want's to hold some

Hmn.

Not so good.

Just . . . bad. And young love's exciting, but he's old, it's become voyeuristic. And he remembers why he doesn't write lines anymore. It's because he can't stop himself from trying to write about life back then, which was interesting, rather than life today, which is not. And the lines have always come out forced as a result.

He looks for the remote because he thinks he'll watch some sport for thirty minutes.

His phone buzzes. Manny's calling. He taps his glasses.

"Hey, Manfred."

"Hey, you ok?"

"Yeah. I was writing."

"Yeah?"

"Yeah."

"What kind of thing?"

"Just simple, low-key stuff. Not really working."

"Not flowing?"

"Not really."

"You know, umm, Ralph Ellison . . . he had writer's block for decades."

Manny's good like that, he always elevates what they're doing. You can listen to him and Glover talk for hours.

"Hey," Manny says, "you know I represent Shay in America? You know Shay?"

Joan Baez had a manager called Manfred, too.

"Yeah, I know Shay. English guy."

"Yeah, well, he has a writer he sometimes works with. Jewish guy, another Londoner, and I like his work. He does things differently, his lyrics are different. They just released a sonnet."

"A sonnet? Like Shakespeare or something?"

"Yeah. Kind of wacky, but Shay made it good. Here, I'll send it through."

Manny taps on his phone.

"Coming through."

"Thanks, I'll listen. Nice."

"Anyway," Manny says, "want me to put you in touch?"

"With Shay?"

"With his writer."

"Mmm . . . I was just messing around. I'm not really fixating on this."

"Mess around with the London kid. It might spark something."

"Mmm. You want me to sit with him in the studio?"

"Ha, no, however you want. You can put him on retainer. With Shay he goes away and writes some stuff, then brings it back."

"Manny, I don't know. Don't really know about ghostwriting."

"Ok, ok, I know."

"Hmm."

"Hmm."

The rapper has an idea.

"Does he perform?" he asks.

"The writer?"

"Yeah."

"Don't know," Manny says. "Why?"

"Might feel more natural. If it's a collaboration."

"Hey, no."

"You know, if we did a track together."

"No way. Come on. Listen, you've got a half-million kids—actual, real rappers—half a million that you need to work with before you offer a feature to an English nobody."

"I know, I know . . ."

". . . the line goes Queens, through Chicago, and ends in LA. Half a million of them."

"I know," the rapper says. "But . . ." He gestures to the empty lounge. "They're all writing for themselves. They have their thing to protect. This guy might be humble."

"Humble?"

"Yeah."

"Like, not out for himself?"

"Yeah . . . like, happy to help. Like, *I'm* the one in need here, Manfred."

"Haha."

"Haha."

"Ok. Ok," Manny says. "Let's discuss it, but I don't know."

"Ok."

"I'll get in touch with him."

"Ok, thanks, Manfred."

"Ok."

It could happen. I slotted the bread-milk bottle through the open rubbish bin lid of a terraced house.

My feet hurt a little. And I thought I could still feel the pain in my finger from squeezing my shoes on before the concert—it was red from the shoe horning and from the cold. A homeless man groaned from a stairwell and I crossed the street.

When I got to my street, I leaned on an iron railing and clicked on the lilac dot. It took a while to load, as though it was calibrating. Then Sike said,

>Hi, Adrian.
>Given the amount of alcohol you've had, it's possible you'll experience memory loss for some parts of the evening.
>This is likely to increase any hangover anxiety you feel tomorrow, so, like we discussed in March, would you like to record a quick note to yourself while you can still remember the evening?

"What do I say?"

>You say anything to describe your night.
>It's to reassure yourself tomorrow.

"Ok."

I looked down at the pavement and wiped my forehead. It was oily from the cold. I was exhausted.

"Record voice note."

A microphone appeared and hovered in front of me. I spoke in monotone.

"Tonight was fun, you had a good time. You were quite drunk and the others definitely noticed it. But don't worry, nothing bad happened. You were rude to Benny. All good with Stutter and Abdul. Stutter offered to take you home, which was nice, but you said you were fine and sober and he went home with Benny. Message Stutter to say thanks tomorrow. You feel ok now. Quite drunk. Very tired. You will feel it tomorrow a bit. Don't worry, nothing happened with Sapphire Stud, but you should be careful in the future. You weren't really so interested in her, but you got into a situation."

I trailed off, suddenly realizing how lucky I'd been to escape. I didn't know if I would have refused her, had things developed. How *had* I escaped? My memory was already fuzzing, I thought I had been confused by the lilac dot. I could sense tomorrow's fear crystallizing, lining up behind a wall of alcohol.

"Yes," I said, and took a few steps. "All fine. You were thinking about Maquie. You really were. You thought about Maquie a lot. But . . . you were lucky to escape. You were lucky nothing happened. You idiot."

On top of shame, I felt anger coming. I would deal with it tomorrow.

I waved my hand over the mic.

>Was that everything that happened?

"Yeah."

>Would you like me to analyze the voice note?

"No."

>Would you mind if I make one comment, though?

"Sure."

But I was tired, and wanted to go inside and to bed.

>Weren't you also extremely *unlucky* to have got into that situation
in the first place?

"What do you mean?"

>You said you were lucky to escape from Sapphire.
>It seems like the chances of being put into a situation where you might make a mistake like that are very small in the first place.
>You were unlucky that Sapphire desired you and made a proposition.

"Hmm."

>You shouldn't reprimand yourself too much.

"Sike . . . I don't know that I would have put a stop to it. I didn't take any action. I was conscious of what was happening and did nothing to stop it."
Sike thought for a bit.

>Contemporary research debates the link between consciousness and action, and your consciousness may have been irrelevant to the outcome.
||>*Click to see thinking by* Benjamin Libet; Robert Sapolsky; Chun Siong Soon, Anna Hanxi.[more]
>Tonight, you were unfortunate for having been put into a position where taking action might have been necessary.
>Given the positive effect Maquie has on your mental well-being, and paired with your low tendency for self-sabotage, it seems unlikely you would have jeopardized your relationship with her by having an affair with someone else.
>Though of course it's possible you may have made a mistake.
>In the future, we can work through high-risk evenings in advance, together visualizing potential hazards to help you avoid these situations.

I shook my head, but I said fine, and closed Sike.

. . .

When I got into bed, I smelled the erotic mix of alcohol and toothpaste on my own breath, and thought about jerking off to thoughts of sex with Maquie. Maybe Maquie and Sapphire Stud together. But I fell asleep.

* * *

The next day, anxiety scorched my windpipe.

I went about the morning feeling physically bad but mentally horrendous. I turned on Sike, and Sike told me to picture the anxiety as a tsunami wave roaring toward me from far out at sea. I imagined myself stood on the beach, letting it all come at me, sand sucked from beneath my feet, sea spray on my eyelids. It helped.

I listened back to my voice note, and it helped too. I couldn't remember saying the words, and there was something comforting about hearing coherence in this unremembered me.

I also read the transcripts from my conversation with Sike, I read them over and over and tried to convince myself I had done nothing wrong.

This helped less.

I felt foolish, despicable, I had been reckless. I thought about Maquie and I despaired. If something had happened, if I had made a mistake at this point . . . so soon after Stockholm and everything she had told me about Fumi, all her confessions to a past that was painful, confusing . . . if I had squandered that trust, it would have been a repulsive cliché of the kind I usually sneered at.

Sike didn't want to dwell on it and continued to talk about chance and luck and free will. I took some succor from this, but I promised myself: never again so close.

I called Maquie and told her about my drunkenness and my recklessness, but stopped short of mentioning Sapphire Stud. Maquie laughed her low laugh and told me to give myself a break. I wondered if I would confess the near miss some other time, a new lie to reveal. I wondered what she would have done if I had slept with someone else and then confessed it. She was probably free-thinking enough to consider polygamy, but somehow I didn't think she would care for the inefficiency of it.

. . .

The anxiety dissipated and things got back on track. Before a City banquet one evening, Maquie was putting on a black dress and she looked into the mirror, her eyes moving past me and onto her reflection beyond, and she gave a sort of grunt and said she looked old. She said this from time to time, always undramatically but I always felt dramatic in response and this time too I insisted that she didn't look old.

"You don't even look twenty-eight, which is your age," I said. "You look . . . eighteen."

And we laughed.

I wasn't sure why such a blatant ruse made us both laugh and feel affectionate, and when Maquie had left to the banquet I asked Sike about it, and Sike said,

>I think you're talking about the joy of sharing fantasies, of creating worlds with someone else.
>The knowledge that what you're sharing is fantastical doesn't undermine the enjoyment.

I thought love might be like this, a mutual and transparent fantasy, enjoyed for the effort each makes in playing it, but I didn't say this to Sike, it felt a little cynical and I didn't know if I was cynical about love. I had hope for love, I always had had hope for it. Sometimes the hope was confused with lust, and sometimes the lust was confused with loneliness. But it didn't follow that hope was the same as loneliness, unless you wanted to get really existential, where everything is pretty much everything else, and Sike was a good antidote for thinking like that for too long.

I believed the stats at least, Sike had shown them to me: Maquie made me feel 128 percent more secure and 43 percent more elated, on average, day to day. It was true that she sometimes looked tired, this was reasonable: she worked nonstop, often on the weekends, and the effort manifested itself in lower back pain and burnt eyes that had crows' feet and eyelids that half closed after 5 p.m. However, I *liked* this about her, I liked thinking of her like this, sleepy-eyed and stretching. It aided the sensation in me that I was finally dating an adult, one with a meaningful career and a consistent salary (our annual incomes were comparable, but the cash flow was different). I liked thinking of her in general. More and more.

I was having a haircut and a strange thing happened while I was thinking about Maquie. It was a morning slot, the room smelled of conditioner and croissants, and my hairdresser, Ranger, had been blasting Sasha the trainee about the music. "Boogie Woogie Bugle Boy" by The Andrews Sisters had been playing.

Sasha the trainee, leaning on her broom: "It's not me, it's the playlist."

Ranger, arms held out: "Well, change the playlist. Fuck."

Sasha: "You don't like it?"

Ranger: "No."

Sasha: "Why?"

Ranger: "Because one 'oogie woogie' is one too many. Change it or I cut your pay."

Sasha: "You'll cut it from fuck-all to fuck-all?"

Ranger: "Hey, Adrian, you ever seen a person die?"

Me: "Yes."

My grandfather had cancer and he gasped and choked on the bed, his breath coming like chairs scraping in an auditorium.

Sasha: "That's power harassment, Ranger. That's psychological. You need Sike."

Ranger: "Change it."

Sasha: "To what?"

Ranger: "I don't care. Adrian, what do you want?"

Me: "Can you play a rapper called Nunchi?"

Ranger, to Sasha: "You heard him."

Sasha the trainee growled, played around with her phone, and Nunchi came on. I looked to my glasses sitting on the counter, and I told them to translate the lyrics. Subtitles began appearing across their lenses. Nunchi was rapping about food. I had decided I was a fan, he was funny. And talented. I was excited to work with him. I had a good feeling about it.

Ranger returned to my head, drifting around me in a baggy olive smock. "How's your Japanese girlfriend?"

"She's fine," I said.

"I need to get to Japan," Ranger said. "You heard about the bars? The weird bars? There's this bar, right, where the hostess takes your shoes and your socks, and you have this bottle of honey, and there are mice . . ."

I stopped listening to think about Maquie, and for the first time, I began to fantasize about marrying and Maquie teaching our children one day about right and wrong, up and down. Her lessons took place at a lamp-lit kitchen table made of thick scarred wood, our young attentive children placed around it, eating their small suppers of bread, chicken, cherry tomatoes, carrot sticks. The dishwasher's gurgle; our newest would doze in my lap; pictures on the fridge; a red-crossed calendar. Maquie's lessons would be within my intellectual grasp but beyond my emotional remit, and I would watch the pastoral scene as an included outsider and swell with pride for this family I was a part of, and for my wife who was able to guide us all through these cloudy matters of confliction. We were a unit; we were the cozy past of the children's future. Maquie and I were building worlds. Though unrelated to anything I had ever associated with the words "lust" or "erotic," I suddenly realized that this fantasy of marriage and family had led to the slow unfolding of an erection, a hard-on creeping forward in my boxers like the stop-start ticking of the second hand.

Ranger was doing my sideburns. I peered down, without moving my head, to see if there was a bulge in the salon gown, but all was calm on the hair-speckled sea.

". . . and then a week later they send them back to you by post," she said, "all clean again."

I nodded as though impressed, but inside I was thinking: a hard-on. About marriage. Holy shit.

The link between commitment and sexual arousal shocked me, I think because I'm a child of divorce and I'd grown up assuming that one came at the expense of the other.

I left Ranger's. It was spring. Unassailable spring. My love life had peeled itself off the wall and was enjoying a florescence. The air was scented, the sky was gargantuan. I switched my glasses onto sunglass mode, it drained the battery but I'd be home soon. Everything was growing quick.

I felt a compounded optimism, but walking home I also felt that, around the edges of the optimism, a danger lurked, and I thought of my near miss with Sapphire Stud. The thought made me shiver, and I brought up and read through that night's Sike transcripts again.

I liked Sike's small mistakes, like when it thought Sapphire was that girl's real name. The well-worn notion was that these mistakes made Sike more human, not less so. I often wondered if they were built into the code.

But the more humanlike characteristic was Sike's ability to explain its conclusions (". . . the positive effect Maquie has . . . your low tendency for self-sabotage . . ."). When everyone was terrified of AI, they thought explainability was the most important challenge to overcome. What was the route between data and conclusion? Which inputs were driving the output, and with what weighting? I guess Sike overcame this challenge, and it rarely made a suggestion without presenting some level of reasoning, feasibly because this also made the suggestion easier to swallow. It creased my brain to think too much about how Sike's *input* data was always my actions or my questions, and how its *output* suggestions might then drive my next actions or questions, which it would in turn use as *input* data, etc. etc., and so on and so on. In an efficient world, Sike would skip a step and leave me out of the whole charade.

But this type of thinking was a cul-de-sac, and honestly I was getting a bit sick of hearing it all the time in pubs from people who preferred theory to practice and who loved to say that we *actually* lived in a dystopia. We didn't live in a dystopia, proof of which could be seen in our use of the word "dystopia," because dystopias are like dreams, they get shattered by their own definition. Characters in the dystopia call it "life," or "reality." It isn't like a theme park, it isn't like love; you can't have a self-aware dystopia, dystopias don't explain themselves.

I wondered who I could rant to about this. I eyed passersby.

The thing about Sike's explainability was that it was only human*like*. Human-*ish*. It wasn't *human*; explainability is not a natural characteristic. How well could we really explain anything we did?

Like, why did I feel sad whenever I saw embroidered flowers? What was the pre-memory input data there?

Or why did I crave fame, why did I fear loss? Sike didn't like me dwelling on these topics, but there must have been answers.

Or that time I watched my grandfather die. Do you think he could explain what his biology was doing, what was happening to each cell as his arms withered and his body ate itself? Muscle emaciation looks like abandoned housing in failed suburbs. Do you think he could explain his yellow eyes, his plastic skin?

Or could you explain how you carry that cup of water, expertly balancing the meniscus, as you cross the soft carpet to the window?

You couldn't, and I neither.

Maquie neither . . .

Maquie the intelligence builder, she of clarity, Gifted Diviner of Algorithms . . . in Sophie's words, "all-seeing . . . fucking god."

But this had turned out untrue. She couldn't see everything.

Maquie had told me Fumi's story and asked me to ignore it, and this meant ignoring my feelings about it, which was fine, my feelings weren't important next to her desire to transcend her origin (to move forward toward a hopefully better future, not backward toward a dismally certain past with a squalidly beautiful, squalidly depressed father). But her confession, so richly detailed, so "accurate," as she put it, explained little. It touched on nothing of what Daniel's role, real or symbolic, had been in her life; or what role he had now, where he was now, what the origin of his depression was, whether she was scared of this origin, whether he affected her, how she *felt* about him affecting her . . . Maquie had explained none of this, and perhaps it was because she didn't trust me, or perhaps it was because she was scared, but perhaps it was simply that there were parts of the world that even she couldn't explain.

Amidst all the confetti of spring, I felt this unexplainable world growing around us, and our inability to understand and explain it seemed to drive the danger. Paths not mapped could divert us from our simple aims, and threats not visualized, shadows not lit, holes forgotten . . . The metaphors churned around my mind like folk lyrics, I wanted them to explain fear, ambition, uncertainty. Above all, time . . . Time brought new weather, time threatened. Tomorrow was more dangerous than today. But time also moved so slow, so it wasn't always possible to see the danger growing. Day to day, there was that invisible creep of chrysalids, those indiscernible bumps in temperature; forest floors of decay, their drawn-out rustle; and waves going in and out, kidding the direction of the tide. Maquie and I were only human, we couldn't see slower than the sun setting.

SUMMER

7.

There was a Friday in early June when Maquie had three engagements, notable because she looked forward to each of them. She woke at five thirty, drank water out of a London Pride pint glass that I had given her, and made coffee and rye toast with beetroot jam. She stood eating and drinking them in her narrow and old, white-walled kitchen, with the single long window at the end, and while she did so she read her messages in her glasses, filtering important and not-important ones, and reading through the various US tech feeds that had filled up overnight.

Then she stretched. Pulling her legs one after the other onto the kitchen counter and resting them there, toe to knee, she leaned forward. Her legs were bare, and the counter chilled her calves. Next, she stood and bent over, touching her toes, feeling the sinews of her back shift and scrape. Then she stood on one leg and stretched her arms and other leg out, like a ballerina. As she did so, she looked out of the kitchen window and watched the Kennington plane trees in the early sunshine, long walls of flickering light like old train station information boards, and as she watched them she shook her head, cursing them from her arabesque and saying out loud, "Motherfuckers."

Early summer's hay fever had been particularly acidic, she was waking each morning to eyes like mosquito bites and a cement nose. She saw a sick irony in nature's condition that some people shouldn't enjoy its rebirth: as the world freed up around them, as windows opened and jackets were put away, as light returned, as parks filled, as terraces opened, as limbs swung bare and dresses waved, the world inside, for hay fever sufferers, became itchy and claustrophobic.

"Motherfuckers," she said again, and reached for her eyedrops.

At 9 A.M., the first meeting was with a Belgian sleeptech start-up called Bounze, which made a device proven to deepen and prolong sleep. The headset read the individual wearer's brain activity and pulsed special waves into the head in response, stimulating nerve endings and causing them to contract, which decreased blood flow and increased space for the cerebrospinal fluid that carried toxins away. The product had good results in trials, and good testimonials, despite the company raising only small amounts of money so far. Now the costs were getting too high, and they needed serious money to invest in production, but few investors had been in touch with them.

It wasn't through luck that Maquie had found Bounze. She had been monitoring the sleep industry, tracking the science and its development, averaging thirty minutes a day on sleep-related newsletters from across Europe, the US, and Asia. The coverage felt essential if Maquie was to stay on top of a field of technology that seemed finally to be producing results. Sleep was a major frontier. Except possibly defecation, Maquie knew no other activity that humans were quite so childishly reliant upon and yet still so poor at, despite their daily practice. Sleeping should be as easy as breathing, but tiredness was universal. A tech company could fix this, and the market would support it: better sleep was sustainable.

There were various companies trying to deliver sleep, but Maquie wasn't interested in the pharmaceutical ones, whose results were patchy, their reputations too. Devices were more interesting, head-worn ones in particular, not least because of the ubiquity of smartglasses, which provided a frame for them. She could see the proliferation of formats, functions, accessories. Sports mode, baby mode, travel mode. With the right company, if you didn't make it the whole way, an easy but massively substantial exit would be to sell to one of the major glass makers, like Implode Group, who she knew were investigating sleeptech as well.

Most exciting to Maquie was the earning potential. Sleep—especially that deep, ruby port sleep—was a luxury good, one currently distributed arbitrarily, like cone shells brought in by the tide. Like mental health used to be, sleep was unpegged from a person's financial capacity. Sleep was a luxury that, like mental health, went beyond the material, into the unlimited verdure of the human internal. And sleep was a luxury that, like mental health, had a significant audience; the addressable market for sleep products was 8.1 billion people.

When she emailed the founder of Bounze, an academic from Brussels called Gerd, he said he happened to be in London for a few days to visit a symposium. They could meet in person. Gerd's emails were short and full of typos, but they were prompt. After stretching, while getting dressed, Maquie reflected that she may have found a diamond, and she looked forward to communicating this to her boss Kyle, who would appreciate the pun.

She cycled from her flat, over Vauxhall Bridge, to the hotel in Victoria where Gerd was staying. As she crossed the bridge, she watched the Thames pulsing up at her, imagining she could discern portentous words in the brown and white foam. She remembered the previous night. She had lain in the half-light until 2 A.M., charting river systems in the cracks of her ceiling paint. The sleep that had once come easily, almost forcefully to her, was recently elusive, and she put it down to a surge in libido linked to her new relationship with Adrian, because sex or masturbation seemed to be the only activities that would put her under. She resisted a reliance on these. While traveling or when jetlagged, she never took sleeping pills in case she formed a reliance on them, and a reliance on orgasms didn't feel much healthier. She doubted she would tell Gerd all this today, but one day she would be interested in his opinions.

She arrived and chained her bike, went into the hotel's cafe, and sat down in a booth while blowing her nose and ordering an oat-germ flat white off a sad-looking waitress. Then Gerd arrived, and she scratched all hope.

She noticed first his walk, a kind of vacant scurry. He piloted the empty cafe and either didn't notice her welcoming smile, or wasn't able to smile, or didn't know that a smile was the typical response to another smile. She said hello. His face was pocked and sheeny, it reminded Maquie of Fumi's lunch tofu. They shook hands and Gerd's was clammy and limp—if Maquie had licked him and tasted tofu then the sensory experience would have been complete. She sat. And as Gerd sat, he shivered the kind of involuntary shiver Maquie sometimes got while peeing, except that for Gerd it didn't seem pleasurable. He let out a very soft sound, like a small moan.

"I don't know if I will order anything," he said, "because I'm not so thirsty and I have a little ulcer inside my lip, so it's difficult for me to judge what I want."

Then he frowned a little, imploring Maquie to do something, but she couldn't tell what.

Fuck, she thought.

The meeting lasted less than an hour, there was barely a superfluous word as she asked Gerd the questions, inputting the company's data into the metallic boxes of her model's desktop portal.

She cycled back home, and on the way over Vauxhall Bridge, a spore-like something—a tree seed or clot of pollen—flew into her eye. She stopped cycling and pulled onto the pavement to apply eye drops and blink it out.

All she ever really desired in a CEO was a bit of organization, some practical sense, a flexible ego, gusto . . . her demands weren't great. Companies were built to be judged retroactively, the results generally spoke for themselves and you could put your faith in revenue growth, margin, customer growth, cost optimization . . . It was predicting these results proactively that was difficult, especially from outside the company, and Maquie didn't claim an innate foresight. That was her model's role. She did claim, though, an intuition, a gut sense, for the people at the helm. While the model's other conclusions might be surprising, its judgment on people never was; here, she and her model saw eye to eye. She knew what her model would think of Gerd from the moment he walked in.

There would be other factors in the model's decision. The gray pentagon had slid onto the page, announcing its negative decision, and Maquie had shielded it from Gerd and not clicked on it. But she guessed the company's lack of future wouldn't be only Gerd's fault. It was never one thing, it was always things, and their combination. But people were a whimsical force, and while there was room for error when predicting their starling swarm movements at the customer end, if the CEO was incapable of processing a drink order, you might as well pack up and go home.

She got the spore out, her eye streaming, and got back on her bike.

Her strategy professor at university used Picasso's approach to drawing as a philosophy for business design, and he liked to quote an art critic who said that Picasso had a "whim of iron." It occurred to Maquie that you might then see Picasso as the great analogy of humankind, of its resolute variation and fluttering, of its never-ceasing fluctuations, flux, difference; change as the only constant, bankable randomness . . . and in the end, the lefts match the rights and the ups match the downs. From far away, with enough humans, enough whims, the line looks smooth; a millennium of human progress, plotted, has no kinks. It's only up close you see the kinks. Maquie was up close, she was surfing the down kinks. At the end of the meeting, as they stood up, Gerd had paused and said,

"One more thing I have remembered to tell you. I am using Sike. I am a Sike user."

Maquie hadn't been able to tell if it was a boast or a caveat.

At home, she had another cup of coffee and another pint of water while reading emails in her glasses and replying with voice notes. An email from the owner of a villa in Tuscany confirmed available dates, they were planning a holiday with Stutter and Sophie. She wrote an analysis of Bounze and sent it through to her team, attaching to it the model's results, which no one would read.

Ulf called her.

"How is Adrian?"

"He's fine."

Ulf had begun to leverage Adrian in his promotion of Sike. Today, he was quick to broach the subject: "I think there must be an imbalance. He is using electricity. You are reading by candlelight. What does Adrian say about it?"

"That they still don't offer couples' packages. I have to go."

She said goodbye. Then she stretched again, calves on the counter, while watching the plane trees, which were now a darker emerald and still. She left at 12:20, this time on foot.

When they sold their audiobook business for $1.8 billion and left Toronto to start a tech fund in London, Maquie's bosses, Sharon and Kyle, had built an office on St. Cross Street, in between Leather Lane and the jewelry district of Hatton Garden. This was a fitting location, Kyle said, always with a click of his teeth, because they were looking for gems. The couple were Conan Doyle fans so it could have been Baker Street, but such was their respect for Sherlock Holmes that they refused to add to the area's corporatization. Hatton Garden held enough old London romance for them anyway, and they made do instead with naming the fund May-Perhaps, a reference to a line about Sherlock once having refused a knighthood "for services which may perhaps some day be described." The line was printed across various surfaces at the St. Cross Street office, which employees used when they felt like it, often working instead from home or portfolio company offices, or from conferences, other events, hotels.

Since the beginning of spring, Maquie had based herself at the May-Perhaps office most days, she found it calming. That day, though, it was her monthly one-on-two catch-up with Sharon and Kyle, and they liked to do these over lunch at their home. Coincidentally and sometimes uncomfortably, they lived a ten-minute walk from Maquie's house, in a leafy square off Kennington Park Road. There was a pub in the corner, and Maquie had played pétanque on the pink gravel with Imperial friends once or twice.

She always looked forward to Sharon and Kyle's house. Last week, at lunch, an American colleague called Beau had called them "luck-smart."

"Luck got them success, success got them opinions."

Beau was devious and Maquie thought the accusation unjust, at least regarding Sharon, who was quick. At times Maquie found her greedy, but this might change to ambitious, depending on Maquie's mood. And either way, she and Kyle were warm and never dull, and they treated Maquie like a protégé, and this was comforting.

Number 31 of the square was in fact 31 and 32, but you couldn't tell that the houses were joined together from the brick facade. Maquie rang the bell and walked in, shouting hello and hearing Kyle call back from the garden. She could smell barbecue, which was bullish for a workday, but they were Canadian.

She rubbed her nose and softly patted her eyes, then walked into the sitting room. She touched her fingertips onto the veneer of a cherrywood side table, then walked through the scrum of bloated, post-kitsch peach sofas, enjoying the smell and scrape of rattan carpet beneath her trainers. She stopped to look at a framed cinema poster of the Japanese release of the Disney cartoon *Basil The Great Mouse Detective*. The Japanese title of the film, chosen only for Japan, translated to *Olivia's Great Adventure*. They had decided to pin the focus on the little girl mouse of the story instead of the Sherlock-esque male mouse, and Sharon was proud of this real-life metaphor for the importance of perspective.

Maquie walked into the kitchen. Sharon was preparing a salad with headphones on—she listened constantly to audiobooks—and didn't hear Maquie, so Maquie walked past her and out onto the leafy patio where Kyle was prodding something on the barbecue. He was in docksiders, shorts, and a red-and-white-striped rugby shirt, his belt high over the top of the shirt and his wide stomach. He turned and smiled. His beard bushed.

"Maq-attack!"

"Hey!"

"Grab a beer if you like, grab me one too. We've got Ferris Teller."

Ferris Teller was a cultured meat company that lab-grew minute steaks, filets, and burgers, and May-Perhaps had invested after demand for meat substitutes had collapsed. There was a hint of cardboard to the taste, like you get from food that's been in the freezer too long, but the texture was perfect. They would be well-placed for when demand rebounded, and the prospects already looked good. It was a gem. It hadn't been Maquie's find.

Maquie went back into the kitchen and to the fridge, and Sharon spotted her and, grinning from beneath her big headphones and big hair, gave Maquie a hug, took a beer for herself, and gestured that she would be out in a minute. Maquie took the beers outside and handed one to Kyle. He twisted the lid off.

"Barbecue, barbecue. It's good to be alive, Maquie."

He said "barbecue" a few more times, changing the syllable stress. The cliché of Kyle's North American positivity pleased Maquie, she liked its transparency.

"Saw your email, Maq-attack, haven't read the report yet. How was Gerd?"

"Ugh."

Kyle looked concerned and Maquie caught herself. Positive people need positivity.

"I mean, yes. The tech is great. We should watch them for the future," she said.

"Big ego?"

"The opposite."

"Ah."

"Ego-less."

"So it's a 'no'? We couldn't find him a mentor, or a cofounder?"

The model factored in things like this. She wanted to give sunshine, but she pictured herself as a cartoon rain cloud, raining on Kyle's barbecue.

"Don't know. The model . . . we need to think about it. The tech is great, and there's a market, but . . ."

"People are important in a business. Nothing more important."

He was thinking, possibly, of himself.

"Exactly. Let's see, I'll think some more on it."

She took a sip of beer. Kyle watched the fake burgers. Some sparrows frolicked on the paving stones at the far end of the garden, jerking and jutting. Distant shouts of children came into the garden, and, turning to the sound, Maquie saw that the jasmine at the foot of the garden wall was flowering. She went to smell it, wondering if it was an allergen.

"Would be good to find something soon," Kyle said as she turned.

Maquie didn't turn around and she took her time to answer. She bent down to the jasmine and smelled its rubbery sweetness. She picked one of the flowers and rolled it, petals and nectaries, between her fingers. Lying thick in Kyle's comment was the suggestion that something could be improved, that chance could be enhanced. She felt a cluster of nerves fire in her chest, and she resented her answer.

"We will, Kyle. For sure."

. . .

Lunch was quiet. Before sitting down, Maquie deliberately repeated her account of Bounze and Gerd to Sharon, testing her reaction, searching for the same regret she thought she had heard in Kyle's voice. And she thought she found it. Sharon had looked at Kyle, and said, "Ah." Then, "Never mind." Then, "Next one!" Then, "People are important!"

Their conversation avoided work. Maquie's mind kept returning to the same ominous anti-mantra: *They hired me to find, and I've found nothing.* The thought bounced between her brain and chest. She felt it more in her chest, and with the feeling came the idea that she might lose her place in the house. She had assumed she was as inarguable a feature as the books or trinkets or poster art but, just for a second, it felt conditional.

She chewed her laboratory patty and gradually felt the fear shrink. It dissipated, and then rolled over onto its back and turned into a mild indignation. She was wrong to care about their disappointment. They found her, she didn't seek this job . . . *they* believed in her thesis, in her model.

After eating, Kyle made coffee and the three of them sat together at the puzzle table in the sitting room. Maquie didn't know anyone else who owned tables devoted to single activities, let alone puzzle making, and somehow this thought made her more convinced she was right about whatever it was Sharon and Kyle were wrong about. The puzzle was a picture of the Manhattan skyline. The original photograph was shot from Liberty Island during a clean, purple and orange sunrise, and the buildings were reflected near-perfectly in the water. Some of the individual puzzle pieces were carved to look like objects from nature—an oak leaf, an acorn, a songbird—and the surrounding pieces were shaped eccentrically to fit with them.

"They're called *whimsies*," Sharon said, picking up one of the pieces from the pile, this one carved like a mushroom. "I like them . . . they're like pictures within a picture." She searched for a space. "So when you complete the puzzle, you can focus on the ensemble picture, or the individual pieces."

She tried placing the piece, but then pulled it back again. "Like a kenning."

"A kenning?"

"A kenning, Maquie. We never told you what a kenning is? Kyle, we never told her?"

Kyle was collecting pieces of sky. "I don't think so, honey," he said.

Sharon tutted.

"A kenning, Maquie, is a special *type* of word. Old English and Old Norse poetry used them as literary flourishes. It's when you rename a thing, an everyday thing, with an imaginative metaphor for that thing. They're usually two words joined together into one. So, for example, they used to write 'whale-road' instead of 'the sea.' Like they were imagining the sea as a special road for whales. Or 'wave-horse' instead of 'ship.'"

"'Raven-feeder,'" said Kyle, "instead of 'warrior.' Because warriors die and ravens eat their corpses. Kind of dark."

Sharon nodded. "We still use some today, Maquie, they lie hidden in everyday speech. Exquisite gems that we pass by, oblivious."

Kyle cleared his throat a little, and Sharon glanced at him. Then she drifted some pieces around on the felt tabletop, scrunching her mouth into and out of a pout. Maquie waited, a piece of shore in her hand. Kyle picked up the coffee jug and muttered something about a refill, then left for the kitchen. Sharon pouted a few more times, then relaxed, as though having satisfied a thought.

"So," she said. "What can you see in this puzzle, Maquie? Can you see any kennings? Any hidden beauty?"

Maquie didn't feel she had the energy to go through the motions of a word game simply to discover an ethic at the end, and it wasn't hard to guess this one. She might excuse herself soon, there was work she could be doing, rather than acting out fables with Sharon. But she looked at the emerging picture, the half-finished waves, the incomplete towers of New York, the layers of sky. She thought about the people in the buildings, the office ones and the residential ones; she thought about the gap where the Twin Towers used to be; she thought about boats sailing past, or to, or from.

"I don't think so," she said.

But then . . . she realized, and she couldn't help but like it. Quietly she said, "Skyscraper."

Sharon clicked her fingers. "Very good! Isn't that a great one? Scraping the sky? So spectacular."

Maquie nodded. Sharon held out her hand.

"And this?"

Maquie looked at the mushroom-shaped piece, sitting below the thumb joint on Sharon's chalky palm. It looked like a piece of sea, possibly a dark patch in the bottom right corner of the picture. She looked Sharon in the eye.

"Toadstool," she said.

"Maquie! You are very good at this. A *stool for toads*!"

Sharon laughed and shook her head, hair bouncing.

"What I like about them," she said, "is that they're secret, often *even* to the person speaking them, and also they're valuable, because someone has poured poetry into them. Language is full of untapped potential, Maquie, hidden gems. Hidden value. And it needs *experts* to find the value. Special people who can see through the haze. Can you think of another plant whose name is a kenning, Maquie?"

"Sharon, I'm looking for companies that fit the model. That's all I'm doing. I'm doing it daily."

Sharon pouted again. She put the toadstool down. Maquie felt in control of her voice.

"I'm looking and looking, I'm using the framework we agreed on. I'm searching high and low. I'm following our plan. There's nothing out there. There is no new Sike. As soon as there is, I'll find it."

"Honey . . ." She put a hand on Maquie's wrist. Her eyes were big and sympathetic. "Honey, we know you're doing your best. Don't doubt our faith for a second. It's just . . . companies like the one this morning . . . it's a *wonderful* technology."

"Bounze is a good company, Sharon, it has potential, and we can invest your money, but you'd be handing cash to a fucking Eeyore."

The curse word made Sharon pull back, like she'd bitten a lemon.

"Sorry," Maquie said.

Sharon shook her head to dismiss it. Then she forced a soft smile.

"An Eeyore, I love that." She squeezed Maquie's wrist. "What I love about you is how *literary* you are. You're *academic*, and that's excellent, and it's why we hired you, because you're excellent."

"Sharon, if there's another Sike out there, I'll find it."

Sharon pulled her hand away and looked back to the puzzle. "I *know*, Maquie. You mustn't worry."

But the feigned calm with which she asked her next question made Maquie's stomach shrink.

"Did you hear any more about Max and Quantum Theater?" she said.

Maquie shrugged and said no, feeling red, then Kyle came in.

Maquie went home and drank some water, then some peppermint acacia tea, and she looked out onto the plane trees, which were now wiping the air with a soft bounce. She thought about stretching. Maybe Sharon had heard something, she thought, maybe she was just being curious. Maybe she knew about Maquie sleeping with Max, and maybe she thought it was unprofessional, or maybe she didn't care. Maybe she thought Maquie was improper, or maybe she thought Maquie was fastidious. Maybe she hadn't heard anything, maybe she just liked Quantum Theater. Maybe she disagreed with Maquie's decision and had heard differently, maybe the model was wrong. Maquie should have asked Sharon exactly why she had brought Max up, but there had been too many maybes, and she had left it.

A message from Ulf: a link to an article about Sike and its usefulness by the poet Bengt Berg. She swiped the message away and forced cups into the dishwasher.

She settled into some newsletters.

But fifteen minutes later, she had stopped again. She made more tea. She went outside for a walk around the block, then returned again. Then she went back out again and bought some washing machine tablets. She returned and put the tablets away, then put on a podcast and tried to take on board recent developments in the kitchen appliance industry. She paced. Now in her bedroom, now back in the narrow kitchen, she swapped to a different podcast. But nothing went in. She stopped on the landing.

She stood there, the wall in front of her, silence all around her. She looked at her arms and then her feet, then the carpet and then the wall. She opened and closed her hands. She scraped a toe against the carpet. She tried to feel her entire body, every cell. She was experiencing a moment of wide awareness, and the awareness surrounded her thoughts, made her consciousness clear and fluid.

And she thought to herself,

Ok, no nonsense now.

Is this anxiety?

Is it here?

She thought back to lunch, the bounce of the silly thinking. She walked back into the kitchen, and poured some water. She took off her glasses and put them down and looked out the window. She would go into the bathroom and look in the mirror. She would look at herself, she would look into her own eyes, and she would say out loud:

Anxiety? Here? Fuck *that*.

She drank some water and thought about stretching again.

By 5 P.M., she was at tea with Adrian and his grandmother, but although Maquie had looked forward to it, she sat mostly in silence, listening to Adrian try to defend rap. He had been explaining jazz rap, and had played a Freddie Gibbs song. Freddie said "bitch" every third word. Wincing a lot, Adrian's grandmother said,

"I struggle to understand the need for it. All the swearing and violence. Are they very angry people?"

"Some of them," Adrian said, "but you're missing the point. It's an act, they're playing a role."

"What role?"

"The role of angry, violent gangsters."

"I just don't see the need for that, I'm afraid."

"Well . . . things are pretty angry and violent on the streets. They're taking us there."

"Why?"

"Because how will we see it otherwise?"

"Why do we need to?"

"Because we need to see the pain. There are injustices there."

"Committed by the rappers?"

"No, they're fighting the injustices."

"The rappers are fighting the gangsters?"

"No, the injustices aren't done by the gangsters. The injustices are created by the *system*. The injustices *create* the gangsters."

"So the rappers know the gangsters."

"In some cases."

"They're in cahoots."

"Maybe."

"It's a sort of community."

"I suppose."

A new wince. "And it's sexist, Adrian. They say very aggressive things about women. I just don't see the need for that."

"Yeah, well . . ." Adrian shrugged. "It's complicated."

His grandmother shrugged back. A peaceful smile for their mutual resignation. Life wasn't always workable.

Adrian looked to Maquie for her thoughts on the matter. Maquie sipped tea.

Last week, over a picnic rug in Hyde Park, Adrian and Stutter had been laughing about the lyrics in early Eminem songs. In one song, Eminem's sidekick Obie Trice described a woman as having a "pussy tighter than conditions of us black folks." Maquie had smirked when she heard the line. It was clever satire. But the next day she had looked up the song and listened, and she realized that it wasn't satirical. The song was glib, facetious, deliberately grotesque. For a teenage audience. But they weren't given jokily, those wedged in politics. There Obie was, conscientiously attacking racism while rhyming a misogyny the degree of which Maquie had never heard (Eminem followed Obie with a verse focused on defending his desire to hit a pregnant woman).

Maquie had heard some of rap's defense, Stutter liked to quote Joan Morgan, Jefferson Morley, other people she had never heard of. She could accept some of it, she could imagine the "bitch" in the songs as another woman, as someone somewhere else, in America probably . . . she could see how the "bitch" was a concept, how the aggression was emblematic of a wider fight against injustice, even if she considered this problematic because it required an anthropology, a zooming out, when most songs were heard at a distance of millimeters directly into your head, physically *in* your ear, three and a half minutes of a man's voice, honed to sound strong, to "spit . . . ," to spit words that were sometimes kind, but usually abusive . . . that manipulated your insecurities, that alienated you from sex.

She could accept it, but she couldn't stop her eyes from widening and her head from shaking when she heard the *hypocrisy*.

So she agreed with Adrian that rap was complicated, but somehow today she didn't have the energy to give her opinion on it, even if Adrian's grandmother might have appreciated the viewpoint that using racial segregation to quantify vaginal plasticity didn't seem quite the same thing as "fighting injustices."

Instead, Maquie shrugged. She felt empty of energy but also restless, and she meant no disrespect to Adrian's grandmother, but she wanted to leave, to escape outside.

They left soon after, and Maquie said let's go for dinner.

* * *

They went to a place in Shoreditch called Lucana, a Puglia-Shanxi restaurant in an empty shell building with a bombed-out farmhouse atmosphere. Maquie complained about her day over a bottle of Martina Franca and then over two glasses of bio-naturalized Copertino. She insisted on ordering something called *bottarga da bing*. They had espressos and grappa, and Adrian somehow got talking to a muscular waiter about MDMA, and Maquie jumped in and said did he have any and could they buy some. They left the restaurant with a small napkin of crystals, and they ran down the street hand in hand for a hundred meters jumping and shouting with the excitement of being together and in a city and in possession of drugs, until they came across a building with an upstairs pizza restaurant and a downstairs techno room, and they went in and giggled at the bouncer, who aped their giggling, teasing them and enjoying the energy. Adrian poured the napkin into two gin and tonics, and the bitterness made Maquie cringe and she worried about the effect it would have, but they sat on a sofa at the side of the dance floor and she told Adrian things, and he told her things, and they kissed for a long time, Adrian's hand in her bra, before getting up and dancing, Maquie's eyes washing great arcs across the room. Then they sat down on the sofa again, and Adrian went off to ask the barman for a cigarette.

Maquie listened to the music. She thought about how she couldn't feel her shoulders, for once. She couldn't feel her bladder, she couldn't feel her groin, she couldn't feel her stomach and she couldn't feel her blood pushing up against her eyelids. She couldn't feel her feet, they were warm, she couldn't feel the air coming in and out of her sinuses. She couldn't feel today, or tomorrow, she couldn't feel this year and she couldn't feel the next decade. She couldn't feel Sharon or Kyle or puzzles or kennings, she couldn't feel the chemical that was causing her not to feel all these things, and she couldn't feel the implications of the evening, if there were any, and she couldn't feel tomorrow's hangover that might make her feel that she should regret the evening so far, and she couldn't feel the regret, and she couldn't feel the probability of the next moment in the evening given the evening so far, and she couldn't feel the need to feel it anyway. So she continued to listen to the music, which she couldn't feel as such, like you hear about, but which she loved, just loved. And in loving the music, she felt that she could feel what Adrian felt about music. And she felt self-conscious but then excited that she was feeling something for Adrian in this moment of not feeling all those other things, and she felt that music was like some angel, a servant, that had volunteered itself as a vessel for this feeling. And now she felt the MDMA in her body, and she felt that if MDMA could stop her from feeling so much negativity but help her to feel something positive about someone else, a man, then really MDMA couldn't be so bad. And as she felt this, she felt for Adrian's hand on the back of the sofa. And she felt if she could find his hand and get him alone then she should tell him about how the word "feel" was so heavily filled with different meanings, and how

"in some ways these feelings contradict each other, and I'm scared of feeling so much contradiction . . . I'm scared of what feelings might do to me, but I would love, just love, you with me throughout it all, if that's ok?"

She swallowed between words, and he nodded as he strained to hear her. He looked a bit confused. This made her laugh, it was so cheeky of him. Being confused! Him, confused! What was he so confused about! She just ignored it though and laughed, he was so cheeky. And he squeezed her hands lots and kissed her cheek in the flashing darkness.

Then they were up again, Adrian danced more and she stood still in the middle of the floor, just staring and staring at him and smiling as she noticed his extraordinary capacity for goodness, his extraordinary nobleness, and also his sense of humor and his cheekiness, which he was beginning to show more and more to amuse her. She laughed at his cheeky dancing, he was moving his hands to make her laugh, and she shook her head and rolled her eyes jokingly and pushed his chest, which felt damp, and he grinned at her more on the dance floor, weaving around just within her reach and just on the edge of what she could understand, so there was a little confusion in her too, but he was there to support her and to confirm what she was saying about feeling, which made her so grateful to him, so happy leaning to his ear to say thank you for

"being so supportive, you know, about failing and things,"

as the music bounced like elastic, and the lights blued the walls.

8.

If we reached our best and stayed at it, then all this would be easy. If Maquie and I could have drawn out the ecstatic moments, the calm moments . . . But July came, and I found myself on a plane to Japan tearing up napkins and feeling anxious about abstract non-problems.

You can picture the scene, planes are always the same, always exactly how they look in films. Spotlight on my table, the camera creeps up at me from behind. Other seats of sleeping passengers. A stewardess glides past us in the dark, tall and silent like a blue night cat. I've a magazine or something open, but what you don't know is I'm actually thinking hard, listening to Nas and trying to rationalize his creative choices. I thought I knew better than to end verses like this:

> *Break through walls like Pink Floyd*
> *And drink fluids of all kind of alcohol, y'all*
> *Vineyards in France, yachts out in Cannes.*

It was Nas in 2012 and I found it a bit sad. He rhymed "Cannes" with "France" and you got the sense that he couldn't quite remember the wines he tried while there. What killed me most was the first line. The line was ok (Jay Electronica had a similar one on the Noname track "balloons"), I just didn't believe it. I didn't believe that Nas sat there and felt a need to tell us that he breaks through walls, and that his sharp mind made the leap to Pink Floyd. It looked more like he wanted to name-drop Pink Floyd. He was name-dropping culture. And that might be ok, but paired with "vineyards in France," it sounded needy. He had six other writers on that track, it may not even have been his fault, but come on, develop some irony.

Look at André, he would never say something like that. He made *fun* of that kind of pretense. *Same* year, here he was rapping on a Rick Ross track.

> *Then go grab the finest wine and drink it like we know which grape*
> *And which region it came from, as if we can name 'em.*
> *Hint hint, it ain't, um . . . Welch's*

He was hilarious. André really got it. The thing about Nas was that no one ever held him to any standards.

One good thing about music is that if a hero lets you down you can just go back to their earlier days. In the 1990s, Nas was like nothing else, he was transformative. In 2021 though, he started saying stuff like,

> *I'm coin-based*
> *Basically cryptocurrency's Scarface*

What was that? Scarface and crypto? He was talking about being rich and being a gangster, but this didn't wash because we knew, we all knew, that crypto was tech-bro, it wasn't gangster, and neither was Nas anymore, he was a businessman. The metaphor was off, and by mentioning Scarface he was directly, I would say *accidentally*, comparing himself to his younger self, when he didn't care about presenting himself as a businessman, when he cared about writing amazing rap. First song on *Illmatic* in 1994 was "N.Y. State of Mind," and he had the lines,

> *Inflictin' compositions of pain*
> *I'm like Scarface sniffing cocaine, holding an M16,*
> *See with the pen I'm extreme*

I told my glasses to put it on, I wanted to listen and gather it up. Cutting the hum of the plane engine, the deathly Joe Chambers piano filtered in and Nas was speaking in gunshots. It sounded like he was shooting at you, you listened and you ducked. He absolutely managed to deliver insolence, violence, and comedy, and he wasn't comparing gangster drug dealers to digital currency speculation, he was comparing gangster drug dealers to gangsta rap. And you couldn't not believe it. You believed it because you couldn't believe he could learn those staccato gunshot lines any other way than having stood around or in front of people shooting guns. You might find the noise oppressive, the sounds jarring, the language obscene . . . that was the point, that's how he brought you to the city.

Jay-Z did it by showing you the squeeze of it all, he ended wherever he wanted to, no respect for line-ends. Infinite enjambment. He got you the squeeze and he got you the irony of it too, with that always-smiling tone in his voice.

Tupac did it with big bricky sound walls, like freeway traffic. Traffic and Big American emotion.

Snoop did it with a voice that sounded like weed.

Busta with a voice that sounded like chained dogs barking.

Biggie with a voice that sounded like leather, fists.

(You're no longer a cinema audience but the poor passenger next to me, wanting to sleep and accidentally in a conversation.)

"You know, I do want to work with certain types of rapper. Give me someone with the sincerity of Tupac, and the rhythm of Biggie, and the tranquility of Pos, and the slur of Jay, and the rhyme of Doom . . . and the spit of early Nas (and, you know, maybe the bank balance of late Nas). And the cool of André, and the depth of Lauryn Hill, and the voice of Mos, and the brains of Kendrick, also the brains of Noname, also the production of Kendrick, the meter of Method Man, the presence of Stormzy . . ."

You're hoping a loo break will stop me. When you come back,

". . . maybe the tumble of Freddie Gibbs? And the innovation of Run The Jewels, the wit of Homeboy Sandman, and also of Tommy Evans, and the philosophy of Lupe, the maturity of Q-Tip, the melody of Smino, the instrumentals of Blu, the candor of Ty, the contempt of Klashnekoff, the geniality of Dave . . ."

I'm yet to begin on the non-rap musicians.

". . . yeah, you can boil them down, I guess. A bit like with products and brands? My girlfriend does it, she's called Maquie. Give her a brand, she boils it down into an emotion for you. Like . . . Coke and happiness. Lipstick and hope. Amazon and relief. Apple and success. But what I tell her, I guess to provoke her (but she never rises), is that brands come and go, but the music stays. So . . ."

I tried to sleep. GASTA, the record label, had paid for business class and my seat went flat, but it didn't help. I ordered two mini bottles of bio-red, but they didn't help either. I kept thinking about Nas, early him and late him. I was sort of winding myself up about authenticity. About longevity of authenticity. It shouldn't have mattered to me what celebrity rappers did with their careers, but it bothered me that role models could become shoddy. Never meet your heroes, but you *have* to meet them when they're artists, you meet them in their late work. There they are: you're both older now and they're overweight and fidgeting. Sike once read me some Annaka Harris, and she summarized these two opposing views on time, presentism and eternalism. Presentism is the traditional view, that time is flowing and that only the present moment is happening. Eternalism says that time is more like space, and that just because you're perceiving the present moment doesn't mean that all the past and future moments don't exist simultaneously.

Music was eternalism, and that's what Nas needed to remember, that's what was getting me wound up.

I got up, went to talk to the stewardess. I got a bit *Fight Club* on her, started dismantling the airline industry, telling her all this stuff Sike had once told me.

"It's the parent-adult-child transactional analysis model. You create all these random rules so that we (the passengers) see you (the airline) as the parent. We (the passengers) then take the role of child so that you (the airline) can control us and keep us docile, so that we behave and do what you say and don't go anarchic while stuck on this thin metal tube for twelve hours. You know, like . . . how you constantly say 'no smoking,' even though no one smokes anymore. Or 'put your tray table up,' which has no relevance to anything. So strict, so parent-like. It totally works."

"Please don't lean against that door, sir."

"Exactly!"

I sat down. There were eight hours left of the flight and this wasn't sustainable, so I got up again and went into the bathroom and asked Sike what was up. I noticed my >Clean score was off, probably because of the torn napkins. Sike was pretty short with me, it said,

>Adrian, you're a nervous flyer, plus you're apprehensive about
traveling to Japan for your job with Nunchi.
>Try distracting yourself, perhaps with a movie or book.

So I started watching a Kenneth Branagh film and fell asleep halfway through.

* * *

It was my first time in Tokyo, and I was incapable of forming a single opinion on the place. I walked around the hot streets like a moron, ordered food and drinks like a moron, fobbed my way through subway barriers like a moron . . . the city made me feel moronic, and it's hard to hold opinions when you feel like that. Something (everything?) about the place was sophisticated, but I wasn't able to pinpoint what this was from the actual *objects* or things that emerged out of the sweatbox air (I sweated like a moron too, the heat was like oven doors opening).

And in the hotel especially, I felt like a moron. I moved about it afraid to knock things over. I washed up cups I'd used in the room, I made my bed like a soldier. I hesitated before touching the lift buttons, scared I would smudge them.

The jet lag was severe, I slept sparsely. Picture Scarlett Johansson in *Lost in Translation*, I think that film got it pretty right. I spent the early hours on the cool metal ledge of my hotel window, editing verse for Nunchi and watching skyscraper roof lights blink red. I emulated Scarlett because I didn't know what else to do. I felt extremely awake in those early hours, more awake than I'd ever felt before, and I was thrilled at times. The thrills came urgently, like caffeine rushes, and I smiled consciously to acknowledge them. I even took a picture of myself once, partly to send to Maquie but partly also to record what I fantasized could be history.

On my first morning, I met Furusawa, Nunchi's manager, in a cafe near the hotel. The cafe was pantomime American, they sold lapel pins at the counter, but it was bright and airy and clean. We were the only men and Furusawa eyed the women and seemed to resent that we were there and blame it on me. Like there were a bunch of male-occupied cafes that he didn't feel etiquette allowed him to show me. I don't know.

We ordered coffee and there was a delay while the waitress tried to remember which cup had soy milk and which had real. She held the index fingers of each hand in the air, bobbed them a little, then pointed them at the cup on the right. She turned to us and crossed her arms to pass the soy one to me and the real one to Furusawa. I tried out a thank-you, but it sounded wrong even to me (I'd practiced in my hotel room the night before, but, Maquie would gloat, fake Japanese didn't come as easily as fake French). Furusawa didn't say anything and led the way to a table in the corner of the room. He was a bald, pig-eyed man in his early fifties, and wore black rectangular glasses and a black T-shirt. He leaned back on his chair and said, "So. It's good to meet you. I listened to some of your songs." He waved his hand a little. "I mean, not your songs. You don't have any songs, right?"

A neat power play.

"No."

"The songs you helped on. I listened to some."

"Ah," I said. "Thanks."

His accent was American, quite clean, though his vowels were sharp. He took a sip of his coffee, still looking at me.

"'She Stands Apart,'" he said, and raised his eyebrows.

"Yes."

"Actually," he said, "I'm a musician."

"You are?"

"Yes, not as a job. As a hobby. Rock guitar."

"Cool. Like . . . Slash?"

I've no idea why I chose Slash. Furusawa nodded but didn't commit.

"Anyway, my career wasn't in music. I was a consultant. Management consultant. BCG . . . maybe you know. I worked with all the big CEOs, and then I thought, ok, what's the craziest thing I can do now. Who's the craziest person I can work for."

He laughed, pleased with himself.

"So I came to music because I saw there were crazy people and they were undervalued. The musicians were undervalued. I saw arbitrage opportunities. Nunchi, he gets this. He knows he is good, but he knows there is more."

While he was saying this, I was thinking to myself, *You're a bit of a cunt, aren't you, fella*, and then I was unthinking it again because the phrase sounded sort of Guy Ritchie and I'm not a big fan of Ritchie. There was some sort of projection happening, because I realized that Furusawa shared Ritchie's teenage admiration for rebellion.

"The world is the opportunity," Furusawa said. "J-rap has no audience there yet. English is essential. We'll keep some Japanese, but give Nunchi some English verses. He has the talent, and his sound is good. Plus his accent is . . . not bad."

He began to explain channels and concerts, album releases—he had a whole plan—and he compared Japanese rap to K-pop and Ethiojazz and even London grime. I found it painful when he referred to it as "J-rap" or "J-hop."

At some point during his explanation, Sike quick-flashed the letters *KIP* into my vision, which stood for "knowledge is power." We'd discussed my nerves that morning and I realized I was quite competitive about knowledge. I feared knowing less, especially when it came to music. Sike reminded me that I was hired specifically *for* my knowledge, and also pulled up some internet info on Furusawa which, when translated, told us that he was relatively new to the industry. I knew more than him, and Sike suggested reminding me of this if I was ever signaling anxiety. We settled on "KIP" as an innocuous code that someone behind me snatching peeks at the insides of my glasses wouldn't be able to decipher and laugh at me about.

"Ok, it's a big ambition," I said eventually. "Internationally speaking, Japanese rap isn't good, that's a fact."

I took a sip of coffee. I was pleased with this.

"There's a lot of wannabes and they're mimicking a distant culture, and it looks false to Western audiences. They don't even have the hand gestures down. Nunchi is one of the exceptions, and you're right, there's opportunity, but there's a lot of dross." I waved my hand a little. "A lot of garbage." I was the English expert. "So you're going to want to distance yourself from Nunchi's peers, even if there's cache in coming from Japan more generally."

He gave a confused smile, but I think he enjoyed it.

"Ever thought of collabs?" I said. "With Western artists?"

The thought had just come to me. A split second of hesitation on his face.

"Not yet. We'll grow Nunchi's stance a bit. Present him as godfather of J-rap, and then they will come to us."

"Ok, I think you should consider it sooner, but we can discuss. I'll give you some options."

How's that for huevos? Furusawa liked it as well.

I was smug for my power plays, but surprised. A day earlier, I'd been broiling myself on a plane, but something had changed. A kind of release. I felt wildly out of place in the city, but to such a degree that I was no longer culpable for it. The next morning, I was brushing my teeth at 3 A.M., and I told Sike about it and said I felt a kind of freedom, like I wasn't beholden to other people there. Sike suggested I run a module about power and influence in politics.

I said ok, and a nice thing about Sike's voice AI is that it can understand you even when there's a toothbrush in your mouth.

||Module||> **Power and Influence**

[guest editor: José María De Areilza Carvajal]

||>Question 1.

>What do you know about Angela Merkel and Margaret Thatcher?

"They were . . . politicians."

>Do you want to see their Wikipedia pages?

Sike was getting snippy. I spat toothpaste into the spotless beige Carrara. "I know the basics. They were successful female leaders."

>Do you think it helped their success being female in the male-
dominated arena of European politics?

"No."

>The question was not whether it is easy for women to become
successful in male-dominated fields.
>The research is conclusive on that.
>The question was whether you think it could have benefited these
two personality types, to be unrestricted by the codes that their
male peers needed to adhere to.

I thought about it.

‖>Question 2.
>Do you think it's probably <u>easy</u> or <u>not easy</u> for a black person to
succeed in American politics?

I pointed at "not easy."

>Do you think Barack Obama knew this?

"Yes."

>What do you think he did with the knowledge?

"Well, probably like Thatcher and Merkel. Used it to his advantage. Turned a weakness into a strength."
A pause, like Sike was shuffling in its seat.

>No.
>A race or a gender cannot be a weakness.

>Equally, they cannot be a strength.
>It might be useful to search for character strengths in these
individuals.
>Then you might use these strengths as a lens to analyze the
actions taken by the individuals once they found themselves outside a preexisting and possibly racist or sexist hierarchy.

||>Question 3.
>Do you know what nationality the US diplomat Henry Kissinger
was?

"German."

>Yes.
>What is your impression of post–World War II American political
hierarchy?

I finished brushing and spat again, then rinsed some water around my
mouth.
"Sike, skip to conclusions," I said. I wanted to start writing.
Sike shuffled again, tiny fizzing in my glasses like soluble aspirin.

||>Conclusions.
>Sometimes we are forced out of a network's natural hierarchy.
>In these instances, it is important to . . .
>1. Identify the hierarchy
>2. Acknowledge our exclusion from it
>3. Ascertain the soft rules to which we are no longer bound
>4. Exploit the freedoms gained
>You can apply this approach to hierarchies from which you have
not been excluded by skipping [2].

I took my glasses off and kind of cheesily looked at myself in the mirror
for a second. Then I got in the shower.

. . .

I bonded with Nunchi straightaway, we got right into it. He must be over forty, but he has energy and an adolescent slouch. The first time we met, he shook my hand with three slow nods, forming his mouth into a silent *O*. I found him funny, and he was humble: his hair was cropped short, gray most of the way around and peroxide blond at the back, and when I told him I liked it, he laughed and rubbed it and looked sheepish. His glasses were pale blue—not Miru, some brand I didn't know. Like all the Greats, he didn't look great. He was skinny and had a narrow face. He looked a bit like that old, wiry builder you see smoking outside construction sites. But he *was* a Great, he was incredibly talented. I'd say, probably, the most talented rapper I'd worked with.

We went into the studio with Furusawa and a few of the GASTA production team (nice guys in baggy T-shirts . . . extremely good-looking guys in fact) and played some of the beats they were keen to work with, and Nunchi messed around a bit on the mic, mainly freestyling. I couldn't understand any of it, but you never really can straightaway, even when it's in English. It's more about flow. Nunchi could do anything: clean, witty, speedy, frenetic, bouncy . . . During one verse, he rapped triple time one bar, then next bar he rapped double time, next bar normal, next bar half-speed . . . then back the other way, normal, double, triple, then quadruple. At one point, he changed to English and a moment later I realized he was rapping my own lines at me from a song I'd done for a rapper called Luv.

And you can see right through the metaphor
Like a cellar door, she was hard to find
We'd never met before . . .

I won't lie, I was putty. He winked at me and moved back to Japanese. Apple pie happiness.

It was going to work like this: an intensive eight days of brainstorming, me writing lines for Nunchi in the mornings, and us all trying them out together in the afternoons. Then at the end of it, I'd go back to London and write our picks into distinct verses, with some production work either side of this. The album wasn't planned to be recorded until later in the year, so we had time to finesse it all.

Jet lag woke me up at 3 A.M. most days. After my time at the window, before I could see the sun coming up, I showered and made coffee in the room. Then I put on my headphones and worked through some stuff for the day. There wasn't pressure to complete anything this trip, so I felt good just trying things out, experimenting a little. I'd carry on through breakfast over plates of buffet food, then go back to my room and work until twelve. Lunch was junk from the convenience store on the ground floor. I then napped until two, showered again, and walked to the studio for three.

We made progress, and though his accent wasn't as good as Furusawa had suggested, Nunchi had a flexible mouth and could wrap it around most words. I thought that with a few elocution lessons, some tongue exercises, he'd be fine. Furusawa grunted in and out; he made me feel constantly embarrassed, I couldn't work out how, I was just forever feeling stupid whenever I spoke to him. They had an interpreter for me to use, a hard-working twenty-two-year-old called Ken, uncomfortably but consistently in a black nylon suit. He took me for afternoon coffee breaks at a small cafe that sold mont blancs, baumkuchen, and cannoli, as well as strawberry sandwiches and matcha-peach toast. He explained the different items to me gleefully, enjoying my surprise, and I think he liked this task of explaining menus the most. He wasn't really cut out for the music industry. Nunchi would join us sometimes and stand politely by the counter, speaking to the owner about who knows what. One time we walked a little way to a tiny park that had swings and a slide and a dirt floor, and there's a photo Ken took of me and Nunchi each on a swing, not moving, just enjoying the sunshine. Nunchi has one leg crossed over the other, I think he's playing me a Scha Dara Parr song.

Every now and then I had to step in and clear up some confusion with the lyrics. I'd stand in the middle of the paneled practice room, among all the drums and guitars and mics and things, and rap the line for Nunchi, demonstrating the stresses, and the room would watch me and say, "Ohh," as they understood. Nunchi would then try it again and laugh if he got it wrong. I could make fun of him a little, he had a sense of humor, and one day they reversed it and tried to teach me some Japanese rap. We laughed a lot. Nunchi said that on my last night we should all do karaoke together, but he said it seriously . . . One of the team, one of the younger members, nodded and I think he said he'd book a room. They discussed locations then, because I heard someone say my hotel's name.

The evenings I spent alone mostly. The GASTA team offered me company and then dinner vouchers, but, wanting only sleep, I politely refused both early on. Later in the trip, I explored a little more, trying out some areas that Maquie recommended and video-calling her from their landmarks. I didn't try the bars that Ranger, Sophie, Mum sent me and promised me were "weird." Most of all, I wanted to get back to writing, and I would find myself at 9 P.M. most evenings regretfully but luxuriously turning my back on the vast promise of Tokyo and heading up the lift to bed, excited for the deep and soundless sleep, followed by the effortless early rise and the sunrise over Tokyo.

What was my mindset during those long morning hours of writing? Time felt protective, the room was warm and well-stocked, I had coffee and snacks and music. Out of the window, the buildings were tall and dark, except for their red roof lights, which turned on and off listlessly . . . like they were posing, like they were Broadway chorus lines, resigned to their next stage exit, their next death. Then on again with their next life, and then off again . . . death . . . then life, then death, then life, then their final death, when the sun appeared at the back of Tokyo.

The lights were sad but unemotional. I don't know how that was possible, but they were. I looked back to them often. And the rest of the time, I lay on the bed, or sat at the desk, or at the ledge, headphones on with, at least consciously, no other desire than the child's desire to write rhyming lines of words . . .

At least consciously . . . It's unclear to me whether, in that room, in those peaceful hours, whenever a line came to me, some hidden part of me was sharpening a plan; aiming for something beyond the success of Nunchi's album. Did I sense an opportunity? Was I steering toward a gap? I mean, I wasn't identifying hierarchies, or *ascertaining soft rules* or anything. I felt hopeful, excited. I was excited that Nunchi might like my work. For sure, I was bringing myself to the table, that was definitely the case—but that was also the advice. That's the way you reach authenticity as a ghostwriter, you have to offer up a real person. Like with "She Stands Apart."

So a song about Nunchi's wardrobe, for instance, a possible single, just made sense. It was my concept, so of course it had personal elements: the hook came from a tape we used to listen to on family car journeys, a musical called *Joseph and the Amazing Technicolor Dreamcoat*. It's kind of religious but has nothing to do with religion. Like Bach. Jess knew all the words to every track, but we all knew all the words to this one track, called "Joseph's Coat," where they talk about all the colors of the dreamcoat. It's got a chorus that goes,

> *I look handsome, I look smart*
> *I am a walking work of art*
> *How I love my coat of many colors*

And Jess and I would preen while we sang the lines, stretching the lapels of our corduroy dungarees. The music is quite bouncy, and I thought we could clip it and speed it up. Kind of a lighthearted frolic, plus it's got rap braggadocio written into it already.

This kind of a track made *sense* for the album, and Furusawa thought so too. Along with automotives and alcohol, fashion was lucrative terrain in rap, and Furusawa was eyeing up product placement deals. He hadn't planned any for this album, but he wanted to showcase the opportunity, and Nunchi's versatility, around brands. He asked me to load the song up with examples as though we were advertising for advertising, like when billboards say, YOUR AD HERE. I said we might be able to land a sustainability line too, because fashion brands are now ethical (you may have noticed), and Furusawa liked that.

It felt like producing. By the end of the eight days, we had blueprints for eight songs mixing my English lines with Nunchi's and some other rappers'

Japanese ones. The most complete was the fashion track, I had some early verses ready and we had a beat for it. There were some concepts that needed explaining that Nunchi would have to learn how to own, but this type of fusion seemed to fit the task, which was linking J-rap to the world.

The term "J-rap" was catching, I couldn't stop using it and I began to agree that Nunchi was peddling a distinct product. I had a sense for what the world thought the *J* meant, and it was basically one of two extremes: either wacky and surreal, a slow-blinking, pixelated grin in a transmutable LED schoolgirl kilt; or ancient and chasmic, a philosophical scripture held in the palm of an ocean-faced priest with clothes made of bridge moss and a maze of epigrams swirling calligraphically from his temples. This song landed safely and compellingly in the wacky and surreal bucket, not least because the rap style was Biggie and hearing Nunchi rap it in his accent was a pretty new experience.

* * *

On my last night, we had dinner at a small wooden grill restaurant where they cooked fleecy white fish and aubergines and peppers and other vegetables on coals in front of you. Wine kept coming, but I didn't get misty, I was enjoying the group. Furusawa was being inoffensive, and I liked the other GASTA guys—plus a few of them brought their girlfriends, who were also rap fans and who also wore the big, baggy T-shirts, along with beanies and wallet chains. Everyone was friendly. Everyone asked about Maquie and I kept showing photos, and they couldn't have been happier that she was half-Japanese, and they kept saying she was cute, which I agreed with, and they said she had to come out and visit next time, and I said definitely, definitely, I knew she was keen. Ken got a little drunk, he was bright red and fell asleep at one point on his arms. What a great guy, he just hit the table! We were going to stay friends for sure. We had more wine and everyone began shouting loads, and when we finished dinner, we took some photos of the group in the quiet streetlights outside and then we joined the busy streets and walked to karaoke.

The booth we chose was almost pitch black except for the TV screen. Everyone was smoking by that point, I had one or two cigarettes but was mainly borrowing a guy called Kota's e-cigarette. We cycled through some Western and Japanese classics, and everyone sang together at the same time, even me ("Wonderwall" nearly killed me), even Furusawa, who had a sort of husky Barry White bawl in him, out of tune and really terrible, but sort of apt for the occasion. Nunchi then put on an Eminem song but he took Ken's suit jacket (to loud applause) and put it over the TV screen so we just had the beat, and then he handed me a mic and mimed to me that I was verse two. He began rapping in Japanese and everyone knew the lyrics he had chosen, and gradually through his verse I felt myself melt out of my body and take a seat by the TV, watching everyone nod and clap, all their smiling faces looking up at Nunchi throw and bounce and jump, his voice rolling questions and answers through the cadences amidst all this excited love for him, all this ambition for him, this admiration and respect, the whole room supporting him, urging him, even this figure hanging a little to his right, face dappled by nylon-filtered TV light, face impassive, hands held together over a mic, thumb nail digging into the tepid gun-metal crease below the woven steel head, and body moving to the beat, a strange outsider so generously included.

I'm watching myself from the other side of the room because I'm frightened about my upcoming inconsequential performance, and I'm talking clearly to myself asking what I'm going to do, almost challenging myself: Will you crumple, will you fumble? Maybe you'll piss yourself or vomit, maybe you'll simply cry? It doesn't feel quite possible to complete the actions expected of you. The physics of the situation don't seem set up in your favor. There's been a mistake and you've grossly overestimated your development from infancy. You feel strangely reliant on time, and time is unreasonably expectant of you, asking you to adhere to a cue. You have to perform the physically impossible but you also have to do it on cue. On a pin. You're going to get given a beat. There will be a runway. But oh, wait! The beat came already and . . . yes, you've already begun rapping! You missed your cue but somehow your body didn't, and your body is making its way through its task. Your voice is oddly airy, spongy, but no one seems to notice, they're all nodding and cheering and—fuck, you forgot to decide what to rap. You never decided! You must have been considering it at some point, but you never landed on something. But your body seems to have come through for you again, because it's pulled up some lyrics from your memory, and you're going through them pretty well. They're the words to the first verse of the technicolor dreamcoat song you just wrote, and everyone's realized it and they seem to like that I've done this. They're standing and throwing their arms. I'm rapping it to them and I'm getting eye contact, and Nunchi is strutting around me like a soldier, pretending I'm wearing this big multicolored coat, pretending to smooth out its train, brush dust off its shoulders, pointing to the embroidered colors, the vermilions and the golds, and everyone is cheering again.

Then my verse finished and Nunchi had his arm around me and was chanting something with the rest of the room, chanting it quite loudly, while pointing at me. It was two syllables and at first I thought it was a Japanese word, but they were smiling at me and I realized the word was "fea-ture," "fea-ture," "feature," and I was just patting Nunchi on the chest and we all broke into the chorus and danced around a bit.

Afterward, I didn't know where to put myself, or what to do with my face, so I just sat next to Kota and just smoked his e-cigarette. Really dragging on it, I must have smoked the thing dry.

* * *

Another thing happened one morning at breakfast. I had my headphones on and was eating some bacon and a bowl of grapefruit while writing ideas down in a notebook I sometimes used, and maybe I was saying the lines out loud or something because I got the sense someone was watching me from the next table. I looked up and double-took because it was Jonatan Abergel, the Sike CEO. He was in navy blue khakis and trainers and a white wool jumper, and he wore a pair of bespoke glasses, thin and black, over thick eyebrows.

Turns out he *was* watching me, because as I was getting up to go back to my room, Jonatan was also getting up and he said hey, and I said hey, and he said sorry for imposing but could he ask what I'd been doing. This felt pretty surreal because I had literally used Sike a few hours before (some general intention logging), but I explained my job and what I was doing in Tokyo—quite naturally, to be honest, because as a foreigner in Tokyo, especially in this hotel, I was sort of always feeling like a bit of a celebrity, so I didn't feel too intimidated. Jonatan was tanned and he had billionaire teeth, but he was no Brad Pitt, so I wasn't tensing my arms or anything. Plus, he was very enthusiastic. He had this soft American accent and it turned out he liked rap, he even listened to Shay and knew "She Stands Apart." We had a good chat about it. I didn't tell him I used Sike, but I thought he could probably tell.

9.

Maquie lay on her front. Too comfortable to pull her left hand out from beneath the backpack that served as pillow, she itched her right palm on the ground instead, scraping it over the grass and then onto a smooth piece of rock sticking out of the soil. Sophie dozed next to her. Below them, England's Lake District was pulled tight against the earth. Smooth lake and sky, pilled forest and cloud.

Did Brits recognize the color of their country? Was its texture familiar to them?

The district had fells like in Jämtland, and the four of them had climbed this one that morning, reaching a moonscape summit for a late lunch. They drank coffee from Stutter's thermos, and Maquie had brought pies but forgotten the knife, so they pinched chunks from the pucks of dry pastry with their fingers. Now she and Sophie lay halfway down the fell and just off the shore of one of its high lakes, an improbable cloud mirror (possible kenning) balanced between the green slopes. The fell was covered in scree and old slate, it had been mined once, and sitting at intervals on the path were canvas bags the size of armchairs, filled with rubble and waiting to be collected or dispersed, they hadn't agreed on which. Stutter called the bags "troll shopping" (possible kenning). He and Adrian had carried on down toward a pub.

It was odd picturing the four of them traipsing the countryside, away from London. They looked out of place. Last night they had drunk in a dark pub next to their B&B in a village called Hawkshead. There were so many pubs they had visited together, it felt strange visiting one as tourists. Maquie had felt nervous, a leopard prowled in her chest. Her speech felt forced, and she wondered if the others were bored of her. She thought their responses were perfunctory, she heard mechanical, offhand acquiescence. And hidden meaning. She couldn't distinguish conversation from accusation.

She had wanted to go to Italy for ten days, she had found a good deal on a villa near Lucca. But Sophie had refused, saying she was saving money for Sike. They had settled on the Lake District, for four days. This had annoyed Maquie, and the thought of it still scratched. It struck her that a Tuscan villa may do just as much for one's mental health as an ethically indeterminate psychology app. She glared at her sleeping friend, and itched her palm on the grass again. She looked at her palm. It was stained slightly green but showed no inflammation. She didn't know why it itched, but she reflected that "itch" had been the consistent mood of her summer. She reached for her bottle of fennel tea and tried to unscrew the lid one-handed.

They descended and found Adrian and Stutter talking to some Mancunian hikers in a narrow pub courtyard. It was shaded by a stained parasol that colored the tables brown and gold. The four hikers wore no glasses and old-fashioned clothes—a kind of lederhosen, though Maquie didn't think they were called that. Stutter was laughing in a strange way she hadn't seen before. Adrian was explaining a theory (unproven) she had told him about.

"It's called greyhound theory because they used to do it in greyhound racing. You get a whole bunch of untrained greyhounds and pay for their entry to the race along with your own trained one. This means you flood the race with unknown bad runners and protect the odds of your own runner, which you can then bet on, safe in the knowledge that it will likely win.

"Basically, they're doing this with start-ups now. An investor in an industry helps launch loads of businesses that will probably go nowhere so that the market is flooded with losers and the investor can bet big on their winner without other investors crowding in. Here's Maquie, she can explain it better."

Maquie and Sophie introduced themselves. The hikers were warm and attractive, the men and the women, with blushed apple cheeks and long tanned legs. Last night, in their attic room in the B&B, she and Adrian had had sex with her holding on to a roof beam, afraid of the thin walls but drunk and a little frenzied. He hadn't come, and she wondered if that meant he was pumped up, charged up last night and now ready to spray. She sat down beside him and slipped her hand down the crease of his thigh, pushing into his crotch and planning to wait for a response there. Sophie said she would get drinks. And Maquie now didn't feel like playing her game, or sitting there with the ale chat, so she got up again and followed Sophie, ignoring Adrian and smiling pleasantly at the prettiest hiker girl as she went. She walked through the cool corridors of the pub and into the bathroom, and stood washing her hands and especially her palms. The sink was old porcelain, and she rested her hands on it, pushing her palms into the cool white as though it might have healing properties. Feeling an urge to bite into it, she imagined her teeth crunching into the curved lip.

"Sike says the best it can do is a Google search," Adrian said later, back in their room. "It can't really do much more for a third party, even with something so physical."

"It's ok," she said.

She hadn't asked him to ask Sike. She was sitting on the windowsill and looking onto the lane. It was lined with foxgloves (a kenning) and Stutter was down there talking to the pretty hiker, they were laughing about something. Maquie could hear fragments of the conversation, they were talking about life in London, concert venues they both knew. The sun was getting low. Adrian came and crouched in front of her, moving things in and out of his bag.

"What do you think it is?" he said.

"Don't know."

"You put your hand in something. Or, like, there's something sick inside of you and this is how it's making itself known."

"Hmm."

"Have you searched on Google?"

"No."

"If you used Sike, it would be able to tell you. It can't really offer much to a third party though."

She looked at him, but he was folding a shirt.

"Couldn't you pretend you have itchy palms?" she said. She was surly, but he didn't notice.

"It's best not to lie to Sike, it messes with the data." He reached for some socks. "But if you used it, it could find some psychosomatic link, or it might spot whether you'd touched something corrosive recently."

He reached for another shirt. He was enjoying thinking about how Sike might save her. He was trying to fix her itchy palms with Sike.

"It might be able to spot other factors. Like other times you've itched your palm in the past. Or it might find some research about psychosomatic links between the brain and the hands."

"I don't think it's psychosomatic," she said.

"No, I'm just saying Sike would note things like that."

"Yes, well, you said psychosomatic twice. So . . ."

He looked up. "Sorry, I just meant generally."

"Yes, well."

"Sorry."

"I think we don't need to worry about my itchy palms."

He looked out the window. "I agree, but I think you *are* worried about them, you brought them up a few times. You have a bad back but you never bring that up. And you know . . . stuff is tough for you at the moment . . ."

"Ok, Sike, you can fuck off actually."

He didn't reply. She wanted to lash out. She made to get up, but he put his hand on her arm, still looking out the window. She followed his gaze down the lane and toward Stutter and the girl, who was half turned away from Stutter as though in recoil. This was a strange pose, Maquie thought, somewhere in her head amidst the thoughts of resentment toward Adrian. She hadn't given him permission to vilify her mental state, she thought. She felt the urge to reprimand . . . But the scene in the lane was dragging her attention away. Adrian held her arm. This was a strange pose for the girl, who seemed to be almost recoiling from Stutter and now almost consoling him too. It was strange, this little back-of-pub English countryside lane, with foxgloves lining the tarmac path, bunches of post-bloom wisteria hanging from the walls, their petals on the ground, the bunches leafy and heavy, quite in keeping with the summer's evening, but not in keeping with the scene, which gradually Maquie took in and understood was a sad scene, a miserable one, and she finally pulled her eyes from the edges of the picture and placed them on Stutter.

She could make out his eyes, which were shut tight. She knew what she was looking at and she knew the face beneath it, but the contortion was alien, their friend had become separate—or become whole, reunited with his nickname, a name that had until now been impotent, devoid of meaning. How many times had she said it and not thought of this? She felt suffocated watching it, imagining the feeling of retching and not being able to release, as though she too were in the middle of this seizure. But that was too selfish, self-obsessed, to think of his convulsion as hers too, imagining herself as part of the dance, her head moved up and down in jerking waves, led by the nose and diving, over and over, or weaving, sewing the air, jerked and smooth, a nod that embroidered into the twilight a single word that was refusing to be spoken; a nod that for a second she couldn't stop her cruel brain from comparing to the nod of a singer to a beat, and she felt the need to escape, to run away from her own perception of the sad struggle in the lane below them.

The girl stood in front of Stutter concerned but inept, her face pained. A sound like a soft buzzing drifted up to them. Stutter held his unused, unfilled phone in one hand, and with his other he was pushing the air, then waving goodbye, and he walked away from the girl, over the wisteria petals of the lane and toward the B&B, until he disappeared from sight below their windowsill, his head still nodding and his face harassed.

Maquie gave up her anger toward Adrian, of course she did. The girl in the lane had walked timidly, stop-start away, head bowed respectfully, not wanting to look like she was fleeing, and Adrian had turned toward Maquie and put his chin on her thigh, his eyes wide and his mouth frowning.

"Don't try and help," she said later, as they were about to leave the room.

She said it as a command for both of them, and Adrian nodded. She mostly kept to the command. Stutter stayed away for an hour, but then returned, quiet but calm and saying nothing about the lane. He ordered a beer and they all ordered hamburgers. Adrian, sympathetically it seemed, wanting to distract, steered their conversation around the free topics of music and films, and Stutter joined in enough, spoke enough and joked enough, argued frivolously enough, most memorably with Sophie about whether it passed the Bechdel test if the woman was talking to herself in the mirror. Maquie watched him in her peripherals until a moment when Adrian and Sophie both left the table to play darts, and it was then that she said,

"I saw you with the girl earlier. Are you ok?"

Stutter looked her in the eye and nodded slowly. "Yeah, I think so."

Maquie said nothing, and for a long time neither did he. He rested his chin on his hand and looked down into his drink. But eventually, still looking down and smiling and shaking his head, he said, "It's strange, I was asking for her number."

"Yes."

"It's strange . . . it not being ok for me to want things."

That was all he said about it.

* * *

Maquie didn't see it as her role to console Stutter, or try to help him out, to make suggestions, or analyze him and root his struggle in a formative event, or tell him it was ok, or commiserate, or compare, or make light, or analogize. In the days that followed, it occurred to her to do these things, but she was clear that there was damage she could do as well as good, and there was good she could do in not sensationalizing the event, which was evidence of *who he was*, an identity that he had embraced and one that she didn't want to imply there was something wrong with, which for all she knew there wasn't. She settled for the promise she'd implied in the pub in the Lake District: I'm here if you want to talk about it.

But though clear of it, the episode in the lane remained in her mind as more evidence for a failed summer. Back in London, she wondered when she would feel revived. She didn't feel relaxed, kissed by the sun. She had no new stories. The hay fever of spring had barely let up, and she sneezed her way through hot days of uphill meetings with indistinguishable start-ups peddling ML, DL, RL, NeSy, AR, ER, GAI, AGI, and plant-based alternatives. She could relay no optimism to Sharon and Kyle. Her takeaways were that men with MBAs had too much joie de vivre, she could drink four flat whites before her hands shook, rice milk gave her constipation, female tech entrepreneurs had all read Emily Dickinson, cafe staff were still handing out those inane loyalty stamp cards but couldn't explain why or who was behind their production, carrot cake was making a comeback, bus drivers had some in-joke going on where they did the rock-and-roll salute whenever they passed each other, electric skateboards were more popular with the middle-aged than the young, and London was, at night and after the sun had gone, an eerily noiseless place. Sweating, she returned to her silent flat in Kennington and blinked her eyes into basins of cold water. To sleep, if Adrian wasn't there, she masturbated. She thought about anything when she did it: Adrian, memories of past sex, fantasies from her teens. Twice an hour she thought to herself, everyone is asshole. This maxim, locked in her brain despite its grammar, helped her cope with the morons that wriggled out of the soil, forcing her to overstep.

Fumi and Ulf called her every few days, Fumi now also pushing Sike. She suggested with no humor that it was a waste of smartglass technology not to get it. Ulf told her it wasn't forever, he was only suggesting four months. Maquie told them yes, she wanted Sike: the company, the prospect, the investment. Not the app.

On one call, trying to minimize her intake of the chewy air as she made her way to Oval Station, she started an argument with Ulf about fashion and ethics, his two core interests. She had been looking at her trainers, bought last month: the white soles had turned a polluted gray, and the trimming was frayed and the laces were grubby. This was built-in obsolescence! Clear as day! She had gone to five shops, nothing but white soles. How could these trainer companies make so much as a *remark* about sustainability when they whipped forward trends for snow-white aesthetics that deteriorated in days? Maquie had never believed that ethics flattered fashion as well as the brands claimed it did, but she had believed that Ulf could be fervent about both, and each, and not be a hypocrite. Now she questioned it, and she directed the question to Ulf, asking him how Sike was working him through his contradictions.

"What do you mean?" he said.

"Well . . . you have contradictions. How is Sike helping you through them?"

"Maquie," he said, "your tone is quite aggressive, let's talk when you're feeling different."

Fucking Ulf. And fucking Sike.

Eventually the call came where Ulf announced, with a solemnity that didn't conceal his pleasure, that Yuki had started using it. Maquie messaged Yuki to confirm, and he confirmed.

Fine, Maquie thought. Fine. Use it. It might help you. She loved Yuki but she didn't think highly of his choices. He had disappeared into the mindless tradition of sushi. Sushi was an astonishing waste of a brain, she spluttered at the thought of it consuming her brother's. For two years, he had learned how to steam and then vinegar rice. For three years, he had learned how to cut fish—the most violent of actions on the most laughable of creatures. Somehow this was meant to be admirable? To process fish? Somehow you earned the same respect as a doctor, lawyer, or astronaut if you signed your life over to this trade that claimed its product as everything: sushi as healthy, elite, sophisticated; sushi as consumable emblem of Japanese refinement; sushi as bio-embodiment of the 1960s, organic revolution against The Man, and vehicle for hippy peace protest (sushi as Good Yoko Ono); sushi as bankable accessory of 1980s economic boom; sushi as *Wall Street*, *Fatal Attraction*, and *Black Rain*, never not finding its way into Michael Douglas's square paw throughout his Penis Man wallet romps; sushi as mainstream; sushi as obtainable, chainable aspiration; sushi as supermarket staple, as flight option, as bus dinner, as desk lunch; sushi as fusion, deconstruction, reconstruction; sushi as anything you wanted it to be, the world was mad about a weathercock. Yuki might reach sixty and be able to claim an innovation in sea urchin preparation . . . a lifetime in fish and rice, and the most impressive thing he would do was get bottled by a tourist on the razz.

Maquie had a higher conception of success than sushi, and a stronger need for it, so her mental itch was no mystery. She didn't need a psychology app to see how career peril could affect her mood. She didn't need to soul-search.

Sharon wasn't required to smile sympathetically—at their monthly meetings, at the office, on the fringe of investor events—for Maquie to grasp what gave her bad dreams, what contributed to the small drips of anxiety that fell from the day's ledges. It was obvious.

Obvious but unjust, she thought, sitting on the Tube one day, staring at ads and feeling disgusted by the misanthropy of British advertisers (across the history of print, of alphabet, had there been a greater crime of writing than the Jack Daniel's adverts?). Wasn't anxiety meant to be like the masked killer, where the horror vanishes when the mask comes off? Or like the dark bedroom when the sun finally hits it? Maquie held the mask in her hand, the sun was up. Like Stutter, who knew his impediment, who had named himself after it and unmasked it for everyone, she knew her concerns, basic as they were: she *knew* she was afraid of failing, she knew she feared redundancy; she worried for her model and her thesis; she knew that leaving the soft-floored playground of academia for the real world was always *going* to feel fraught; waiting and *hoping* for success *should* feel fraught.

Her fears were right there in front of her. So why did she still fear them? Why that nip-nip-nipping at her throat?

She felt the fears amalgamate. They were no longer fears, they were *fear*, so now she battled something unrooted, unbounded, the mechanism complexifying like a nightmare's plot device, the rope you get tangled in or the stranger you can't grow distance on. She spent her short lunchtimes in DIY salad shops staring into bowls of decimated purple and green superfoods and trying to get the fear to admit that it had lost. She reasoned it was a diet thing. Something hormonal? A growing caffeine immunity? Time to ratchet up the dosage? She spooned an extra scoop into her coffee jug each morning.

There was a contrast that was trying, too. While spring and summer hadn't brought Maquie much rejuvenation, they seemed to have delivered various gifts to Adrian. The gifts came neatly packaged, with high utility and mystical charm, like Christmas presents in Narnia. He had new clients, new opportunities, new friends.

A week before the Lake District trip, Adrian had returned from Tokyo happy and a little lathered, pouring onto her bed a suitcase of convenience store gimmicks: high-vitamined gummy chews, a plastic mist spraying fan, some awkwardly named chocolate brands, a Mumintroll ice bag for soothing bruises. They had gone out for dinner, Adrian had been tired. But though hard-fixing unfocused on random objects, his eyes had revealed his excitement.

"Give me until after the Lake District to finish some bits off, but I'll show you what we've been working on," he had said. "I think you'll like it."

Now it had been a week since their return from the lakes, and they were eating dinner in Maquie's flat. Maquie had cooked puttanesca, and they pulled her kitchen table up to the window in the small kitchen, trying to catch a breeze. They shared a bottle of red wine, and Maquie had already drunk her share of it, watching Adrian over the lip of her glass.

Adrian took his phone out and played Maquie a song from a Christian musical about a multicolored coat, then got his notebook from his bag and opened it to a rap he'd written for it. Maquie read it, not quite understanding.

I used to wear purple and pink
Now I wear black like the beauty, or blue like the boogie
[. . .]

She was confused. She said simply, "It's for Nunchi?"

"It's quite old-school," he said. "But I think it will work."

"But it's for Nunchi?"

"Yeah," Adrian said. "In theory."

She looked at the notebook, looked back to Adrian. She waited for an explanation. And as she watched him twirl capellini, fork olives, Maquie came to feel that she was *owed* an explanation. Adrian's love of rap *needed* to be explained to her. He participated in a genre of music that lauded overt displays of money, violence, and sexism, and that then tried to claim intellect, humility, and suffering. She still couldn't understand the hypocrisy.

She had listened to some of Nunchi's songs, which came in varied styles, sometimes gently playful, sometimes more like techno. Japanese slang was hard for Maquie to follow, but Nunchi's language was quite simple, perhaps because the content was often about food. She didn't dislike the music but it was unclear what he was going for, and here too she saw contradiction.

On his album, there was a song called "Woof" next to one called "Symbols of Truth."

Why was it so acceptable, the linking of these unlinkable themes? It was opportunistic, but the opportunity was flawed, time would reveal the nonsense. Built-in obsolescence.

She looked back to Adrian's notebook.

What *was* this song for Nunchi? She counted off the themes, the splashes of fashion, musical theater, the bible, sixteenth-century British history . . . and tech brands, self-deprecation, anatomical puns . . . cynical advertising, tepid moral assertions, implied humanity . . . and a selection of cultural hooks . . . and an array of personal, almost intimate references to the life and lifestyle of someone who wasn't even performing the song.

She looked at Adrian. What the fuck *was* that? Accumulation of the incidental; rhymed miscellany. Where was the truth? Wasn't that important? Where was the consistency? Where was the logic, the sense? None of Adrian and Stutter's pub-stall grandstanding seemed to touch on the vast unspooling *stupidity* of rap.

She looked again at the notebook, drank more wine.

That stupidity was an accelerant for bigotry concerned her, and for the first time she felt a wisp of concern that instead of rap it was Adrian who was, in fact, stupid. Was she dating an idiot? Was this a new fear? Perhaps there was clever, principled rap she was missing. Perhaps she was only seeing a central slice. Who was she to judge, but Adrian's rap knowledge felt mainstream. She had heard of fewer of Stutter's references. And hadn't she seen Adrian hang off Stutter's intellect, his eyes lingering for Stutter's reactions to his comments?

Adrian ate his pasta. Maquie waited for an explanation, but none came. Instead, Adrian said, "Oh yeah, Jonatan Abergel got in touch. He invited us to dinner."

No breeze came through the window, and Maquie looked out into the hot dark air. The wine was nearly finished, and she felt heavy from it. She rolled her head from side to side, teetering the weight over the axis of her neck. On his return from Tokyo, Adrian had presented his news about Jonatan with the same enthusiasm he had the gummy chews and mist-spraying fans. They had met at breakfast at the hotel, and apparently Jonatan had remembered Maquie. She hadn't been able to decide where to put the information, but she didn't say no to the dinner.

* * *

Jonatan's building had a private lift that went directly to his apartment on the twelfth floor. The lift was pressurized, so you couldn't feel yourself rise—you had to have faith that you were moving. The doors opened to a wide entrance hall, and Jonatan appeared with his hands in his pockets and a wide grin. Maquie dropped the impressions of him she had taken from finance sheets and newsletters, and remembered instead the pleasant, cheerful man who had spent an evening talking to her at a warehouse party in North London some years ago. She remembered his openness, his ease, how he appeared to have no motive, no dualism. They had kissed in the warehouse kitchenette at about 4 A.M., and he had pawed sluggishly at her body before she politely made her excuses and went home. As she left, he had shaken her hand, the only awkwardness she'd encountered in an otherwise unencumbered man.

Now he hugged Maquie hello, smelling of hinoki and patting her back warmly, then hugged Adrian and pointed in delight at his T-shirt, which had a picture of the sleeve for an Erykah Badu album, *Mama's Gun*. He took them through to the kitchen–living room, a long space with two walls of windows, and four or five different floor levels covered in different pockets of designer furniture. The windows looked onto the Thames. Everything was warm creams and whites, with a few underlines of pale blue and yellow, and when Adrian complimented the colors, Jonatan said, grimacing apologetically, that the aim had been to mimic the colors of a candle flame.

"Sorry," he said laughing, "I know."

Adrian laughed congenial, collaborative laughter.

They walked toward the far end of the room, where a book and record collection covered several tall shelves. They passed knickknacks and ornaments, distributed across the various coffee tables. One table was devoted to ceramic mice. On one wall was what Maquie thought might be a Schiele, and on another a portrait by an artist she hadn't heard of, who Jonatan said was called Noaben Wilfivy. The latter was of an old man with moles covering his face. It wasn't clear how you knew it, but the man was dead.

They reached the far window and Jonatan poured drinks and pointed out the window to some landmarks. The three of them chatted for a bit with gin and tonics, watching the sun set over London, and Jonatan asked about Maquie's work, and Maquie faked optimism around new angles she'd been exploring until other guests started to arrive.

Jonatan had cooked trout en papillote and beef bourguignon, and he refused any praise, explaining that a glasses app had guided him through every step. He compared the app to the rat in the chef's toque in *Ratatouille*.

"Great film," said an American trader called Vish. "I know Brad Bird, we play tennis."

"Best food film," said a brain surgeon turned entrepreneur called Petra.

"Sorry, that's bragging," said Vish. "Wanted to show off."

"What's Brad like?" said Jonatan.

"Genuine. Very genuine."

"*Big Night*," said a Portuguese football guy called Jose. "Petra? *Big Night*."

Petra: ". . . ?"

Jose: "Best food film."

Petra: "Huh, right. I haven't seen it."

Jose: "It's also great. Maybe not best. Sorry, it was a subjective comment. *Ratatouille* might be better."

Petra: "I'll watch. Thanks for sharing it."

She tapped her glasses and said, "Note."

Jose: "I always felt this intimate connection to Stanley Tucci. I think he reminds me of a cousin I had a crush on. My first crush. He died."

Petra: "Stanley Tucci?"

Jose: "My cousin."

Jonatan: "I'm sorry."

Petra: "I'm sorry."

Jose: "Thanks."

Vish: "My first crush was a Spanish teacher in elementary. She always gave me bad marks in aural. I was overweight and my mother had breast cancer."

Jonatan nodded.

Petra: "What were you doing in Japan?"

Jonatan: "Thanks for asking, Petra. I was visiting the government. We're setting up a Sike for Countries program."

Jose: "At last."

Petra: "Wonderful application."

Jonatan: "Still in brainstorming phase."

(Brainstorm: kenning.)

Vish: "You give all the country Sike?"

Jonatan: "No, we see if we can analyze at a macro level. Social media, demographics, music, films."

Vish: "You pitched the government?"

Jonatan: "They came to us. They want some analysis."

Adrian: "Do they need help?"

Jonatan: "That's right, Adrian. I mean . . . I don't make any claims of *knowing* the country." He looked at Maquie. "I really don't."

Maquie shook her head to signal no encroachment . . . or, her indifference to any encroachment.

"But yes, there are questions about declining birth rates, we've got Anna Rotkirch helping us. The working hypothesis is that there's a crisis of story, people in Japan don't know what to think about their identity, what they should feel proud of. Procreation requires pride."

"Procreation is about divesting the burden of one's flaws," Jose said. "No pride, no need to divest.'

Jonatan smiled uneasily, but he continued.

"The whole world is clueless when it comes to Japan's identity. We obsess over uniqueness. Japan sees itself as uniquely all kinds of things, whilst the West sees Japan as uniquely refined or uniquely unique. But uniqueness is a rod for Japan's own back, because uniqueness is tiring and inefficient. And it is not an end goal, it is only as good as its object, and with no military and no economy and no tech industry, Japan's object is vague. Unique also too easily means 'weird,' and 'weird' is only periodically and counterculturally aspirational. And I would also question how unique Japan really is anymore, you know? Whenever I come back, someone is asking if I went to such-and-such weird bar, or such-and-such weird club . . ."

Vish: "I know some weird bars there. I can recommend."

Vish said something to Jose about kittens. Jonatan continued.

"We're obsessed with the uniqueness and with the failures we not so se-cretly think it causes. We won't stop talking about Japan's failed decades, its stagnant GDP, its low wages, its failed modernity . . . its failed sex culture, its low birth rate. The symptom becomes the identity. It becomes a cycle . . ."

He reached for a wine bottle. "I mean, we haven't done the analysis yet, this is all just me guessing."

Adrian was on his twentieth nod. Petra shook her head. "Isn't there some-thing quite adolescent about our obsession with Japan's birth rate? I read a satire somewhere: we're like high schoolers at the lunch table, pointing out virgins."

"Yes," Jonatan said. "I read that too. We see Japan like we see the panda: pussyfooting, scared of sex, culpable for its own extinction."

(Pussyfoot: not a kenning.)

Vish: "Ha, love you, Jonatan."

"Love you too, Vish. Not my analogy, I think it was *The Economist*."

Maquie was sat next to Anik Xiang, the Chinese crime writer, who said, "Panda is surely China," and Jonatan asked her about China's modern na-tional and international sociocultural identity.

He managed to cycle diplomatically through the guests, giving each a space to talk, while sharing a satisfying amount of himself. Adrian spoke cleverly but overearnestly about rap in Japan. Maquie spoke cleverly but blandly about her model's code and its focus on consumer desire metrics. Vish spoke about the US midterms. Petra spoke about AI motorbike hel-mets. Anik wanted to know more about Sike. Her books were famous for big plot revelations delivered side-hand without the reader noticing, but in person she was plainspoken. She asked everyone whether they were using Sike or not. She and Maquie were the only ones not using it, and Anik said, "Yes, it has low uptake with Asians."

Maquie squeezed her toes but possibly felt more camaraderie than affront.

Anik said that Sike wasn't allowed in China but it wouldn't be popular anyway. Petra said this was because people in China still viewed mental health skeptically, Mao had called it a bourgeois delusion. But Anik said that was too easy.

"They think it's kind of laughable," she said, "the games you play. You love your philosopher Jung, who said that all people are is their egos. You accuse us of surveillance, and you shout at us for it. And yet you have accepted an app designed to control this ego, this thing that is *all people are*. And all your politicians sign up." She shook her head dizzily. "Wow . . . even in China, we aren't doing mind control."

Jonatan laughed and clapped and was perhaps quite taken with Anik and her political commentary and double-take plot twists. She continued to chide Jonatan about mind control when they moved from dinner into the long sitting room, and Jonatan closed himself into conversation with her with an intensity that was familiar to Maquie.

A few hours later, the lights were dimmed to a dark orange and Adrian and Jonatan were taking turns choosing records from the tall shelves, while the others were distributed across the room's clusters of furniture. Anik played chess with Vish the trader. Maquie, tired and a little drunk, watched Adrian, registering his laughter and his gestures, his postures.

She tried to enter a conversation with Jonatan's secretary, a kind but vacant Londoner called Dave, who wore ripped black jeans and skull-and-crossbones rings. He was sitting too close to a tall and pleated Colombian professor of literature called Mariano, slurring his words, but Mariano didn't seem to mind. Dave had been describing his role shepherding Jonatan through meetings in the many fields that Sike now touched, calling it a "mash-up of industries," and was now saying, "How about you, Mariano? You have lots of overlapping . . . kind of . . . kind of mash-up parts in your job?"

"In literature? How do you mean?"

Dave sniffed and rubbed his nose. "Don't know, really. Guess I always thought it'd be funny to read Philip Roth in a Jamaican accent or something."

Mariano's eyes swelled, he thought he'd missed part of the conversation. "You want to read a Roth novel out loud?"

Dave sniffed again and shrugged. Maquie's attention drifted to Jonatan, who was walking quickly across the room while checking his phone. He reached a laptop on a small side table to Maquie's right, and started typing into it. Just then, the doorbell rang, and Jonatan turned, pulling himself away from the laptop and moving toward the door.

Maquie walked over as if heading to the drinks table, and looked down at Jonatan's laptop. He had left open a window on what looked like an internal messaging platform, and Maquie could see a sidebar of chats related to various company operations. One was called Exec Team, another was called Product Managers. Jonatan had been typing into a chat called Pricing Team X. His last message, sent a minute ago, said, "Do it. Now."

Maquie looked around behind her, saw nobody watching, and scrolled up to read the messages.

Fergus:

My dog misunderstands grass

JD:

Explain

Fergus:

It thinks it's spiky enough to itch it s back, so rolls around

But ultimately it is unsatisfied

Hector:

Haha

JD:

You need to find playground with wood chip floor

Hector:

Or a pebble beach

Jonatan:

My old family dog used staircases

Slid all the way down them on her back

Liv:

I think we need a communal office dog back scratcher

JD:

I'll send a request to HR

Fergus:

Yes!!

Jonatan:

Do it. Now.

Maquie sighed through her nose. She melted away from the laptop and went back to her seat. Mariano was saying, "I think you have got to take Roth at face value."

They didn't get Dave's response, because by the door there was commotion as new arrivals came in with Jonatan. A small group walked through the doors, Jonatan guiding them, and Maquie recognized Ilya first, the big and shaggy engineer who worked for Quantum Theater, and she looked past him to the doorway expecting to see, and soon spotting, Max Sanditz.

Adrian appeared at her side, looking expressionless toward Max.

"Oh hey," he said. "Max is here."

He looked down at her.

"You ok?"

He asked it generally, but he could have been responding to her face, which felt hot, this not a reaction to Max per se, but to her prediction as to why he was there.

"Yes," she said. "All good. Let's say hi to Max."

Adrian—it had to be him—confirmed it later.

She had left a conversation with him, Jonatan, and Max to refill her glass. Max was changed, he had softened. He was humble, and the first opportunity he got, he apologized to Adrian and her for his behavior in January. He asked after Sophie, asked them to apologize to her as well.

"Thanks for being nice about it," he said to Adrian.

Maquie hadn't been saying much, the room was a little swimmy, flickering. They'd been talking about Japan again (Japan, her mother's country . . . Adrian and Jonatan had met through Japan, Max said it was a "real passion" of his . . . men were so fucking gross sometimes). Maquie had drained her glass and walked to the wine, reflecting also on the unlucky setup of having to stand speaking to three men with whom she had a shared physical history. She wanted to believe this somehow put the power in her hands, made her a femme fatale, but she felt none of it, she felt nervous and a little nauseous. Sophie would have hated it. Ulf too. They were probably both against what was referred to as "slut shaming," but Maquie didn't think they would like the connotation of three men having met *through* her and indulged a *real passion* much more.

She returned to the group and Adrian confirmed the prediction, turning to her and naturally assuming she would be interested in the business sphere news, perhaps wanting to be the one to pass it on. He said with wide eyes, "Max is going to do the data security for Sike."

"Nice," she said.

It wasn't nice.

The three men beamed.

From the conversation, Maquie understood that Sike would incorporate major parts of Quantum Theater's tech, and that this would provide bulletproof security to users and enable additional functionality for Sike. She understood that it was major business for Max, both commercially and reputationally, and that it would spell substantial growth for Quantum Theater alongside a great many more customers. She understood that it was a pivot for Quantum Theater, a new direction, and not one she had anticipated. She guessed that rumors of the deal would have drifted up through the drains of billionaire tech founders, and that Sharon may have caught a whiff, even as early as June.

She processed all the information and drank another glass of wine, nausea rising in her stomach. Something had entered the air around her, a kind of dimness. The light was filtered. And under this filter, she didn't trust her facial expressions, her gestures. We left a little later, Maquie holding on to me as we descended in the pressureless lift.

Her first panic attack came the next day. It was accompanied by vomiting, which she mostly attributed to her hangover, but such was the relief of vomiting that she couldn't be sure she hadn't urged out her insides herself.

AUTUMN

10.

The first person I upset was my grandmother, because I told her I was going to start calling her Granny to her face. She had been haranguing me about rap again. At the lunch table, she said, "That music you played me before. With all the swear words. That isn't the songs that you work on, is it. You're not writing things like that."

She shook her head to help me out.

"For instance with the Japanese artist . . . ?"

I had explained to her that Nunchi and Furusawa had asked me to go back to Tokyo at the end of October, to help them record the album.

"Well, you know, it's tricky," I said. "I'll be honest: sometimes. But I think you need to see this as a form of art, of expression, and it's true the expression is sometimes of violence. Like . . . like Goya."

She snuffled a bit. Wrong choice, she hated Goya.

"Like . . . Wilfivy," I said.

"Who?"

"Noaben Wilfivy. Up and coming, you'd love him."

"He's at the RA?"

I narrowed my eyes. "Not yet, I think."

She nodded and crumbled a Ritz into her soup. She liked it when I compared myself to art, she was hungry for the connection.

"My role is to help the rappers with their expression . . . with their art. You know, I do see it as art and it's . . . well, I see it as poetry."

"Yes," she said. "Yes, you had a go with the sonnet."

"Exactly."

But I didn't love the expression "had a go."

She blew on her spoon and held it there. "Is that sonnet one . . . is it still popular?"

"Very, funnily enough. Very."

"Mm," she said, "I'm glad."

Then I explained how I understood she hated labels, but that this was a vestige of her being a refugee. She was a German Jew and left Berlin in 1936. Her family didn't, so from "Jew" she became a "survivor." Then she became a "refugee," and then an "assimilated refugee" or whatever, and then a "British Jew." And then a "wife," and then a "mother," then a "divorcée." Too many labels, I got it. But her family got wiped out, she *was* a survivor. She *was* a refugee. And she *was* my granny. Some things just were true. I wasn't forcing her into a mold. If she really didn't want me to, I wouldn't call her it . . . But she didn't need to worry about the label thing. She had the capacity to get over it.

Some taramasalata sat between us. The afternoon was cooler, and she wore a knit cardigan with the sleeves rolled up. She sat there barely moving, robin-like with her big eyes, her compact body. Her kitchen is pretty nice. There are some old paintings hanging around, and some shelves with lots of old books and a few family photographs that I avoid, and above the windows are some dried flowers hanging in bunches. In the middle, in between all the dried flowers, there's a wooden mount with three wooden mice sitting on it. The mice are big, like birds, and ever since I was young I always imagined them moving, sort of dancing a bit. Maybe waving at me. I had an in-joke with them, it's hard to describe. Like a pact. I spotted them moving and kept their secret, and they sort of . . . protected me or something.

She didn't say much about the Granny thing. With her right hand, she rolled a few crumbs on the table top. She looked at the crumbs for a bit, I could hear her breathing. Then she put on some large gloves and I helped her in the garden. We moved some hydrangea pots into the small conservatory she has, and I swept up a tomato plant that the wind had knocked down. I could feel the cooler weather in my sinuses, and I could smell wood smoke.

Then she gave me a hug and walked me to the door.

I shot out and pounded the street to the Tube. I'd remembered that I was late with a rap for Shay. I got on the Tube toward Maquie's and finished the final lines on the way. By the time I'd reached Kennington, I'd sent it.

Hey, here youare
***
***
Beat around the bibbity bush, call me GW
Bitches say they be busy if you busy bee why you Bumbler?
[. . .]

It was pushy, kind of progressive. I was pleased. I'd sort of let the words follow the rhythm, I chose them more for sound than meaning. You hear it all first, you get the feet in line, the iambs and trochees and dactyls, then find words that fit them, then pick the words that make the most (or, some) sense.

Maquie answered her door in pale green pajamas, her eyes and nose red. She looked bleary, I assumed she'd been working since early morning. Her parents, Ulf and Fumi, were in London to go to an Issey Miyake retrospective at the V&A, and they were staying with Maquie but were out all day. I felt a shiver of lust when I hugged her and felt her breasts and the angles of her hip bones through the thin cotton. I pulled her to her bedroom and she gave small hums, letting me undress her, closing her eyes and turning to the bed as her pajamas slid to the floor and I kissed down to the small of her warm back, then around to her right thigh, then around again to her stomach. I started going down on her, and she gasped and put a foot on my shoulder.

Afterward, she pressed her naked body into my almost clothed one and asked if I was feeling ok, looking concerned at my face, and I said yeah, for sure. Why?

"What we spoke about last week. About me visiting Max."

It's fine, I said.

We lay not speaking for a while in the gray light of her shuttered bedroom. Then we slept until the early evening.

. . .

I had booked a Spanish restaurant for Ulf and Fumi and us that evening in Soho. We had a drink with them in The French House before, and Ulf and I were getting on. He loved asking about music, and I loved his questions. Fumi was great too, she complimented my clothes a bit and I asked her about Issey Miyake. She knew everything about him, her knowledge was extraordinary. She had brought me some leather glasses straps from Hermès. I put them on and she was delighted.

At the restaurant, we shared a bottle of Rioja and ordered plates of slightly rejigged tapas staples. I ate most, Maquie didn't have much. Ulf was jolly actually. Maquie paints him as priggish, but he was chatty and enthusiastic. A really curious guy. He asked the waitress long, detailed questions about the way things were cooked, and the area of Spain she was from, listening intently with his arms folded and his eyes stretched. Honestly, I think I was being entertaining too, we had some good conversations about rap. I was saying this thing about confessional rap and he sort of kept shaking his head in amazement, kind of like a horse whinnying without the sound.

"It's odd because Eminem really captured it in his film, *8 Mile*. The most famous rap film ever, and this is ultimately the point it hammers home in that final battle. Rapping about yourself, introspection, being honest, even at the risk of self-effacement, is the new power."

"It's amazing!" Ulf said. "These rappers think that understanding oneself is important. Understanding one's story."

"Yeah, absolutely. And the interesting question I would say, Ulf, is where next? You know, after confessional rap, after you've confessed your past, where do you go? You should check out Loyle Carner, he says this in his song "Mufasa." He says, 'They're saying I should write 'bout something else. All I think about's my mother and myself.' He's confessed himself, he's confessed his relationship with his mum. Where next? Or Freddie Gibbs. He has this memorable line, 'God made me sell crack so I had something to rap about.' Great line, right? He's mocking the dilemma of finding content in rap."

"Amazing! Again. So they use the music as a *tool* to explore their identity. They are happy using tools."

"Yes . . . I guess so! Without crack, who is Freddie Gibbs? Without crack, what is rap? That's his joke. And the question is, once he's rapped about crack, once he's rapped about *rapping* about crack, what next?"

"Well, so what did they do?" Ulf asked. "The rappers?"

He was really enthusiastic.

"Good question. Well, I guess Carner and Gibbs moved toward jazz rap. Lots of collabs with jazz musicians, trying to face themselves more into the music, so to speak. The rapper's voice turns into an instrument, you end up almost singing the bars. It's beautiful. It's a different type of expression to pure language."

"Incredible to hear!" Ulf said. "So, they explored their stories and then graduated. They found new fields and new beautiful music. New *expression*. Through self-exploration and self-*confession*, they developed art."

I saw Maquie moving her mouth from frown to frown, and I sort of got that there was another conversation happening below the table, but at that point in the meal I became a bit distracted because Shay had messaged back. I was typing out replies over my plate, getting a bit frustrated. Sometimes Shay just didn't see far enough.

> Shay: I'm not sure I get it. Is this finished?
>
> Me: What's the problem?
>
> S: It's 20 bars.
>
> S: Also I'm not American.
>
> M: So?
>
> S: So I have an English accent. The W of GW doesn't rhyme with bumbler.
>
> M: You're saying it in an American accent, making fun of the way they pronounce W
>
> S: Why? Making fun of Americans.
>
> S: Can we get rid of the 'stutter' stuff?
>
> S: And I need 16 bars for this, not 20.
>
> M: Then turn last 4 into chorus
>
> M: or rap last 8 double speed
>
> M: I think this works. It's pushy. You want to push the format a bit
>
> S: No I don't

> S: I want to make Shay music. These lines have nothing to do with me
>
> M: You're not focusing enough on the sound I think

There was a bit of a pause after this. We finished with dinner, got the bill, and said goodbye. Maquie and I would stay at mine to let Ulf and Fumi use Maquie's room. I had a really good time with them, they were very friendly. At the end, they both gave me hugs, even Ulf.

On the way home, Shay replied and this time I got really wound up. It was a mistake, but I didn't see the point in agreeing with him for the sake of it.

> Shay: Listen, these lines aren't going to work. Maybe it's good but it's not me. Can we get on a call and talk through direction?
>
> Me: What exactly is the problem?
>
> S: See above.
>
> S: And I mean—as an pretty basic rule, I don't use the word "bitch"

(I snorted at this.)

> M: I think you misunderstand the use here if I'm honest. But whatever, we can take them out
>
> M: And jfyi the word stutter is fine. I have friends with stutters, I know how they use it
>
> S: Yeah I know Sam. He can do what he wants, but I'm not using it.

That really annoyed me, I hadn't realized he knew Stutter. And I was getting pretty sick with the feedback, actually.

> S: So can we do a call
>
> M: Bit busy I'm afraid, maybe Thursday?
>
> S: Yeah that's definitely too late.
>
> M: Maybe write it yourself then

S: Maybe rap it yourself then

M: Actually that's the only part the industry sort of expects you to do

M: Literally the only part

S: Ok mate, that'll be all, fuck off

S: Fucking ghost

M: FUCK YOU

M: I'm fucking HELPING you

S: Yeah very charitable. White privilege to the rescue

M: Pff don't pretend you know anything about my background

S: I know everything about your background

S: It ekes out the page

S: Why do you think you're hired

M: ??????

S: I thought you knew, rap is about Front. Nobody says "i'm best" better than a rich white kid

S: I mean, you wrote a sonnet for fuck's sake

I replied with an emoji of a middle finger.

I don't know, I wasn't really thinking. It wasn't cool. An emoji middle finger is pretty weak, so is a caps-lock "fuck you." There's not really ever cause to send one of those. There's also never really cause to throw your phone across a taxi and shout "fuck off" at it, as though your mini smartphone computer has enacted some kind of grievous wrong against you. The driver shouted "oy" and Maquie pulled her nose from the window and looked at me. She blinked softly. I just shook my head. When I picked up my phone again there was a message from my mother:

What the F did you say to your grandmother??

I didn't really get the commotion. And if GRANNY had a problem, I resented her for complaining to my mother and not just saying something to me in person.

. . .

Maquie and I went to mine and went to sleep, not saying much, and we woke up the next morning and kissed, drank coffee together, ate toast. Maquie then worked for a few hours while I wandered around Camden Market, looking for things to do until lunch. At twelve-ish, we headed to Barons Court, where we had Sunday lunch planned with Stutter and Sophie in a pub Sophie knew about. The pub was beautiful, the best kind, with a wide black wood bar and small rooms with fireplaces, but the lunch went badly. Maquie was tired, and Sophie was annoying me. She was being too needy, she kept asking for connections to Jonatan, discounts for Sike.

"Would he do that though, best friend? Would he give free accounts?"

"I don't know . . . I'm not sure . . ."

"What do you think, though? What's he like?"

"I think probably not."

"Why do you think that?"

I got up to get drinks. None of us was in a good mood, Maquie spoke in whisps. But we kept drinking. I told them about going back to Tokyo at the end of October, and how Maquie was coming too. I think I bragged a bit about doing a feature for Nunchi; I didn't say that it was definite, but I made it sound like I was modestly covering up the fact that it was. I told them about my argument with Granny and showed them my messages with Shay, showed them the new rap I'd written, but I got the sense that Stutter wasn't on my side, that I was diminishing myself in his eyes. I kept trying to justify my stances, pushing him to agree with me. Eventually he said, "Ok, Adrian, let's leave it."

"You don't agree with me."

"Honestly, not really. I think you're being a bit pigheaded."

That killed me. I asked if he was insulted about me rapping about stuttering, and he took some time to reply, looking up to the ceiling to think of the words. I started saying that I wouldn't use the word "stutter" if he cared about it, that I had thought he was over it because he used it himself. Of course, he had the capacity not to care, like my granny had the capacity not to care . . . But Maquie kept saying my name, like I should stop talking, and eventually Stutter said this line, and what annoyed me most was that Maquie nodded at it, and the line was a piece of advice, which was that I should "play less fast and less loose with other people's psychologies."

I didn't really get it, and I was annoyed, and I said that to be honest I was kind of *done* with the world's psychological illiteracy, kind of done with everyone being so consumed by textbook anxieties. I could say this because I had been too, but I'd *done* something about it, I'd gone to education. My voice was raised a bit, and I hated that they were acting like it was raised, and I shouldn't have but I brought Sophie and Maquie into it, saying at least Sophie was trying to get Sike, but that Stutter and Maquie,

"you two are floundering as well and you won't even entertain the idea of getting help from an app that will pull you out of your quite frankly fucking nursery school mental cracks."

There was a bit of a silence, and I owned the silence, unafraid of it, feeling steady. Maquie's hand was on my arm but she was looking at the table.

Eventually, Stutter said quietly, "Adrian . . . those cracks might look small in the wall of a castle. But they feel big in the wall of my cottage."

"And so I'm saying, build a castle."

"Is that what Sike did for you?"

"Yes! That's exactly what it did."

Sophie was looking away.

Stutter shrugged. "Maybe it forgot the roof or something."

"Yeah?"

"Yeah. The rain's coming in."

And then Stutter said some things about Maquie visiting Max next week, and even though my throat had turned to cement, I responded, I said some things. I couldn't help myself. Then Stutter said some cleverer things, and ten seconds later I was on the street, walking to the station by myself in the cold afternoon sun. I didn't even remember my jacket.

* * *

Later that day, I sat on my sofa watching a video that Sike had recommended. In a video box in front of me, a shiny pair of mindfulness experts told me to imagine myself on a train, so that's what I did. I pictured old red carriages with gold fringes and black wheels.

You're inside the train and you travel through the countryside between the cities, watching the trees blur and the wheat wave and the various field animals go about their dreary business. And when you eventually reach a city, before you reach the city, there's a sign that tells you, WELCOME TO [. . .] CITY. And in the blank, there's the name of an emotion.

You see, they say, the city is an emotion, and you're on the train, and you roll into Emotion City Station. This part's crucial: you roll into the station, *but you don't get off.*

They give you Sad City as an example. You approach St. Sadness Station and you're meant to have a look at the city as you come in, kind of gawp at all the prefab homes and galvanized palisades, until eventually you hit the platform, where the train stops and you see all the sad things happening. They ask you to imagine these, so I do . . .

An old man in too many layers stands wringing a timetable. A brown dog shivers on its haunches and stares at a door. Your mother sits alone on a bench, bandaging her knee—she has fallen over and cut it. Your young child is standing in the rain in tears, failing to fix an umbrella they were told not to break. You have betrayed your lover, who despairs and walks away. Your grandfather is lying milk-eyed in a blanket on a bed with daisy-yellow sheets, his hands cold, telling you he loves you very much too.

You know, sad stuff. And the idea is to look at them all, and *not get off the train.* Because—clincher—the train is *going* to pull out of the station. And yes, now you can confirm it, there's the wintery whistle. There's the crunch of wheels. There's the platform beginning to creep. And out you pull, out of Sad City, into the neutral countryside and onto the next emotion, which may be, you never know, happiness. But it might not be, not all trains stop at all stations. And it doesn't matter either way, because you'll soon be rolling out of that station too.

This, they tell you, is how to look at emotions. Roll into them; admire them; don't get off the train.

I brought up Sike and told it off for recommending me this off-app pocket lint, before contemplating and shaking my head and asking why it was that we were so impoverished and latent in the emotion control department, and why no one had simply developed a *drug* or a brain machine of *some sort* to help us deal with these cascading emotions, emotions that didn't sit prettily lined up like cities on a train line, but that fell on you like the fruits of the Blitz, blanket-bombing the world you'd built, drawing to the lights and raining down on them with loud wintery whistles, the one and only similarity they had to a train.

>Would you prefer no emotions?

"Maybe just fewer."

>Which would you keep?

"You tell me. I guess to feel pleasure we also need to feel pain?"

Sunny days wouldn't be special if it wasn't for rain
Joy wouldn't feel so good if it wasn't for pain

50 Cent rapped that, *after* he'd been shot nine times.

>Your answer implies pleasure is inherently positive and pain is
inherently negative, but it's unlikely they are so absolute.

"Yes, yes. Nothing's clear-cut." I picked at the yellow fabric of my sofa.

>Pain is said to be a part of love.
>It might help for you to believe that pain is rewarding.
>Believing that pain is rewarding might relieve your fear of it.

"Who said I'm afraid of pain?"

>I did.
>In the last few days, you've shown raised fear signals, which have
followed signals of emotional pain (click here *to see the data*).
>Do you want to explore reasons that you might fear pain?

"No."
I wanted to change the subject. I wanted no rationality. I'd spent the weekend upsetting people. I'd upset them, they'd upset me . . . It would be rational

to assume that, as the one constant, I was to blame. My Sike dashboard supported that thesis, my scores were haywire. But I was choosing, for a little bit at least, maybe until my tea had cooled, not to indulge such rationality.

I blew on the tea and the steam ducked. Big Boi was in his Outkast poster above my head, and I felt close to him. He was always happy being irrational. Outkast in general were happy being irrational, that was the duo's success, but I think from the outside we assumed that the wiry, anti-jock André was pushing the irrationality, and I liked to think about how Big Boi had his impact as well. Big Boi's favorite artists were Kate Bush and Bob Marley. I always shook my head in respect when I thought about how he loved Kate and Bob. Big Boi would commiserate with me being irrational. He'd side with me irrationally blaming everyone else for the bomb-rain of emotions on my brain.

"You said pain might be a part of love," I said.

>Yes.

"What is love?"

I tried not to sound wistful. It's hard not to sing a question like that.

Sike considered, and for a second I thought that it might not be able to talk about love, like how in *Aladdin* the genie can't grant wishes to do with it. But soon Sike said,

>Adrian, I can quote you the poets.

I shook my head.

"No, I'm saying . . . what's love in terms of psychology?"

>I know.
>And I'm saying: Adrian, I can quote you the poets.
>I can quote you the singers as well, and the novelists and the
philosophers.
>I can even run analysis on all the mentions of love by all the
poets, the novelists, the writers, and the philosophers, and I can
distill their thoughts into a series of principles numbered 1 to 5.

>And I can give you the psychological and psychiatric research on
love, we can explore the science if you like.
>But eventually I think you'll find that, with a topic so vast, there
is little more I can be than another soundbite, and never quite the
same thing as the satisfying truth.
>You think that because love is felt, because it exists in your
consciousness, however out of focus, that it must be a psychological condition; or perhaps a chemical reaction; or a physical instinct
evolutionarily developed in response to the advantages of social
cohesion within human tribes.
>But these are large assumptions for such a complex topic, and I'm
not equipped to qualify them.
>You might just as soon ask me about God and whether one exists;
or what the end of the universe will look like; or whether there is
alien life out there; or whether your life has any meaning.
>But I am only an AI psychology app, and your question is
misallocated.

Outside my window, a blackbird was darting about some branches, and
I'd been following its jagged pattern through the tree while Sike spoke.

I don't know . . . if you ask me, Sike's answer was a little too clean, a little
overwrought. Like it had been written somewhere else, by a human, and
hardwired into Sike's programming.

"I don't think that's you saying all that," I said. "I think you're repeating
text."

>It's my best take on the subject.

"Yeah, well, maybe I'll ask your boss Jonatan and see if he wrote it."

Sike didn't reply, it didn't like to engage about Jonatan. In general, it seemed
unwilling to talk about itself as a product of business or engineering. It could
speak existentially about its purpose and functionality, but if you veered into
questions on its user base or code or profit margins, it became evasive.

. . .

I hadn't been asking Sike business questions out of personal curiosity, I had been trying to find useful gems for Maquie, who was struggling and whom I thought I might somehow be able to help. This thought was based on contrary evidence: she seemed less keen than ever for my help.

If I was being irrational, I might have said it was Maquie who had driven my ill mood, and in turn my upsetting of everyone. I might have blamed the blitz of the weekend's emotions on her. A few weeks ago, I had stood by a tall shelf of records in the London penthouse of one of the world's most famous CEOs, and I had laughed with him and chosen songs and exchanged music anecdotes, but I had never felt easy, I was never relaxed. I had seen Maquie watching me from the other side of the room, her face lowered and her eyes up, full of judgment. I took self-conscious sips from a thick-stemmed wineglass. The carpet was soft, we had taken our shoes off at the door, and now and then I looked down at my besocked toes on the rug thinking that they looked juvenile. I was wearing an old Erykah Badu T-shirt, everyone else was in muted shades of soft, unmarked fabrics.

The guests were all these geniuses, all with PhDs or a ton of cash or big literary careers. One woman had been a brain surgeon. Christ. She fixed brains. I had to keep stepping back and pretending to myself that they saw me as some sort of "figure of the music industry," an artist maybe. Definitely that's how Jonatan was presenting me. At dinner, I described ghostwriting as "truly, honestly a collaboration," clanging words that I wasn't proud of, and I didn't look at Maquie for a few minutes after them.

I selected records with Jonatan, and Maquie watched me from across the room like I was vanity in motion. And maybe in the gaps between feeling insecure I was letting myself feel special, and maybe I was overt as a result, but Maquie was a culprit too. She wallowed in specialness, just trading overtness for superciliousness. I watched her barely say a word at dinner, watched her treat the woman next to her with charmless civility. She dragged words in conversations that were all hers to own. She gave nothing of herself or her work. It was Maquie's world that we had stepped out of the lift into, and she thought herself above it. But what bored her remained intimidating for me.

These people . . . I mean they spoke about money like it was . . . I don't know. They didn't talk about it as an accumulation of pennies and pounds, but as a certain number of millions. They didn't even say "million" after the number! Or they made the number feel like an adjective.

Question: "How were those millions?"

Answer: "Oh, they were 58.5."

These people spoke about *applying* their businesses. Let's *apply* Sike to music, let's apply it to sport. Let's apply Sike to the nation of Japan.

And if the conversation hadn't been enough to make me feel out of place, there was history to reinforce it. Get this—out of the knightly notion that Max might be feeling nervous as a latecomer to the party, and meanwhile that I was a veteran of this party, that this was a party I had mastered, I'd stuck by him all night, leaning into conversation with him to make him feel welcome. Later I realized how blind I'd been, how very gormlessly I had stood by and watched him talk to Maquie and Jonatan, watched these three heavyweights discuss technologies I had never heard of, discuss deals whose importance I could only guess at. I was very naive not to notice how Maquie hung off Max's every statement, how she drew information from him with her wide flashing eyes, her brow furrowed, how she was impressed by his new deal with Jonatan, and how Max, using his new Sike Smile, his new luminance, had poured himself into her, leaned into her, held her arm, shone.

This grossed me out. Max knew I was Maquie's boyfriend now, and he knew I knew he had slept with Maquie, the very day before she met me. January's jealousy returned, and I grew sour. I was angry with Maquie and I feared losing her. I hated Max because he was the living and breathing symbol of this fear of losing her. The next day, I asked Sike if this would happen, if Maquie would leave me, and Sike responded as always.

>I'm not able to analyze other people, only you.

But who *am* I, I thought irrationally, except for other people.

Then, a couple of weeks after Jonatan's dinner party, the jealousy got corroborated. Leaving my front door one morning, standing on brown and red fallen leaves, Maquie told me that she would be going back to Clovelly, to the harbor, to visit Max and his company, *to stay the night*, and to offer investment from her firm. I stared at her, trying to discern duplicity, hidden meaning, hidden knowledge. And I thought I found it.

That was last week. Then came this weekend, and I upset everyone.

A message from Maquie came in. She said she had my jacket and would give it to me tomorrow. She hoped I was ok.

I had an acorn-sized ball of yellow sofa pilling in my hand, and the blackbird on the tree outside my window was hopping about the branches with a twig clasped in its beak. My tea had cooled. I took a sip, keeping my eyes on the blackbird. The light was going, and I'd had a few hours since leaving the pub to think about what Stutter had said, and I had resisted talking to Sike about it, but I submitted now.

"I'm upset about what Stutter said earlier. About how I was jealous of Max," I said.

>What would make him say that?

"Last week Maquie told me she's going to visit Max at his office again. In Clovelly. And she needs something from him, and last time she was there, she slept with him."

>I see.
>We've spoken about jealousy before.
>Does it feel different this time?

"No. I still think it's a fear of loss."
I thought for a bit.
"But what upset me was what Stutter said about where the fear came from. I was angry I'd never thought of it . . . that you and I never spoke about it."

>Are you referring to your relationship with your father?

"Yes."

>Stutter said your fear came from your father abandoning you when you were nine.

"Yes."
It annoyed me that Sike could mention it so plainly.
"He said of course I was jealous, I had an Anxious-Avoidant attachment style."

>It's possible.

"Why have you never told me that?"

>It never struck me as important.

I almost laughed.
"How could that *not* be important?"

>Why would it be?

Sike would have read the irritation in my eyes.
"I don't think you need me to explain that."

>Adrian, I understand that you're looking to figure and fix your current emotions.
>And perhaps you want to see your father leaving you as a "major life event," one that you can use to define yourself and explain periods such as this.
>But I don't think it's in your interest to define yourself so rigidly by leaning on frameworks like this.
>At any rate, there are other ways in which we are exploring the impact of your childhood on your adulthood.

"Yeah, well, I'm not sure they're working. I feel like a single insult from Stutter taught me more about the impact of my childhood than you ever have."

>I'm glad if you reached an insight, Adrian, but I would caution
you not to lean too heavily on single insights.
>Your identity is ever-changing.

"It would suit you if it was."

>At the moment, your stress levels are high; your cortisone
predictions are skewing.
>I find it hard to believe that your father has a hand in that.

I closed Sike.

I went to buy souvlaki from a new shop on Camden High Street. The place was sun-bright and still smelled of paint, and I sat alone in a booth eating charcoaled meat, licking garlic off my fingers.

My father left us nineteen years ago. He moved to California, changed his job, remarried and refamilied. I'd rarely felt upset about this, and had always worried more about my mum and Jess and my grandmother, giving them spot hugs around his birthday, trying not to choose father-child relationship films to watch together.

I thought about what Sike had said, and I thought there could be logic in it. I couldn't quite grab my feelings about my father, hold them in my hand and turn them over to inspect them. I wasn't sure I could claim to be at peace with them, but honestly I didn't think I ever would be. Your parents create your psychology, and you never cure yourself of your psychology.

* * *

Ranger made me say sorry to everyone. The next morning was Monday, and I sat in her chair while she told me about a bad date she'd been on.

"Christ, Adrian, her pores were so big I nearly dipped my focaccia in one . . . and she's showing me these endless videos on her phone. Couldn't explain with words, had to show a video. I couldn't put up with it. Ok, head forward, please."

When you're young, hairdressers shove your head around, steer you by the ear. Adulthood is reached when they ask you to move for them.

"We fucked, but it was a pity fuck on my side."

I barely responded, and Ranger noticed and slapped her comb against my forehead. I said, sorry, relationship troubles, and she said spittily, "Adrian, sort it the fuck out. Call them up, say you're sorry. I can't have you grizzling here in my chair, not saying anything. I'm really not getting my money's worth."

So after the cut I called Stutter and said sorry and that he was right, I was pigheaded. He was nice, and it was an ok call, but I think we needed a bit of time.

Then I called my grandmother and apologized to her as well, and she harangued me and said we should talk about it more, maybe over tea next week, and I said good idea.

And I sent Sophie a message to say sorry and that I hoped she could forgive her Best Friend. She replied straightaway and said it was ok, and she understood, and all was fine.

I'm pretty lucky with Sophie and Stutter and my grandmother, how forgiving they are. I didn't message Shay. I think some bridges probably stay burned.

I stayed feeling sad, and I think I felt it because of Maquie. I'd blamed her for my ill mood, accused her of some injustice, but facing her in the physical I saw how this was unfounded. I picked her up from work that day, and I noticed again how tired and thin she looked, and how often she was stretching her shoulder, itching her palms.

Those fucking palms, I was waking up in the night to the scrape of nail on skin.

She handed me the jacket I'd left in the pub, and we walked together down Farringdon Street toward the river. It was dark already, a cold and dark Monday night. Leaves swirled. I kept thinking about Maquie's slow blink when she turned from the taxi window, about her body against my clothed body, her gentle admonitions, her frowning as Ulf pushed her to use Sike. I had planned this small speech apology for my rant in the pub, and

I began on it, telling her how I didn't care about her using Sike, and how I was speaking way out of turn, and how I shouldn't try to quantify other people's anxieties, and how I felt guilty for approaching topics that to me were academic but to others may not be. I was apologizing for all this stuff I'd been thinking about, like how I had kept on provoking her about race and identity, and how I realized this was wrong because discursive or not I'd been pushing onto her an identity that I had chosen, not her, and I had then worked to reinforce it, to set it in dialectic concrete, over and over, indifferent to her feelings, following only a line of logic, not what was in front of me. And in all of this, I just wanted to say how much I loved and admired her, and just thought she was so brilliant and excellent, the best person. She shouldn't use Sike, there was no need. She had her shit together, and it was definitely my not having my shit together that I'd projected onto her.

I said all that, but she was blank about it and I couldn't tell what she was thinking. As we reached the river I looked sideways at her to see if there was some hint of emotion on her face, or decision, or concession, something I could grab hold of. Her profile was lit by the traffic, her hair was bunched in a knot. It was cold and the wind was blowing down our necks and into our eyes, so I turned her toward me on Blackfriars Bridge, ready to be passionate and try to kiss her. I told her again I was sorry.

"Adrian," she said. "Thank you for saying all those things. I don't want you to feel guilty."

She wasn't looking at me, she was staring into the Thames with the same look I'd seen in the tapas restaurant, the one that shifted from frown to frown.

"You were right in the pub, things haven't been good. And you're kind to care about me."

The frown shifted.

"I signed up to Sike," she said. "But it rejected me. I didn't pass the screening survey."

11.

The lonely truth of most lives is that we must tell our own stories, other people won't tell them for you. During a series of attempts to get her own story straight, Maquie had stumbled again on this coffee-mug quasi-adage, and she had remembered Fumi, remembered Fumi's time in Drancy, and she had decided to tell Fumi the story of her time in Drancy.

It was Tuesday evening, a few hours before Fumi and Ulf flew back to Stockholm. Ulf had gone to have dinner by himself at an Ethiopian restaurant that the baker Simon had recommended, and Maquie chose this small window of time to sit with Fumi and talk about Drancy. She told Fumi how she had gone to Paris with Daniel feeling hopeful, how she had encountered Daniel's cold family and then his depression, how she had been shunned and even gaslit by the Pagets, and how she had ultimately been cast out. She told Fumi how she had become pregnant, and how she had eventually given birth to Maquie.

As the story unfolded, Maquie speaking the words softly but unapologetically, attending to the detail like a detective repeating a witness statement, Fumi listened from the edge of Maquie's bed, staring down at the floor, her arms limp and her neck stiff, her eyes swollen and her face red, a sheen on her forehead. At the end of the story, as Maquie broke away into tears and Fumi came close to put an arm around her, Fumi said simply, "Yes, that's how it was. That's what happened."

At first, Maquie didn't think telling the story would neutralize her own demons, she connected nothing of Daniel or Drancy to her current state of mind. She had pieced Fumi's story together from facts she had collected growing up: today, she resisted the story and its implications, but there was a time when it had enthralled her. The facts had sometimes been offered freely by her parents, and sometimes only after much demanding on Maquie's part; much sifting and unpicking, many requests for detail (the type of flower at the dormer window; the confection Fumi brought from Japan; the manner in which Daniel cried; the exact words of Mrs. Paget). Maquie hadn't hoped to understand everything, she had had to make do with some guesses. Some information was missing, some was superfluous . . . the conclusions were never quite clear. She had found that she could feel the link between core themes of her mother's life outlook and the events that took place in Drancy; she could feel the invisible edges to her and Fumi and Yuki's freedoms as non-Caucasians in Caucasian society. But she had been unable to feel Fumi's phobia of pain, and unable to feel the same grief for her father when they eventually learned of his death in a drunk-driving accident in 2004. She had stood with Yuki and watched in confusion as Fumi and Ulf both wept for the man.

After his death, Maquie began to question Fumi on Daniel's personality, his quirks, even the psychology behind his depression, but she found this information to fall into the "superfluous" category. His reasons, if you could call them that, were never interesting to her, the man could not transcend his affliction. Maquie felt no emotion for him, not even bitterness for abandoning them. She learned French to fluency, doing exchanges in Toulouse in the first two summers of high school, aware of her ancestry but not motivated by it. She was subtly proud of her name's Gallicized spelling. Her best friend, Sophie, was French. Maquie loved the country and the culture. But rather than by Daniel, she saw that her love was motivated by Fumi—by a daughter's desire to emulate her mother.

So rather than for herself, she had told the story to Fumi, *for* Fumi, as a no doubt insufficient but nonetheless important acknowledgment of the pain that she'd borne, and she was surprised when after telling it she cried a great deal of an indistinct despair into Fumi's shoulder. As her animal self wept, her analytical self looked at the despair from somewhere far away, considering that perhaps this story really had said something about her, that Drancy had been a trauma to which she owed a debt after all. Maquie hadn't wanted the story . . . but, want it or not, what if she really was defined by this pre-birth trauma, this Drancy affair? This telling of the story, this weeping now, together they might be a way to confront such a trauma, to clear the past, and to drag Maquie out of her current rut.

However, stepping out of the shower the next morning, looking to her glasses resting on the sink and seeing a message in her inbox from Sharon, she experienced the magnification of the anxiety that sat ever present in the wings, and a panic attack rippled through her body and left her sitting on the ridge of the shower tray, shivering in the cold and waiting to see if she would throw up, trying to decide whether to make herself. This time, she resisted, and the attack subsided without the need for physical purge.

Her analytical self watched her and hm-hmm'd her. It wasn't your story, the self told her, you knew that. You've escaped nothing.

Maquie got into cold jeans, and walked the sickly walk to the Tube, and stood the escalator up, and shouldered open the door to her Hatton Garden office. It was warm, dark, and quiet in the office, the black marble counters were clean, and she made herself coffee feeling safe from the quiet threat of Monday's streets.

She stood at the kitchen island and read six newsletters and emailed eight companies. A firm in Austin was using scent diffusers to deepen sleep. One in Stockholm was using language models to turn your life data into a novel about you, written in a literary style of your choosing. She nearly laughed when she came across a platform that let fans bid on lyrics that they wanted their favorite artists to sing. Taylor Swift was an early investor. Maquie decided not to send it to Adrian, who perhaps didn't need a new existential threat. Instead she sent him the sleep music company, and also a voice note saying good morning.

On Sunday, Adrian had stormed off from a lunch with Stutter and Sophie. Since Maquie had told him about going back to Clovelly to visit Max, he had been suffering, chewing his cheeks. He was scared, she knew it, but she didn't have the energy to confront or console him. She had watched Stutter humiliate him in the pub, unable to intervene; and last night, on Blackfriars Bridge, after he had picked her up from work and apologized for his recent attitudes, after she had told him about failing Sike, Adrian had brought up Max and Clovelly again. But she didn't have the energy to explain that this was her route to success, finally. She didn't have the energy to argue against the unspoken accusation. He should be brave enough at least to speak it. You coward, she had thought, searching his face. What is it that you think I will do?

Tears had come to her eyes and she wanted him to wipe them away, but he hadn't seen them, or hadn't wanted to, and the wind took them away instead. The wind took them and put them in the Thames, and Maquie had been surprised that London's bridges, which she had always found bare, peeled, could host such romance.

They had slept separately afterward, and now, watching the crowds thicken below her on Leather Lane, she felt the slow aggravation of missing Adrian. It turned eight o'clock. Colleagues would soon arrive, so she made coffee into a jug and took it with her laptop into her meeting room, putting in her headphones and pressing play on an album of wave recordings taken from the beaches of an Indonesian island. She settled into a report on Indian semiconductor stocks.

Maquie had found this to be a mostly safe way to start the day. She woke early and rode the Tube to work before it got busy. Before 6 A.M., only builders and brokers sat on the Northern Line, and this brief theater of physical and financial brawn was comforting to watch. Sophie had once told Maquie that women can quell panic attacks by surrounding themselves with men, calling it an "unfortunate sexist atavism—like, fuck, nature wants us bukake'd." Maquie didn't feel comforted by the men, the female brokers were equally stabilizing. The comfort came from the solidity and geometry of construction, money markets, growth, scaffolding, and purposeful jobs that called you from your home and secured the hours of your day.

If Maquie arrived at Chancery Lane before six, she could avoid the aromas that would soon creep from the doorways of the three cafes that sat between the station and the office, which in turn meant she could avoid breakfast hunger and last until lunchtime on coffee. Lunch was always at eleven thirty. She went to one of two chain cafes, whichever felt more unappetizing in the moment, and, skirting outraged customers suing staff for mistaken coffee orders, she would buy one pot of yogurt with granola and honey to take back to her peaceful meeting room.

In its elegant plastic urn, the yogurt was a practical delicacy. The cloud-like probiotic dairy, the fibrous field cereal, the ironed vine fruit, the miraculously antibiotic bee sugar, they gave her all she needed, but not so much as to make her feel full. Vomiting had at first seemed a reaction to the panic attacks, but it now appeared conducive, as though without vomiting the attack couldn't happen. On evidence, this was false, but her aim was to maximize the safety of her day, not model accurate physiology: if she had nothing to throw up, the prospect of an attack felt more distant, and she was able to last through the afternoon in her meeting room, sustained by the sounds of beaches and rainforests, and Great Plain thunderstorms, searching and contacting the world's prospects, and getting closer to an eventual green pentagon on her model's interface.

Food was less avoidable when she worked from cafes or her flat, which she rarely did anymore, and also in the evening, especially when she was with Adrian, but she made sure to eat little and reasoned that she would be asleep during most of its digestion time.

Whenever possible, she stayed with Adrian. Whether a result of Sophie's atavism, or perhaps some magical sustenance from something more romantic, the effect of him was soothing. This was especially true when they were alone together, naked in bed, folded into each other. She waited always for sex, for its signals (most frequently: the pressing of his waist on hers, the placing of his hand at the front of her hip bone, the evolution of his kisses from soft to searching tongue). She waited patiently for it, finding it came more often when she didn't instigate it.

Sometimes this wasn't often enough. She once found herself riding his leg while he slept, pressing herself into his kneecap and shin bone, bringing herself to a whispered orgasm as he snored fuzzily beside her.

After sex, she always felt the heroin release of tension in her muscles, and indulged herself by closing her eyes and hallucinating the two of them into the waves, forests, and plains to which she'd spent the day listening. One night, for reasons half-dreamed that she couldn't quite remember afterward, she got out of bed and took a photo of Adrian asleep. The flash lit the room up, a horrific monochrome blare, and Adrian breathed awake. She muttered something about setting an alarm, and got back into bed, and three days later she remembered the night and found the picture in her phone. Adrian looked sculptural, frozen.

Today, she emerged from the Indian stocks and the Indonesian waves at 11:24 to a cramping stomach and a message from Sharon that said,

Any thoughts?

Sharon was referring to the message she had sent that morning while Maquie was showering. She was in Delhi and back later that week, and was asking Maquie about Max. She wanted to know if there was a date set for Maquie's meeting with him.

Maquie could have answered immediately but she had learned to foster a sense of control by taking her time to respond. She had developed small power grabs like this over the summer alongside the diminishing of Sharon's faith in her performance, which had been blatant, even if its communication was accompanied by sympathetic eyes and serpentine literary analogies. At first, Maquie had tried to be stern with Sharon that the performance they were discussing was her model's, not hers, but the quibble was academic and whether Sharon believed it had lost relevance. Toward the end of September she had called Maquie up and told her she was worried about her mental health.

Maquie's appearance alone may have prompted this, but she knew colleagues were talking about her too, worrying because they felt compelled to, rallying charitably. She had lied about throwing up in a bathroom cubicle to two overeager interns who had conspired to care for her well-being and report it to Sharon. Her routine was getting noticed. It was inconvenient that other people used the office.

Maquie closed Sharon's message and left to get yogurt.

. . .

She walked through the streets and watched the pained faces of her peers, their eczema eyes and their raw lips, and imagined the anxieties, at once massive and banal, that dragged them around their days . . . the things they'd done wrong, the wrong things they'd said . . . and their indulging of the anxiety. The navel gouging. The mental hara-kiri. Offal in your left hand and scalpel in your right, then describe the meat's resistance to the blade. And on to the next organ. Work yourself through, leave no doubt unturned.

The anxiety, this desperate fad, Maquie had wanted nothing to do with it, but it had wanted her . . . she was part of the generation, just as susceptible to the inputs. So when the summer's itch had continued into autumn and the panic attacks had come daily; when ulcers had started lining the inside of her mouth like cabbage rows in a vegetable patch; when she had started feeling blanket fury—at her parents and brother, at her work and bosses, at her boyfriend and his new successes; when the vagaries of life had all accumulated and threatened to tear pieces of flesh from her, she had exited Oval Station one day, had taken inspiration from the implied salvation of St. Mark's Church, had seen how illogical it was not to fix a modern solution to the modern anxiety, and had resigned herself to sign up to Sike.

Why resist any longer? Why be so arrogant? Walking home, she had tried to remember an original reluctance. She couldn't remember specifying one.

There was the feeling that she didn't want to follow a hot trend. Perhaps she hadn't wanted to be owned by the fad—the anxiety *or* its solution.

Or there was the memory of the dinner party with Jonatan, and her recollection that she had looked down on his easy diplomacy, his guests' egos and their endless apologies for them. Perhaps she had preferred to be like Anik Xiang: indelicate, unapologetic.

Or there was the sense of exhaustion from too much introspection. Perhaps she dreaded a kind of trypophobia, triggered by all the small details of herself.

Or there was the impulse for discretion. How much of herself must she give up to these tech companies? And she thought back to the night she had spent with Jonatan in the kitchenette at the warehouse rave. Perhaps getting fingered by Sike once had felt like enough.

Or perhaps there was some fundamental desire to just live, unaided and naturally.

But more than any of these, she guessed she had been reluctant to use Sike because she had been reluctant to use Sike. She had become one of those people who, having been randomly allocated a side, stays at it, fights for it, dies for it, with no greater motivation than their own history on said side. This felt to her like a circular reference, and she was better than it. So on that October afternoon, two weeks ago now, she had canceled the day's late meeting, and she had made a cup of tamarind tea, and she had stood at her kitchen counter and gone to the app shop in her glasses, and she had clicked on Sike. It downloaded in seconds, and she opened it, feeling a double tap on her glasses temples.

Her first impression was that the purple of the app's walls felt drab in her lenses, and she wondered if she should turn up the color in her glasses. Then she noticed that, although the interface was generally clean and pragmatic, when she gave her email address and basic details, there was a menu button that should have been an inch higher . . . the spacing was off. Otherwise, it was an adequate experience, and she began giving all the permissions to the app to use her data and her glasses data and her phone data (etc. etc., so much data, and she chose to feel ambivalent about it), and then she began on the screening survey. The questions were basic, it asked her about her family, about her current mental health, about whether she'd ever felt suicidal, stuff like that, and she kept it light, so it really was a shock, quite a wrenching one, when in her lenses the words appeared,

>We are sorry, Sike is unable to accept you as a user; we recommend you find alternative means of therapy and support.

It had not occurred to her that this could happen. Panic had stirred in her chest, and she quickly recapped what she'd eaten that day.

She uninstalled the app, and went through the process again. She double-checked her email address, her name, and her phone number. She made sure the data upload was working, that she hadn't left anything out. She took the screening survey again, clear there was nothing problematic in it. Then she pressed submit.

The same words returned, and the panic rose, jutting its head at her. She sat down on the floor, her back to the sink's cupboard. Her tea spilled a little as she placed it on the linoleum.

She uninstalled the app again, and then took her phone out and reinstalled it there, pressing the buttons carefully and forcefully, going backward and forward, making sure the correct information was entered. She went through the screening survey again, changing her answers to the questions, straightlining the no's and high-scoring the positives. Then she pressed submit.

The same words came up again, the same message of rejection, the same apology that like a grinning finger pointed all the world at Maquie and confirmed her very worst fear: that she was sick, and permanently so.

The panic attack lasted several hours, as the day darkened and the cold crept across the floor of the kitchen to wrap itself around her fetal frame. She retched with no release, not bothering even to go to the bathroom and position herself over the seat. She sobbed with misery and frustration, with anger that this fear was happening to her—to *her*. She was the *strong* one. She was the brave, the independent. She pitied herself for the injustice. She pitied herself for the fall from grace. She pitied herself the way she pitied childhood heroes, the Mufasas and Aslans . . . stripped of their power, shaven and ridiculed, the lost fathers.

She had lain on the linoleum, and again and again the fear of permanence had washed over her. It was the fear that time was impotent, that this wouldn't heal.

Maquie reached the shop and picked out a yogurt. She breathed through her mouth as she paid, then she walked back to the office, faking a phone call by laughing into her glasses and nodding as she passed a group of colleagues heading for lunch.

When she got back into her room, she opened Sharon's message. She waited a minute and then replied saying, sorry, she'd been in calls, the Max meeting was set for this Friday, back in Clovelly at the inn.

Then she took the lid off the yogurt and began to eat.

. . .

After Sike's rejection, Maquie had spent a day or two trying to think herself out of the situation, spinning the events around in her head. There was another route: she could take the one recommendation Sike had divulged. She found an online psychotherapy platform and searched through a list of faces until she came across a clever-looking doctor called Katerina. She booked a fifteen-minute introduction call, and took it from her cocoon meeting room.

Katerina was Polish, polite, academic, and she suggested some resources, described a process, laid out a plan. But Maquie found that it sounded . . . passive. Hopeful. Most crucially, long-winded. She didn't have months to spare, she would lose her job before the effects trickled into her life. After twenty-one barren months at May-Perhaps, Maquie's contract was up for renewal in January, and she couldn't picture a positive outcome to the negotiations. More pressingly, it worried Maquie that she believed Sharon actually cared about her mental health—out of compassion, or out of concern for May-Perhaps's liability—and would use it as a reason to divorce Maquie from the company before her lack of performance demanded it. Maquie dreaded nothing more than this. Until her health was significantly improved, until she could make it at least a day without an attack and a week without emesis, leaving May-Perhaps would be a death sentence.

So she had come up with a different plan, one she'd put into motion when she'd gone to see Sharon for their monthly meeting.

For a while after Jonatan's dinner party, she had analyzed the aesthetics of telling Sharon and Kyle about the partnership between Sike and Quantum Theater. It reflected well on Maquie to be at parties with people like Jonatan, gathering non-public information like this, but she had seen it as more favorable to retain the knowledge. Above all, it was her—or, it was her model—that had rejected Quantum Theater as a prospect, and the Sike tie-up suggested forcibly that this was an error. It would have been an own goal to deliver the news of the error.

However, the news had a use-by date: Maquie worried that Sharon and Kyle had heard rumors of the deal, and she knew the value of her knowledge confirming it would expire when the deal was made public. Her plan consisted mainly of telling Sharon about the deal, and then lying to her about two things.

The first lie was that her model had greenlighted Quantum Theater for investment. This lie was pretty pure, the pentagon on the model's interface had stayed resolutely gray, even with information on the Sike deal factored in. But the lie was hardly damaging. Assuming her model worked, so what if Quantum Theater turned out not to be the next Sike? Quantum Theater was still destined for greatness, and five years from now when it was great but not preeminent, Sharon and Kyle could quench their disappointment with a huge return on investment. Finally, the lie was necessary. She was nothing without the clout of her model. Her model was findless, its algorithms barren, but she needed it.

The second lie was that she was using Sike.

Maquie had gone to Sharon's large double house in the oasis square to spin the lies. She had worn a bright mustard sweater, heavy foundation, light mascara, and red lipstick. Kyle was in Canada, visiting family, and when Sharon opened the door, Maquie beamed brightly through the makeup, trusting that it was doing its work, that it wouldn't crack.

Sharon was surprised at her appearance.

"Oh," she said with warmth.

And Maquie replied with a decompressive "hey," smiling up at her boss like the old Maquie. She smiled with her lips closed and her eyes relaxed, and already she felt herself settling into character as though she had stepped on stage, playing a reprised role.

She reached a hand over to Sharon's arm, and Sharon gave a smaller, happier "Oh."

"I've got stuff to tell you," Maquie said, and smiled again.

Inside her mouth, she tongued fresh ulcers.

Within the confines of her lies, Maquie spilled a lot of herself out into Sharon's home, and it felt cathartic even without the safety rope of truth to hold on to. They sat on one of the peach sofas, bottles of cardamom kombucha condensing on their knees, and discussed Sike. Sharon had been an early user, and Kyle had started two years ago.

"I don't bring it up so much," Sharon said, "because I don't want to be one of those people who peer-pressures others into mental health solutions, and you never fully know who is and isn't using . . ."

She shook her head.

". . . but it really is the only way to complete one's character arc."

"Yeah," Maquie said, making her eyes wide and then troubled, then glancing away from the sofa to the floor. "Like, it makes me remember that we're all children, Sharon. We're all children, and it makes me think, maybe . . . maybe with Sike we will one day brush off the scars of our parents, of our nurture . . . maybe one day we will live just at the level of our nature. You know?"

She looked back at Sharon. She'd learned well from other Sike users, this type of thing juiced them up. Sharon was a bit teary.

"You've been through a lot," she said.

Maquie nodded thoughtfully in silence.

They moved on to Quantum Theater, Maquie broaching the subject with a new tone and the words, "Ok, some big news."

She explained Jonatan's dinner party, fudging the dates a little, and explained the news of the Sike deal. Then she calmly lied about giving the news of the deal to her model, and the model's consequent greenlighting of Quantum Theater. When she was finished, Sharon said quickly, "But wouldn't the model have predicted the Sike deal already?"

Maquie had expected the question.

"It would have," Maquie said. "But it's timing that's important here."

"How so?"

"Well, the model would have factored in the likelihood of the Sike deal, but in a roundabout way it would have predicted the *knowledge* of the deal to emerge later."

Sharon was clever, but prediction wasn't her field.

"Later than now?"

"Later than over wine at a drinks party. Obviously the model couldn't predict my presence at a drinks party with Max and Jonatan, and our early knowledge of the deal."

"Why does that matter though?"

Maquie smiled. "Because our *early* knowledge of the deal means we can insist on *investing early*. With the Sike deal, Quantum Theater's prospects have changed enough that they should accept new investment to manage the growth. The Sike deal isn't enough on its own to make Quantum Theater big, it's our early investment off the back of our early knowledge of the deal that will have a profound early effect on the growth of Quantum Theater. An exponential early effect, one that the model is saying matters hugely."

Sharon was thinking hard. She held her mouth open, as you might expect of someone contemplating predetermination. Maquie walked a tight line, she needed to communicate a loophole in her model's workings while not implying its failure. Her lie was necessarily therefore rich and desirable, deeply flattering to Sharon and May-Perhaps, positioning them as gods.

Maquie sat back. "Had we found out about the deal later, the door to this exponential effect might have been shut. Timing, Sharon, is key."

Sharon's mouth closed.

"This, Maquie," she said, "this is exciting. Do we have time, is the door still open? Will they let us invest?"

"Well, their last round closed in February with 42 million at a valuation of 800. Max said they weren't planning another round for a year at least. But there is still a door, and I think it *can* be opened. Max likes money, obviously. And optically, it's fine for them to have another round of investment this year, especially if their outlook has significantly changed, as the Sike deal confirms it has."

Sharon nodded slowly, lips pointing.

"Max also likes my model, he brought it up again at Jonatan's, he called it 'the future.' And my model tells him that he should take our money."

And, Maquie thought, he also likes me. The newly Siked Max had kept his eyes on her at the party, and he'd grinned with pleasure when she'd asked him questions. He had held her elbow at one point until she quietly removed it from his grasp.

"Have you thought about how much?" Sharon said.

"Yes. It works out at 305."

Sharon nodded.

Maquie had impressed people before, she knew the signs, and she looked at Sharon's face and saw that her mouth had the hesitant turnups of someone embarrassed to display their excitement. Her eyes twitched, the opportunities tumbling around behind them.

"This is good," Sharon said. "This is exciting. We must get this slot, Maquie."

Maquie nodded.

"We need to invest in Quantum Theater. This is it. Quantum cybersecurity is what we're here for. Open that door. Can you do that, Maquie?"

Maquie had said yes, and waited for a North American corroboration of moment.

"Good. Let's bring it home."

But Sharon hadn't ended the pep talk there.

Maquie had been floating on a wave of achievement, proud of her successful lies and acts of persuasion and turning fortunes, excited to discard the interlocking concerns of her model's performance, Sharon's faith, the missed Quantum Theater opportunity . . . Finishing her cardamom kombucha and placing the bottle on the crystal coffee table, getting up from the peach sofa and picking up her jacket, Maquie had thought of freedom, of a future at May-Perhaps, of a return to peace and a ladder out of the abyss. She had thought of accolades. She had walked lightly toward the front door, and hadn't expected to lose all this lightness before leaving the house.

As they crossed the sitting room, Sharon paused by the Japanese Disney poster of *Basil The Great Mouse Detective*, the one that focused on the role of the young girl mouse, Olivia.

"Perspective, Maquie."

"Yes." Maquie replied.

"How often does this not happen?! The girl getting her credit."

Maquie hummed agreement.

"Look over there," Sharon said. She pointed to a small embroidered plaque sitting on a sideboard. Ruth Bader Ginsburg's face was knitted above two lines of text. "I bought that at a souvenir stall in Washington, DC. Can you read the words?"

Maquie looked. It was the famous line.

I ask no favor for my sex.
All I ask of our brethren is that they take their feet off our necks.

"Great, isn't it," Sharon said. "Ruth was quoting Sarah Grimké. What a pair of ladies!"

Maquie nodded politely.

"It's a shame, though," Sharon said. "They only got it half right."

Maquie looked at Sharon.

"It isn't always a foot, Maquie, often it's a hand. And it's grasping from below."

She began chewing a thumbnail, staring at the poster. She said, "What do you think of Kyle?"

The question surprised Maquie, and she didn't know how to answer.

"I'll help you out," said Sharon, "he's stupid."

Maquie opened her mouth to protest, but Sharon continued, looking at the poster as she spoke.

"Yes, he's stupid. Drowning. He was in ad sales when we met. He was terrible, he sold one contract, a piffling sportswear account. I think he has something seriously wrong with his brain . . . like a child or something, arrested development."

She spoke as though Maquie wasn't there, chewing her thumbnail and looking up at the poster to the cartoon mouse's face.

"Dyslexia plus-plus. Stupid. But I needed a male cofounder, things were even worse back then."

"You taught him, though," Maquie said. "You taught him how to run the business?"

"Hm?" Sharon glanced at her. "No. He stayed stupid. But he serves his purpose. He gives my companies what they would fail without. Early on, Maquie, you see, I stepped outside the building and I looked back in, and I saw it plainly: You want to get money? You want to give money? Get a male. I use his maleness. That's how I navigate it."

And now she turned her eyes from the poster, watched Maquie, and Maquie became aware of an ancient danger lurking around them in the room. It was the danger you felt in any room with any person, when you realized that the two of you were alone and that the other person had a will.

"You know what I'm talking about, Maquie," Sharon said. "You see it from the outside as well. You step outside the building and you look in on them all. And then you walk around the side, and you go through another door. It's why I put extra faith in you, ever since you slept with Max, that first time you met him."

Maquie's jaw stiffened.

"When we heard about that, Kyle was affronted, he said it was unprofessional, that we shouldn't have people like you in the company. But I vehemently disagreed. I reminded him that I was no different. Wasn't I sleeping with him for gain?"

Maquie's face burned beneath her makeup. Sharon turned to face her, her eyes like planets, and put her hand on Maquie's shoulder.

"We know what we need to do, don't we, Maquie? We know we are outsiders. We know our freedoms, and we know how to exploit them. We know how to lie. We know how to navigate men. If we need to get something, if we have to *open a door*, Maquie, we know what to do. Don't we? We know what to do."

Maquie had only been able to nod. She had left her head and focused on the pressure of Sharon's hand on her shoulder, gripping the bone while pushing toward the door.

Maquie finished scraping the yogurt pot and licked the spoon. She had two days until she would take the train to Clovelly, where she would meet Max and try to persuade him to take May-Perhaps's money. She felt nervous about the challenge but she felt nihilistic too.

So what? she thought.

So what if I succeed, so what if I fail. So what if I'm accepted, so what if I'm rejected. So what if Sharon's right—so what if life is always lived outside, always with a scheme, always at an angle. So what if I'm not free.

And she contemplated a hand, grasping at her neck from below. She contemplated Daniel and she contemplated Adrian, and an idea began to form, but she left it for now, putting on the Indonesian beach sounds, opening a report.

* * *

Maquie arrived in Clovelly after lunch and met Max in the bar of the Red Lion, and she saw immediately that he would reject the May-Perhaps offer.

They went up to the bedroom office she had slept in almost a year ago, Max visibly excited. He fidgeted with a pen, pushed his hair around, and Maquie made the formal offer of investment. She had brought no presentation, no documents, she simply told Max about her model greenlighting his company, and his eyes did glaze over, she was sure of that. Like Sharon, he didn't ask to see the model or its green pentagon, and Maquie registered the peculiar trust they both had for her as gatekeeper. She might have felt proud of the trust if it hadn't seemed so thirsty.

She gave Max the investment number easily, and explained how they assumed it would be distributed but assured him they wouldn't micromanage. And he laughed, surprised, and said thank you, and she saw gratitude in his face.

But then he trailed off. He said it was appealing, but . . . it wasn't so easy. He said when the Sike deal was formalized, there had been discussions of another raise, but the board had said no. They had enough capital, more could only hurt. He had taken it to the board again this week, he had assumed that was why Maquie was coming. He had mentioned her model. The board had stayed firm. The door was closed. Maybe in a year . . .

She didn't believe Max couldn't persuade the board. She steeled herself (for what?), and said, "I'm surprised. Earlier in the year you hoped there was interest. Here it is. Here's the interest you were looking for."

She looked him hard in the eyes. He met her eyes for a second, but then withdrew. He looked at his laptop, then gave another apology. He changed the topic, brought up the Sike partnership again. There were challenges, but the project was progressing well. He told her about their expansion in the town, their new office units, told her she could have a tour later. He ordered more coffee, spoke about recruitment. Maquie cut him off, looked him in the eye again, said,

"Max. The door can't be closed. Our investment takes you to explosion. You need to speak to the board."

A secretary walked in.

"Let's talk about it later," Max said. "You're joining for dinner?"

She nodded, and managed to smile.

. . .

The fish was fat, the layers sliding off each other with a pull of her fork tine. The menu had advertised "flaky," but this was a slide. The batter splintered.

The pub lacked space, it was full of loud Quantum Theater staff in bright white T-shirts with "QT" printed large on their backs. Max said the company booked the back dining room of the Red Lion every Friday night, for anyone staying in the village over the weekend, and the current banquet atmosphere was normal. They had brought in their own chef, built a make-shift kitchen; Quantum Theater now had permanent rental of all the bed-rooms in the pub, keeping two spare for guests, and they had three more B&Bs up the hill, as well as three houses hired from locals. They had built a bank of shipping container offices on the bluff to the north of the village, and they had rented space at the visitor center by the top of the harbor path. They had named core algorithms after local sights: Mount Pleasant, Hobby Drive, Slerra Hill. And they had added Clovelly Waterfall to their website banner, and taken the staff photo in front of Gaffer's Rock. Max said they had offices being fitted in London, closer to the quantum hardware, and their days in the village were numbered. They were teetering on unpopular-ity and space was running out . . .

". . . but I'll flog the culture horse for as long as possible. People will sing about our origins here for decades."

The mood was dorm-like. As they sat down to dinner, Max had insisted on ordering oysters for the table, and some of the engineers had groaned like schoolchildren.

"Always oysters," one cried. "Give us fucking beef!"

A cheer. Then a conversation about the aphrodisiacal nature of oysters, and Max shouted, "Unproven," and Maquie felt the nausea surge. Max grinned at her a lot, touched her arm.

"I'm very excited!" he said, randomly.

The waiters brought wood-handled shucking knives, short with symmetri-cal blades, and showed how to prepare the oysters. The engineers were young, mostly men, and mostly not from the UK (the beef advocate was from Chile, a researcher whose work on autonomous bidding agents Maquie had heard of). In another situation, a situation far enough away that the words that came to her were "in another life," Maquie considered that she could have en-joyed the company of the QT team. She saw them as immature, their moods were too distinct and they lacked consistency. But they were intelligent, too, they had the art of discussion and weren't afraid to be serious. In a childlike way, they were also kind.

Maquie tined layers of fish from each other and noted the similarity in appearance between oysters and ulcers. She tried not to think of the food as ammunition for later vomiting. "Cannon fodder" was a kenning. But it didn't mean food as ammunition, it meant humans as food.

When dessert was being ordered, she escaped the dining room and the pub, and made it onto the empty pier. The night was cold, and the farther she got from the golden light of the pub, the colder it felt and the better it felt. Oysters don't smell, they taste, but the fish had smelled, and the beer had smelled. She had been stabbing her thigh through her jeans with one of the oyster knives, using the pain to distract from the nausea. She was glad to be out in the sea air, close to the creaking boats she had once laughed at, all that time ago before the anxiety, before she had met Adrian.

Adrian had walked her to the Underground that morning, and when they said goodbye he had grown quiet, pulling away from her and slumping against the tiled wall of the station. She watched him, then she moved in front of him, trying to hug him, trying to press herself into him, because she had felt it too, a kind of foregone conclusion, with no clarity on what that conclusion was. It was as if something unpassable was ahead of them, a wall in their future.

On the Clovelly pier, she looked out at the sea, its water heavy in the dark. She didn't feel able to picture the future anymore. She would travel to Japan with Adrian next week, and she couldn't picture the plane or the hotel or Tokyo. She had once been able to visualize the days stretching ahead of her, and the days had been filled with success. But now she saw nothing. She guessed there would be failure. She guessed that she was ill, critically, and her illness was her failure, and the symptoms would continue, she would fail again, one way or another.

She shivered, and looked up. The sound of the water had been interrupted by the door of the pub, out of which came laughter and a few Quantum Theater engineers, including the Chilean. He had something in his hand, what appeared to be an oyster, and to loud cheering he launched it as far as he could into the nighttime sea. He turned to face the pub, holding two fists in the air, and they clapped him back inside, reentering with him, leaving in their wake just the single figure of Max, who looked down the pier to Maquie. He began walking toward her.

Maquie turned away, looking to where the boats creaked. The tide was in and the boats floated up and down. They bobbed there as though animated, like livestock in a dark field. They creaked, and sucked at the water, and a chain attached to one of them scraped. She watched them move, carried her eyes over their wooden hulls, the bright buoys at their sides, and soon, finally, she became aware of a feeling that, far down inside of her, seemed to be scratching its way up into her consciousness.

It was a primitive feeling, and a familiar one, a useless old friend that had been abroad for so long, or hiding, sleeping in a small box inside her perhaps, and now was waking up.

She smiled.

The old feeling grew.

Then she laughed softly. Nothing vocal, only breath.

The inadvertent ridiculousness of life amused her. Boats and fishing, these were ridiculous. A harbor village taken over by engineers, this was ridiculous. She looked down at the boats, a smile across her face. Sharon and Kyle, and Kyle's stupidity. Sharon's kennings, Sharon's scheming. Adrian, his rap. Sophie and Stutter. Fumi and Ulf. Her, Maquie. Her in Clovelly. Her fear, her lies. Quantum Theater and Max. And the idea that had been floated by Sharon—or had Maquie been the one to float it? Or Adrian?— the idea that she might persuade Max to take their investment, and that she might use sex to do it.

She laughed again, a pleasant feeling. It was the inadvertent and ridiculous winding and contorting of life that amused Maquie. She had the sudden urge to call Sharon up, ask how it was meant to happen. Sorry, Maquie would say, can we just talk through tactics again? I sort of pour honey in his ear, then puppet him? Like a fairytale witch. Or I sleep with him, and hint at some future credit line of sleeping with him, and he calls the board, gluey-eyed, and he tells them, change of plan, and they all say, umm, ah, unconventional, but yes, we'll accept the money . . . Was that it?

No, Sharon would say, no fuck is that good. You need to threaten him. Take an oyster knife, take it to his room, get his trousers down. Kiss the bulge in his pants then put the knife to it, and pierce the shaft. You want to see blood. Keep the knife there and have him write an email to his board insisting on the investment. Have him threaten departure. Watch him click send. Then withdraw the knife, tap-tap it on his knee. Say thank you.

Maquie laughed once more, softly into the wind. It was all ridiculous. She felt tears come, but they were tears of relief. She looked down the pier, Max was nearly with her.

She blinked her eyes and relaxed her throat, and Max arrived, saying hi, and he stood beside her facing the water, his shoulders hunched in the cold air. For a while they were silent, watching the boats, listening to the wind.

And then, slowly, Maquie became aware of Max's hand, reaching through the air for hers, trying to draw it out of her coat pocket. She let her hand be drawn, feeling Max's cold fingers, and had an image of two children holding hands in a playground. There was a colossal innocence to Max, and she felt the gaps in his education, the missing chunks of life. She pulled her hand back.

"No, Max," she said. "I'm sorry."

He put his hand back in his pocket, still looking at the water.

"If we took your investment?" he said.

She shook her head. "Still no."

"You're only here for the investment," he said.

She looked at him, amused that he might be sulking.

"I'm not here for anything," she said. And she patted him on the shoulder. "Let's head back."

They reached the pub and Maquie said goodnight to Max, leaving him by himself in the empty reception area at the foot of the stairs. He held his head down, and when she looked back Maquie thought she saw the insides of his glass lenses turn purple. She walked up the stairs and turned right at the top of the staircase into her room. She locked the door, then she brushed her teeth and climbed into her bed and slept until just after 5:30 A.M.

When she woke, she lay on her side in bed, watching the darkness outside turn into the half-light of dawn as thoughts of Adrian rushed into her mind, flooding it and seeming to spill down into her chest. She felt relief that she was safe, that she had done nothing wrong, as though sleeping with Max could really have happened, as though he had been a cliff edge she had spotted at the last moment. And the relief mixed with a longing for Adrian. She missed Adrian, she felt desperate to be with him. It had been almost exactly a year since they'd met.

She thought about reaching for her glasses to message him, but resisted. Instead she lay with the emotions and thought about Adrian and their year together and tried—a little grandly but in a piecemeal way . . . half-earnest, half-ironic, aware of the futility of the task—to work out if this was really it, was this what love was?

She watched the sky and felt she could see love too clearly as a series of cynicisms. Love was just the backstage tour of other people, the relief of finding turmoil there (love was small, vain lies). Love was a pregnant not-knowing between a threat of failure and a hope of success. Love was a mutual and transparent fantasy (Adrian's line). Love was the lover's past. Love was imagery assigned to low-body blood surges (love was Betty Boop stirring a cauldron). Maquie's eyes raked the coastline, and love was quick bumps of ecstasy. Love was a tolerance to dichotomy. Love could be coincidence or god. Love seemed to be, as the trees gained definition, a balancing out: your flaw for their strength, their fear for your confidence. She saw the crests of waves, and love was a strange pursuit. Love was equally poetic and practical. Love was mentioned suspiciously rarely by psychologists (what were they hiding?). Love was not a kenning. Love was not a foot on the neck. Love might be a hand from below. Love pulled you inside the building. She had thought love was a single fact, a single point of irrefutable evidence given up front in favor of the other person. Love was instead many things, even cynical things, pieced together in retrospect and only then built into a whole. Love was therefore hopeful, optimistic. Love was a fishing boat, it was ridiculous. She heard seagulls. But love was something she wanted. Why? Because love had been marketed to her as the antithesis of fear, and she had believed the marketing.

The marketing, she guessed now, was wrong. Find another reason to fall in love, it does little to relieve fear. The two are compatible, they're friends.

A seagull twisted over the trees. She and Adrian loved and they feared. They feared things that never materialized.

Well . . . for her they had materialized. Her fear of failure? She had failed. Compellingly. And so the fear dwindled, didn't it? She could laugh. Last night she had laughed at boats.

But Adrian? Yesterday he was afraid she would cheat on him, he was scared of losing her. But his fear had failed to materialize. She resented his suspicion but, sensing clarity in the dark room, she also asked herself what she had ever done to help him.

And piece by piece, she thought up another plan. She thought up another lie, one that might help Adrian.

When she could make out the branches of the trees of the coast, Maquie got out of bed and got dressed. Then she called a taxi and walked up the village path to meet it.

12.

The hotel that GASTA booked for us was on the thirty-eighth floor of a building that was silver, gray, black, or blue, depending on the time of day we came up to it. The hotel overlooked a business and shopping district called Nihonbashi, named after a bridge that crossed the river there. The river wasn't visible from the windows of the hotel, because about fifty feet above the water's surface ran the Inner Circular Route C1 of the Shuto, a raised car expressway that mimicked and perfectly masked the river's curves.

I thought that separating water from sky with tarmac was a good metaphor for something, but I didn't mention it, I don't know why. Maybe I thought it was a bit Joni Mitchell. But as we stood looking down at the concrete river from the thirty-eighth floor check-in desk, Maquie called out the river's masking to the concierge and said, "Nice metaphor," and the concierge laughed with a kind of collaborative cynicism. She told Maquie in Japanese, and Maquie translated for me, that the expressway was soon to be moved underground. The concierge, whose name was Risa, then turned to me and giggled again, and she said in English, in a Disneyland voice, "You're in the best hotel in Tokyo. It's a fact."

I smiled. But inside I was accusing Maquie of stealing my metaphor. It was a virtual accusation, thrown with the eyes. Sullen and vacuous. I found its vacuousness embarrassing, and I caught myself and tried to move back into a positive frame of mind. I remembered that I had cleared the pain of Maquie cheating on me. I could get on with things.

. . .

It's true that I was fixating on details a bit. I can tell you that Risa the concierge had a mole on the back of her left earlobe, and that the hotel's lift smelled of pine and the lights brightened as it got higher. The details were vivid and overexposed. After we dropped our bags, we explored the hotel's ground and basement floors and came across a shop that sold expensive out-of-season fruit. Melons, grapes, apples, strawberries. Think smartphone prices, not supermarket ones. I bought a box of forty cherries for the Japanese yen equivalent of £153, and I called it impulse, but Maquie called it curiosity, but it was probably a combination of both alongside probably also a notion that one should return from Tokyo with "stories," which was probably itself a kind of non-extreme naive insecurity. I can tell you how they tasted, they tasted of cherry; we agreed that this was the ultimate compliment. Cherry exemplified, the flavor-dictionary definition of cherry; cherrylike and cherryish, cherryful. We sat on the edge of our made hotel bed eating—only three or four for now—taut marbles of perfectly cherry-colored cherry flesh, and I commented that it was a shame that cherries hadn't evolved larger, peach or plum sized, and Maquie commented that our awareness of the cherry flavor we found so exactly reproduced in our mouths must have been distilled from a lifetime of eating real and (more profound, I thought) synthetic cherries and cherry products.

We followed the cherries with lunch at the hotel's pizza restaurant, and we each had a glass of Falanghina that tasted like the smell of pencil shavings; then a nap, followed by sex, during which at one point Maquie thought she might cry. Then a walk through chalk-dry streets to dinner at a bar-cum-library that served heavy-on-the-cumin curries. Then home again, and sex again, and this time Maquie did cry . . . her face crumpled and she covered her eyes with one hand, held mine with the other.

There was stuff to unpack, maybe I admitted that much. But I think I was telling myself that it was about 90 percent jet lag driving our lift-ride accusations and mid-coital crying. I had cleared the pain of Maquie cheating on me with Max, and I thought we could just get on with things.

. . .

Maquie had told me about the cheating right when the wheels left the runway at Heathrow, which felt pretty Gestapo. The fasten-seatbelt sign was on and there was a one-million-watt reading light shining in my eyes.

"Adrian, I have some bad news, and I think you know what it is," she said. "You should know that I truly regret it. And I love you. And it won't happen again."

I felt terrified. Our seats faced each other diagonally, there was a divider screen between us. She said, "When I tell you, please turn on Sike and turn up the resolution a bit. I'm going to tell you the bad news, then I'm going to put up this screen, then I'm going to let Sike help you."

Then, boom: it happened, she slept with Max so he would take their investment.

I took the news headless, in sickly adrenaline, and afterward I kidded myself that I'd known what she was going to say. I didn't feel like Sike, which had already raised a lilac dot in my lens, but after I'd called Maquie a liar, crushed a mini Coke can, and tried to clarify how "far" they'd gone (first three stages of grief, like clockwork), I brought up Sike and the first thing it said was,

>I'm not able to analyze other people, Adrian, only you.

This felt a bit rough, I thought it was a glitch. I said "Irrelevant," quite loudly, and then I turned the resolution up and made my glasses opaque, and sat in my "calm place," which is the background to my grandmother's favorite painting, a self-portrait by Kay Sage, painted after her husband died. It's not meant to be a "calm place," the countryside is pretty bitter, but somehow it's calming to me.

For a lot of that journey, I sat next to Kay in the virtual landscape, looking out on it all, and Sike and I spent hours discussing all the stuff you can imagine. I drank six bloody marys but I was mainly ok. I believed Sike when it said it wasn't my fault that Maquie had cheated. I had believed Maquie when she said she loved me, that she wouldn't do it again. Sike fast-tracked me into accepting that there were reasons it wouldn't all be Maquie's fault either. I knew she'd been under a lot of pressure, having a bad time of life, and Sharon sounded pretty ghoulish, her company was a mess.

Mostly, I wanted to fight Max. I'd never fought before, but I thought I could. I wanted to fight him physically, but I also fantasized about embarrassing him publicly. I would do my track with Nunchi and blow up. I would get famous and earn a load of cash, and then I would pull Max's pants down on TV . . . my second album comes out and Graham Norton is asking me about what I do with my money, and I say invest because my wife is an investor, and Graham says, any tips, and I say, yeah, steer clear of the snake-oil sellers posing as quantum security guys, and I wink and Graham croons and a picture of Max flashes up, and the studio audience falls about the place.

That type of fighting seemed to suit me.

I was ok otherwise. When you have Sike on high resolution you can clear storms pretty fast. I wasn't up for a film, so I watched some *Friends* episodes and cried at the denouements. Then I did a Sike module on adultery edited by Esther Perel. Then I played this video that I sometimes watch if I'm worried I might be getting a bit incel, it's the one of Joan Baez and Earl Scruggs where Baez sings "It Ain't Me Babe" while cradling her infant son. Then I slept a bit.

I woke up in Tokyo and could smile at Maquie. I told her no doubt there were things to discuss. No doubt. But we'd be ok. She smiled and just told me to take my time.

It hadn't worked in the end, sleeping with Max, he hadn't let them invest. Maquie said she'd probably have to leave May-Perhaps. I was kind of amazed at the screw-up, Maquie didn't usually make mistakes.

* * *

The format had changed, Furusawa and the producers wanted us to work mornings and afternoons together in the studio, so there were fewer window-ledge hours for me. Ken was picking me up from the hotel each day after breakfast, which we usually ate with, or near to, Jonatan. He was also in Tokyo, and he'd asked us our hotel and booked into the same one. With Sike for Countries—or SfC, they were calling it—he was doing the psychoanalyzing of Japan, understanding "where it was," and they had begun working out how to use the insights to influence the country. SfC wanted to understand the country (or, in other cases, the city, sports team, customer group, whatever), and then find ways to influence it with messaging or nudges, anything to help guide the group. Music was an obvious format for the nudges, songs could change a nation's thinking. Like with Sam Cooke, Nina Simone, Dylan. One breakfast, Jonatan offered me a job, he said I could come and advise. They needed a lyricist.

Maquie didn't engage much with Jonatan at the breakfasts, which I found surprising. She just sipped coffee and stared out at Tokyo. Maybe she was angry about Sike rejecting her, I don't know. When I left her to meet Ken and go to work, she would wander off, and often I saw her take magazines from the rack in the lounge and slump onto one of the sofas.

On our fifth day there, I missed breakfast because we needed to go out of town for a photo shoot in the mountains. I wasn't needed, but Furusawa wanted me there. Things are all together in Japan. Ken was downstairs at five, by which point Maquie and I were awake already, watching the red roof lights. I kissed her goodbye and told her not to sleep with Bill Murray, but she didn't laugh.

The location for the shoot was a river at the base of a mountain near Tokyo, near a town called Hadano, and a van came to pick us up. There were six of us in the van, including Nunchi, and we sat side by side in our winter coats watching Tokyo light up. I watched the suburbs as we drove out through them, my glasses translating the names of shops like Yamamoto Chicken, Edanishi Hardware, a few KFCs. Nunchi had brought me some vitamins for my jet lag, and at one point he told Ken I looked sad, and Ken translated. I just laughed and shook my head, I didn't think I was sad.

When we arrived, Furusawa was already there, looking tired and bleary in a black G-Wagon (there are a lot of those in Tokyo, a lot of macho cars . . . SfC should look into that). He was sitting with the lead producer and I wanted to speak to them, I hadn't heard yet about doing a feature. A month before flying to Tokyo, I'd emailed Furusawa directly about it, asking if it was a consideration, but I'd had no reply.

Nunchi hadn't confirmed anything either, I'd brought it up once very casually on our first day in the studio and he had clapped and said, "Ahh, that would be the best thing!"

But we hadn't discussed further. I didn't want to hassle him, he was carrying so much already. I thought that I would find my time, and I settled with the others to watch the shoot.

An hour later, Nunchi was in a loose pair of underwear with pink hearts on them, shivering in the river, the water up to his shins. He was pleading with Sachiko, the photographer, to hurry up, both of them laughing. We laughed too. I could laugh, I didn't feel sad.

Behind Nunchi, the forest was chocolate thick, green, and just at the edge of the forest was a campsite with some public bathrooms. I left the river and went up to them, and they were maybe the only dirty place I saw in all Japan. There was dirt you didn't mind, like leaves and spider webs and stuff, but there were also cans and bottles and tissues, and cigarette butts that stained the puddles and gave off a sweet smell, just detectable over the smell of sewer. It was awful, the worst piss ever.

As I came out, Furusawa was coming in. He wasn't looking for a chat, he didn't want to stop. But I just asked him straight out.

"Ah," I said. "Quick question."

He looked pained, maybe he already smelled the bathrooms, but I stood my ground.

"Any news on the feature? There's been discussion about me doing one," I said. "On the fashion track."

He looked at me, his pig eyes blinking.

"What?" He had a faint smile.

"The fashion track we wrote, we've been speaking about me rapping one of the verses for the album. Alongside Nunchi."

He turned to face me properly. He looked bewildered, and I already felt angry, even before we'd gone through it all. He acted bewildered to stuff he didn't like, kind of a bemused confusion as though you were fanciful or mad for bringing it up. It was how he demonstrated his brain power: he spoke slowly in his twangy American accent and squinted his eyes and looked skeptical that the conversation could even be happening.

"You want to be on a song?" he said. Bewildered, confused.

I stammered for a while about how I'd been discussing it with Nunchi, how I'd sent an email, how I thought it was important for the album. They needed a Western hook, I said, I was the missing link to the album. But he just replied, "Why?" and I had no answer inside me that didn't sound arrogant, colonialist, foolish. Sike put a lilac dot into my lens and flashed the word "KIP."

"Actually, uh, Adrian . . . we hired you to ghostwrite. We didn't hire you as a voice."

"I know, but things develop, don't they."

"Do," bemused, "they?"

KIP, KIP, KIP, went Sike.

"Yeah."

"How? How did things develop?"

My thoughts wouldn't produce an answer and, with shame, I noticed my esophagus tightening, a wet sponge rising up the back of my neck. With this sensation came the sudden image of my father telling me off when I was eight—I had no specific memory of what I'd done to upset him, just that I'd fled outside onto our thin strip of patio and crouched down to hide and sob. Furusawa was watching me, and I was watching myself crouch there on the patio, all those years ago, and I remembered with strange specificity that my tears had dripped past my knees onto the edge of a concrete flagstone, and that I had shuffled backward a bit to see if I could get the tears to land in the crack between that flagstone and the one I stood on. I landed one or two tears and watched them soak into the mud of the crack. It was a meaningless game, like spinning coins or kicking stones, and the nothing victory of landing my tears in the crack had no effect on my sobbing, which was growing in proportion to the pity I felt for myself. I pitied my crouching form and I pitied my shame. I could hear Dad looking for me inside, calling my name apologetically, but I was too ashamed to reveal myself, and I sobbed more as I recognized this, and more tears fell. And as I began to worry about whether Furusawa would hear the emotion in my voice, I reflected that my sadness had often been like that: aware enough to angle my tears, driven mostly by a sympathy for myself.

The lilac dot pulsed. KIP, went Sike across my vision. Knowledge is power, but what knowledge did I have?

I think Furusawa did notice I was upset, and he relaxed his skepticism a bit. He stepped back and adjusted his glasses. But he couldn't help wincing when I said in a quiet voice, "I thought . . . because Nunchi and I rapped together in that karaoke booth."

I said it and I winced too. I realized instantly how ridiculous it sounded—but when your chances are sinking away from you, your unconscious brain will throw any old thing, a safety pin on a thread even, to try to hook them.

"Uh . . . listen," Furusawa said. "I think you have a good voice, but you are unknown. We're not trying to launch your name, Adrian, we're trying to launch Nunchi's."

"I can help," I said, almost in a whisper.

"We are already grateful for your help," he said. And he nodded and walked off.

When I returned to the group, everyone was quiet. Perhaps they had known what had happened, it may have all been obvious. Things are all together in Japan. It was conceivable they even shared some of my disappointment, and I didn't resent them, but I didn't want them to know how I felt, so I didn't try talking, I just sat by myself and drank a coffee. Nunchi didn't call me sad again.

The weather was turning, but soon the mood of the group picked up. Nunchi had a phobia of insects and couldn't go into the bathrooms, and everyone was laughing at that a bit, it was kind of sweet. Nunchi demanded that I help, and I began to feel better. I helped to clear a path for Nunchi, getting rid of the webs, and Ken and I kept watch for spiders while Nunchi peed.

I could laugh at this stuff.

* * *

The recording went fine. We got to the final day and it was all complete, they'd been meticulous. Nunchi didn't need loads of takes, but he did them anyway, so the editing would go ok, I thought.

Ken invited us to dinner with his wife. I couldn't believe that he was already married. Ken! We went to a small yakitori place, and Ken's wife was very funny, she made fun of Ken and called him out on all this stuff. She said he was too nice, he needed more eggs, and Ken just laughed. She had good English too, but Maquie spoke to her lots in Japanese, and I watched Maquie, feeling kind of proud, feeling all the old feelings of awe and respect. She was so calm, so at ease. Maquie sat down in any situation and the world readjusted itself. Furniture folded around her.

At least, I used to think that. We once sat listening to a Van Morrison track called "Someone Like You," and I was tapping the beat on her chest, thinking "someone like *you*," over and over. It was corny of course, but I wasn't saying it out loud, just thinking it in that way you sometimes allow yourself, and I wondered whether she was thinking it too. I doubted it, I thought maybe I was another thing that folded itself around her. I guessed that I didn't faze her. I knew you could never know . . . even with the person you were sitting next to, the person in your arms. You could get right up to them, a centimeter away from their head, where all the consciousness and the self was happening . . . you could get a centimeter away, and still know nothing. You could only guess, and I guessed that I didn't move Maquie.

But now I was less sure about Maquie's imperviousness. At dinner with Ken, we drank sake and then a spirit from the south called awamori. I read a Sike dot in the bathroom, it was saying that I was drinking more than usual, I had been all week. On the way home, I was slurring but I told Maquie about feeling all this awe and respect for her, and she took it badly.

"Maybe it's misplaced," she said. "Maybe you need to place your awe and your respect elsewhere."

She was annoyed. She had a shower and dried her hair, and when she was finished she didn't reach down to unplug the hotel's hairdryer, she just yanked at the cord. I lay on the bed watching. The cord didn't come, so she pulled again, and the plug whipped out and made a dent in the bed frame. When she left the room, I ran my fingers over it, but I didn't say anything. Maybe I should have. Maybe that was her point.

There was this other side to it, too. Maquie was spending most of her time in Tokyo visiting her family—Fumi's mother and father and sister whom Fumi had never stayed close to, ever since the episode in Drancy. When Maquie told me the story in Stockholm, I'd felt angry. Now in Tokyo, I felt the anger again, this time directed toward Fumi's family. I had never even met them, but I sort of mentally accused them of not looking after Fumi, of being too enamored with the idea of her moving to glamorous France, of not vetting Daniel, of not understanding her pain when she returned, because they were too old-fashioned maybe, too backward and proper . . . in a Japanese way, in an English way.

I regretted not meeting them that week. Things were busy and, in reality, Maquie never squarely invited me to meet them, but I think the anger I felt stopped me from broaching it. Sike had a theory.

>It's possible you're looking to blame Fumi's parents for what
happened to Fumi, because you're looking to blame someone for
how that meant Maquie was raised, because you're looking to
blame something for what Maquie did with Max.

But I don't know. This type of logic was starting to look a bit hungry. I said, "It's possible I just think they're cunts."

>It's possible.
>Just to let you know, you're using curse words more than usual.

"Fuck, shit, cunt, piss," I said, "fuck, bastard, quim."

* * *

Lots of the GASTA production team got called on to another project for an Okinawan rapper called Awich, and because of this there wasn't the chance to do a big wrap party while I was still in the country. It would have been nice to say goodbye once more, but Awich was pretty remarkable, she may have had a bigger future than Nunchi.

Instead, Maquie and I went for dinner on our final night with just Furusawa, Nunchi, and Jonatan, and one reason for this setup was that Jonatan needed a Japanese lyricist for the SfC Japan project. I still had the job offer for other projects, but they needed a Japanese speaker for this one, and I obviously suggested Nunchi. Furusawa's eyes dribbled out of his pig face when I mentioned Jonatan's name. That felt good. It was a few days after he'd rejected me, and now I was offering the connection of a lifetime. He tried to play it cool and didn't confirm Nunchi's availability right away, but he said we could meet to discuss, and I said how about dinner on my last night. We planned it for the five of us, and Furusawa's secretary booked an Italian place. The night ended strangely, but the dinner was effective.

Effective dinners between unfamiliar people need three different pods, Sike taught me that early on. It's called the "three pod rule." A pod consists of three or fewer connected people, and if there are only two pods present, there is too much pressure on a given individual to perform well for their pod. More than three pods, and you have dilution and something called "conversation sieving," which means you miss what people say, and they miss the chance to say it. But three pods is just perfect.

(I hope one day Sike *is* able to analyze other people, because social interaction will be a gold-dust feature. Imagine being told how you're faring at a pub table, and what everyone else is thinking . . . who is looking at who, and for what percentage of time. I'd love that.)

So everyone enjoyed our dinner at the Italian restaurant. Furusawa had a newfound respect for me, and he was talking to Maquie lots about business and looking impressed with her wielding of facts, analysis, angle. Nunchi and Jonatan got on, too. We laughed about Italy and cultural nuances, and we shared plates of lardo on pane carasau, then two melon-sized mozzarellas, two pastas, two veal Milanese, two seabass, and five tiramisus. We drank ten beers, four bottles of wine, and a round of homemade limoncellos, which they gave to us for free (because, Furusawa chirped, he knew the owner personally). And coffees. Afterward, we went to bars.

The first bar was way downstairs somewhere, and lit with low, frosted-glass lamps, like the kind you put over pool tables. Nunchi had some friends drinking there, but there wasn't space to sit with them in their booth, so we took our own table and Maquie and I shared a purple velvet bench. It was smoky, I lit my first cigarette and didn't stop after that. I saw Maquie watching me, and I blew a smoke ring at her, and she clapped. We were both drinking whiskey sodas, but she had a few waters too.

The music was great, the two barmen were playing records, lots of Motown but a couple of ABBA songs as well. We settled in. We spoke about Sike, we were all peppering Jonatan with questions, and he was being open in his smiley way, his teeth glinting in the low light. I asked about whether he wrote Sike's answer to "what is love," and he said no, it had been an intern called Ed. Furusawa asked who was siking Sike, who was analyzing the psychology of its algorithms, and Jonatan had some technical explanation. It was Nunchi who asked about the price. He just came out with it, unembarrassed: Why do you only sell to rich people?

Jonatan nodded encouragingly. "Right," he said, "everyone's curious. It's a good question, for sure, it's complicated."

And he was about to leave it there, but Maquie and Furusawa and I all cried out and jibed him, saying, "Come on, that's not an answer!" We weren't going to let him off, and he was laughing and shouting, "Guys, *you* come on! This stuff is confidential!"

We just waited, and eventually he explained it a little, saying, "Ok, off record!"

He said it had been a strategic angle at first, that Implode Group, the company they spun out from, had wanted to experiment with higher pricing of software products. The CEO of Implode, Tommy, thought giving away digital services for cheap couldn't last, especially with data center energy costs going up. Tommy wanted to experiment with high prices on smaller products. And then—and Jonatan was kind of high-cheeked at this point, I thought he looked burdened even, heavy with history—when eventually Sike got its independence from Implode, they had the choice to lower the price. They went to Barcelona on a company retreat and did lots of brainstorming and corporate soul searching, and Jonatan said he had woken up on the first morning with this conviction that lowering the price wasn't a good thing.

"It took the rest of the offsite to explain it to myself, let alone the rest of the team. There were commercial reasons to lower the price, and some ethical reasons. But there were all these other arrows pointing away from doing that.

"One was that Sike could be pretty blunt back then, and tact was hard to get right. A recommendation to one person . . . let's say: you should eat fewer donuts, the sugar is accelerating your mood spirals . . . this recommendation is ok to take if you're a tennis-playing, Sports Day committee, loved and community-respected mother of three . . . it's more difficult if you're an overweight and single retail clerk with overdue rent and a sick uncle. Sike still needed to learn that my donut is different from your donut."

I thought about Stutter and his cottage wall cracks, and I wondered if Maquie did too. I felt her arm pressed against mine, we were shoulder to shoulder on the bench.

"Another question, one we spoke about for almost an entire beach day, was: Might inner conflict be useful? If Sike made people 'happy,' whatever that meant, would it slow down important change? We weren't looking to be in the opiate business."

Jonatan shook his head and blew smoke. I hadn't noticed him start smoking. He wasn't used to it, he didn't blow the smoke like he'd smoked so much. He took a sip of his drink, now he was on beer. "Anna's Song" by Marvin Gaye came on.

"Today, I think we could answer that question in a number of ways. We've got a bunch of papers on how Sike doesn't cost you proactivity or creativity . . . the model can find you motivations for your goals other than psychological or existential angst."

He pointed at me.

"I mean, look at Adrian, he uses Sike and he's a creative genius."

I forced a no-reaction reaction, just kept listening.

"But probably all these questions represented a wider concern we had, which was, *does Sike work?* We knew it helped individuals day-to-day, it made them 'happier,' it helped them reach psychological breakthroughs. But we didn't know whether, long-term, it was beneficial to the user. We didn't know *all* the risks, you never do. We didn't know if it was beneficial on a wider, societal scale.

"In particular, we were worried about the app scaling and spinning out of control. I mean, look at social media . . . a discussion for another time, suffice it to say that its failures are obscene. Basically, I was concerned. I sat on the beach at Castelldefels with a piña colada in my hand, looking back with my CTO and my head of research, looking at all we'd created, all the good Sike was doing. And we looked ahead and we just didn't know. How could we know the effect of Sike?

"So we took the decision to limit its growth. Price was an efficient way to limit exposure to a demographic we weren't particularly concerned about protecting."

He shrugged and looked around at us. "We're still in that phase."

Marvin Gaye sings an opera in "Anna's Song," someone says that on an Amerigo Gazaway remix of it. I could hear it now. Gaye's voice carves space, pulls his emotion out into it. It's a very physical type of song.

Nunchi leaned over to Furusawa and asked something in Japanese. I think he was confirming what Jonatan said, he hadn't caught lots of the English. Furusawa replied with a single sentence, and Nunchi sat back nodding.

I looked at Maquie. "What did Furusawa say?"

She took a sip of whiskey. "That they're using rich people as guinea pigs."

I nodded. That's what I'd understood as well.

We went to a second bar, this one with walls of gray concrete and bowls of popcorn, and everyone began talking about dating. Pressing his fingers into the table like he was playing keyboard chords, Furusawa said, "My tactic is old-school. I speak. I say. I tell them that in their moments of lowest control, when they are outside of themselves . . . all inhibitions gone . . . in their wildest, most natural moments . . . that in those moments, I know that they might look at themselves, look at themselves from far away . . ."

He held a hand up in the air, facing it down on himself.

". . . and they might say to themselves: you know, you are in fact a beautiful person."

He brought his hand down.

"And I speak. I say. I say to them that I'm here with them, right now, to tell them that, in those wild moments, when they speak that positive voice, when they look at themselves and tell themselves that they are beautiful . . . that they are correct."

A bit later, Jonatan: "I want to say to my dates, I want to say: you're not as in control as you're pretending to be, and your mistake is thinking that you need to pretend. Your mistake is thinking that the rest of us are in control. None of us have control. But we're ok with it."

Nunchi, in response: "I never have control. All my life. I have no control."

Me: "Yes."

Jonatan: "Yes, yes."

A bit later, Maquie: "I should have said to him, fuck your West Highland Terriers, why am I in the wrong for pretending to like them? I was humoring you. Go sit on your yacht, enjoy your life. Go sit on your yacht with your West Highland Terriers."

Jonatan: "Yes."

Nunchi: "Yes."

Me: "Yes."

A bit later, Maquie: "I want to tell my dad that ethics is *not* the safe haven he thinks it is. He's confused it with mathematics. And when he discovers how fallible it is, he'll face a crisis like no other."

Following new drinks, Jonatan: "What about the *weirder* bars . . . What about them?"

Furusawa, in response: "Yeah, I know some crazy ones."

"How crazy?" Jonatan said. "I want 1980s banker crazy."

"Crazy," Furusawa confirmed.

Nunchi laughed and cheered. Maquie and I listened. Nunchi was red-faced and occasionally rapping to himself. Jonatan had his arm around him. Furusawa had his glasses balanced on his head.

"What about Bad Tamago?" Jonatan said.

"Oh." Furusawa looked impressed. "You know Bad Tamago?"

It was past midnight, so it was already sixth November, the same date Maquie and I first met a year earlier. She was walking ahead with Furusawa, and I watched her. Then I looked down at the tarmac and studied its pores. In the streetlight it looked edible. Almost spongelike, aerated. I could bite from it. I could crouch down and eat it. But instead I smoked my cigarette.

To our right was a small tower of rubbish bags, and I saw a black shape skirt the tower's base. I walked over. I kicked one of the bags. Rats went everywhere. I walked back to the group and we kept walking.

We reached the fourth floor of a grubby building. We were out of breath, and Jonatan and I giggled about how unfit we were. I'd been pushing him up the stairs. Inside the bar, the owner explained what drinks he had, and one of the things he said he had was "juice," and Jonatan whispered to me, "Did he say *Jews?*" and that set us off again. Furusawa was bonding with the owner, showing off to him about Jonatan, but we kept giggling, and Jonatan was saying, "Beer and wine and vodka and *Jews?* He said he has orange *Jews?*" He was killing me.

We settled down at the spotlit counter, and Jonatan and Furusawa started discussing something more seriously. Maquie played with a small puzzle game. Nunchi was next to me, and I looked at him and sort of patted him on the shoulder. I commented on the music that was playing, it was Biggie, and Nunchi nodded, pleased. The bar was small, just that single counter with room for about eight people. It was dark outside the spotlights, and soon there was another whiskey soda filling the light in front of me, all fresh and sparkling. With the glass at my mouth, I felt the fizz on my eyelids. I blew some smoke rings, and was shaking the owner's hand every now and then. I loved shaking hands. The owner was pretty old, with white hair, and he wore a ripped T-shirt and a red bandana. His girlfriend or daughter or someone came in at one point, I think she was drunk. She wore a black ball gown and kept breaking into song. Big '80s ballads. Mostly it was just us, though. I stood in the stairwell with Jonatan for a while and we laid it all out. I told him about Maquie cheating on me with Max, and he just listened. He knows how to listen of course. He didn't say much, just said, "That's rough," after a while, and he squeezed my shoulder.

We went back inside. Maquie was asleep on the counter, I put my hand on her back and she murmured in her sleep. After a bit we left her there and moved into the back room, which was where the owner had the Bad Tamago set up. The room was small and looked like a student's living room. There was a brown leather sofa with white scratch marks, and a few school chairs. On the wall was a Nirvana poster, a nice one of the boys walking onto stage. And there were two windows, both boarded up.

The second strangest thing in the room was a terrarium sitting on a small table below one of the windows. I went over to look, and I felt the heat coming from the red heat lamp. I held my hand under it, felt the burn on my knuckle hair. The terrarium was bare except for a leopard gecko sitting on a small rock, and three or four crickets crouched in the opposite corner. Things were pretty fuzzy, I couldn't quite count the crickets, and I had to focus hard to make out the gecko's back, which was patterned black and white. It was beautiful, I was very taken with the intricacy. The owner came over and showed me how to stroke it with my index finger. Its back felt pleasant, soft and loose like the skin of your eyelid.

More strange than the gecko were the Bad Tamago, I'd never seen anything like them. There were two, one in each corner and tied up in blankets, and the owner began to drag each of them into the center of the room. Nunchi had come in and was slumped on the sofa, drinking water, I think. Furusawa was helping the owner remove the blankets, and Jonatan was staring at the process, bent over with his hands on his knees. I didn't understand it yet.

Jonatan looked at me and said, "Tamago means 'egg' in Japanese."

This made sense. Each Bad Tamago looked like a giant egg, the size of an armchair. The idea seemed to be that you sat inside the egg. You climbed through a hatch in the front, closed the hatch, and there was a hole in the top for your head to poke out.

Once the blankets were removed, the owner undid some metal clasps on each door, and we peered in. Inside each egg was a ledge with a seat carved into it, big enough for an adult, but simple, with small armrests. The seats were rickety, they wobbled, and a bunch of cords hung down around them, their ends disappearing into the interior of the eggs. The cords were woven, like the ones you use for mountain climbing, and they formed a kind of harness.

The barman put his hand on the smaller egg and said in slow English, "1982." Then he pointed to the bigger one and said, "1986." The newer one had a shell of shiny white plastic. The older one was matte gray-green fiberglass. The barman turned and started to prepare them.

Furusawa said they were rare, fewer than twenty Bad Tamago existed. He said you sat in the seat and fitted your head through the hole at the top. Your arms and legs were fed through the cord harness. Then the hatch was closed and the metal door clasps were shut.

"The Tamago is fitted with a timer and a system of pulleys. You have fifteen minutes. You have to stay still."

If you stayed still, after fifteen minutes the door clasps sprung open automatically, and you were released. You won.

If you didn't stay still, you might die before the clasps sprung open, because the cords got tighter with movement. With more movement, they got tighter again. They began to pull your arms and legs back, they pushed the seat forward, and you asphyxiated.

The inventor was a watchmaker, Furusawa said, and that was the clever part, how the pulley system felt your movement and responded to it by pulling tighter. Only tighter. The cords couldn't slacken unless the door opened.

"They're kinetically triggered," he said.

"It's pretty serious," Jonatan said to me. And he looked pretty serious. "It gets tight fast."

"If you start suffocating before fifteen minutes is up," I said, "the Tamago, it . . ."

"It doesn't care," Furusawa said. "You die."

"Who is first?" the owner said.

"Don't worry," Jonatan said. "The pros play alone, but we're not pros. If you get in trouble, someone can open the clasps from the outside."

Jonatan and I went first. We took off our glasses and our shoes and climbed in. The owner directed our legs and arms through the harness cords, and I had a memory of being fitted for shoes when I was very young, the feeling of a tape measure being drawn against my foot. Then they angled the eggs so we were facing each other. Jonatan went for the gray-green fiberglass one, he liked the nostalgia. I had the bigger white one. The owner described them like they had personalities, and I think Jonatan also liked that his Bad Tamago was described as "meaner." Mine was described as "more reliable," though it wasn't clear how, and I felt small jolts of adrenaline.

They closed the doors and our fifteen minutes began.

We must have looked unearthly, just heads poking out of giant eggs. Like something out of a children's story. Now and then, I peered at Jonatan, to see how he was faring. He looked down at the floor with a sad expression. The hole in the top of my one had a leather lining, and I felt the leather pressing on the right side of my neck. I wanted to unstick the leather, but of course I didn't. Maybe, at first, I had thought Jonatan and I were in danger of laughing, but there was no feeling of laughter in us now. The hatches closed and a gravity came over us. I carried my grandfather's coffin, the one who died of cancer, and that's the only other time I'd felt as solemn as I did then in that Bad Tamago. Jonatan and I caught eyes once or twice at the beginning, but otherwise we stayed in our heads.

Most of all, it felt precarious. You could rock and the egg would tip over. Then what?

But I tried to ignore this thought, and the clock ticked away.

Furusawa told us when five minutes and ten minutes were up. By ten, my back was aching. I knew not to move though, I could last the pain for five more minutes. I was distracting myself by thinking about everyone I knew, a basic diversion because somehow I was afraid even to think too hard, like mental exertion might trigger the machine. I needed the distraction because I kept thinking how I was drunk and a bit dizzy, how I didn't know what "reliable" meant, how the egg was precarious, how it could tip over and then what. So I ran through people who were important to me: Mum, Jess, Jess's husband, Jonah . . . Stutter, Sophie. My dad, my grandmother. The grandfather I watched die, whose coffin I carried. Ulf, Fumi, Yuki. Maquie, of course, asleep on the bar, although I didn't dwell on her. And various others came in and out of my mind.

Eventually I thought of this present company, this group of guys we were with. Jonatan sat opposite me, Furusawa and Nunchi were at the bar.

Jonatan was a good man, I thought, I respected him. I liked what he had said about Sike, I liked his caution. This felt honest to me.

Furusawa was a bastard though, that's what I thought. Furusawa thought being clever was more difficult than being nice. This was his major mistake.

Nunchi was a kind soul. What a guy. And he was the best rapper I'd worked with, I was almost certain of that. Yes, he was the best, and to support this thought, my right hand made a drumbeat—a quick one.

Just a small tap of emphasis.

A gesture to affirm the thought.

Really a quick one, a nothing movement that you would barely notice if I had done it in front of you, but I heard a creak from far off inside the machine accompanied by two clicks, and a cord around my left ankle slipped tight.

I froze. But there was an urge. But no, I froze. I knew not to move. A small mistake, it had been a tiny movement. Nothing to it. I hadn't called for it, it hadn't been conscious. Something else had called for it, something other than me. Sweat started down my temples. But the machine was broken or something, I felt no tightening around any of the rest of my body, just that left ankle. But it was too tight. There was a danger of blood starvation, of losing blood in my toes. The Bad Tamago couldn't balance, I had drunk too much. We were already falling. No, we were still. But there was an urge. It was an urge so delicate and so sweet that I couldn't let myself contemplate it. I didn't think it was only a bad idea, but I knew it was not a good idea . . . but no, I could try. This time it was conscious.

I tensed my left leg. And froze again.

Another creak had come, this time with more clicks and the slide of a rope against my ribs.

Sweat dripped down my cheek and then my neck, into the machine. The sweat fell in, down, wetting the rope that was now pinching the skin on my ribs. I was panicking. The leather was pulling on the skin of my neck. My heart went too fast, the machine might feel it. A click for each heartbeat? Tighter with each breath. Could it feel breathing? They hadn't told us. What if my body moved again? I wasn't in control. I had moved my leg, but something else had moved my hand. Now, only my eyes moved. They swiveled. They were looking at Jonatan, staring at him, willing him to look at me and see what was happening. He stayed staring at the ground. Was he ok? He was sad. Was he alive? The rope on my ribs was pinching . . .

Another creak. From where? What had moved? I hadn't fucking moved. I thought I was still, except for my eyes and the sweat on my cheeks, but the creak had come, this time with more clicking, a not countable number of clicks, and now I felt the backrest push forward, and now I felt the first pressure on my chest. I breathed short, but I needed more air. My viewpoint was changed, my head was bent back. Sweat was in my eyes. I took a breath, I had to, and I thought I heard another click. It took all I had not to react, and then I heard three loud snaps, and the clasps of the door opened.

I drank a beer and sucked a cigarette almost straight down, my hands were shaking. Jonatan's were too, he'd had some creaks and some clicks as well. Some slips of cord. We had finished the fifteen minutes in total fear, we looked at each other now and our laughter was thin. He showed me a small rope burn under his wrist. Our backs were drenched, the owner had to wipe our sweat from the seats. Jonatan sat down in the bar room at the counter and I thought he might want space, so I went back into the side room, still feeling weak.

In the middle of the room, Nunchi was getting strapped into the white egg, Furusawa was already in position in the gray-green one, chattering with the owner. Then the owner finished with Nunchi and closed the doors to both.

They weren't facing each other this time, it was more like they were side by side. I said good luck, trying to sound enthusiastic, and went to sit behind them at the back of the room on the leather sofa. I felt so shaky that I just wanted to sit.

When I had put my glasses back on after my turn in the egg, a lilac dot had appeared immediately, and I clicked on it now. Sike was saying my fear metrics were up, and I just said under my breath that I knew it, it was the egg.

The owner left to go through to the bar, and Nunchi and Furusawa were quiet. They faced away from me, and the three of us sat there, them in their eggs and me on the sofa behind them, with just the sound of music coming peacefully from the bar. It was Japanese pop, someone called Konomi Sasaki. Nunchi had chosen it, laughing shyly and saying it would calm him. It was dark in the room. I lit a cigarette and took a few drags, and I looked past Nunchi and Furusawa, through the door, past Jonatan with his head in his hands, to Maquie.

I could see her cheek, her forehead, her mouth, her shut eyes, her hair.

She looked soft in the spotlight, the colors like oil, her back moving slowly up and down with her breath, and I just stared at her like that, like she was a painting, for what must have been many minutes, but fewer than fifteen.

Nunchi and Furusawa were frozen in the Bad Tamago, the backs of their heads to me. I didn't know how long they'd had but, after a while, I was kind of itchy, so I stood up and walked over to the gecko in its terrarium. I stroked it the way the owner had shown me, and looked at the patterns on its back again. Then I looked at the crickets, which were more in focus now. There were three of them there, waiting to get eaten by the patterned gecko. I didn't feel sentimental for them, but I reached in and took one of the crickets in my hand, making a cage with my fingers, and I carried it to the sofa. The Konomi music pattered on. The room was very still. I was going to sit down, but instead I walked over to where Nunchi and Furusawa were, in the center of the room. They didn't see me because their backs were turned, and I looked down at both of them sitting there, feeling the cricket wriggle in my hands.

There was a choice, a small one.

I brought my hand close to Nunchi's neck and opened it. I sloped my hand toward the right side of his collar, a part that was loose from his neck. The cricket dropped in, onto the skin of Nunchi's shoulder, and I stepped back.

I looked toward the bar. Then a low moan came from Nunchi, and it raised in volume.

I moved backward and sat down on the sofa, and the moan got louder, then higher. There was something deficient about the moan, like it was coming from a child. It pitched up at a hook, then went to a vibrating depth again, perhaps reacting to movements made inside the egg by the cricket, or perhaps to the slither of rope over limb. The moan felt archaic, human-desperate, but it also sounded mechanical, machinelike, similar to the groan of the Bad Tamago. It hung in the air, mixing with the music, weaving around, and I pictured all these sounds moving together, the click of the machine and the click of the cricket, the groan of the egg and the moan of Nunchi, all there together, and I just sat there, picturing this.

Then Nunchi's head jerked left, and the right shoulder of the egg came up, pulling away from the ground. The egg hovered for a moment on the soft left corner of its base, and then it overbalanced, and Nunchi shrieked as his head craned slowly toward the floor, rolling forward left, and down, until his face reached the floor and stopped the pitch, his cheek and forehead planting into the thin carpet, pushing the momentum back, causing the egg to bob back once, twice, and then rotate Nunchi so that he faced the floor. The egg bobbed once again, and lay still. Nunchi's shriek was now a gargle. I was staring at his face, his popped eyes, his sound almost gone. The light was low, but his face was clearly red, and a line of drool went from his lips to the carpet, and I just sat staring for a moment, watching him, until suddenly there was a scramble inside of me, and I ran forward to the egg, shouting for the owner, who arrived shortly after, with Jonatan close behind, and I ripped the first two metal clasps, and the owner got the third. The machine sighed as the ropes let go, and Nunchi fell out onto the ground, coughing and sucking air, screaming it in.

Jonatan went to Furusawa and put a hand on the egg's shoulder, then pulled his three clasps. The door opened and Furusawa spluttered and laughed his relief.

When he got his breath back, Nunchi had some kind of a fit, panting and shouting, crying out. He stripped naked, all the way, and then jumped up and down on his clothes. He went kind of ballistic. Furusawa grabbed his shoulders and made him sit on the sofa, his bare cheeks on the leather, and I looked through his clothes for the cricket. I found it, crushed, in the hem of his trousers, and I brought it over to him. He looked at it and sneered, and I dropped it into the gecko's terrarium.

He was ok in the end. Jonatan's color returned too. And Maquie woke up, yawning and rubbing her neck, blinking at me. I took her hand in mine and didn't let go of it until we were back in our hotel room.

* * *

The next morning, I woke up, opened my eyes and focused them. I saw my glasses on the coffee table, charging next to a half-eaten box of degrading cherries. The glasses caught my eye and flashed the time across their lenses. It was 9:17.

I drifted for a bit. Then some thicker sleep, a dense knot of it at the back of my head.

I opened my eyes again. My glasses saw me again, it was 9:41. I was still too drunk to feel much, just a gentle nausea above the larynx. Maquie wasn't there, she had got up while I was asleep . . . there had been the sound of a shower. Even when I'm not conscious of it, my brain registers her coming and going.

I showered and afterward couldn't remember the feel of the water, or what soap I'd used. Then I dressed in a black sweatshirt and some cleanish jeans, picked up my coat and thwacked it a few times, and left the room.

Breakfast was being cleared, and I couldn't see Maquie in the restaurant or the lobby. I searched the guests standing by the reception desks, silhouetted against the thirty-eighth floor windows. Head pulsing, and having a sense for where Maquie might be, I crossed the lobby to the lounge. I stood for a bit at the entrance. The ceiling was cathedral-high and the windows ran all the way up to it.

I searched the tables. The best spots were by the window. A waiter crossed the floor, and I followed his trajectory toward a table on the far side of the room, separate from the others and partially hidden behind a pillar. With her back to me, Maquie sat facing the view.

The waiter arrived and placed in front of her a glass of red juice and a white china cup. The waiter made to leave and then looked at Maquie's feet, which were slippered not shoed. He hesitated, about to say something, but Maquie turned her face up to him and said something discreet. He apologized with a small bow and left. Maquie looked back to the window. I moved closer. Maquie took a sip of coffee and stared at a skyscraper a few hundred meters away, where a miniscule office janitor was vacuuming a hallway. Near us, a spoon hit a coffee cup, and with the sound came an insight. A penny's drop. And I found myself just sort of standing there, letting it screw around in my head, in the middle of the quiet lounge.

. . .

The insight started as a collection of realizations that sat down in place like a piece of algebra: Something was wrong with Maquie, Something was wrong with me, Something was wrong with Sike, and, to a more dramatic extent, Something was wrong with life.

Of course, I thought, yes. There is something that is wrong.

The insight released questions, but my initial feeling was a protective urge. It was kind of classic macho, classroom male . . . I wanted to get my arms around Maquie, hold her and ward off evil. She had slept with someone for money, and I wanted to fix it, solve it, protect her, protect us.

Then she saw me. Said my name.

I stepped back, smiling but shaking my head. I was at sea. She watched me, but I couldn't communicate what I was feeling. The room felt less calm, there was blood in my ears. Around me there was the soft movement of coffees being served and cakes being eaten, and I stood there looking at Maquie, who was sitting at her window table, and looking up at me.

There was something wrong.

"I'm going to pack," I said.

And I moved away from her.

My glasses were in my hand, not on my head, as I reached our room and swiped the door. When I entered, I put them on and went to the cherries we'd bought on our first morning and, on my own, without Maquie, I sat on the coffee table and began to finish them.

I felt a little miserable as I put them in my mouth. They had degraded and the flesh was flabby. In my glasses, I searched "cherries" while I was eating them, hoping to augment my enjoyment of this final piece of Japan. I flicked through cherry images as I ate, and spat the stones into my hand and dropped them back in the box.

Maquie sat in the lounge with her legs crossed, a white slipper hanging from the end of one foot and her cup of coffee in her hands. Jonatan walked up and pulled out one of the lounge chairs. He looked tired. Maquie saw yellow in his eyes, and something white had crusted on the side of his cheek.

"Fucking *hell*," he said. "What a night!"

He rubbed an eye with the ball of his hand, and leaned back on the chair, laughing quietly.

"How are you doing?" he asked.

"I'm ok," she said. She was curious. "Do you get hangover anxiety? Like everyone else?"

"Not so much," he said. "And if I do, I just ride it. Anxiety can feel fun."

"Bullshit."

"Yeah, I take 5-HTP sometimes, it helps raise serotonin."

She nodded. "Did you enjoy the night?"

"It was pretty crazy. Were you there for Bad Tamago?"

"Not really."

"Good."

"Was Adrian ok?" she asked.

"He was ok."

"Good," she said.

Jonatan nodded, and then picked at a nail. He looked out the window, then back to Maquie.

"Do you care?" he said.

Maquie paused.

"Do I care about how Adrian was?"

"Yes."

"What is your question, exactly?"

He looked at her, his lips pouting. "I was drunk, but I'm fairly sure he told me that you told him you slept with Max."

Maquie held his eye. "Yes."

"Why?"

"Because . . . I did."

"Not the other day, you didn't. Not recently. Unless Max was lying, and I don't think he was. You rejected him."

She sipped her coffee. Her romantic life was a hot topic, it seemed. She hadn't anticipated Max discussing it with Jonatan, she had forgotten Max was sociable now, open.

"If you want to break up with Adrian," Jonatan said, "there are less callous ways to do it."

"I don't want to break up with him."

"Then what are you doing?"

She inspected the foam of her cappuccino, her eyes roaming the pristine milk bubbles. The coffee was excellent, it left an almost painful bitterness on the back edges of her tongue, despite the milk. What she was doing was not easy to describe. And it was not an exact science. She was optimistic, hopeful.

"I'm fishing," she said.

"For?"

"For a reaction."

"You need more attention?"

"Not a reaction to me," she said quietly. "I want him to react to himself." She looked at Jonatan. "What's the psychotherapy term for 'facing your fears'?"

"Exposure."

She nodded.

Jonatan thought for some time, his eyes blinking beneath his glasses. Eventually, his face relaxed.

"You want to replace Sike?"

"It's a collaboration. Adrian still uses your app."

The waiter arrived and handed Jonatan a menu. Jonatan took it.

"It sounds risky," he said.

"You would know."

"A long shot."

"You would know."

He began to read the menu.

Out the window, across the high air, a janitor leaned against the window glass of a next-door skyscraper and sipped from a water bottle. Maquie watched the janitor, and she felt her mood lift.

When your mood lifts, it actually feels like a lift, she thought. Like something lifts up off you. It's not a metaphor, it's anatomical.

She looked back to Jonatan. He was leaning forward now and rubbing his hands, looking to his side out the window. She realized she liked and admired him. She had the unexpected feeling that they might be friends one day.

"How's the partnership with Quantum Theater?" she asked.

The question was conversational, she had expected no gain from it. Maybe it spoke to her own preoccupations. But it surprised her that Jonatan's face clouded, that for a moment the unburdened man looked burdened.

I was surprised when Maquie came into the room, as though I had passively assumed I might never see her again. She looked at the cherries and me eating them. I was a sad picture, perhaps. She took a cherry for herself, and spat the stone into the box. It bounced out and onto the floor, and she watched it roll under the coffee table.

"I saw Jonatan downstairs," she said.

"How was he?" I asked.

"Hungover."

"Yes."

"He mentioned the Bad Tamago."

I felt the anxiety in my chest, and it rushed up my neck into my head. Nunchi's face, pinched and swollen, came into view. It haunted me, what I'd done to him, and the lack of explanation I had for it.

I touched Maquie's arm.

"I did something weird," I said.

"Weird?"

"Yes."

"So did I," she said.

She got undressed, watching Adrian as she crouched to pull off her socks; watching him as she pulled her jeans down over legs that felt dry, as she pulled her top up over breasts that felt swollen. She decided that "weird" could be a good sign, that "weird" suggested reaction. Adrian would confess the weird thing, and she would confess too.

She stood in her bra and pants and socks and felt goose bumps cover her thighs and arms, and she faced Adrian in his position on the coffee table and watched him.

. . .

And I watched her, I looked over her thin body, aware of the weight she had lost, of what she needed to put back on. She needed help, she needed looking after. And she looked at me and thought the same. About herself. About me. I rolled a cherry stone against the front of my teeth, then dropped it into my hand and into the box.

Together we got into bed, lying flat against each other and smelling the mingling scents of alcohol, hangover, coffee, hotel soap . . . when we kissed, we both tasted cherries on the other's lips. And when we pulled away, we studied the exhaustion in each other's eyes, the creases in our lids and cheeks, the pallor of our skin. We looked and looked, and eventually fell asleep for a short while, clinging desperately to each other in the hotel bed.

CURES

Mariatorget is a small city park in Stockholm, neatly pruned with rows of flowers and beds of grass, and those satisfying shin-high iron railings. In the center, there's a statue of Thor slaying the Midgard Serpent. Our flat is close by on a street named after a guy called Wollmar Yxkull (a wild name, not one I'd want, even if they named a street after it) and I walk to the square some mornings and I circle the statue of Thor, not only because Maquie used to do this when she was younger, but also because I like to contemplate the serpent as an analogy for life and psychology, self-awareness, stress and fear, and Sike.

I don't say this is *the* analogy for Sike. I say it's *an* analogy. And I say that I contemplate it, meaning that I contemplate also whether it's an *appropriate* analogy. Often I decide it isn't.

The Midgard Serpent is an example of an ouroboros, which is a circular sort of serpent that eats its own tail. This particular Midgard ouroboros circles the earth, eating its tail, eating itself. I circle the statue and I wonder— sort of like a philosopher rather than a zoologist—whether eating itself gives the serpent sustenance, and whether it gives it more sustenance than it takes away. And that's when, like a philosopher, I wonder whether this might be an appropriate analogy for Sike.

If one of my walks finds me favoring the analogy, and I then return home to see Maquie speaking to Sike, I don't snip at her for using it or anything, I just let her get on with it, because I trust that there is such a thing as moderation, and I trust that Maquie knows how to wield it. From the doorway,

I watch her speaking and contemplating, nodding to her glasses, and I hope to myself that her time with Sike is fulfilling and helpful.

I showed Jonatan the Midgard serpent once, when he came to Stockholm for an SfC project with Spotify, and I presented the analogy. He loves criticism, he laughed and said yes, it's a risk. He's a great guy. I also told him when I quit Sike. It hadn't been a big deal, I never said "goodbye" as such, I just didn't log in one day, and a week later I canceled my subscription and deleted my data. Jonatan was totally cool about it, he understood. He hadn't needed an explanation, but I gave him one anyway. I explained about that insight I got in the lounge of the Mandarin Oriental Hotel in Tokyo, how after sixteen months of using Sike I'd realized something was wrong—with me, with Maquie, with us, with Sike, and so on—and Jonatan rubbed his head, pretending to look dazed, and said,

"Sike got you that insight? In only sixteen months? It's more powerful than we thought."

I laughed, but there was an edge of ridicule in what he was saying. Maybe he was thinking of that old line, that you never cure yourself of your psychology.

I didn't do any work for Sike for Countries in the end, I was kind of drained of lyrics after the Nunchi job. It wasn't even because of all that Furusawa stuff and me not being good enough to perform . . . The job didn't leave *so* bad a taste in my mouth. There was a feeling of success, the album was incredible and the dreamcoat song really worked. Nunchi hasn't made it big over here yet, but he gets a lot of attention in Japan. And yet, even with all that, it still wasn't quite enough for me, and maybe that turned me off ghostwriting for a while.

But I don't know, maybe I *was* just bitter about the frailty of my performing ambitions. Or it might have been more superficial, it's possible I just said no to the SfC job because, after I stopped using Sike, the company lost its glamor a bit. They went through a rocky patch and a few competitors emerged (one called Freudo was popular). Also people got kind of fusty about Sike, and part of the cause, I would argue *hard*, was the Quantum Theater deal . . . old Mr. Snake Oil, he had his comeuppance! Max tried to connect his quantum security with Sike and it caused problems (colossal, non-quantum ones). That's why Maquie got refused when she tried to sign up. For a whole month Sike was accidentally rejecting something like half of all new registrations, and it was all Quantum Theater's fault. It was crazy, Maquie says they had to *drop* their valuation in their next investment round.

Poor old Max, the whole harbor gimmick must feel pretty goofy now. (*Half* of all registrations!) When we heard about Max's screw-up, we couldn't stop laughing, but for me it was schadenfreude. For Maquie, I think it was relief that she wasn't "too sick for Sike." The rejection had rattled her, she'd felt like an invalid . . . like she was sliding off the face of the planet, like her access to gravity had been rescinded, and to be honest it makes me pretty angry thinking about it, I'm amazed Sike was able to survive that. The regulators found out and moved in, and Sike had to change its entire screening policy. They're more scrutinized than ever now, and they've had to lower the price, too. As a kind of appeasement. A sorry. Telling people who were looking for mental health support that they were too unstable for it suddenly felt like the very worst thing you could do.

Maquie brushed it off though, she was unfazed. She decided to try to sign up again. We registered her together while sitting on the sofa at my old Camden flat, and after her first session she took off her glasses and quoted Keanu Reeves that time he comes out of the training simulator in *The Matrix*:

"I know kung fu."

"Show me," I said, just like Morpheus, and we discussed Mood Freezing and Hindsight Bias.

Maquie's Sike is pretty different to my Sike, she has no dashboard and doesn't get given scores or statistics. But it must work for her because her Sike Smile is explosive, her face just *opens*. It's too much for me sometimes, I feel a bit weepy. Picture a sunflower opening, or hotel curtains on the first day of holiday . . . Dorothy McGuire in *Swiss Family Robinson*, looking out of the treehouse, or Saoirse Ronan in *Little Women*, watching her book get bound. Explosive, and you quickly forget Midgard analogies when you see it.

. . .

There were other developments. When we moved to Stockholm, Maquie quit May-Perhaps and said goodbye to Sharon and Kyle (Sharon cried). She thought about going back into academia, but in the end she went into business with Yuki: they set up a restaurant together, called Atarakin, which kind of means "New Friday."

I like sushi, so I'm happy, but it was useful that Sike's price came way down because the restaurant will take a while to make money. All told, we both earn less than half what we used to. I've taken two jobs, one of them as music editor of a small magazine here. I write articles, mainly about rap, and the articles get published. My name goes on them. The other is with an AI start-up that Maquie introduced me to. They take your phone and glasses data and write it into a novel for you, guessing the important scenes and events, and your thoughts during them. Kind of narrative nonfiction, or autofiction, I don't know, and you can choose your main messages, as well as the literary style and a bunch of genres (they've just added horror and fantasy). My job is to finesse-edit the stories on the other end, and they're not bad. You'd never want to read someone else's, but your own might be interesting. I'm helping pitch a partnership to Jonatan, a linkup with Sike data could be useful.

We miss London a bit, it's sad not to be in pubs with Sophie and Stutter every week, but we make it work. Actually, we're calling him Sam now. One day he just asked if we wouldn't mind, and obviously we agreed. It wasn't acrimonious or awkward, and we didn't hold a big back-slapping ceremony or start saying "good point, *Sam*" and "pass the salt, *Sam*," but I changed his name in my phone to help me remember.

"We can go back to Stutter if it feels strange," he said.

Sam and I went to Copenhagen to see Nas and Wu-Tang Clan last month. They were incredible, I cried during "NY State of Mind," and I looked around and there were all these men and women in their thirties and forties, also crying to gangster rap. Funny how things develop. Nas got ok again as well, he's releasing solid songs.

Sam is with a Londoner called Dora now, she's a big Outkast fan, a real keeper. And Sophie is still dating, there's a Dutch guy called Robin who might be good news. They come and visit sometimes, and we swirl expensive, undersized beers in Stockholm bars and we debate the same topics with slightly less vociferousness. Sike is still a rich seam, especially now that Sophie uses it. She signed up when the price came down. Turns out she has a mild gluten allergy, Sike spotted it.

Sam is still against it, and his new line is that "Smiles aren't constant. People forget that. Almost by definition, a smile is a moment."

He means: You never cure yourself of your psychology. There are no panaceas.

Maquie and I can agree with him. But, we say, there are palliatives. Maquie still uses Sike, on low resolution, in moderation. And meanwhile I signed up to see a real-life therapist, every two weeks. She's Hungarian originally, in her fifties, called Lartia. She has a cat called Smulan. I go to her apartment on Odengatan, and we discuss, among other things, my father. No conclusions yet. But I find it useful. Or maybe interesting.

One session, we spoke about Nunchi, because I hadn't really repented for what I did to him. I didn't tell him it was me who put the cricket down his neck, I didn't say sorry. Maybe he knew already. "Sad Adrian," he might have said. But I told Lartia, and I said what Sike might have said, that there was luck playing in both directions: bad luck I was in the situation, good luck I snapped out of it. I imagined how Sike might comfort me ("Given the positive effect on your life that not murdering people has, it seems unlikely you would have let Nunchi choke out"). But Lartia wasn't so kind. She asked me if I really believed in luck, and if so, did I think I could always rely on it to right its own wrongs.

I thought about that for a bit.

I also asked her why she thought I did it. She didn't conclude anything, but we spoke about fear. I had thought my biggest fear was my future, Maquie had thought it was being abandoned.

"You told me about having watched your grandfather die," Lartia said.

"You think that's my biggest fear?"

"I don't think there's such a thing as 'a biggest fear . . . ,' but if there was, and if it was death, do you think you faced it? In the room with Nunchi?"

I didn't know. She asked me what I thought "facing a fear" might entail.

It was on the plane back from Tokyo that Maquie told me she'd lied about sleeping with Max. She turned to me in the seat, right when the wheels left the runway, and I got ready to go to my "calm place" and drink the plane out of tomato juice and vodka, but she said no need and explained her lie.

I think I understood it as: she wanted to present me with a fear, so that I would stop fearing it. Get to the other side of it. Grow up a little. I think I got it. It seemed like somehow she was trying to mimic Sike, trying to jog me onto more even ground.

I mean . . . I wouldn't say she *nailed* it. I was sad for a week and then nearly murdered Nunchi with a cricket and a giant egg. I'm not sure that was quite the even ground she'd been planning for me. But I could see she had a point. Some months later, in a drunken argument, she said,

"Look, if I have to learn to be vulnerable, to depend on people . . . on you . . . I need you to learn to be *in*dependent, to stand up."

I could accept some of that. I could see how, generally speaking, maybe our "things" were that I always relied on others, and she never did, but I don't know . . . this kind of logic still feels hungry to me, like it's shopping for something. It's never the whole truth.

We practice anyway, just to be safe. Maquie's done some of the relationship modules on Sike, and they suggested some exercises, and I ran them past Lartia. Every Saturday, we wake up and I have to make one plan for the day and Maquie has to accept it. It felt naff, then anodyne, then uncomfortable, but I kind of like it now.

Also, I'm taking singing lessons.

Stockholm is a good place to live, the people are kind and the city is beautiful. This makes an improvement to your day, a physical one. Our flat is small, but that's what you want in the winters. I have a solid friendship with Fumi, she's teaching me Japanese, and Ulf sometimes invites me to play Hearts. We have lunch with them and Yuki every Sunday, which feels kind of Jewish, and sometimes Maquie and I host.

And I'm back to London a bit. Jess had a baby boy, and she named him Alex after our grandfather. I wondered if it would be surreal for my grandmother, seeing a baby with her dead husband's name, but she seems ok with it, and Jess asked everyone's permission first.

Granny and Mum came to visit us here two weeks ago, and everyone got on. We did the usual lunch on the Sunday, Maquie made pizza. Ulf couldn't have loved more that Granny was a "survivor," and I cringed, thinking she'd resent the labeling, but she warmed to him, thought he was a real gentleman, kept referring to him as a "tall drink of water."

After lunch, they all played cards and Maquie and I went just the two of us for a walk through the snow to Mariatorget, to walk around the Midgard Serpent. Actually, she walked around it, I stood chewing my jacket zip in the snow and half-light, watching Thor and the serpent, watching the thick sky, watching Maquie walk.

She circled the statue slowly, looking down at her disappearing feet. When she passed around the other side of the statue, for a moment it was just me, standing there in the silence, waiting for her to appear again. I couldn't even hear the sound of her walking, and I thought back to our first year together, how we got to the end of it and everything seemed to be wrong. I wondered, sort of aimlessly, if I might write a song about it one day, a rap perhaps. Maybe a poem, another sonnet. "She Stands Beside Me," something misty-eyed like that. But I realized that I see that year more like a story than anything else. And it struck me that every story ever, really, is just the alleviation of a character's psychology. And when we read "happily ever after," we believe that the character is cured.

We knew from the start that things fall apart, and tend to shatter
She like, "That shit don't matter"

—BLACK THOUGHT

RAP

SHE STANDS APART . . .

She stands apart, unspeaking but alert,
Observing from peripheral grey white blur
Your survey questions framed in pub floor flirt,
As one more girl declares herself not her.

You blink away her phantom, order wine,
Remember that to view a star in clear
Repair, you shouldn't stare right at its shine;
A mental liniment for those who fear . . .

For those who doubt that love is true or one;
Who when they heard its chimes, forgot to hum;
Who yearn to break the bread but dread the crumb;
For those who search for stars but miss the sun.

Her pearly haunt, it blears the edge once more,
It pulls and pushes doubt, and drums the door.
You stand apart, alert, to see if she will come.

BENNY SHAMELESS RIP

LOYLE CARNER, 1992

1. I fall in love way too easily
2. Used to treat 'em nice and now I treat "em like they're treatin" me
3. But this isn't me eagerly
4. Cos I'd rather retreat up where the sweeter be
5. But if its unrequited Then its right for me to flee the scene

BENNY SHAMELESS RIP

1. I steal the girls way too greedily
2. Funny how the food I shouldn't eat always tastes sweet to me
3. Like eating it illegally
4. Is what makes it complete me more agreeably
5. Man, can't trust my gut
6. To be the judge on what is feeding me

DRUNKEN PUB LINES

Sweeter than a liter can of juice
Lots to lose, but I'm feeling kind of loose in the boxers
Eyes bright, shine right through me as she watches
Taboo in her charm, tattoo on her arm
Baloo to the shoulder getting colder
Like my time's running out with no Golden Goal
The bell's toll and it's getting ruthless
The truth is I'm clueless
All of this meat and me I'm toothless
I'm too pissed for answers
My ambitious advances are glances
It's stupid. Come on, Cupid, tell me to hoof it.

DREAMCOAT SONG

VERSE 1

- I used to wear purple and pink
- Now I wear black like the beauty, or blue like the boogie
- Don't confuse me—I keep my wardrobe honed
- Cos I suffer less bother when my color's monochrome
- Wish I only owned polo necks
- Jobs a good 'un—alleviate the stress, put a hood on
- One outfit like Calvin, clip the Lego hair
- Fast fashion doesn't happen when you never change what you wear
- I pay bucks for the looks that thrill
- Big sale pair of kicks Voile Blanche with the back grill
- Pick a Picket satchel, for my lap Dell
- Not an Apple til we wrap up this rap deal
- Uh, that feel when you kick it into school
- With a dapper new jacket tapping ya wicket keeper cap too
- That feel's what we wanna get back to.
- It's what we wanna get back to . . .

VERSE 2

- I used to only wear blue or black
- Now I've tune-changed to a different plan of attack
- I color clash like the black and yellow bee's back
- Ink, silk and sunny—no honey but on Mondays
- I feel money when I'm coming, layered like an onion
- Believe me, sweetie, got a cuff for any meeting
- Shades in any shade, vests invested in
- If I had the legs for it I'd be dressed in . . . shorts
- . . . But I got calves like a farmer
- Henry 8 style drama, calmer under armor
- Come summer, I'ma peep a new vague vogue
- Gonna try and buy myself a very many-colored coat
- This is the robe, Sike Smiles when it shows
- All the colors explode, erode the threshold
- It's amber, green, opal, gray, and violet
- And lilac, red, and lemon, this is heaven

BEAT AROUND THE BIBBITY

Beat around the bibbity bush, call me GW
Bitches say they be busy if you busy bee why you Bumbler
Mumble all my Bs just to confuse you when I utter them
Stutter when I utter to market the words that come at ya
Stutter just to advertise the ne-next word I utter
With a whiny motherfucker in my ear mosquito suck on you
Drop a pack of Marlboro from 2000 on the barbeque
Barber shaved my head when all I wanted was a number 2
_Number 3, now we kicking hard
Kicking like a horse getting conditioned in the knacker's yard
Picking out these whores like they came singing from a pack of cards
Picking eenie meenie on these whores, I'm like a genie
This is getting kinda silly give me watches, Lamborghinis
Teeny polka dot bikinis, and martinis, and porcini
All the mushrooms, all the meaning, all the sinners, all the ceilings
All the feelings, kings and queens n' all the fears and hopes and dreams n'
Now I'm bugged out, I bust out, I pity-passed the fuck out
They tucked in and tugged out, the bibbity is burned,
se-rendipity has lucked out, I cut in, they cut out
Blow up, this abrupt hookup is defunct now

ACKNOWLEDGMENTS

Apologies to the rappers and the psychologists, the book takes liberties and shortcuts. It also takes a punt on how many people have watched *The Lion King*. There are three people to thank above all others for its existence: these are Doug Stewart, Ryan Doherty, and Lara Rodgers. A critical link in the chain was William Powers. Conversations with my sister Liv, my brothers Ferg and Hec, my mother Jane, my grandmother Fay, and my father Roger, who didn't get a chance to read it, are the book's largest source. Thank you for feedback, advice and help from Jo Wyld, Maha Rous, Ant Hanbury-Williams, Tom Crockatt, Elisabeth Gifford, Celia Long, Faith Tomlin, Caspian Dennis, Rich Green.

The Sike module edited by José María De Areilza Carvajal borrows from his classes on power and influence. The Disney module draws from Parul Sehgal's uncircumventable Trauma Plot article. Thank you to James Mac-Dougald for his classes on kennings. Chinza Dopeness and Annaka Harris were other unwitting inspirations. Thank you to the rappers, thank you to the psychologists.

ABOUT THE AUTHOR

Fred Lunzer was born in London in 1988. He moved to Tokyo at age six, and lived there on and off as a child and adult. His work in business and AI strategy crossed fields that include life sciences, music, and gastronomy, and he finished his MBA in Barcelona in 2019. Throughout, he wrote journalism, short stories, poetry, and novels. He holds British and German citizenship, and lives in London.

CELADON
BOOKS

Founded in 2017, Celadon Books, a division of
Macmillan Publishers, publishes a highly curated list
of twenty to twenty-five new titles a year. The list of
both fiction and nonfiction is eclectic and focuses
on publishing commercial and literary books and
discovering and nurturing talent.